DANCING IN
THE DARK

DANCING IN THE DARK

*A Novel About the Civilian
Conservation Corps*

Winston Lavallee

To order additional copies of this book, contact:
Xlibris Corporation
1-888-795-4274
www.Xlibris.com
Orders@Xlibris.com
28643

For Ken and Isabelle who always taught
that the art of survival can be an act of love.
And for Richard, who proved it.

PROLOGUE

A cold March sun hung yellow in the crack between the western cloudbank and the Green Mountain ridges. Wet snow had fallen off and on during the day, a final threat from Champlain and the Adirondacks to the northwest that winter might be waning, but was not over. Fuscous and stretching for miles in every direction, the forest was a tumultuous sea of hardwoods, pierced here and there by islands of evergreen and jagged outcrops of granite. Swift-falling streams, until recently locked tight in winter's grasp, murmured under the thin white coverlet. The sun slipped a little lower behind the hill, casting the ravine in the brief, pearly light of dusk.

From within a cluster of balsam fir, an antlered head poked out cautiously, sniffing the wet wind. Sensing no danger, a buck and three does, one a juvenile, proceeded across the clearing, the crunch of their tiny hooves muffled by the spring snow. The young Mohawk brave, well hidden within a hemlock clump, nocked his arrow noiselessly and waited for a clean shot. He had visited the deeryard twice before this day, hoping to get some meat for the long trip north. The sun was nearly gone now and cold drafts lanced down the valley, portending sudden change this night. His fingers numbing from the pressure of the rawhide were impatient to release and send the arrow home. He had planned well. The wind blew in his face and the deer continued past his blind.

"Now." His lips moved silently as the eagle-feathered shaft whispered across fifty feet of moist Vermont air. Struck clearly in the heart, the small doe leaped wildly and ran a dozen paces before collapsing in a writhing heap of fur and snow. Dropping his bow, the brave leaped at the wounded animal, lost his footing and sprawled in the snow. Back on his feet in a twinkling, he literally flew through the failing light and tackled the doe, wrapping his legs around her belly. The tiny hooves flailed, tore his leggings and bloodied his thighs, but the brave clung like a leech, thrusting the knife once, twice into the furry neck below the jaw.

It was over quickly, the doe unconscious and limp in the bloody snow. The young man now threw ferocity aside and grasped the doe's head gently in his hands. A soft moan rose from the Mohawk's throat as he thanked both the deer and his gods and raised his eyes to the heavens where stars were now punching through wisps of clouds. In darkness, he dressed the deer, carefully removing his arrow and ritually consuming a bit of the heart. The deer was well-fleshed, telling that the winter had been mild and light of snow. He skinned the animal and slung as much meat as he could carry around his waist and neck. Then, by starlight, he moved across the valley to the forested hill, putting two miles between himself and the scavenging wolves, which would soon find the remains of the doe. He stopped when his moccasinned feet told him where the moss grew thick. There, sheltered by granite erratics strewn in a rough horseshoe shape, he built a fire in the snow-free area beneath a huge white pine. After hanging his extra meat in the deer's skin by means of a rawhide thong tied to a high branch, he devoured nearly a whole leg, which he had first roasted on the fire. Tired from the hunt and bloated from the meal, he used his snowshoes to pull a thick carpet of pine needles into a pile over the moss, making a rude bed as close as he dared to the coals of the fire. Wrapping himself in a single blanket, he slept beneath the thin moon oblivious to the faint howls and growls down near the deeryard. He was up before first light, stirring the ashes of his fire in hopes of finding a spark. Luck was with him as he turned over a charred knot. Piling on some of the pine needles, he soon had a hot blaze, which warmed him through. He took down his cache of meat, sliced off only a small portion and cooked it. He must travel far and fast this day and a full belly was but a hindrance.

Slowly the surrounding drumlins hove out of the mist to delight his eye. In the terse, slanted morning light, the harsh and unforgiving landscape was the shade of ripening blueberries, mauve and vulnerable. From his hilltop vantage point, the brave looked east, savoring the glory of this fine day. Much snow would disappear down rocky clefts, for the sun even at this hour was warm on his face. He could hear melt water moving down in the glen where he had slain the doe. Looking further off he could see the cleft threaded by the Saxton's River, a roaring tributary rushing away to its concourse with the wide, south-flowing Connecticut.

Once his people had roved at will far down this long tidal river and cultivated its lush valley, aptly called "the smile of the gods". Then came the English up the valley from the sea to practice their strange "work ethic" alongside these agrarian folk and for fifty years there was relative harmony. But Massasoit, the savior of the Pilgrims, had a son, Metacom, or King Philip, who resented the loss of his peoples' freedom by Puritan encroachment on land and wildlife. All New England and especially the Connecticut Valley frontier exploded during "King Philip's War". Deerfield's Bloody Brook ran scarlet with English gore and the Great Falls Massacre in 1676 nearly exterminated the Pocumtucks, a small river tribe of Native American farmers. Revenge and atrocities on both sides destroyed forever the tenuous goodwill fostered by Massasoit. Redmen were ever afterward held to be something less than wild beasts, truly "Satan's children".

To the redman, these English were strange ones, always searching for the big trees and laying them low, taking all the fur and game they could without a thought for tomorrow's hunger. Chopping their way through the forests to feed their hungry mills, making fenced fields for their cattle and burning, always burning to produce charcoal, they devoured everything in their path. The Mohawks, fierce themselves and once the proud and powerful heirs to these woods, were revolted by such habits. "Fat caterpillars", the sachem had said scornfully. But the white man in his greed had slowly pushed back all the tribes, first into the Berkshires and the Green Mountains, then into New York and wild Maine and finally to the more hospitable French Canada.

The brave pondered this sadly, knowing that the redman was helpless before the European hordes. Then his eye caught something that made him cringe with fear and superstition. A King's Broad Arrow had been harshly adzed years before on the trunk of a big pine though white with age, the wound now oozed tiny droplets of golden pitch in response to the sun. This mark was the ancient symbol of naval property belonging to the King of England. His agents had fanned out across New England branding all the substantial first growth white pine trees they could find. The finished mast of His Majesty's ships had to measure 108 feet high and 36 inches at the butt which was the standard length for a seventy-four gun vessel. But the King's subjects had revolted, declaring that these forests belonged to them alone and this marked tree was never taken. Perhaps it was too far inland or too high up on the hill. In any event, no one found it useful as its entire top was now antlered, the result of some severe storm or insect blight. The brave's fear turned to smoldering anger. Redmen of any kind were barely tolerated in this wilderness. Mohawks were an anathema. As mercenaries in the colonial rebellion they were scorned by all, including the British who paid them. Many scalps, mostly Rebel, but more than a few Tory, had hung in Mohawk wigwams. And after Jane McCrae, whose beautiful, bloodied hair hung from a Mohawk's outstretched hand, there would never be forgiveness.

These things the brave had learned from his father, a Pocumtuck captured as a boy and adopted by the Mohawks. The father had fought alongside the Hessians at Bennington and had never forgotten the savage anger he saw in the faces of Seth Warner's Green Mountain Boys who stormed that little hill above Walloomsoc's Creek. He and a few others broke and ran back to Saratoga. Then, when Burgoyne capitulated, he and his surrogate kinsmen fled north. Their remnant lived precariously on the fringes of Quebec farming villages. Thanks to French largess, some became semi-permanent residents, adopted the veneer of local civilization, took wives and began families. The Pocumtuck was one of these whose Mohawk wife bore him a strong son.

Retaining the old ways, father and son would run south to the mountains as coureurs de bois and hunt through the deep Vermont forests as their ancestors had done, but only in the Time of Darkness when winter locked the Yankees into their villages and farms. Then the white man's pox claimed the father as it had taken thousands of others and for three years the brave had come alone to this place. Once, at Ascutney, he ventured too close to the village and stumbled onto a hunting party of farmers. Their eyes had met his with loathing and he knew that only his courage had saved him. Like a defiant animal he turned his back to their muskets and walked slowly into the thick pines, expecting shots to ring out. But none did. The manitou had been kindly that day.

His heart now grew heavy as he gazed for a long while across the ridges warming in the sun. It was time to quit these beloved hills for the St. Lawrence Valley. Somehow he knew that neither he nor his children would ever return. He thought of Dipping Bird, his friend's half-French daughter, and his spirits brightened. She, who often chattered to him while he worked among her father's cattle and granted him secret smiles as she wove at the loom or prepared the family supper. A metis, with the often superlative features of mixed race, he had never known so gentle a creature, with eyes more luminous and round than winter moons and skin the texture of fawnhide. Often, at day's end when her father stroked the strange wooden box he called the fiddle, her tiny feet would tap, then she would prance lightly round the sand-packed floor, increasing speed with the music until she collapsed in laughter, a sound not unlike the summer wind in the aspens. Oh, how she and her father had laughed when, after the first time the brave had heard the music, he peered cautiously inside the instrument half expecting creatures to emerge. The Frenchman had then let him hold the fiddle under his chin and move the horsehair over the strings. Her nose had wrinkled at the raucous sounds he made and again the laughter, including his own.

She would be waiting for him again in her father's hayloft, warmed by bodies and breath of the beasts below. They would make love there, and, in time, she would cook his meals, share his bed, and bear his children. But she would care little for his need of mountains and wildness. Despite what he would teach children about the hunt and the woods, they would become farmers confined to milking cows and tilling soil, preferring to spend their winters reveling at village dances and keeping warm in snug houses. This was the Frenchman's way. With some reluctance, he would plant and harvest too, and perhaps even learn to play the fiddle. But in his elder years he would sit in silence with pipe and memories, gazing from time to time at the same stars that hung here, recalling the old ways, listening to the wind.

The sharp crack of an axe biting into yet another maple far below warned the brave that he must move on quickly. They would soon find the mangled entrails of the deer and hate him. He dispersed his fire, gathered his load and took off at the trot northwards towards the Black River. He would unerringly follow his secretly blazed path up the river valleys to Lake Champlain, to Montreal, to Dipping Bird.

1

The sun had nearly set as two soldiers sped along the deserted highway approaching the town of Saint Omer. Driving the motorcycle was a slender youth of eighteen wearing the uniform of a private, Canadian Army. The sidecar vehicle bore a middle-aged captain of infantry, also a Canadian. The vehicle careened from side to side attempting to avoid debris and gear, particularly helmets, discarded by the retreating French. Here and there gaping holes were blown in the roadbed and destroyed trucks and autos, some still smoldering, littered the shoulder. In the distance, across fields blooming with May flowers, the town appeared as serene and unoccupied as the others they had passed this afternoon. Attached as liaison officer to the 51st Highland division, British Expeditionary Force, the captain was on his way to B.E.F. Headquarters, or what was left of it, in Dunkirk.

The vehicle slowed and cautiously approached the outskirts of the village. This was no-mans-land, the German Panzer units having crashed through on the tails of the French. But they had negotiated other hamlets that day and, sensing no danger, the captain urged resumption of speed. They took the town square at forty miles per hour and saw too late on the side street the squat, armadillo-like armored scout car bearing a swastika. Fortunately, their speed carried them well beyond the enemy who was caught off guard. Pouring on more gas, the private sought the protective screen of houses at the bend in the road onward just a quarter of a mile. They both heard the growl of the scout car and bleakly envisioned the cat and mouse game that was to come. Without the sidecar, a motorcycle might easily outrun the predatory vehicle, but that route closed, escape lay in reaching the open countryside where the Nazi machine might dare not venture.

Just 500 feet short of the turn, a light machine gun fired a searching burst. Dust danced up from the debris in the road. Suddenly, a tremendous flash split the twilight followed by a double roar and concussion which nearly felled driver and passenger. By sheer strength, the private wrenched the machine into the turn and, glancing swiftly behind, noted that the scout car was no more. The remains of a house were settling crazily across the narrow street. Munitions must have been stored there and either a stray shot or a landmine hit by the scout car had set them off. The motorcycle continued at a fast clip into the dusk, slowing only when it was apparent that no one was in pursuit.

Trembling and giddy from fear at the close call, the private cut the engine and, gliding to a halt, dismounted and ran to the ditch where he vomited. Slowly, his system returned to normal and, between retching and gasping for air, he turned back to the passenger who remained motionless in the sidecar. Only then did the youth realize that his captain was unconscious. Reaching across the dashboard, his hand became smeared with blood barely ebbing from the officer's tunic. A single wound just below the collar had resulted from the short burst in the village. The scout's gunner had done his job, even if he never lived to know it. With great effort, the private lifted the unconscious man out of the sidecar and laid him by the roadside. Attempts to revive him were useless and panic gripped the youth when he saw the glassy stare of death becomes fixed in the captain's eyes. The boy had seen this more than enough times when farm animals had been slaughtered. The sheen suggested tears that would soon flow out of increasingly lifeless orbs and he looked away in horror. Then, grasping the dead man's shoulders, he shook the body and pounded on the chest, screaming, "You can't die like this, Captain. You're a cheat and a coward and I want you to admit what you've done." But his cries soon broke into weeping. The pummeling ceased and he hugged the lifeless corpse.

As the rush of grief subsided, he let the captain go and breathed deeply. He was still in danger of being discovered, and panic was fast robbing his senses. Quickly searching the dead man's pockets, he found a sizable roll of francs and an unsealed letter, which he stuffed into his own tunic. Looking farther down the road, he spied some farm buildings and decided to seek shelter there until dark. No point in starting the motorcycle, the gas gauge was nudging empty. So he pushed the machine into the farmyard enclosure and collapsed on pile of straw. Numb with exhaustion, he tried to decide what to do with the captain's body. His sixth sense suddenly told him that a door had opened to his left and he scrambled to his feet, realizing that in his distress, he had foolishly forgotten to arm himself.

A boy of about twelve stepped toward him, face frozen in fear, mumbling that he would do anything if his life could be spared. The private spoke to the lad in French and allayed his concern. In the confusion of the blitzkrieg, the boy had been told to stay with the farm animals until someone came for him. But no one had and he was running out of food. Glancing about, the soldier saw evidence that most of the animals were gone or slaughtered, probably victims of deserters or refugees.

It was dark when they returned to the body with shovels and a crudely made wooden coffin. The private carefully cut the shoulder straps bearing three gold pips and the 1st Canadian Division crests from the captain's uniform. He then removed the identification tags and the Sam Brown belt, attaching the pistol and holster to his own belt. These personal effects would be added to the pouch still in the sidecar. They buried the body beside the road on a little knoll beneath some apple trees. It was hard work, but they finished before midnight. Returning to the farm, the private collected the pouch and strapped it to his chest. He handed some francs to the boy and told him to draw a map of his village and the farm to which he noted the location of the grave. He then returned alone to the knoll and stretched out on the grass and fallen petals.

The private had served as batman to the captain since their arrival from Canada the previous October. They were immediately attached as interpreters and advisors to a Scots battalion leaving for France whose ostensible mission was to support the French at the northern hinge of the Maginot Line. But the dull garrison life in Longwy had been an exercise in dissipation. The Phony War of 1939-40 gave them too much free time with too little to do. The young private had grown weary of defending his virtue against the teasing and taunts of the earthy highlanders, many of them heavy drinkers drawn from the warrens of Glasgow. One night, fortified with wine, he'd followed one of their easy women up the side street to her small apartment. His had been a bumbling performance, but she was experienced and adept at her trade. He paid the usual amount and while the woman tidied and dressed behind a screen, she chattered away, grateful for the opportunity to converse in French and amused by her patron's Canadian accent. But when she let slip that another Canadian, an officer, came to her often, he was jolted from the wine's haze, knowing that there was just one other Canadian in Longwy.

He had mulled endlessly on what to say to the captain and how to say it, but within days, the Phony War was over. In the dark hours of May 9 and 10, 1940, Hitler launched the invasion of France, one of the most astounding military campaigns in history. The captain roused him before the gray light from Germany was in the eastern sky. An unexpected German thrust had captured half a dozen pillboxes in the hastily fortified area flanking the Ardennes forest. French infantry backing up the fortresses had panicked and fled the sudden and savage onslaught, leaving the overrun defenders to hold out alone. A company of highlanders, supported by tanks were to join a squad of Belgian Ardennais Chasseurs in an attempt to relieve them. The two Canadians went along to interpret for the Scots.

Without breakfast, the unit moved out in lorries and as dawn broke, they joined a column of five French Souma tanks several miles down the road. The French seemed in no hurry to finish their breakfast and took no notice of the hungry highlanders. A lorry with prepared food had been sent to join them, so there was nothing to do but sit in the trucks and wait for the French to organize. At nine o'clock, the tanks finally moved out. The Soumas, capable of making better than 30 miles per hour, set a march speed of only 10. Travelling a circuitous route, their progress slowed to five miles per hour with frequent stops at crossroads and checkpoints for the refugees who increasingly were clogging the roads in a constant stream to the west. It was now noon and still no sign of the promised food. Tempers were getting short in the unusual spring heat.

By one in the afternoon, they reached the attack zone. Some French infantry were lined up at a bend in the dusty road intermingling with a knot of nervous civilians. Off to one side under some trees stood the disciplined squad of Belgian chasseurs commanded by a sargeant. The Canadian captain spotted a French officer and strode into the mob, learning little before returning to the Scots commander to plan strategy. The slim, taciturn Scot, possessing little of the bombast and rank consciousness so often seen in garrison, signalled the Belgian sargeant to join him. From the sargeant, they learned that the pillboxes were about a mile down the road just beyond a wooded ridge. The French officer confirmed that the area had been quiet since mid-morning, but that he had been sent from another unit to reorganize the scattered French infantry and take them to another sector. The Scot had hoped for French support for their attack, but after looking over the poilu, most of whom were old and conscripted, saw little chance. These soldiers, derisively called "crocodiles" by crack French outfits, were thoroughly broken in spirit. Their officers had disappeared early in the fight and were presumed dead or captured. Rumors of the Germans using tanks with flame throwers had produced a mad exodus. Some poilu had even donned civilian garb and joined the tide of refugees.

The silence was unnerving, but the Belgian sargeant, showing no disrepect for the officers, scoffed at these reports. He predicted that the Germans, infiltrating the Ardennes with its narrow valleys channeling their armor, were already gone since they would have to retreat across an open valley to the safety of another ridge, leaving their tanks exposed. Impressed with the man's knowledge of the terrain, the Canadian translated this to the Scot who, while still apprehensive, pressed for an immediate attack under cover of the tanks, insisting on a flanking movement to sweep the crest of the ridge up ahead by one of his platoons led by the chasseurs. The Canadians accompanied them after working out a visual signal system with the French tankers.

Everything seemed just as the Belgian had said. What they hadn't foreseen was the mining by the Nazis of the trails leading to the pillboxes. They were deep into a minefield before the first casualty, a point man who miraculously was only scratched by debris from the explosion. The platoon quickly dispersed to the sides of the trail and halted. They could make out the pillboxes on the downslope ahead, but the Soumas were nowhere to be seen. The captain told his batman to stay off the mined trail and accompany the Belgian sargeant to the rear, find the tanks and get them moving. The day continued hot as they waited and still no Soumas. The pop of several suspicious explosions to their rear raised hairs on the necks of the platoon and near-panic in the Canadian captain. After informing the platoon leader that he would verify this threat, he raced back down the ridge, oblivious to mines or possible foes, certain that the Belgian and his private had come to grief. In heavy brush, he nearly collided with the private and seeing him unharmed and whole, embraced him. "Thank God you're O.K., Paul", he puffed. They stood there, sharing sweat for a time, the young Canadian holding his commander's shoulders until the officer was able to catch his breath and ask about the tanks.

This bizarre skirmish actually came to nothing as the Belgian was wrong about the Germans. They had indeed used the Ardennes as a perfect cover for the armor, but slamming west through the

Maginot Line hinge, they swiftly moved on and broke all the French defences at the Sedan River.

All night he guarded the grave like a dog, but sometime in the dark hours of the new day, his soul became less wretched as a strong resolve grew within his breast. His grief remained, but Private Paul Boisvert knew that he had been spared for something more. In the first light of morning he spotted far off the field gray uniforms of a Wehrmacht patrol probing along the road towards Saint Omer. Like a wild animal at bay, the private raised his head and sniffed the breeze. Then, slinging the pouch over his shoulder, he turned and quickly melted into the hedgerows making a line west for the coast.

2

Pierre Boisvert and his wife arrived in Vermont late in the nineteenth century as part of an exodus of French-Canadian tenant farmers. No less than other immigrants from across the seas, their imaginations had been fired by tales of a better life than that of the St. Lawrence River region from whence they came, where the sparse soil had run down, winters clung too long in the spring and vestiges of the seigniorial land system common to French Canada discouraged new beginnings. Experienced and strong as a bull, Pierre easily secured work as a hired man on a dairy farm flanking the Black River. The owner, a respected banker in nearby Springfield, lived with his wife in the large main house set on a hill overlooking his many acres. He demanded and got a dependable man who allowed him to spend most of his time in town, yet play the role of gentleman farmer.

The gentleman farmer class was the successful result of several preceding generations in the trades and commerce. Early on, these sharp-eyed Yankees had tamed the river's energy with a series of dams and waterwheels, taking advantage of the thunderous Contu, a 100 foot drop of water in a linear distance of less than a quarter mile. The milling of seed and sawing of lumber gave way in time to the more sophisticated metal turning and weaving trades. The result was a swarthy but successful little industrial center crimped onto the steep hillsides cleft by the Black River. A single rail line ending abruptly south of Springfield provided an umbilical cord to the considerable prosperity of the much richer Connecticut River Valley.

The work was hard and although the Boisverts saw many of their earlier dreams turn to dust, they counted their fortune in secure employment, abundant food and good health. A small house was provided rent-free as part of the remuneration. They withstood the occasional slurs hurled at them by native Vermonters and kept their dignity through a tiny circle of friends in economic circumstances nearly like their own. The Boisverts learned to be thankful that at least here in the rural Vermont they need not run the daily gauntlet of derision and blatant discrimination, which befell Canucks, working the grim spinning mills of southern New England. Additional strength came from their parish priest whose dingy little Saint Boniface church down beyond the railroad tracks and the coal piles on the banks of the Black River served as a rallying point for French-Canadians each Sunday.

A daughter was born to Pierre and his wife in 1904. Following the pattern of the day, she grew to become part of the family team contributing labor to the running of the farm and the upkeep of the banker's house. During the period of the Great War, the banker prospered and living conditions all along the Black River improved. The young girl was both energetic and bright. Though only French was spoken by her parents, she easily mastered English with the help of a teacher and the parish priest. This pleased the banker's wife to no end and by the time the girl was fifteen she was indispensable at the homestead. She saw how the moderately wealthy lived and each evening, upon returning to her modest quarters, filled her mother's ears with tales of how she would live if ever given the opportunity. No amount of reasoning by either parent could convince the girl of her place, given her common Canuck heritage, but she knew she was anything but common. Tension and apprehension soon rose in the little farmhouse as the girl argued more and more against her parents' ideals and constraints while she sought in desperation for some of her own.

Times were good in 1920 so the banker decided to enlarge his holdings and hired a contractor from Bellow Falls to erect the new barn. The contractor's crew included a tall, sandy-haired carpenter's apprentice, recently returned from military service in France, who soon cast a roving eye over the girl as she passed on her way to and from the main house. She did not object to this frank attention and rather enjoyed listening to the dropped g's and nasal Vermont twang of the workers. To her it was like hearing new and intriguing bird sounds after years of the rough, stubby Canuck French. As summer wore on she beamed winning smiles and inconsequential French chatter to the young man. He, having learned a few Gallic phrases, taunted and flattered her with mock professions of servitude and concern. This seemingly harmless flirtation led to their spending a long August evening together in one of the banker's haystacks.

By September, the barn was finished and the contractor and his crew left abruptly for another job in Rutland. The apprentice was not seen again. Cold winds were ripping leaves from the scarlet maples when the girl realized that she was with child. And an even more bitter day it was when she grew so large as to have to tell her parents. Shock and shame led the Boisverts to concoct a tale that the girl had gone back to Canada to visit relatives, while all the time she was kept out of sight in the little farmhouse.

Somehow the awful secret remained intact. The Boisverts had seen no one at their home since the girl went to seclusion, but with the bright, warm days of spring the probability of unexpected visitors increased. The banker's wife, eager to begin spring-cleaning, began asking when her best help would return from Canada.

On a humid evening in late May the girl gave birth to a healthy boy in the loft of the small cattle shed behind the house. It was not planned that way. The Boisverts, after evening chores, had gone to visit friends in Springfield. Although her time was near, the girl's pregnancy had been singularly uncomplicated and there had been no signals of imminent birth. Just before dark, she was startled by a rap at the front door. Her parents had forgotten that the parish priest was starting his census early this year in hopes of garnering some extra support for church repairs. In a flurry of panic, the girl gathered herself together and slipped out the rear entry. Keeping the house as a shield between her and the caller, she ran to the cow shed. Sharp pains shot through her belly as she hoisted her swollen self up the loft ladder and rested in last year's straw. She heard the priest drive away and wished she'd remained silent in the house as her innards writhed with contraction. Bitterly reflecting on the irony of this sour smelling hay, she recalled how her agony had begun in the sweetness of curing grasses. Was it all to end here trapped in this stifling little hovel among the cattle? She was convinced that she really would die as the massive contractions came regularly and with increased tempo. She whimpered through clenched teeth and howled openly when the pains became unbearable. This hideous hurt, this impending death might even be tolerable if only someone was near. To be alone in this hell like a common animal was unforgivable. She grew black with anger and deep down in her soul cursed the apprentice, his passion and flight and her parents for their abandonment when she most needed them. With rage came resolve and she knew then that she would not die.

Upon returning home, the Boisverts searched frantically for their daughter, calling out in the darkness. The mother hearing the girl's moans from the loft knew at once her error. Dashing into the shed and up the ladder, she found the baby already in the swooning girl's arms, bawling loudly. She shrieked at her husband to get towels and wrapping for the child, then joined her daughter in the musty straw. She wiped and wrapped the boy with the cloth Pierre brought, then yelled down for her sewing scissors, which were to be thoroughly flamed in the lantern. Guided only by instinct, she snipped the umbilical cord, tied it as neatly as she could close to her grandson's belly and laid him in the straw out of the way. After covering her semi-concious daughter with the blanket her husband had thrown up onto the ledge, she helped the girl expel the afterbirth, then rocked her to sleep in a maternal embrace. All night the three generations remained in the loft while the elder Boisvert paced the floor below.

In the morning the mother cleaned the girl up and prepared her to feed the newborn. After feeding, grandmother Boisvert gently passed the boy to his grandfather and with considerable effort carried her daughter down the ladder, into the house and put her to bed. The girl slept soundly, but at midday the priest returned and to his great surprise and embarrassment discovered a new candidate for his parish.

Despite several days of pain, the girl completely rejuvenated within a week. She nursed her son well and set him on the road to health. But her physical trial was but a prelude to a more lasting affliction. Her secret was no more and each day seemed to bring additional recrimination on her and the Boisverts. Tongues clacked until the shame seemed overwhelming. Worst of these critics was the parish priest who, as a man of some learning, had always been the girl's ideal of what a Canuck with a brain might be. But his wisdom took wing when confronted with an illegitimate addition to his small flock. He showed no compassion for the girl and mercilessly scourged her fall from grace. It was clear from the start that he was far more interested in the squawling male life in her arms, as yet nameless, than with her own anger and suffering. She learned to avert her eyes from her father's sad face. He had never been one to show his feelings easily, but this cross stooped the once proud shoulders. Her mother tended the boy with care and gentleness, but said nothing. Inexplicably, the banker's wife never called to see the baby and by her absence became yet another mute critic of the girl's misfortune. Despairing in her rapidly contracting world, it was hardly surprising that the girl ultimately rebelled. A life so utterly devoid of support and understanding called up yet again that resolve she had found in the cow shed loft.

With no warning to her parents, she awoke very early one morning in late August, pushed a change of clothes into a gunnysack and tucked a little hoard of money into her pocket. She nursed the boy until he was satiated and asleep, then ever so tenderly held the pudgy little hands a final time before letting herself quietly out of the house. She faltered just once on the road and with moist eyes observed new haystacks in the meadow, misty in the sparse light of early dawn.

Making her way quickly into town she passed the dingy woolen mill and was startled to see a boy called Raymond looking out of an open upper story window, waiting for the whistle to end his shift. She and the boy had never spoken, but she knew from his furtive glances in church that he had taken more than a passing interest in her. In the dim, half-light she turned her face upwards, but the boy was looking beyond her. Perhaps he never saw her at all for at that moment he spit as far as he could over her head, the moist corners of less vigorously propelled sputum peppering her face. That done, he turned abruptly and disappeared.

She bought a one-way ticket and boarded the 5:06 southbound for Massachusetts. In Holyoke she would begin a new life in the mills and like hundreds of French-Canadians before her take a flat in "Little Canada", that ethnic warren down by the canals. No scorn of bleak city life would bruise her after what she had endured. She was beyond vulnerability and caring.

The banker's wife finally realized her error and paid a rare visit to the Boisvert home offering assistance in the search for their daughter. Eventually, the girl was located in Holyoke and the woman provided money for Pierre to retrieve her. But no amount of coaxing on the father's part would make her return. All ties had been irrevocably severed and the harshest words that Pierre was ever to hear were those of his daughter suggesting that the boy be placed in an orphanage as she never wished to see him again. Despondent, Pierre returned to Vermont, but long before he reached Springfield, he knew in his heart that this boy was to be the son he never had.

They called the boy, Paul. Actually, it was the priest who suggested the name, reasoning that one with less than auspicious beginnings must have a name to which he might aspire. The lad was healthy and grew like a weed under the careful eyes of his grandmother. He had his mother's dark eyes and sensitive lines about the mouth which might have been mistaken for weakness should the casual observer fail to see the firmness in the tilt of the chin. His frame was light, but had a breadth that promised he would one day flesh out like his grandfather. No likeness to his real father could be found save the suggestion of auburn in the hair, which was secretly noted by only his grandmother.

Paul followed in the same family tradition as his mother, gradually becoming an integral part of family toil needed to make the farm profitable. Grandfather Boisvert loved the boy in his aloof way and taught him all he knew about tilling the fields and husbanding cows, noting that, like his mother, Paul learned eagerly and quickly. As Pierre's half-Indian father had done, he showed the boy how to hunt and fish, emphasizing that he take only that amount of food which could be immediately consumed or safely stored. On winter evenings, Pierre would play Canadian country tunes on the old violin he kept in a worn case on the dining room mantle. The grandparents marveled at Paul's quick ear and he was soon singing and playing everything he heard.

The lad became a solitary creature, but not withdrawn or lacking humor. He experienced wholly the harshness and rough living of tenant farming, but always enjoyed the friendship and good nature of his grandmother who became the dominant influence in his life. She engendered in him a love of the fields and forests, which complimented Pierre's hardheaded practicality. Early on he became an expert reader of nature and no berry or edible plant on the rugged hillsides of the Black River escaped his sharp eye. He learned to amuse himself by stalking small animals, even deer, just for the thrill of being close to them without their detecting his presence.

Forever stung by his daughter's shame, Boisvert refused to send the boy to public school and kept him busy on the farm away from town contacts, save the few family friends. But his grandmother saw that he attended church and its social events for youngsters his age. She also taught him to read and write French as best she could for upon Pierre's decree, not one word of English was ever to be spoken in his house again. But contrary to her husband's edict, she never admonished Paul for the few English phrases he uttered, knowing full well that his survival might some day depend on engaging the wider world.

The parish priest took over Paul's education when Grandmother Biovert, who was unschooled, reached her limit. Weekly drill and Sunday sermons in French helped expand the boy's vocabulary and it was through this provincial cleric that Paul learned of books, writing, culture and the mysteries of an abstract God. Full of somber warnings that sin in all its forms made eternal damnation in Hell extremely likely, this man generated both respect and fear in the boy. Paul's head often teemed with contradiction, but the old priest's interpretations, rich and ridiculous, were all sorted out by simple, solid Grandmother Boisvert who never once doubted that God had both a great sense of humor and an immense love for the boy.

3

Harwood snubbed out his third cigarette of the day and looked at his watch. It was already ten o'clock. Rising only thirty minutes earlier with a head roaring from too much whiskey, he had barely made it to the overstuffed chair by the window. Without thinking, he had lifted the thick drapes just a crack to peer out, but the dull, gray light had driven jagged slivers of hideous pain through his skull. Mustering more courage, he now raised the drape again. The pain was tolerable this time, but all he could see were grotesque figures in the street below made squiggly by the rivulets of sleety rain on the glass. He blinked several times to assure himself that his eyes weren't malfunctioning, then dropped the curtain in disgust.

March of 1936 was not particularly pleasant in Springfield, Massachusetts. Unemployment and disillusionment were as widespread here as in other tough river cities in New England. Roosevelt's alphabet soup of federal agencies hastily thrown together to pull the country out of the Great Depression were, after a brisk start, losing steam and coming under vicious attack from Republicans and even a few maverick Democrats. No matter that the number of families on the federal dole were decreasing and farm prices, those elusive bellweathers of the nation's economic health, had risen and held steady, national statistics out of Washington created not one ripple in the lives of poor folks rubbing their pennies together along the banks of the turbulent Connecticut. To add to their woes, winter was slow in leaving. Snow and bone-chilling rain fell heavily through the month raising the water level and fears that another flood like the one back in 1927 was in the offing.

The bed against the wall quivered as the sleeper turned over and heaved a sigh. John looked across the room at the sleeping woman whose bed he shared. She had been a regular at the Red Sails Ballroom out on Boston Road. Late one evening the police had arrived unannounced and ushered her and three others into the waiting van. John trailed the paddy wagon to City Hall and waited patiently while they wrote her up, then stepped forward and bailed her out. In handing over the fee he cast a casual eye over the blotter.

Name: Hazel Hopkins   Age: 33   Sex: Female. No family relations.
Address: 179 Linden Street, Apt. 16 Springfield, Mass.
Background: Graduate of Springfield Business High School with
     Honors. Class of 1920.
Former occupation: Chief Clerk/Bookkeeper, Adams Boiler Co.
Present Occupation: Recepshunist

The last entry had been crossed out and replaced with Prositute, then lined out again and the word Doksee pencilled in. The desk sargeant was not a whiz at spelling, but Harwood got the drift.

That was last October. He'd become weary of his room at the LeRoy and the greasy food at the chop shop half a block away, so moving in with Hazel was easy. She assuaged the blues and loneliness that sapped his spirit and asked no questions about either his past or his heavy drinking. His presence in the apartment was a relief for her as it discouraged her more randy patrons, many of whom wished their pleasures at any time and in any place. He was clean, occasionally thoughtful and demanded little restriction in her life. She was grateful for his paying his share of the rent and she rather liked fixing meals for someone beside herself.

He usually rose early, made his own coffee and breakfast, then went out looking for work. He would return in the afternoon, edgy, taciturn and nearly always with a bottle. She never asked him where he went or what he did, as she was from the start a little afraid of him, especially just before he commenced drinking. Never one to be garrulous, he would slip by stages into inexpressive eclipses and oppressive silence, the likes of which could nearly be sliced. After a few drinks he might grow more biddable and come to supper with a bit of gleam in his eye. She liked his drollery and even found herself looking forward to their mealtime banter. But she loathed his morose periods when he remained in the bedroom. somber, lost, self-separated from self, sipping the ever-present whiskey. She found it best to let him be, eat a fast supper and depart early for her rounds of the bars.

As on so many other nights, she had come back about three in the morning slightly inebriated, removed her dress and crawled into bed beside him. Long gone, Harwood was unaware until the mill whistles and traffic sounds at daybreak stirred him awake. He avoided rousing her. She not only needed the sleep, but also could be most bitchy until noon. Haggard and sullied, she wanted to see no one, self-isolation being her way of purging residual guilt and self-doubts about the carnal life.

The hurt inside his head was intensified by pangs of hunger. He made his way to the kitchen, quietly closing the door behind himself. Reaching into the cupboard for the coffee, he elbowed a stack of pans onto the floor.

"For Christ sake, do you have to be so clumsy?" she rasped from the bedroom.

He said nothing, cleaned up the clutter and put the coffee on. She emerged minutes later, face set like a stone and went into the bathroom for aspirin. He heard her shaking the bottle and slamming the medicine cabinet door. It was going to be a good morning, he was sure.

She stood next to the table looking at him through puffy eyes. "Why aren't you going out?" she asked hoarsely.

"Decided it wasn't worth it."

"So you'll be around here all morning waking the dead, I suppose." The last few words caught in her throat and she coughed dryly.

"I'll leave in a while after I eat".

Her eyes narrowed and he knew she was bringing up the heavy artillery.

"What the hell do you do everyday, anyway? I don't think you're looking for work at all. I'll bet you go to some dive and soak up beers till its time to refill your belly."

"That's really none of your business, is it?" He skewered her with a frosty glare.

She averted her eyes for a moment, but added scornfully, "Most men are out honestly looking for work. All you seem to come back with is a bottle of Southern Comfort. But, then, you don't really have to worry, do you, with all that support your mom sends you? Don't think for a minute that I haven't noticed the letters with the checks coming in regularly every two weeks or so from up the valley. If I were her, I'd wonder when this investment was going to pay off."

"You're not her and the checks are accounted for", he muttered.

"But you don't even care enough about her to go see her." Her voice was harsh with anger.

"That's enough", he snapped, coming out of the chair like a shot and slamming its back against the sink. She cowered slightly at this, but her inquiry persisted albeit in softened tones.

"Look, maybe it's that wife who's left you, but whatever's bothering you, get rid of it. Go somewhere, do something with your life."

"Like you?" he retorted viciously then regretted it immediately. Her mouth hardened, and he knew she was wounded. She turned to go back to the bedroom, the smeared lipstick and unkempt hair adding unfair years to her appearance.

"There's a couple of letters for you on the icebox, one of them with the check in it", She announced wearily over her shoulder.

"Hazel", his voice trailed off. She hesitated. "Sit down and have some coffee", he continued more gently.

"No, no thanks". The wind was out of her sails, the fire gone. "Leave some in the pot and I'll have it later."

She closed the door and he heard her get into bed. She wouldn't sleep and he felt angry and miserable for what he'd done to her, recognizing full well that her attack was at least clean and forthright while his response had been specious. He picked up the letters. The smaller of the two, bearing his name in a womanly scrawl was, as Hazel had said, right on schedule. But the larger envelope caught his eye. It had been forwarded from the LeRoy Hotel and was typically governmental in size, edging and opacity. The return address read: Headquarters, 1st U.S. Army, Boston, Mass. He'd nearly forgotten the inquiry he'd made back in September about requesting a return to active duty. He tore it open, read a few lines and sat down. The crucial paragraph at the bottom caught his eye.

"Sign the agreement below and report to Camp Devens at 1600 hours on 20 March 1936. After conditioning and preparatory training, you will be assigned to a Civilian Conservation Corps unit in the First Army area".

"As simple as that," he told himself in amazement. He smiled, recalling his friend's admonition prior to their discharge many years before that "No captain in the U.S. Army Reserve ever gets rich in the peacetime army."

"But what the hell would it be like baby-sitting a bunch of leafrakers in the woods? Well, it couldn't be much worse than the life in this brownstone," he thought, rubbing the back of his neck. He cast an eye toward the calendar on the back of the cupboard door.

"Cripes, today's the 20th!", he muttered. Moving easily now, he went to the bedroom to pack. Hazel raised her head and asked what he was doing. He didn't answer until everything was in the leather suitcase. "Joining the Tree Army, love," he said simply as she sat up, her face a mask of disbelief.

"I'm putting my share of the expenses for the rest of the month here on the dresser. Give my regards to the Red Sails barkeeps." He left in a downpour, clearing the city just ahead of the wall of ice and flood waters roaring down the valley.

4

July was being kind to no one. The sun had raised blisters of pitch on the wooden ties in front of the Northampton railway station. Professor Stone could smell the sharp odor of released hydrocarbons and removed his straw hat for the third time that afternoon, wiping graying hair with a handkerchief, then moving a bit farther down the bench into the shrinking patch of shade cast by the platform overhang. He fretted. The heat always bothered him and the train from Hartford was unaccountably late.

Stone was the sole survivor of an old Yankee family, which had for generations wrested a poor living out of the bouldered hills of western Massachusetts. As a youth he was precocious and had achieved a brilliant high school record, earning him acceptance as a town scholar at Williams College. There he continued to distinguish himself in science and philosophy by earning a Phi Beta Kappa key. But his success and identity with the "other world" of academics and science weaned him ever further away from the hard, but uncomplicated life on the farm. Psychologically and quite literally, like his hero, Gregor Mendel, he moved from one life to another, becoming an exile of his own making. Such was the price of scholarship.

Yet, there was no estrangement, no chasm, between him and his unschooled parents. Ashley had always returned four-square the love, care and respect his parents gave him. Despite the farm's nearly having failed in his last year of college, his father saw to it that the young man was given both time off and sufficient money to complete his education. Ashley had then contributed his next year's labor free of charge to stabilize the farm.

There was never any doubt about Ashley Stone's ultimate lifework. Indeed, the parents were both proud and enthusiastic when Ashley finally announced that he would be a scientist, not a farmer. Their blessing was enough when he left for Ithaca the next fall. Penniless, except for the niggardly scholar's stipend, he entered Cornell University to work with J.H. Comstock, one of the pioneers in the infant science of entomology. He emerged five years later with a Doctor of Philosophy degree and membership in Sigma Xi. With Comstock's help he had become established in the research literature of forest entomology. His work caught the eye of B.E. Fernow and Gifford Pinchot, the founders of the U.S. Forest Service and they brought him to Washington, D.C. to help flesh out Teddy Roosevelt's grand design to protect land and forests against exploitation and ruin by the timber barons.

Stone worked doggedly with Pinchot's brilliant team, but soon saw the golden days turn to brass when Roosevelt left the White House and the back-scratching bureaucracy began to swallow up conservationist ideals in a morass of compromise. Then the Great War in Europe turned heads one hundred and eighty degrees. Conservation gave way to patriotism and holy victory to make the world safe for democracy, a "war to end wars". The nation's natural resources so recently cherished became objects of personal and corporate profit, fuel for the flames of the Western Front. Stone knew his days in the capital were numbered and when the United States entered the war, he signed on for the duration as an officer in the Quartermaster Corps and monitored grain shipments from the mid-west.

With the Armistice, he returned home, married his boyhood sweetheart, Grace, and took her to Amherst where he had obtained a faculty appointment at Massachusetts Agricultural College, With Grace at this side, he was finally doing that for which he was best suited, scientific research. The year was 1919 and Ashley's cup overflowed.

The Spanish flu pandemic changed everything. It had carried off millions, but by early 1921, the worst was over and the newlyweds thought themselves spared. The sniffles and chills started in April. Ashley fought it off, but Grace suddenly worsened, lingering for a month like a flower burned by a late frost. Stone would never forget the panic-filled nights when sleep was unthinkable, the breathing of his gentle wife, coarse and obscene, like a swimmer drowning, as fluids filled her lungs. When her face finally took on the dreaded heliotrope pall, he knew that the valiant fight was over. Still, it took two more days for the pneumonia to squeeze her life away.

Grace's death ravaged Ashley. He refused to mourn and totally immersed himself in his research, rarely speaking of his wife again. Outwardly, Stone carried on as if the grim reaper had never harvested. He chose to live alone and as the years passed, even his colleagues often forgot that he had once been married. His research became his life and the carefully honed methods and incisive logic applied to forest insect problems regularly yielded such accurate and valuable information that his name became commonplace in the science literature. He retained no close friends and, typically the reticent Yankee, he shunned desultory talk with colleagues. Totally oblivious to modes of fashion, his outfits came to qualify him as a legendary campus figure. Ancient wire-framed glasses constantly slipped down his nose and his speech consisted of low, guttural monotones occasionally punctuated by a mispronunciation suggesting a childhood impediment of some sort. Student wags fondly, but secretly, referred to him as "old cheese mouth".

Yet, with students he was always affable. He might drive them to distraction by seemingly endless lectures on warm summer afternoons, yet none disliked him and nearly all came to respect his fair and thorough pursuit of the truth and austere personal honesty. The few who succeeded in peeling back his hide were pleasantly surprised by the wealth of natural warmth and good humor they found. He gave generously of his time with these students and spent many unrecorded hours working beside them in field and laboratory. Those who sought his counsel left his cramped little office with increased confidence in themselves, relieved not so much by any special wisdom that Stone might have divulged as by the undefined twinkle in his small myopic eyes. Like Comstock, he knew how to turn out able graduates. Yet for all of this, there resided in Stone's personality an irritating bur. His reclusivity and denial of Grace's death cut neatly in one direction as he relentlessly molded his life's work to perfection. But this same stoicism hacked silently at his peace of spirit. In dreams, Grace would come to him. So clear would she be that he would smile at the sweetness of her voice. But too many nights were wracked by a mute demon.

As a young boy, Ashley had witnessed the destruction of the favorite family mare after it had gotten loose in the stable and over-consumed on oats at the storage bin. Ashley was responsible for excluding such animal raids on the fodder, but had just once neglected to lock the bin door. He willingly walked the animal day and night as the father forced periodic swallows of mineral oil to rid the horse of the fermenting oats and the deadly bloat. But by the second day, the mare lay down in agony and rolled furiously, twisting the gut and sealing her fate. In horror, Ashley endured the anguished, near-human cries of the animal brought on by the blocked and bursting intestine. His father accepted the inevitable and put a deer slug between the mare's eyes. The boy was aghast and shed long and bitter tears. Although no one blamed him, in his secret core at a tender age, Ashley had become his own merciless critic.

This unresolved, nearly forgotten guilt quietly festered. After his wife's death, in disturbed sleep, Ashley would find himself walking the shore of a quiet Berkshire lake, when from the deep, dark water Grace would appear riding the dead horse. No matter where he turned or ran, the galloping specter horse gained until he could see his wife's face twisted with hurt and anger, the horse pounding over his helpless body, savagely tearing him from sleep and causing him to cry out in the darkness. In self-defense, he

developed the habit of working late into the night after which he
dropped into unconsciousness from sheer exhaustion.

Sam Chapman was now dead. Ashley had personally seen him
tucked into the corner of that tiny Boston graveyard where his
many forebears lay. Sam had been his best friend at Cornell and
Ashley had always envied him his Boston Brahmin upbringing,
which early on had bestowed both a superior education and super
ego. Sam's interest in insects had seemed almost an afterthought as
he would read deeply of the classics in the original and quote
endlessly therefrom the foibles and fortunes of Greek and Roman
heroes and deities. Nor was he a stranger to the more pithy works
of Pliny, Vergil and Plutrarch. This detachment and a dry wit
balanced against Ashley's cold sober approach to learning and the
two got on incredibly well. Even after Sam went to Iowa to teach,
they corresponded often, Sam in his expansive, rich language, Ashley
in short, terse prose. Over the years their paths had occasionally
crossed at professional meetings where they had spent a number of
late hours reminiscing over good whiskey. Even now he could taste
it, but his doctor had told him not to push his luck. That little
flame beneath his breastbone could be ominous.

Stone could not recall the exact date that his friend's letters
had stopped. Two years ago perhaps, but only for a short time as
they began to appear again in the hand of Sam's niece, Sarah, the
one for whom he now waited. It was she who had cared for her
uncle in his remaining months, supporting the two of them as a
teacher in a rural high school. She had asked Stone to arrange the
burial, but did not accompany Sam's body to Boston. Stone
surmised that finances were the problem. Sarah, at age ten, had
become Sam's ward. Sam had never married and instantly became
the doting father to the girl. His letters had proudly reflected her
growing up, her progress at school and her musical talents. In
keeping with Sam's love of mythology, he always referred to her by
the nickname, Demmie, for Demeter, goddess of the earth and the
harvest. She had matured and entered the State University where,

much to Sam's delight, she completed a degree in music. Stone reflected on this for a moment as he shifted on the hard bench. "Yes, that was like Sam," he said almost aloud, "rather disorganized himself, to encourage discipline and study in the finer arts." Had it been Ashley's diligence and focus that Sam had most admired, the professor wondered? No matter. Their friendship had endured. Stone would honor his lost friend's request and oversee Sarah's enrollment at Mass Aggie where in two weeks she would begin graduate study. It seemed the least he could do. "God, how he missed hearing from old Sam!"

The whistle and clatter of the approaching train interrupted Stone's reverie. He stood up, adjusted his glasses and, as the engine hissed to a stop, searched the steps of the coaches for his student. Knots of sweating, exasperated passengers disembarked. From the rear coach a young woman emerged and made her way up the line of cars. Despite the heat, she appeared composed. Her long-sleeved, light-gray dress, decidedly out of season, was gathered at the throat by a tasteful bow and white collar. Her hair, the color of basswood honey, was neatly tucked over her ears and curled in modern billows beneath a matching gray cloche. Not even the smallest details escaped him. His training as an entomologist gave him a penchant for such things. She stopped for a moment on the platform to get her bearings, then turned toward the baggage car.

Although Sam's descriptions of Sarah had been extensive, they had in no way prepared Stone for this meeting. The queer feeling below Ashley's chest was totally unexpected, a strangeness that recalled days long ago. As she turned and looked at him on the steaming platform, he raised his hand to her and smiled. She caught his eye and came toward him, her movements suggesting a vulnerability or trace of insecurity. Yet, to his surprise and delight, he would soon learn that she was uncommonly strong. There was hidden energy and intensity that shaped her life, but would never constrain her sincerity or grace. She was without artifice and the outward manner served only to nurture and protect a deep and lovely sensitivity, too tender and precious to be cast willy-nilly under the feet of the mad and scrambling world. There was humor and warm cheer in those intelligent eyes, for hers was a spirit of happy, rippling waters and unfathomable pools.

In this moment before their meeting, Stone knew these things in his heart. He tried to compose himself and muttered, almost aloud, "You damned old fool!!" What he didn't know until much later was that Sam's ward would become much more than a twist in his gut.

5

The Civilian Conservation Corps was a hastily organized conglomerate built on lofty ideals by government bureaucracy. In 1933, newly elected President Franklin D. Roosevelt faced a bankrupt, dispirited nation and an entire world entering a dark economic valley, The Great Depression. In his first 100 days in office, he cobbled together and sent to Congress for approval many programs aimed to relieve the troubled economy and people suffering in it.

One of the first of these, the CCC, was unveiled on March 21, 1933. FDR signed the act, setting it up by the end of the same month and appointed Robert Fechner as Director. This man, a labor organizer from Boston who knew little about science and conservation, proved to be a superlative choice who devoted all his energy, time and skills to making the program work. With Fechner's advice, FDR instructed the Department of Labor to enroll youths ages 18-25 for work in forest camps. The War Department was to operate and maintain discipline in the camps and the Departments of Agriculture and Interior were to supervise camp work under civilian direction.

Despite earlier suggestions for conservation work and preservation of natural resources by William James, Gifford Pinchot and others around the turn of the 1900's and some existing examples of youth work camps in Europe and Canada, there was no "how-to-do-it-kit" for this new and bold experiment. Yet the strange combination of government agencies worked amazingly well under Fechner's discerning eye.

The major purpose of the CCC was economic relief. Each enrollee was paid $30 a month of which $25 had to be sent home for family support. This left $1.25 per week for spending money, but food, medical care, lodging (such as it was) and clothing (two dress uniforms, two sets of work clothes and two pairs of Army shoes) were provided by the government. For many of the young men enrolled, this was the best wardrobe they had ever had.

The typical camp was loosely based on the U.S. Army company unit plan and was self-supporting and autonomous.

Organizational Chart—CCC Company

Commanding Officer	Work Supervisor
(Military)	(Non-Military)

Executive Officer	Forester(s) Blacksmith/Mechanic

Mess Officer Medical Officer	Tradesmen (Local Experienced Men)

Mess Sargeant Infirmary Staff

Top Senior Leader
CCC Enrollee

Barracks A	Sr. Leader & Jr. Leader in each barracks

Barracks B

Barracks C	50 men in each barracks

Barracks D	Total of 200 men in a fully manned company

Many companies operated at less than full strength. Executive officers and mess officers were not always provided and medical officers were often assigned on temporary duty or as floating doctors among several camps. Many companies also had full or part-time civilian educational advisors.

The daily work schedule was dictated by local camp needs, but followed a relatively uniform and typical pattern.

CCC Daily Work Schedule

6:00 am Rise	1:00 pm-4 pm	Work
6:30 Roll Call and Calisthenics	4:00	Recall
7:00 Breakfast	4:30-5:30	Clean up
7:30 Inspection	5:30-6:00	Supper
8:00 Formation for Work Assign	6:30	Retreat
8:00-12 Work	7:00-11	Free Time
12-1:00 Lunch (usually sandwiches at work site)	11:00	Lights Out

Between 1933 and 1942, nearly 3 million men worked in 4,500 separate camps across the United States and generated an admirable record in human and natural resource conservation. Work was completed in national and state forests and parks, on private farm land, in wildlife refuges and in rivers, streams, on ocean shores and in arid regions. The CCC planted more than 2 billion trees and constructed more than 125 thousand miles of roads and trails. They spent more than 6 million man-days fighting forest fires, built more than 6 million check dams for erosion control and fought insects and plant disease on more than 20 million acres of forest. The cost of the program over its nine-year existence was estimated at nearly $3 billion, but considering the lasting benefits to both men and the land, Roosevelt's "Tree Army" certainly earned its stripes.

The July heat wave had been a terrific experience for them all. Three men and two nearly grown boys sat in a Boston & Maine railway coach, which had been sandwiched into a freight train bound for Vermont. Part of a crowd which had boarded at Camp Devens in Ayer, Massachusetts, the men had remained aloof and apart, belying their Yankee heritage. By reason of someone's poor planning or ignorance, the coach had been coupled behind a cattle car. No straw had been provided for the wretched beasts, fully half of which were suffering from summer diarrhea. A little speed might have wafted the odor away from the open doors and windows, but the train was abysmally slow, creeping along, stopping at each tiny depot across northern Massachusetts to take on freight or to disgorge passengers. In Gardner, three hobos had furtively made their way to the cattle car to hitch a ride. They stopped twenty feet from the track, looked at each other, then faded away across the railyard.

At Greenfield more boxcars were added and a Central Vermont Railway engine came on as replacement for the trip north. The switching permitted enough time for a walk up the shady boulevard to the drugstore for a cold soda and sandwich. Returning from their stroll, the boys chatted volubly and made rude jokes about their plight. The brief respite from the smell had been merciful, but aboard and underway once more, they found that the sickly, bovine air had saturated the car clear through its buttoned and well-worn velveteen upholstery.

Two hours and forty miles later, the five disembarked at Bellow's Falls. The station master came out, but after one whiff waved the engineer quickly on. With immense relief they all watched the locomotive chug away over into New Hampshire with its fetid cargo. The stationmaster went back into his office without a word and the four lay-abouts, totally unconcerned by the midafternoon arrival of the men, resumed their card game in the cool of the station overhang. One of the arrivals carried a leather suitcase and duffel bag. The others carried their few belongings in gunnysacks. All wore light summer clothes, but the man with the suitcase was better dressed than his companions.

Older than the two boys by at least 15 years, John Harwood knew the instant they all left the train together that they were headed for the same place. It was also obvious that the promised transportation had failed to arrive. Dropping his suitcase and bag by the door, he walked into the station and up to the railway clerk's barred window.

"Where can I find the Conservation Corps camp?" he asked the back of a small, white head.

Without turning to face the ticket window, the clerk answered, "Fairgrounds", in a tone that might have been used to give the time of day.

"Which direction", John pressed, correctly sensing this would be a short conversation.

The man turned. He had sharp features and leveled a pair of piercing, porcine eyes on John's sweat-streaked face, seeming to take especial notice of a drop of John's perspiration about to land on his polished counter. The silence was broken only by a fly buzzing angrily against a glass somewhere.

"You a C.C. boy?", the clerk said eventually.

"You might say so. I'm the commanding officer of the company."

The clerk registered no more interest than before, but John's companions standing inside the doorway exchanged surprised looks.

"Up the hill by the bank, turn left. 'Bout a mile you'll see the tents, if you don't hear the commotion first."

The clerk's lips remained taut and the level eyes didn't bat a lash. John knew that there would be no more directions.

"Thanks for the help."

"Come on with me", he said, turning to the others who quickly picked up their sacks and followed him out the door.

"Them boys been raisin' hell, the past couple weeks", scratched a dry voice behind them as they stepped off the platform into the glare.

John strode up the hill into town following the clerk's directions. There was little activity at this time of day, the heat keeping everyone in the shade or under the fans in the dry goods store and the grocery. The clerk's attitude and the anonymous criticism of the situation up at the fairground quickened John's pace and his comrades fell in behind him, sensing that the cool reception at the station gave them no reason to linger in town. Upon reaching the bank, John turned and addressed the men directly for the first time.

"Since we're all in this together, we might as well introduce ourselves. I'm Captain Harwood, newly assigned to command the company."

The men shuffled up and shook John's hand. He noted that they were a mixed lot. The two youngsters were probably away from home for the first time in their lives and, while self-concious in the presence of their commander, exuded excitement and a spirit of adventure. The man named Walsh was in his late thirties, furtive, watchful and unsmiling, almost sour, but appearing more sad than resentful. John decided on the spot that he was among the many who had probably lost job after job until he had finally swallowed his pride and joined the Corps. Fred Hurlburt, a bit older than Harwood, had a bright and level eye. He met John easily and as an equal with no obsequities or fears, obviously has own man. Further, he was built like a bull, of medium height, but broad of shoulder and thigh. Great physical strength lay behind that handshake and the confidence in how to use it emanated from the robust, smiling face. Here was a man he could count on, thought John, as he sized up the crew.

They were soon in sight of the camp and John breathed easier when he saw that spanking new tents were pitched properly if a bit unevenly in a flat hayfield alongside the deserted fairgrounds.

As if in mockery to the clerk's warning, nothing appeared amiss. The utter quiet itself was the only thing disturbing. Striding through the crushed and lodged clover that formed the company street, John, by habit, made mental notes about lining up the tents and improving their spacing. There was no tent identified as headquarters so, upon reaching the center of the encampment, John sent the two older men towards either end of the lines to find out who was in charge. Walsh came back with a bearded giant who had obviously just waked up. The squinting eye and drooping lip told that his slumber had been assisted by alcohol. Upon learning John's identity, the big man's face grew dark and wrathful, but he kept the harsh words in. When asked where the commander was, he thumbed in the direction of the woods across the field, turned on his heel and, without a word, made for his tent. John watched him go, decided against taking him to task and told the men to find an empty tent for themselves.

On a slight rise just within the woodsline, John found a single unoccupied tent. A uniform blouse bearing new second lieutenant bars hung from the ridgepole, however, so John sat down to wait on the well made bunk. In minutes, a young man of twenty-two dressed in undershirt and work denims rounded the corner of the tent and, after an initial start, tumbled to the fact that the man sitting on the bed was both his superior and replacement.

"Relax", said John gently to the shavetail, now standing ridiculously at attention. "How long have you been commanding here?"

The young man slowly regained his composure and seemed visibly relieved that the new C.O. was not a pettifogger.

"About two weeks and I'm glad to be leaving", he said." My orders read that I report to Camp Devens for reassignment day after tomorrow at 0800 hours."

"You'll need to catch the noon train tomorrow, then. Right now, tell me all you can about this unit and where the hell everyone is", John said quietly.

Sheepishly and with considerable confusion, the lieutenant painted a bleak picture of the unit's activities. The company had been on site for a month and a half and had not received one single assignment from headquarters. During the first two weeks no one had been in command as the captain originally assigned had been seriously injured in an auto accident on the way to the encampment. Men had arrived piecemeal bringing the company to half strength on the same day the lieutenant arrived. By this time one of the local experienced men, a fellow named Bush, had taken matters into his own hands and was telling everyone what to do. The lieutenant, fresh out of Dartmouth with no command experience, was completely ignored by Bush who, to his credit, had achieved some semblance of order, but only by bribes, threats and violence. By now Bush had consolidated his power and answered to no one.

"That fellow must be the one I just met in camp", John interrupted.

"He's a devil, that one", blurted the lieutenant. "Kicked my ass right out of camp and had his boys stick my tent here in the woods where he thought I couldn't see what was going on".

"Why didn't you have him brought up on charges of insubordination?' John retorted.

"He threatened me if I did. I knew my assignment here was temporary and his word at headquarters would have finished me", the young man said, eyes averted.

John knew the lieutenant was right. The ambiguous lines of responsibility drawn between civilians and the military in the C.C.C. had gotten more than a few officers in hot water and had finished some of them. Oddly, staff officers in headquarters often went out of their collective way to castigate fellow officers in the camps. Few paper pushers back in the corps area near the cities ever served in the woods or took the time to visit the camps to learn what conditions were really like.

"So you dropped the whole damn thing in my lap", John's voice rose ominously. "Where the hell is your backbone?"

"Sorry, sir", was the tight-lipped reply.

There was more. After the tents had been pitched and the mess tent and kitchen fly erected, no further camp preparation had taken place. Water was gathered from a small creek beyond the edge of the clover field and consumed untested and untreated. No latrines had been dug, the men crowding into two privies at the fairgrounds. As these were quite insufficient for their needs and full from a previous season, men took to relieving themselves in the woods by day and behind the tents at night. Naturally, flies were drawn to the area and were now a constant problem in the unscreened mess tent.

"Where are the men now?" John cut in again.

"You won't believe this", the young man said, coloring slightly. "Bush has them out working on local farms fifty at a time with a day off every other day. Five trucks depart mornings at eight o'clock each with ten corpsmen aboard. Each truck goes to a separate farm. Two of the farms belong to Bush's relatives, the other three pay Bush two dollars a day for each batch of workers he sends.

"So Bush keeps his kinfolk out of the red and makes six bucks a day at government expense," exclaimed John in disbelief. "How does he keep it from the men?"

"He tells them that these are temporary orders from headquarters. Most of them are young and impressionable and the older ones who are onto Bush's game either fear crossing him and play along or just don't give a damn", said the lieutenant uncomfortably.

"What about the other half of the unit? Where are they now?"

"Bush lets them take the trucks over to the lake at Londonderry for swimming and fishing. It's far enough away to go unnoticed by the local folks and no one is about to complain of a vacation three days plus Sunday a week. You'll also find a number of them over at the River View, a booze palace about five miles from here."

"Damn, what a situation", seethed John who leaped up suddenly and strode to the tent opening where he could see the sleepy encampment in the field.

"Sorry, sir", was again the whimpered reply.

After a long silence, John said evenly, "You may be leaving

tomorrow morning, but until the time you depart for the station, you'll do exactly as I say."

The captain's face revealed little, but his eyes gleamed with determination as he outlined his plan. The lieutenant was to pack immediately, then go to Bush's tent and tell him that there would be an assembly at seven the next morning. He would then find Walsh and Hurlburt. Walsh was to check on the conditions at the mess tent, inform the cooks of Harwood's arrival and bring Harwood's gear from the company street. Hurlburt was to report to John immediately. Hurlburt stood by the tent flap five minutes later and nodded silently while Harwood told him the situation.

"We've got to get the unit to take care of itself properly", John explained. "Latrines have to be dug by noon tomorrow and fresh water brought in for the evening meal. I want four Lister bags set up on the company street before the afternoon heat. I'll give Bush a chance to get the men in line at morning assembly when he's sober."

"You could get a jump on things by calling assembly right after supper tonight", offered Hurlburt respectfully."

"You're right, I could, but I'm sure Bush would react differently than if I let him think I'm a soft touch like the lieutenant. "Hurlburt caught Harwood's eye and with a slight smile gave his affirmation of the plan.

"Would you be sure that the two youngsters and Walsh share your tent, Fred? And don't tell them the situation. The lieutenant and I will eat our supper up here." Hurlburt nodded and stepped outside the tent. John watched him go, then began searching for linen and a khaki blanket, which he found in a footlocker. He set up the cot found collapsed beneath the lieutenant's bunk and just as he was completing this chore, Walsh stepped into the tent with Harwood's belongings.

"There's no proper shithouse here, sir", he announced.

"I know," said John, "but there will be by noon tomorrow and you're going to see to it. I want you to organize teams to dig four big latrines behind the tent rows." Walsh stared blankly at Harwood.

"Come on, now", urged John, "you've got more experience than any of those young chaps out there. They need direction for their energy and if we don't get some semblance of cleanliness in this camp soon, we'll all look and smell like those cattle we came up here with."

"I built a privy once back on the farm, but not for an army", drawled Walsh a bit sourly.

"Same thing, only bigger", John responded. "Here, take this manual and check on size, depth and the materials you'll need." He tossed a book from his duffel bag to Walsh. "If you get stuck, let Fred or me know. We'll be around to back you up."

About five in the afternoon a few trucks started pulling in. John watched as several off-duty men in the first wave pulled up by Bush's tent and dropped off some suspicious looking packages. "That will be the River View run", mused John. The men, who had been on the farms arrived at five-thirty, hot and dirty from the day's toil. Although tired and hungry, most of them simply grabbed towels and went down to the creek to wash. Harwood noted that they would stand little chance of breaking into the rapidly forming mess line filled with loud, tipsy men.

Night fell on the encampment with very few of the men even knowing that Harwood had arrived. Bush, convinced that his meeting with the captain was just another small ripple in an otherwise regular day, poured himself an ample measure of Jim Beam and slept undisturbed. At five thirty the next morning Harwood roused the sleepy lieutenant and told him to be ready for roll call in full dress uniform. John himself had already washed and shaved at the creek and was sliding into his polished boots. The lieutenant didn't need to be told twice and at six o"clock both men were on the company street getting more than their share of attention from the few men stirring at this hour. Someone must have informed Bush of what was going on for fifteen minutes later he stumbled from his tent, bleary-eyed. It took the next twenty minutes to organize the men falling in on the street in various stages of dress and demeanor. Harwood was sure that some were still in their tents, but that could wait. John moved to the center of the assembly and addressed the men, completely ignoring Bush. "My name is Captain Harwood and I have been assigned to command this company. For the past month and a half you have not been acting under any official orders. This is not the normal procedure and with my assumption of command we will immediately make improvements in this camp and await orders to move to a more permanent site. All work and activities you have been engaged in will cease at once."

Harwood paused to let this sink in awhile and, hearing a commotion behind him, turned to meet the puffy eyes of Bush, who rasped loudly, "What in hell do you think you're doing? This ain't a military parade, it's a work crew." He was flushed with uncontrollable rage and spattered Harwood's face and uniform with spittle as he yelled.

"You're through, you drunken swine. You've swindled and bullied these boys long enough", Harwood said quietly, but with utter disdain.

Bush literally hissed with hate and raised his hand menacingly. But in the split second that this took, Hurlburt, moving surprisingly like a cat, was at Harwood's side. Bush barely knew he was there when his jaw disintegrated under Hurlburt's fist. Coldcocked, Bush fell like a loose sack of turnips and was unconscious before he hit the ground.

No one stirred as Walsh bent over the fallen man, examined his face and rose slowly, eyes wide in amazement.

"Never seen that done before, Captain. His jaw's severely dislocated and may be broke, but he's breathin' regular through them broken teeth."

"Take him out of here and get him to the hospital back in town", Harwood instructed Walsh. "Tell the admitting clerk that he fell off a truck."

While Bush was being carried away, John continued to address the assembly. "From now on Hurlburt here will be my immediate subordinate and you will do as he directs. This camp has got to be cleaned up and you men have to be in sound physical shape for our future assignments in the permanent camp. Hurlburt will give you further instructions as needed. Despite what's happened here in the last, month, none of you are to blame. The fact that Bush was using you improperly should not discourage anyone. I saw the work crews coming in last evening from what the lieutenant tells me was a good day's labor."

Some smiles broke out at this. John beamed, too, adding that there would be time for relaxation. After praising the cooks for turning out wholesome meals under most difficult circumstances, John summoned Hurlburt who, wincing from his sore hand, explained the reorganization of the camp.

After breakfast and when the work was well underway, John drove the lieutenant to the train station.

"That was some ruckus this morning", said the young man, still somewhat dazed by events.

"Yes, Bush acted just like I thought he would, but thank God Hurlburt was there."

"You mean you didn't plan it that way?"

"No, I really didn't know how to handle Bush at that point. I probably would have had to call his hand on the illegal activities in hopes that the men would back me."

"Bush has some influence in these parts and may cause you a lot of trouble."

"I doubt it. Before he leaves the hospital I will have given him an extended leave and an unfavorable report with the request that he be assigned to another unit. If he protests, I'll drop a gentle hint that his illegal activities are known and that I'm requesting an investigation."

They had arrived at the station and John helped the lieutenant carry his footlocker to the siding. No one was on the platform, but as they passed the clerk's office, the terse little man threw them a fishy look. After shaking hands, the young man said, "I hope I can do a better job at my next assignment. After seeing the way you handled things, I'll be more careful."

"You'll do all right so long as you learn to trust the right people. I was lucky this time." And with that, Harwood turned abruptly towards the truck and left the confused and speechless young officer without saying goodbye or good luck. A massive dark cloud spilling over the Green Mountains to the west began to obscure the sun, but not a breath of air stirred round the hot platform. If anything the humidity had been increasing all morning, promising rain, which never seemed to come. Glad to be heading for Boston and civilization, the lieutenant sat on his duffel bag to await the train whose whistle could be heard flatting off low-level clouds far up the valley.

6

The company remained at the fairgrounds for the rest of the summer. The transition to Harwood's leadership went smoothly and without incident after the Bush episode. In short order the tent city was completely self-sufficient and, under Hurlburt's sharp eye, a number of repairs and improvements had been made in the fair buildings themselves after Harwood had carefully cleared each project through the selectmen and town clerk at city hall. Even the fair ground pit privies had been scraped clean and the contents buried in one of the latrines. Harwood was glad for the opportunity to keep the boys busy and out of mischief. Company numbers, meanwhile, continued to grow piecemeal and by mid-August had reached three-quarters strength. Still there were no orders from headquarters, not even a statement of mission. Harwood's calls for clarification yielded nothing but promises of subsequent orders, which never materialized.

"You know, Fred, we could be here all winter at this rate. I think the Army's lost our records in some staff officer's dead file." Hurburt didn't bat an eye.

"The county fair opens in September. No fair committee is going to tolerate our being under foot when all those farm folk descend on this place".

Hurlburt was right. Within two days of his prediction, a letter came from the selectmen asking when the camp was going to move. Harwood went to city hall to explain his dilemma and was informed that a gentleman named Perry Merrill would be in touch with him concerning his new assignment.

"Who's Perry Merrill?" John asked blankly. The town clerk looked at him with raised eyebrows.

"I can see that you haven't been in these parts very long. Merrill's probably done more in this state to save our land and forests than anyone else. His planning group up in Montpelier comes up with more schemes than you can shake a stick at. And most of them work. As soon as he finds out that you're sitting down here twiddling your thumbs, he'll be ringing your superiors."

As Harwood pulled the clerk's door shut behind him, he saw the man reach for the phone. He knew then that his questions should have begun here. As foretold, a vaguely worded letter came from headquarters within the week referring to a new site in Grafton, Vermont which would be occupied "in accordance with a timetable specified by the state forester." Then silence, which had Harwood on the edge of thinking that his unit once again had been forgotten.

But early one morning in late August a pickup bearing the logo, State of Vermont Forestry Department, pulled into the tent city. A slender young man in a soft felt hat and wire frame glasses stepped out and asked for Captain Harwood. He was dressed in field gear and high-cut boots whose condition implied that he spent little time at the desk and conference table. He was clean-shaven and alert, however, belying any false impression of sloppiness. When Harwood appeared, he introduced himself.

"I'm Chuck Hollis, engineer for Perry Merrill. I'd like to show you where your permanent camp will be." The voice was soft Vermont drawl, but full of confidence.

Harwood's eyes lit up as he shook the man's hand.

"Now that's good news for a change. I thought we might be in these tents till hell froze over."

The engineer's eyes twinkled. "The spot we've selected is a bit primitive and until it's developed and barracks built, you'll have to keep your tents." John's smile faded.

"You mean there's nothing there to move into?"

The engineer looked away at the activity in the company street for a moment, then continued in his soft, Vermont drawl. "That's right. The Grafton camp will be built from scratch, but I promise you that the camp and Hyde Pond have the top construction priority in this area. With luck, there'll be a roof over you head before the snow flies."

"You're God-damned encouraging, Hollis." Harwood laughed. But at least we'll have seen the last of this place and these boys will have something to do besides keeping their buttons shined."

The engineer's face relaxed into what looked like a grin. "Perry and I thought that you might agree. Can you spare some time now to go look at the site with me?"

"Sure, but I want my foreman, Fred Hurlburt to join us. He's got a good head for sizing up a job."

The three of them climbed into the forestry truck and for nearly an hour climbed northwest out of the valley through the tumbled hills towards the spine of the Green Mountains. Passing several dirt-poor hamlets, they at last entered Grafton, a sleepy village, authentic Vermont and well-kept by its thrifty residents who recognized the cash value of being a choice spot on the tourist route. "Not bad," mumbled Hurlburt as they passed the old town inn with its brace of sugar maples in the front yard.

"That's the old Phelps Hotel, chimed in the engineer. "It's seen better days."

Hollis said nothing more and drove on out of town, turning off finally onto a dirt sideroad that climbed up the edge of a hilly cowpasture. They continued through a thick stand of hardwoods where the road was deeply rutted and grass grew between the tracks.

"Where the hell are you taking us?" growled Harwood.

"Won't be long now."

They broke out of the forest into abandoned farmland where scattered trees were reclaiming the weedy meadows. Hollis shifted the pickup down to negotiate the final rise of land and several massive bumps, then brought the vehicle to a halt in an old apple orchard. The road continued down the other side of the hill and ended abruptly at the edge of a swamp. Beyond the orchard were the remains of a cellarhole and behind that the forest began again rising up yet another hill to the azure sky.

"Well, this is it, the old Wade farm", quipped Hollis brightly. John looked around in disbelief. They were at least four miles from the nearest neighbor and half again that distance from a surfaced road.

"We know it's a bit far out", the engineer remarked, reading Harwood's mind, "but that swamp over there is part of an old lake bed that we want to make into a pond. There's more than recreation involved here as we need the water for fire control and will eventually pipe it down to Grafton. C'mon down with me and I'll show you why we selected this place."

A natural ridge underlaid the swamp's entire eastern edge, but was cleft in one spot through which a steady flow of water passed even in this dry season. Below and east of the ridge, the land dropped away sharply through which the old lake's overflow had etched an even deeper glen.

"With a minimum of fill and some concrete, we can flood this swamp back about a mile. The two main brooks and the natural springs out in that pucker brush will keep it full year round", Hollis continued pointing out across the scrub. He seemed oblivious to the swamp mosquitoes that pounced on the three sweaty bodies disturbing their lair.

"I'm a believer", Harwood confessed hurriedly "Now where can we put the camp?"

Hollis chuckled and led them back to the truck. On the rise, the wind kept the mosquitoes down and after the gloom of the swamp, the old farm looked a lot better. Hurlburt was already casting his eye about, searching for level ground and protection from winter winds. The engineer watched him for a moment.

"What do you think, Fred?"

"Well, if the mosquitoes don't carry us off the first night, I'd say we could put the camp out there beside the apple orchard. Land's level, yet high enough to drain properly."

Hollis lit up with enthusiasm as he turned to Harwood. "You're blest with a sensible foreman, Captain. I'd suggest that same place for a lot of reasons. If we leave that northwest wooded slope alone it will help break up winter gales. Most of those trees are fifty or sixty feet high, which should give us a windbreak zone of about 600 feet. Snow drifts back of that break will help insulate the buildings. If we're careful with the cutting and keep some trees along the company street, you'll even have a bit of shade next summer." Hollis reached into his truck and grabbed some maps and a penciled sketch of the area.

John's mouth opened a bit as the engineer continued. He'd not thought that this laconic Vermonter had much grasp of the needs of his company, but the homework he was showing them was clearly impressive. Hurlburt was amused, but only his eyes gave him away.

"It may be chilly next winter down in the swamp where the cold air collects, but not here on the rise. You should be warm, especially if we face most of the buildings southeast and put the larger windows and doors on the south and southwest walls. You'll get the early sunlight that way and better warming when degrees are the lowest."

"Christ, Fred, it looks like we've got an offer we can't refuse." John finally responded with mock seriousness.

"And don't forget the apple blossoms in the spring," chortled Hurlburt.

"There's a catch you should know about", continued Hollis, matter-of-factly. "Normally we would send in special crews to set up your buildings, but with all manner of projects going on, all in a rush to finish before cold weather, you'll have to do the building. The plans are all done and I'll spare you three experienced tradesmen plus the material, but the rest is up to you."

John pursed his lips and looked at Hollis for a long time, then did the same to Hurlburt who shrugged and looked away off at the hill beyond the swamp.

"It doesn't look like we have much choice, does it?" His voice was so soft that the other two men barely heard.

"But how the hell can we get these city boys to pound nails straight when they don't even know which end of the claw hammer to use?" They had no trouble hearing him now.

"They'll learn, Capn", muttered Hurlburt, still counting pine trees on the far ridge.

"Damn right they will, Fred,"John exploded, "especially after a few frosty nights in those tents. But we'll really have to kick ass to get enclosed by Armistice Day. I can see us now sweeping tent canopies with snow up to our knees." Turning to Hollis, he retorted, "I don't guess you will expect us to build your pond right away?"

"Nope. Just so long as you clear the trees out of there this winter when the ground's hard, we'll get going on that in the spring."

They all climbed back into the pickup and started down the slope towards Grafton. John braced himself as they slid over the bumps and made a corkscrew turn around a big rock outcrop that came within inches of the fender.

"One condition, Hollis", Harwood muttered through clenched teeth. "Fix up this damn road."

7

The removal of the CCC company to Grafton was achieved in one day, much to the relief of the Bellow's Falls town fathers. With the fair scheduled to open Labor Day weekend, there was precious little time for the transition of military to circus tents. Supervised by Walsh and Hurlburt, the olive drab canvas was folded and tucked away in the trucks in jig time. Harwood himself made the final tour of the area to assure that the site was left spotless."Neat as a pin, dammit," he said to himself as he jumped into the cab of the last truck to leave. He allowed himself a small smile of pride as they roared past city hall.

The month of disciplined tent living had paid off. Before sunset, the old farm orchard was neatly dotted with canvas and a hot meal was available in the mess. John, Fred and Hollis labored long after dark by lantern light over the plans for the camp layout. Some of the company could immediately begin clearing land for barracks and a mess hall. Others would be sent back into the forest to begin cutting firewood for winter heating. A state forester had already marked dead and cull trees for felling. Hollis kept his part of the bargain and more. He had his team on site within the week to tap the stream northwest of camp and lay pipe and a water cistern up on the ridge behind the proposed mess hall. A week later gravel was being dumped and graded on the road to Grafton and a row of utility poles had sprouted on which linesmen were busily weaving a power supply to the campsite.

The tradesmen, two carpenters and a mason, were on the job before the cistern was laid. They were local Vermonters and a taciturn lot, but each knew well his craft. After a lot of pushing and yelling of recruits, they got the job done, but did not relish the prospect of several months in the wild with 150 brushmonkeys, most of whom hadn't the foggiest notion of manual labor. Top priority for construction was the mess hall, the largest building in camp, the single structure capable of sheltering the entire company. Hurlburt assigned thirty men to the mason in the morning and had them draw shovels from the tool truck Hollis had sent along. They would be spelled in the afternoon by another group of thirty, the morning crew and the remainder of the company going back into the woods to cut under the supervision of Walsh and Hurlburt. In no time, the dirt began to fly fast and furiously, prompting Harwood to caution them on their over-eagerness and profligate burning of strength. They nodded and kept on, but by eleven their pace slackened and the mason was now haranging them about not going deep enough.

"I want five foot ditches so the footings are below the frost line." The boys had little comprehension and after wiping the sweat out of their eyes stared at him in disbelief.

"You heard him", goaded Harwood. "Do as he says."

By afternoon roots and rock were encountered and the inexperienced diggers flagged seriously. Progress slowed even more the next day when they hit a buried ledge right where the footing was to make a corner. Somehow, the mason's initial probing had missed it and they either had to get through it or start another dig.

"God-dammed territory", muttered the mason.

But it was Hollis, visiting the camp that day, who solved the problem.

"I'll be seeing the county dynamiter on my way back to Bellow's Falls today and I'll have him come right up here." The tradesman glanced knowingly at each other when they heard this. Harwood picked up the look and asked what it meant.

"Little Almond Cross is a real character in these parts. Tries his damndest to live up to his name. He don't work with no one. Worse then a bull moose in rut and has the mouth of a spurned streetwalker."

Even with this vivid introduction, Harwood was quite
unprepared for the diminutive man who arrived mid-afternoon in
a dilapidated van. Communicating by grunts, Cross took a quick
look in the trench and, without a word, went back to his truck for
explosives and detonators. Noticing that he had a withered arm
and missing fingers on his healthy limb, one of the diggers rushed
up to help him open the van's rear doors.

"Get your ass out of here and stay out"; he barked so all those
assembled could hear. The boy jumped back and melted into the
crowd of watchers, not one of whom made a peep. Dragging his
materials and lines into the trench, Cross clawed away at the base of
the ledge with his two good fingers, then slipped the charges under,
attached the blasting caps and strung out his wires. A little way down
the hill he attached the wires to the detonator and yelled for everyone
to get back behind him. The crowd moved only a few feet. Turning
beet red, Cross leaped at them, gesticulating with his good arm.

"Move, you dumb son-of-bitches or you'll lose some of your
parts."

Most everyone ran for cover. Cross pushed the plunger on his
box of batteries and the ground trembled, the roar muffled by the
earth. There was thick smoke in the trench, but Cross jumped
right in, examined his work and bounded back out.

"Stay the hell out of here til the smoke clears," he warned as he
recovered what was left of his wires. He picked up his batteries,
lurched over to the van and threw the gear inside. He was about to
start the engine when Harwood laid a hand on the hood and asked
if the outcrop blocking the site entrance might be dispatched as
easily as the one in the trench.

"Not in my contract," he retorted testily. Harwood wasn't so
easily deterred and kept his foot on the runningboard. Coming up
the road were Hurlburt, Walsh and the timber crews. The mason,
eager to get his footings in place, set the boys to work again with
sledges and picks to remove the fractured rock and continue the
trenching. Most of the smoke from the dynamite was dissipated, but
its odor was still strong and the diggers were not all enthusiastic.
Some hung back, letting the eager beavers fall to the task. In time,

several of these wandered away to pass comments with the returning woodcutters.

Harwood's nose twitched at the odor emanating from the cab of Cross's truck, but he remained eyeball to eyeball with the man until, after a score of grunts and expectorations, Cross muttered, "Let's see what you got."

The outcrop was more complicated than the trench, but Cross found a number of cracks in the stone which when teased with Hurlburt's crowbar, opened sufficiently for the dynamite sticks. Cross upped the charge, laid out a longer roll of wire and warned everyone back behind the rise. Harwood ran a quick mental check on his men, but Walsh was already one step ahead of him.

"Where's young Borowski?" he asked, his voice taut. It was too late to get Cross' attention and to everyone's surprise Walsh leaped up and sped down the hill towards the rocks. He'd spotted Borowski straggling in late from the forest, waltzing uncomfortably close to the charges. Walsh grabbed the boy and pinned him flat in the grass just as Cross flicked the switch on his batteries. The blast was terrific and sent shards of rock in every direction. When the dust cleared, the outcrop was level with the ground, making a clear passage for vehicles. John could care less now as he hurried towards the prostrate figures of Walsh and Borowski. Both had dozens of small puncture wounds from the rock dust and a dark stain had begun to spread down Walsh's trousers. The young man stirred first, sat upright and rolled a piece of granite the size of a football from Walsh's leg, John helped Walsh sit up and breathed a massive sigh of relief that the gash just behind the knee was not spurting.

"Dammit, Walsh, I thought you'd lost your mind until I saw you grab this man. He owes you one hell of a debt of gratitude." Walsh smiled out of one corner of his mouth and brushed some rock dust out of his hair. Harwood beamed with pride and helped the man to his feet.

"Can you make it to my tent so I can properly dress that wound?" Walsh winced and said he thought he could. By this time Hurlburt and the rest of the company were crowding around.

Hanging between Borowski and Hurlburt, Walsh hobbled towards the tents as the boys commenced to whistle and give him a cheer.

"Let's hear it for Scooter," one of them yelled.

The ovation ended in some good-natured laughter. And while no one dared use it to Walsh's face, the name stuck.

Harwood found Cross drawing on a bottle of Four Roses behind his truck. The cussedness was out of the little fellow and he made much of the hand he'd maimed in an old accident. Both his hands were shaking and he couldn't look Harwood in the eye.

"Look, this thing was probably more my fault than anyone else's, Cross. And you can be sure that nobody away from this camp will hear it differently."

The dynamiter's eyes softened for a split second, then he tossed the empty bottle into his truck, jumped in himself and without so much as a farewell, clanked his way down the rubble-strewn road.

When three boys on the trenching crew failed to report for supper and Hurlburt found them moaning in their bunks with splitting headaches, he sent for John who pried out of them that they were the first three into the trench after the blast. Dynamite headache was Harwood's diagnosis.

"I've seen it a few times when I was in France. Give them some aspirin and plenty of water. If they eat, they'll only lose it. Have whoever is on first aid duty check on them a couple of times tonight for fever. They should be good as new in the morning."

After he and Hurlburt were in the company street, Harwood muttered, "The mason shouldn't have pushed them so quickly after what Cross told him."

Hurlburt nodded.

"Guess everybody wants to get this place organized in a hurry." John caught the irony and smiled. They both knew this beginning was less than propitious, but they were learning. They were all learning.

Throughout September and on into Indian summer the company slowly transformed the old Wade place into a working

CCC camp. The few good apples in the unkempt orchard were quickly depleted by the hungry lads scrambling to and fro with materials and lumber at the behest of the tradesmen. Most of the boys were clumsy with tools, but within a few weeks they could be counted on to follow directions tolerably well.

Hurlburt and the tradesmen grew to understand each other and took delight in keeping the brighter youngsters on their toes. When it came time to square the corners for the mess hall loading dock, Hurlburt gave the job to the sharpest team, handing them string and batter boards. The boys stared blankly at him when, with no further instructions, he walked away. A half-hour later he returned with a twinkle in his eyes and found them arguing heatedly. They had already set the boards half a dozen times to no avail.

"How much is 6 plus 8?" He asked the one who seemed to be convincing the others.

"Anybody knows that. It's fourteen"

"Wrong", chirped Hurlburt. "Get out your measuring tape, and I'll show you". Hurlburt measured off 8 feet out from the mess hall foundation, set a stake and tacked on a string. He then ran the string out another 22 feet from the building and told the open-mouthed boys to set up their batter boards in an L-shaped angle. He tied the string to one of the boards, went back to the foundation and measured 6 feet along its edge where he set another stake.

"O.K. Now, Raymond, I want you to tack another string to my first stake there and bring the loose end to me."

Raymond did as directed and tied the end to Hurlburt's second stake.

"O.K. Now measure your string and tell me what you get".

Raymond came up with 10 feet.

"Told you 6 plus 8 wasn't 14. Now, you believe me?"

"But, but," the recruit stammered.

"Oh, your math is fine. Just be careful and use the 6-8-10 method I'm showing you when you're building something with 90 degree angles," chuckled Hurlburt.

"Now put your other batter boards out at the far angle of where the loading dock will be and string it to the foundation in a square. Run strings at diagonals from each foundation point to the opposite sets of batter boards. Each of these strings must be the same length. When they are, the loading dock will be exactly square".

In no time the boys had the proper measurements and were digging holes for the dock support pieces.

"Now don't forget to use your plumb bob and level often and don't waste any boards. The Army makes us account for everything, including the sawdust." He turned to go, then stopped and gave them a final admonition.

"And blunt your nails before using them. I don't want any split lumber on that dock." The boys continued to dig, but watched him go out of the corners of their eyes. When he was out of earshot, one of the crew cracked good-naturedly, "He sure fixed your wagon, Ray".

Raymond frowned sheepishly. "He always does. Someday though, I'm going to stump him for a change."

"Good luck," someone scoffed.

"Shut up and get those pieces in before he gets back here again," Ray ordered with a grin.

8

Harwood drove south in late September just as the leaves were turning, the irregular Vermont countryside gradually giving way to the smooth drumlins and broad fertile plain of the Pioneer Valley. Tobacco sheds dotted the neat fields still hung with netting and a noon sun splayed wildly from horizon to horizon dispelling the claustrophobia John had felt in camp.

He'd caught a bus in Chester two weeks before and picked up his Ford at home in Burkett, but had no time to linger there with all the camp building going on. There was very little traffic at this hour, so he pulled out the Ford's hand throttle and stretched his legs, letting the exhilaration of the car's speed melt away the tension of too many responsibilities for too long. His original plan was to go directly home, but instead of turning onto the cutoff towards Amherst, he continued south towards Northampton. Shortly, the Mount Holyoke range came into view with its bleached summit house standing out against the brilliant blue sky. Across the meadowland he caught sight once more of the Connecticut River lazily meandering its way towards the Holyoke dam and canals. Thence sullied from tons of mill wastes, it would ooze itself down to Springfield, becoming thoroughly disreputable before passing the state line at Longmeadow.

He crossed the ox-bow and passed the amusement park, stopping for a hotdog at a tiny diner he knew called Nick's Nest. He needed sleep badly, but a greater need drove him to make a short telephone call after which he continued south to Springfield. He used the Deady Bridge, entering the heavy traffic of downtown, then went up the hill to Linden Street where he parked in front of the modest brownstone block he knew so well. Using the main entry, he climbed two flights and proceeded down the passageway.

Just as he remembered it, the corridor was clean, but dimly lit and smelling of food and old wax. At the corner apartment he raised his hand to knock on the door, hesitated a moment, then rapped softly. The door opened a crack, still held by the night latch. John responded to Hazel's unspoken question, "It's me." She slipped the latch and let him enter.

"Where've you been keeping yourself, Johnny?" She inquired rather listlessly, her tired eyes giving him the once over.

"Up in the woods, but not on vacation. They gave me weekend leave to get some rest."

"Nice of them," she murmured sardonically. Then brightening a bit she added, "Well, I *am* glad you decided to call me and come down here. It's been nearly a year hasn't it?"

"Not quite that long, Hazel," replied Harwood ignoring her manner and taking off his jacket which he hung over the back of a kitchen chair.

"How have you been?"

"Look around, Johnny, and you can see for yourself that things are not so bad as they used to be. New furniture, new curtains, a few bucks in the bank. I work four nights a week and pull in as much as I did last year for two weeks work."

John grinned. "I guess that means either Roosevelt has gotten lucky or that you're getting better."

"You are disgusting as usual. How about some coffee?"

"To start with."

Hazel managed a cryptic smile as she turned the gas heat up under the coffeepot. Reaching for some china in the cupboard she deftly fixed a few stray hairs, patting them back into place behind her ear. She set out the cups and took a seat directly across the table noting that John's eyes had never left her.

"I thought maybe you went back to your wife."

"That's not going to happen," he said matter-of-factly, but with a nervous twitch in his stomach.

"What's she doing now?" Hazel persisted cautiously.

"I'm not really sure since she moved to Hartford a while back. We don't write, so I rely on my mother to keep me up to date."

Hazel saw his discomfort and changed the subject.

"You're on your way home now, I take it?"

"Soon enough." Harwood never dropped his eyes from hers.

She got up and poured the coffee. As she was returning to the safety of her chair, he caught the sash of her kimono and drew her close.

"You've been in the woods too long. A little brandy in that coffee will do you good," she suggested and hid behind a generous draft from her cup.

"To hell with brandy! God, you're a provocative woman, Hazel."

"Oh, that's what I'm told often," she responded lightly.

He smiled. "What they don't tell you is that there is more essence in your left earlobe than most women can muster in a lifetime." His voice softened. "And that compels the likes of me."

"That can't be the way I am," she demurred softly, losing a bit of her control.

The sash slipped its knot and he grasped her waist inside the gown.

"But it is, Hazel, and you can't help it."

He rose and kissed her gently. She let him, her mouth gradually parting, but before his tongue could find hers, she broke away saying, "The stove is still on."

"So let it be awhile." His need for her was overwhelming.

"I should have known that a cup of java wouldn't satisfy you," she teased. The ferocious flame in his eyes told her how he enjoyed this banter, this age-old pavan.

Hazel's face was soft, yet pensive as she looked him squarely in the eye, saying finally, "It's so good to see you let down your guard, but you'll never really change, will you, Johnny?"

It was Harwood's turn to drink. He emptied the cup and put it on the saucer. Ignoring the question, he said, "That's what I like most about you, Hazel. You never pull a punch."

He shut the gas off with his free hand and she slipped away from his other arm, but caught his hand and led him to the bedroom where the sun beamed through two corner windows. Patterns and the shifting fall afternoon shadows crawled ever so slowly across the room while traffic and school children bustled noisily by two stories below. Together embraced, they noticed such things not at all.

Harwood dreamed he was lying paralyzed in a shell hole. Searchers were everywhere crying out his name, but his throat was so parched he couldn't respond. Then his brother's face appeared over the edge of the hole, innocent and wholesome, but when Harwood made an effort to reach up, there was nothing. The searchers moved off still calling as panic and desolation welled up and overpowered him. His eyes clicked open to darkness broken only by the intermittent flash of a red neon light at the cafe down on the street corner. Hazel had gone on her evening round of bars leaving the odor of harsh perfume which permeated the air even though she must have left hours before. John rubbed his eyes, breathed deeply to quell his racing heart and lay back on the pillow. He was still dog-tired, but his psyche felt renewed. His mind raced, savoring the pleasant afternoon. He let sensual images wash unfettered for several minutes before catching himself absently counting the neon flashes.

He arose, dressed and remembered to put the ten dollar bill beneath her jewelry box on the dresser. He went into the kitchen, the noise of his footsteps sounding harsh and forlorn in the stillness. He shuddered and was gripped by conscience, thinking of Hazel's lonely, tawdry life in the flat. She, too, must be haunted by that same awful emptiness which blew through his soul like a wind from hell. He was lucky to be in the Vermont camp, however hectic and exhausting it had made his life. Hazel was not getting younger and soon that vibrant, sexy click, click of her heels he had known so well would slow to an agonizing shuffle. He found a pencil and began writing a note to her, then paused and tore it up, realizing that it would only complicate her life.

Jacket in hand, he slipped carefully out of the flat letting the lock bolt slide home behind him. Its soft click sounded like a shot in the deserted passageway and Harwood shuddered again as the hairs raised on the back of his neck. He hunched his shoulders and ran a hand over his head, then lost little time leaving the brownstone. Gunning the Ford, he turned the corner by the cafe and raced in the dark toward home. But after only a few hours sleep and breakfast, he bade his mother goodbye and returned to Grafton.

Indian summer left suddenly with an early frost. Human activity in camp was feverish, like wild bees putting away the stores for the winter they all sensed would be immediately upon them. Few of the boys or their leaders had time to note the glorious hills in fall foliage. Roofs were raised and doors and windows hung to keep out the frosty air. They were beating old man winter. That was enough in the fall of 1936.

9

Foresters from Merrill's office showed up the first day of December and began to train teams of recruits for forest thinning and culling on the hills and for clearing the swamp. There had been a hard freeze right after Thanksgiving, which made most areas accessible. Before long, additional fuel was stacking up in the wood yard located safely on the camp perimeter.

One forester named Johnson, who worked out of Mass Aggie, was most knowledgeable and loquacious, keeping up a constant commentary on his profession. He was also precise and made sure each recruit knew how to handle and measure wood.

"You'll be using about 20 cord per week just to keep warm up here. That's about 40 decent-sized trees. Remember what I told you about a cord. It's a stack four by four by eight feet. Now, Borowski, what does that figure out to be per month?"

Borowski heaved another log into the pile and thought for a moment, then replied smiling, "A hell of a lot more than I want to chuck. I guess about from here to that birch down by the dam".

"Not bad. Try 640 feet, which is one long pile!" Another skid of logs arrived and the forester directed its deposition.

Borowski let out a whistle of exertion and remarked to his compatriots, "I sure see what that guy means by wood warming you twice. Oh, oh, here he comes again for another lecture".

"As I was saying, it depends on what you're burning. That hickory that just came in will get you nearly twice as much heat as white pine. But if you handle hickory all day, you'll wish for something else. It's heavy and tough. The trick is to mix them, but you have to know how to tell them apart. That's why I'm here working with you and giving this harangue. Next November when these piles are properly seasoned, I won't be around to tell you what to put in the barracks wood boxes. You'll be on your own. Now take this elm here. Ever try to split the stuff?"

Borowski rolled his eyes at the others and continued to heave logs on the lengthening pile.

Up on the hillsides, several teams were hewing fire logs and cutting brush. A roaring bonfire was kept going to warm hands and feet during the morning and afternoon breaks. Another of Merrill's foresters held court next to the blaze.

"Better get used to keeping a fire going. In the middle of January those chicken houses you boys are building will be colder than a well digger's tail. Hey, throw one of these pieces of spruce on the fire".

The boy next to the stack pile did as he was told. In no time the piece caught and was consumed almost instantly accompanied by vigorous snapping and popping.

"Now, there's the reason we haven't sent any spruce down to the wood yard. Burns very hot and easy so it makes a good kindling, but its full of resins and is a real flash in the pan. It also chucks out sparks to beat the band. A couple of these loose in your barracks would make a barbecue. On the bottom of that fire is oak. It's hard as hell to coax into flame, but you can't beat it for uniformity and coals. Properly banked it will keep you warm all night".

Their luck with the weather lasted. Despite dustings and flurries, no snow stayed on the ground until Christmas. By that time, the mess hall and two barracks were finished and the headquarters building was completely enclosed. Walsh and Hurlburt were each assigned a barracks and Harwood slept in and operated out of the mess hall office until his suite in the headquarters was complete.

Hurlburt came in grumbling. "We've got about a month, with luck, to get that swamp out there cleared for Hollis. After that the ice won't be good enough and it'll have to wait until next year. What we need is a real tit chiller to get onto that ice."

"Do what you can and let the rest wait, Fred", Harwood returned easily. "We made no promises other than to work at it."

"Yeah, but if we want any peace, it'll be best to get the heavy grading for the dam done come spring so the pond can fill. Laying pipe is their concern after that. Besides, we've got the manpower now. Who knows what it'll be next winter—if we're still here."

"What has Hollis promised us for machinery to get them out?"

"Nothing and he's not returning telephone calls", Hurlburt sighed.

"Then that's it. No tractors, no trees," Harwood shot back.

Walsh rolled his eyes. He was usually content doing what he was told without comment, but he decided to put in his two cents worth now.

"Snake 'em out with horse and chains. Ice can be thin and still hold. It'll take a little longer, but will get the job done."

Hurlburt looked at him a little non-plussed. "Not a bad idea, but who's going to handle the teams? And I don't think many of the locals will lend us their animals to take chances on the ice."

"I don't like the idea of freezing my tail in that swamp, but I've driven teams plenty before."

"Well, so have I, but we can't do the whole damn job."

John looked up from his paperwork. "Hollis gave us a little kitty for supplies and wouldn't miss it. Go hire some of the farmers with their teams. That way they take responsibility for the animals. I'm sure a little part-time work in this season would be welcomed."

"I suppose your right", Fred responded with hesitation. "But I'd still be nervous about that ice cover, especially near the shore."

"Use bridges," retorted Walsh. "The horses keep their feet dry that way and no one goes through ice. I'll bet there's half foot or so out there right now, plenty for horses."

Fred mulled it over. "O.K., let's get us a hatchet and check."

Walsh was right. There was more than enough to support horses and men, but on the shy side for motorized equipment. Hurlburt bought the idea of simple bridges to span the area near the shallows where the ice was rough and full of shards and air pockets. In a week, Hurlburt's hoped for cold snap put a lot of insurance under the horses and soon the operation was in full swing. With plenty of hands to trim and stack, the local farmers and their horse teams snaked load after load of logs out of the swamp with no mishaps while roaring bonfires of brush and slash kept the fellers and trimmers warm. By the time Hollis got around to returning Hurlburt's phone call, the clearing was nearly complete. Hyde Swamp would be ready for the earth-moving equipment, dam builders, pipe layers and anything else the engineer wanted to bring in. Then, two weeks later, Harwood gave Hurlburt some good news. "You've been promoted to Camp Forestry Superintendant, Fred. Seems that Merrill likes what you're doing."

10

Pelham McGarry returned from Spain in January of 1937. An early supporter of the Loyalists against Franco, he had shipped out with the Abraham Lincoln Brigade, but soon was flying infantry cover in a biplane fighter squadron. A hell-for-leather officer, he tangled once too closely with the Messerschmidts of the Condor Legion and narrowly escaped death. He spent a month in a Loyalist hospital with a serious leg wound, then was sent home for additional surgery and recovery. Never one to stay put or take advice; he was riding a motorcycle by mid-March. The letter he had sent to John telling of his planned visit was dated April 1st and right on schedule, he roared into camp on a Friday, just before supper. The boys flocked out in droves to see his machine, a brand-new, top of the line Harley-Davidson. Harwood met him at the flagpole.

"Damn good to see you, Pel. Come over to the office and give these lads room to worship your bike." John noticed the stagger as Pel dismounted and caught the flyer's arm as much for assistance as in greeting. As they crossed to the headquarters building, John acted as crutch for the exhausted McGarry.

"Just give me a drink, Harwood, and I'll be as good as new." Harwood sent a nearby recruit to get a bit of ice at the mess hall. "And tell Sergeant Blantin that we'll dine here tonight," he added quietly as the runner departed. John splashed some Scotch into glasses and when the boy returned minutes later, the two officers relaxed in wicker chairs.

Maybe you're on your feet too early, Pel." John noticed the winced face as McGarry took a huge draught. "Hey, take it easy. That stuff is neat," he added with a grin.

"You're telling me how to drink, Harwood?" McGarry was in good humor and his face relaxed a bit as the liquor smoothed him out.

"Not at all," John said good-naturedly. "One thing the Army hasn't shut off is my source of good Scotch. How are things in Springfield?"

"Just great, Jack. Say, do you remember that knockout brunette we knew in high school, Gladys—what was her name? Well, she's shed that banker husband and is back in circulation. We took in a couple of nightclubs last week."

"You haven't changed a bit, Pel, God help you," said Harwood with a grin. "Now how were you able to hobble around with dynamite like that?"

"Easy. She came to my flat and helped me into her own car, then lent me a heavenly shoulder and shuffled me in and out of the bars like a pro."

"Lucky for her. She's safe so long as you're on one leg."

Pelham grinned broadly, the scotch now unbuttoning his lip. "Just wait til this bone heals and I'll give her a run for her money."

"How long is your sick leave?"

"They've given me through Thanksgiving for some reason. Hell, if I can ride that contraption up here, I ought to be back in the saddle before summer."

"It must be worse than you think, Pel". John scowled.

"Now don't pull a sober-sides on me, Jack. We've known each other a long time and you know I'm going to be back flying real soon. What I need is a place to relax. How about letting me stay here for a couple of weeks? I'll pay for everything, of course, so the government won't hang you."

"They haven't yet for much worse than that," John laughed, and the Army has yet to send me an Exec. Why don't you take his room?"

McGarry beamed. "That'll be just fine, Jack. Thanks."

After the supper meal the two officers had sherry and played chess. They were evenly matched and the contest became protracted.

"What is going on in Spain, Pel? The papers are so full of conflicting stories one doesn't know what to believe."

McGarry didn't respond right away and seemed to be in a deep strategy. After a drag on his Dutch Master, he answered, eyes on John's bishop.

"Murder, rape, child mutilation, you take your pick from day to day. Politics and religion are in bed together like oxygen and gasoline. Their issue is guaranteed to be a bastard. No one will win anything in that war save Hitler or Stalin." The vehemence in Pel's tone stunned John, as did the agony burning in Pel's eyes as he snuffed out another of John's pawns.

"Things you and I in our most troubled sleep would never dream of are happening, Jack, and no one can stop it. Last year we were bivouacked outside a small town near Toledo when Franco's bombers came over one afternoon and leveled it. Nothing was spared, not even the school which was clearly identified. We picked up the pieces of the children in baskets. This was in retaliation for the sacking of a monastery by our forces. Only the week before I was flying cover for a Loyalist battalion which had pushed the Falangists off a fortified hill position. We strafed their rear guard as our troops secured the high ground. They also secured a nearby church where they found nuns hiding. We returned from routing the Falangists just in time to see our troops pass the nuns around like hors d'oeuvres. Several of us buzzed the bastards, but they only thought we were cheering them on."

He paused and drained the last of his sherry, then continued, "There's a harvest of hate being sown, John, ideological hate, the worst kind possible. And it's all being exploited by men on horseback who are garnering their power from confused and failed leaders. Propaganda has replaced political courage. Slogans, half-truths and lies are becoming ideals.You'd have thought that we were fed enough spread eagle in the last war to be immune to such nonsense, but once around doesn't satisfy the gullible and the ignorant. It's almost as if we just have to espouse a cheap cause and hate somebody, especially if it takes our minds off our own problems and failings. What we get are bogus substitutes for confidence."

"What about Guernica?", John interjected.

"Proves what I said before. Sure, the Germans were responsible and may they rot in hell for it, but I know flyers, American flyers, who would have done the same insane thing. It's too simple up there to throw a switch and zoom away. Reason becomes a will-o-the-wisp when mendacity and jingoism unleash their poisons. Pilots become monsters bent on cutting down anything moving in enemy territory. The strategy, the mission is all that counts and lives become the cheap currency of power-hungry men."

"So you won't be going back?"

McGarry rose stiffly and limped to the window. Down the company street boys were returning from the rec hall and library. Somewhere a small group was crooning hillbilly to a guitar accompaniment. The few lights on the narrow barracks stoops were winking out, making each spring star in the heavens appear to burn more fiercely.

"No," McGarry said at last. "The Loyalists will never stand up to the Fascists. Their organization is riddled with distrust and suspicion and the Fascists know it. In another year or so it will be all over except for the revenge. And that will be ghastly."

"But if the Fascists win, it will only encourage more saber rattling and bullying, like Mussolini in Ethiopia."

"Precisely, John. The democracies will hem and haw and be out-bluffed by the dictators. Then sooner or later, someone will overstep and we'll be right in the cesspool again, just like 1917."

"You're wrong there, Pel. Not us. There's too much talk about isolation. Congress passed the Neutrality Act and Roosevelt signed it. Besides, France has it all over both Hitler and Mussolini in military equipment and standing army."

McGarry yelped, "Neutrality, ha!!" His face was taut as he met Harwood's eyes. "I wish I could believe that. You're right on the French hardware. Whatever we got our hands on was good, but I'm not sure if they really know how to use it, tanks in particular. Their generals are still debating things like Verdun. Why do you suppose they spent a fortune the Maginot Line? And the poilu, especially the reserves, could care less. No, I'm not so sure about the froggies. They may have won the last one, but lost almost a third of their young men doing it. They won't stand for that again."

Brightening suddenly, he swept away the somber talk with a grin.

"How about another spot of that sherry. Then I'll turn in and give this bum leg a rest."

"To a quick recovery," John said cheerfully as he filled their glasses.

11

"Lieberman, Joshua M., Master of Arts in Philosophy", intoned the Dean, his rather plummy voice with just the right pause and inflection. Joshua rose and made his way forward amid polite clapping from the audience. How he'd longed for this moment. Somewhere in the back of the hall, his mother and father were watching his unhurried ascent of the platform. With what pride they would write of this occasion to the grandparents and family back in Poland. For a decade the Liebermans had shared a crowded little flat on New York's Lower East Side, working extra hours in the hot, stuffy tailor's shop below so that their boy might be educated. And for seven years Joshua had studied, excelling first in political science and history, graduating B.A., magna cum laude, and now the M.A. He'd make them proud of each of those years they had given him.

But how? The 1929 Crash had changed everything. Even his professors were taking pay cuts or losing their jobs to younger, cheaper men. Though he'd worked summers in woolen mills as an underpaid fill-in for vacationing laborers, he had no trade, no mechanical aptitude. Words were his tools and well did he know how they might be used to construct elegant ideas and to convince others of them. After the cogent and spirited oral defense of his thesis, his committee had drawn him aside and urged him to stay on for the PhD. But he would have none of it. Despite his considerable abilities, he had no interest in ferreting out dusty, old ideas in some library's catacombs. There was more important work waiting to be done.

In the mills he had seen men and women exploited, their years and energy thrown away by greedy men. Men with families had lost their jobs for mere idle talk about solidarity. It was the same system that had doomed his parents and grandparents to lives of squalor and indignity. He knew that a Jew, no matter how able, would always be laid low after others got what they wanted. Yet, even this stigma of his heritage might be mitigated if only the workingman could wrench the oppression of wealth and power from the exploiters. Marx had opened his eyes—"to give the masses the control of production". Lenin had put flesh on these bones and, to Lieberman, the current condition of capitalism was just as he predicted, an overripe fruit ready to fall, even now rotting away inside. Socialism, in time, would end this corruption. Communism would be the catalyst.

Shinsky's course in Modern Political Systems had homogenized all of these injustices, all the hurts of ghetto life in Cracow and the daily taunts and slights of New York. There was the professor now on the platform, clapping, smiling, proud of his star pupil, the bewhiskered face radiant with enthusiasm. Joshua mounted the steps, looking boldly at the assembled faculty, and took the proffered sheepskin from the red-robed President's hand, feeling his own palm gripped and shaken vigorously. Continuing across the platform, he stopped in front of Shinsky, bowed his head and leaned into the old man's embrace. The Dean looked their way, but if he was irritated with the interruption of his name-calling cadence, his sugary smile hid it well. Shinsky pushed him away to arm's length, but did not let go his shoulders and by this ambiguous laying on of hands, sealed their unspoken pact. Then, in deference to the Dean, whose teeth were now showing through the sugar, he sent him on his way. Lieberman returned to his seat exuberant. He eye caught his mother weeping in her joy, completely unaware of his real thoughts, his resolution. Few noted the look of utter satisfaction on Shinsky's face and those who did mistook it for commencement euphoria. But Shinsky knew his feelings well. They had occurred before and would repeat with each new convert he won. Yet this one, this Lieberman, would outshine them all.

A week later, on June 15, 1936, Joshua left for Chicago ostensibly to work for a government relief agency. The appointment was lowly and ill paying, but he was used to doing with very little and the position put him in direct access to workers and their families. In his free time evenings and weekends he would help organize the disenchanted. Backed by party headquarters, he'd have a cell going at Republic Steel in no time. The so-called captains of industry would deny workers nothing once labor was pulling together. If they balked, the workers would strike and bring management to its knees. It had worked against Big Steel in Pennsylvania and would work in South Chicago.

Memorial Day 1937 was nearly idyllic. The summer sun made the harsh reality of the striker's life almost tolerable after a winter and spring of deadlock and intransigence at the bargaining table. The rank and file did not know it yet, but Little Steel had no intention of restoring any strikers. They were doing just fine with scabs, who, desperate for work, could easily be found. Further, the police were in their pocket and for weeks had surrounded the steel mills, effectively sidelining the small bands of pickets trying to break the stranglehold of scab labor. But today would be different. Whole families turned out for a holiday picnic on the flats beside the mills. Baseballs and horseshoes were sailing through the balmy air while children shrieked and gobbled hotdogs. Women, amused by the playfulness of the afternoon and relieved that their men were out of the house and doing something besides brooding, gathered in small groups to chat and gossip.

"Where were they?", Lieberman growled to himself. He'd been waiting for nearly a half-hour for the other pickets. This would be easy, he thought, to confront those damned scabs when the shift changed. He had yet to see a cop this holiday. Maybe the bosses had relented after all and pulled their cronies out as a gesture of good faith. "Fat chance," he smirked, remembering the wall of billy clubs that had met their last venture. The police were spoiling for a good melee so they could knock a few heads. Of that he was sure. On the flats at the other side of the mill complex he could hear the crowd cheer and whistle. He looked at his watch. It was time for the shift.

It sounded at first like firecrackers. Then the silence, soon to be replaced with what seemed a collective moan, followed by shouts and screams. Lieberman could see nothing of the flats, but knew something had changed over there rather quickly and he didn't like it. Still no one had showed. He looked over to see the scabs lining up at the gate. Suddenly, about 20 police poured out of the mill with weapons drawn.

Lieberman froze. He saw the first of the pickets rounding the storage sheds and coming up the company street. The scabs were blocking his joining the marchers and the police were fanning out to stop them. The pickets hesitated, then surged onward like they had done a number of times before. A police pistol cracked, but no one stopped. Two shotguns cut loose and a man marching on the flank clenched his arm. The column stopped, but the police bore down on them, muzzles to the front. The front row of pickets turned and ran, colliding with those behind. In no time, the entire column was in flight. But the police continued, running among them, flailing left and right with billy clubs. Other shots were fired. Lieberman thought he saw a man running ahead go down, but in the confusion he could not be sure and was acutely aware that his position was extremely vulnerable. He casually joined the scabs, most of whom were in a shocked state watching the attack.

The ruse might have worked but for a scab who shouted, "This one here is trying to hide. I've seen him before on the picket line."

A cop looked around, brandishing a shotgun. Lieberman turned and walked in the other direction toward the rail yard. Hearing footsteps behind him, he started to run.

"Oh no you don't, you goddamn Red!", came a voice. Lieberman increased his speed. Fortunately, no one was around the tracks and he nearly made it. He felt a heavy blow to his back before the roar of the shotgun reached his ears. He stumbled, but kept running, around a boxcar and down the narrow space between two idle trains. He stopped only when it was clear no one pursued him. Grasping the iron of a sliding door, he braced himself and panted for breath. The pellets had torn away his shirt and his hands became sticky as he tried to assess the damage. Only his fleet running had saved him from a mortal wound, but those pellets and the bleeding were serious. He'd need help and soon, but the rail yard inside the Little Steel mill complex was hardly the place for improving his lot. He felt very tired and thirsty. The burning pain would only get worse. He looked about for somewhere to hide. In no time they would come looking for him. An open door three cars up the line might do temporarily. With great difficulty, he hoisted himself in, lay face down on a pile of empty feed bags in one corner and lost consciousness.

He thought he heard voices way off, but did not open his eyes. His mind raced, trying to think. Then they were standing over him.

"Looks to me like he caught a load of lead", the closest voice muttered. There were two other grunts of agreement. Lieberman was trapped and knew it. He tried to turn over and fell back wincing in pain.

Suddenly, the car lurched, throwing the trio off balance. A bale of hay tumbled down and landed on Lieberman's back. He screamed in agony before a grimy hand was clamped over his mouth. The car eased forward, slowly increasing speed.

"If he lets out another howl, we're in bad trouble", said the talker. "Keep him quiet until we get out on the open road."

Through the nearly unbearable pain, Lieberman began to put things together. These men were not about to turn him in. They had to be hoboes picking up a little free transportation. The train was on its way and that meant out of the rail yard. He could never have made it out of the mill complex under his own power and these freeloaders were going to be his ticket. He lay still. The filthy paw in his mouth was nauseating. After a while the hand was withdrawn.

In a half-hour they had cleared the city limits, gathering speed in the night. Lieberman had not seen his benefactors yet, but he felt watched. After a while, one of them lit a cigarette and for an instant he saw a lined face looking back at him. Lieberman eased himself up so he was kneeling on the pad. Sitting up was unthinkable as each twinge of his back muscles set off new fires of pain. He could hear them over near the door eating in the dark.

"Hey, city slicker, want somethin to chew?", one of them hollered. Lieberman knew he needed something to keep him going.

"How about some water first?", he said weakly.

"Oh, cat doesn't have his tongue, after all. And it sounds like he's had some book learnin'". It was the smoker talking.

"Look, I'll give you a quarter for something to drink." He carefully reached in his pocket and found nothing. There had been thirty dollars and change earlier in the day. They must have frisked him when he was unconscious. There was a chuckle from the other side of the darkness. They had left his watch and identification probably to avoid a confrontation should the law start asking questions. A tepid fluid was put to his lips. He drank eagerly, not caring what it was, then rocked back on his haunches, the only position he could tolerate. A piece of bread and a chunk of chicken were thrust into his hands. He ate without a word and settled back to the swaying of the train. He couldn't think right now. In the back of his mind the annoying refrain from that last union meeting repeated over and over . . . "Freight train, freight train going so fast." God ! Shinsky had never mentioned this part of union organizing. He slept between fits of wracking pain.

Just before dawn the freight slowed down and stopped. Lieberman opened his eyes and lifted his head from the feed bags. Bright lights of pain ran through him, but he bit his tongue and listened. Only gentle snoring, but he was sure one of the trio was on guard. Light gradually increased and he could make them out near the slightly opened door. He moved to a crack in the wall and peered out. Nothing but flat cornfields, but the sun was just over the horizon. That would make their direction approximately south.

"There's nothing to see here." The smoker had spoken.

"Where are we going?", Lieberman ventured.

The lined face studied him carefully. "What's it to you, anyway? Judging from that flayed back, you won't be heading towards Chicago for a while."

The smoker was right. Lieberman felt the edges of his wound. The bleeding had stopped, but the crust forming over the embedded buckshot was not promising. Already he was running a fever. The sooner he got medical attention, the better and if he waited too long . . . . but there wasn't time to think about that.

He caught the eyes above the lined face and took a shot in the dark.

"The way I figure it, we should be in St. Louis by afternoon."

"Try midnight", came the scoffed reply. "This here freight is a slow mover and sidetracks for everything." Lieberman nodded. He now knew his destination and began to plan accordingly. Just then the train lurched again and continued south. He had to hold on until dark.

By noon, it had become nearly unbearable in the boxcar. No one had offered him any more drink and Lieberman was feeling dizzy. But the freight began to slow again as they pulled into one of the small river cities. It stopped on a siding not far from the main street. He could hear mid-day traffic on the closed side of the car. The smoker opened the door a bit wider to catch the humid breeze blowing up from the river.

"You boys get going and see if there's a grill nearby. We're going to be stuck here for a couple of hours. Just don't get anyone riled up. I'm not ready to spend the night in the lockup."

The two hoboes moved out to panhandle lunch, under pain of vengeance by the smoker if they didn't bring back something good.

"Now it's just you and me, stranger." His eyes got narrow and weasel looking.

"You're a Red, ain't you? And you was stirring up things back at the steel mill. I'll bet there's a bunch of folks who would like to talk with you about what happened." Lieberman shifted his weight to ease the pain. The smoker started and raised his voice. "Oh no, don't think you're going anywhere." He produced a wicked looking section of pipe and swung it around his head several times. Lieberman said nothing and knelt on his bags. He almost wished for railroad security or a brakeman to come along, but none did. There could not be much of value on this run.

They both heard footsteps on the gravel and the smoker leaned his head out the door expecting to see his cronies.

"Well, what do we have here?", he smirked.

Two young women, poorly dressed, appeared head level with the bottom of the door. It didn't take Lieberman long to gather what they were looking for. The smoker gave them a hand and pulled them up through the door. They glanced furtively around the interior, their eyes gradually becoming accustomed to the gloom.

"It's just me and that Commie over there, but he's hurt and won't bother you."

Lieberman judged that they couldn't have been more than fifteen, but with the makeup could pass for 25. The smoker wasted no time.

"What do you charge for going around the world?"

The women snickered and cast a glance in Lieberman's direction.

"Don't pay him no attention. He don't have any money." The smoker pulled a wad of bills out of his pocket. It had to be what he took from Lieberman.

"Tell you what. I'll give you each a quarter."

Lieberman was disgusted and looked out the crack in the wall. A roll in the hay with an ageing bum and all his likely diseases for just two bits. These girls were very desperate. They finally settled on a half-dollar each. The hobo led one of them to the far end of the car and dropped his trousers. While she began to work him over, the other stood watch at the door.

Lieberman saw his chance, but he needed help. With the smoker distracted, he called the girl over. She stood her distance like a wild animal, wrinkling her face when she saw his wound.

"Don't worry. I won't hurt you and the back is not as bad as it looks", he lied. "But that old bastard over there is keeping me prisoner in this boxcar and I need to get out. There's five dollars in it for each of you if you'll help me tie him down so I can get off this train."

Her eyes widened and she looked toward the couple rutting like curs on the moldy hay.

"Get me that pipe by the door and while I hold it over him, you tie his hands with his belt. We'll wrap some of this baling twine around his ankles and it's done. You both get a fiver."

"Give me the money now", she demanded. He could see that she had experience.

"It's in his pocket. He took my money when I was asleep." She was still doubtful. Lieberman sweated. Any minute the cronies might return.

"Here, take my watch as good faith, but be sure I get it back." She snatched the watch and went to get the pipe. The hobo was panting and beginning to moan over in the corner. The timing was perfect. Once Lieberman had the weapon he eased onto his feet, gritting his teeth in pain. The box car appeared to tilt from side to side, but he was determined and in a flash was standing over the hobo who in haste had left his pants around his ankles. The girl under him let out a shriek and rolled away, but he was hobbled by the pants. In short order he was bound securely, but not before Lieberman had taken his shirt and retrieved his money. The shirt was vile, but would protect him against the sun and unwanted questions. He paid the two women, told them to get out, then jumped out himself, but before closing the door, threw a dollar in the direction of the hobo.

"For the meal and the shirt", he said carelessly. He caught the furious glare and heard some muttered obscenities, but slammed the door shut just in time to see the women and his watch disappear behind the roundhouse. He thought he might pass out again from the exertion, but recovered and set off down the track in the other direction. Another train was just pulling out headed south and he barely managed to swing himself up into an empty cattle car. It smelled horribly, but the open-slatted sides made it comfortably cool. He made himself inconspicuous in one of the corners and dared not close his eyes.

Nobody asked questions in St. Louis. It was too large for people to know or to care about another's misfortune. Lieberman first bought a Chicago paper and had no trouble getting up to date on the massacre at Republic Steel. Everything was being blamed on the rabble-rousing strikers and their Commie instigators. He'd be among the hunted, but the anonymity of the city would protect him for a while. He found a Jewish doctor who gave him a safe house while he mended. The infection gradually went away, but left major scarring. So long as he remained covered, however, no one would be the wiser.

Using the alias, Liebowitz, he sought jobs about as far away from Chicago as possible. To his surprise, within two weeks, he received a letter from the Department of Education in Washington, D.C. informing him of the need for educational advisors in the Civilian Conservation Corps. They were looking for vocational trainers, but he certainly had the teacher qualifications and the irony of working for the U.S. Army amused Lieberman no end. He sent his vita to Army districts far removed and waited. Shortly, he was contacted by 1st Army area to come to Boston for an interview. There were several openings in New England. Liebowitz, nee Lieberman, was on his way.

12

In the summer of 1868 Professor Leopold Trouvelot of Medford, Massachusetts glanced warily out the school window at the darkening sky. It would rain before he reached home and he'd left his project unattended in the backyard. So far his French tussock caterpillars had given him little of the silk he was hoping for and he'd nearly given up trying to mate them with the silkworm. It was true that his imports did not need mulberry leaves and fed on almost anything, but the silken nests they wove for their pupae were stringy and sparse. He'd give them one more generation to prove themselves. At this point, the gong sounded in the lecture hall telling him that his class was imminent. He hurried off to his students, giving not another thought to his insects.

Back at the Trouvelot household on Myrtle Street the family prepared for the storm.

"Shut the upstairs windows", the mother commanded. The hurrying feet of children thumped overhead, then the bang of window frames.

"The wind is blowing rain right through the screen door", excited voices shrieked with tension as the little ones danced about like mischievous kittens.

Under the oak tree, the moth cages swayed to and fro. Suddenly, a great gust blew three of the cages over, popping open their gauze sides. Within, full-grown caterpillars with strings of red and blue jewels down their backs squirmed to right themselves and, finding their prison rent, marched out by the score and up the trunk of the oak.

The storm died away and the sun came out. Mrs. Trouvelot opened her windows and spotted the smashed cages. When the professor came home for supper she told him he had better take care of his pets and clean up the debris. He did so, realizing that his experiment was ended. He killed the few remaining caterpillars he found and burned the cages.

A week later, up in the oak, after a long feast on the lush leaves, the three-inch caterpillars became sluggish. They sought protection within leaf clusters or dropped to the ground and secreted themselves beneath stones in the rock garden. The birds had taken many of the escapees, but many more had survived by climbing down into crotches and fissures in the tree trunk. There they remained by day, feeding only at night. Now, in relative isolation, away from the eyes of marauding birds, the caterpillars spun their dingy silk from labial glands, walling themselves into golden-brown cocoons. Inside, their fleshy bodies shrunk down into brown, hard pupae. Here they rested through July, transforming from the brightly patterned and hairy ever-hungry larva to the non-feeding, lackluster adult. In late July some of the cocoons cracked open to emit the smaller, dusky males which skittered about by day searching for the female. They had not long to wait before the big, cumbersome females emerged. Unable to fly, they sat in wait for a male, dousing the passing breezes with an aphrodisiac that would call mates from afar. Frenzied males soon zigzagged among the perfumed Brunhilds, mating to exhaustion after which they skimmed weakly away to an inglorious end in a vireo's stomach.

The females began laying their chamois-like egg masses almost immediately, packing their little purses with as many as 500 eggs and dying in the effort. Stuck tight with the mother's body fluids and often covered with her hairs and scales, the eggs now lay dormant under rocks and debris, on the tree trunk and even up under the eaves beyond the branches of the big elm where it overhung the barn.

Fall and winter passed. Then in early May, tiny larvae popped their heads out of the eggs and clustered in the sunshine on the remains of the mass. As light waned, they marched off to supper with no special goal in mind, but always against gravity and with unerring confidence burning out from genes honed by several million years of evolution. Some tired and died. Others perished in the cool night air. But many found the lush spring leaves of the beech or spinning gossamer lines of silk, lowered themselves into the apple tree. A few were blown by breezes out across the railroad track to the brush lands of Glenwood. The neighborhood was being infested, but no one realized there was a problem. Not even Professor Trouvelot who, after duly reporting his plight to state agricultural authorities, was now occupied elsewhere.

Twelve years later Medford residents described their summer streets as "being black with caterpillars—so thick on trees they were stuck together like cold macaroni." The huge, hairy caterpillars were constantly dropping upon people on the sidewalks. Trolley cars had no purchase on tracks made slimy with their crushed bodies. The foliage was stripped from all the trees and "little was spared but the horse chestnut and the grass in the fields, though even these were eaten to some extent."

Thus was established one of the worst scourges to sweep New England forests. The gypsy moth is a member of the lepidopterous family Lymantriidae. Bearing the scientific name, *Porthetria dispar*, Linnaeus, the alien gypsy was one of a number of foreign pests which were introduced to the United States before much was known about insect and other pathogen invasions of forests. In its native territory in Europe and Asia it caused only moderate damage, as its natural enemies seemed to hold it in check. In the favorable New England climate, especially among the oak-covered hills, the gypsy moth not only found a home, but free of natural checks on its population, became a viscous and costly enemy. Only the chestnut blight, that fungal invader which unknowingly slipped ashore in nursery stock from the Orient to decimate the American chestnut, would rival the damage of the gypsy. But at least the blight attacked only one forest species. The gypsy moth was attracted to more than 15 highly favored hosts in addition to oaks, pines and hemlocks and to more than 25 slightly less-favored trees.

By 1889, more than 360 square miles north of Boston had been defoliated and the state was finally moved to begin an extermination program. This appeared to succeed so well that work was scaled back in 1900. After five years, however, the moth had rebounded and spread into neighboring states causing the federal government to enact a quarantine. But nothing seemed to slow its spread. Moving at a rate of about seven miles per year, it soon infested every New England state. By 1922, the insect had entered eastern New York and, in desperation, a barrier zone 25 miles wide east of the Hudson River and 250 miles long from the Canadian border to Long Island was established. But within a decade, a 400 square mile infestation was found in northeastern Pennsylvania, proof that this frontier, too, had been pierced. Time was fast running out to establish any hold over the gypsy.

In the fall of 1936, the United States Department of Agriculture was being nudged hard by professional foresters and a disgruntled citizenry to do something once and for all about this rampant defoliator. Many southern New England CCC locations were dubbed "bug" camps whose main job was to contain the damage, but they made little headway. It was apparent that simply applying old pest control methods, many of which had been called into question during extended outbreaks, was not enough. New information was needed. Recognizing the vast labor resources of the CCC camps and their strategic locations in forested areas, U.S.D.A. plans were devised to get more data and to explore new methods of control. The department needed a man who knew the pest and its environment, could deal with the many personalities and lines of authority in the camps and who was not afraid to be an original thinker. Scores of names were screened, but one kept resurfacing—Dr. Ashley Stone.

Early in 1937, a team from the United States Department of Agriculture conferred with Dr. Ashley Stone in the Entomology Library at Massachusetts Agricultural College. He'd been awarded a grant to coordinate research and gather data on the gypsy moth infestation in Central New England. Stone recognized their leader as one of the men he had served with long ago and who handled this team with great skill. He had been lucky to get their support without the usual grant restrictions and red tape. By the time they broke for lunch, he'd been given broad latitude on the conduct of the research. They had insisted only that he make use of the personnel in existing CCC camps and to demonstrate active application of standard and new control techniques. He immediately grasped their meaning and, while he didn't much care for the not-so-subtle propaganda value of the make-work project, it was clearly one of the quid pro quos to live with. The rare opportunity to gather some basic biological information and enlarge the knowledge of the New England forest insect fauna was not to be sneezed at.

Later in the afternoon, they had settled on a location in southern Vermont for the project. Not coincidentally, it was in the electoral district of one of the members of the U.S. Senate who served on the governmental committee for agriculture. When this became apparent, Stone looked sharply at his old acquaintance, then smiled and silently counted his blessings that he was no longer a government bureaucrat. After some study of maps of the area, Stone laid his finger on Grafton, pointing out that it was well within the infested area, had both old growth and recently cut forest and could be easily reached from the Amherst campus. All agreed and, after the ritual handshakes, Stone arranged to have the team chauffeured to Northampton so they could catch the late afternoon train departing to Washington, D.C.

When they had gone, Stone returned to his office and called Sarah in to explain the new venture. From the start, he'd kept an eye on her progress in classes, noting how she mastered information and got on with teachers and other students. Now he wanted her to work with him. The Grafton project would open up many areas for a research thesis. Besides, without any fawning or truckling between them, they understood one another and he had to admit that her regular visits to his office most often plucked him up.

The department head called Stone to his office just as Sarah arrived at the door. He motioned her to come in and wait, as he would be back presently. She settled into the only chair not stacked with bulletins, file folders and research paraphernalia. The clutter was overwhelming but for a space in the middle of Ashley's roll-top desk. Nearby, unhidden, was a yellowed photograph of a young woman in a handsome wooden frame. "That will be Grace", she said to herself and retrieved it for a closer look. Sarah had learned of Grace from Sam and a few cursory remarks from Stone's older colleagues with whom she had taken courses, but never a word from Stone. The woman smiled out at her, charming and refined, obviously happy with the man she had wed. "A pity", Sarah thought, "that this man had spent so many years alone". She admired her professor, but thought him quite set in his ways and suspected that he didn't always listen to her, preoccupied as he was with some aspect of his research. Often, to her surprise, a week or so later, he would ask her specifics about what she had said. She replaced the picture and spotted a small volume nearly disappearing under a stack of folders. Sliding it out, she was a bit astonished to see that it was a well-worn copy of the Divine Comedy.

Stone came through the door as she was carefully leafing through the pages. Feeling slightly guilty, she closed the book and placed it on the folders saying, "I don't know how you ever find time for Dante with all you do." Stone smiled sheepishly. "A holdover from Sam's influence years ago. You may borrow it if you wish, although, knowing Sam, I'm sure that it was part of your required reading." She nodded that this was so, but thanked him for the offer.

"I've got a proposal for you to consider, Sarah," Stone began immediately. "We've been funded for the gypsy moth research." He gave her the details and was pleased when she immediately accepted. "Sure you don't want to think it over? It's a rather long commitment." But she shook her head, eager to get on with the project. She would have to complete her spring semester classes with the additional burden of preparing herself for fieldwork in the forest. He gave her a prodigious list of background reading in forest entomology and asked her to free up time to act as teaching assistant in one of his laboratories. She'd need to hone her previous teaching skills in the direction of science and technology. In Grafton, he'd have to rely on her to handle much of the CCC recruit training for the project. He was impressed that she didn't flinch at this suggestion.

"I must be honest about the work in Grafton," he explained. "We won't know what we're getting into up there until we start and even then we'll have to tailor things as we go. That's often the nature of fieldwork and this will be no exception." He reached into the small bookcase over his desk, withdrew a fat volume and, crunching it open, handed it to her. "Better start reading this in your spare time," he suggested, chuckling under his breath. She looked at the spine and read, Massachusetts Board of Agriculture, *The Gypsy Moth,* Forbush & Fernald, 1896.

"It's old, but is still a definitive work on *Porthetria dispar,*" he continued. "We'll be verifying or challenging some of their findings, but if we're lucky, this Vermont work will be a rare opportunity to enlarge our knowledge of gypsy moth population cycles, something my colleagues have yet to deduce.

She merely nodded and smiled. He again felt the way he had at the train station. "Humph," he snorted. "Then the next step is for me to meet with the CCC folks at Grafton to see how the ground lies. Let's talk again next week, same time." He waved her away.

Leaving, she glanced above the doorjamb, spotting a small, yellowed sign, easily missed in the clutter by those coming and going. It read, "Listen once, look twice, think three times, but then get on with it!" She smiled on her way down the corridor, thinking of how well this fit her professor.

13

The Spring of 1937 brought a contingent of new recruits to Camp Grafton. Fully 75% of the original assignment reenlisted, as there were precious few jobs for anyone, let alone young men with virtually no job skills. The Great Depression continued to suffocate whole families and only those who were needed immediately at home were packing their bags. The new allotment was right off the Boston streets. There had been rumors of them as toughs who had reputations for petty crime, car theft and worse, but Harwood judged that so long as they did not constitute a majority of the replacements, they could be kept in check and perhaps even rehabilitated once they got into the work patterns and saw opportunities for bettering themselves. He was not prepared for what he got.

It all started benignly enough, the boys arriving by train directly from Devens as had most of their predecessors. That is, save one, named Sean Rafferty, who came up right from Boston via personal auto complete with chauffeur. The young man's father, Harwood would later learn, was a member of the Massachusetts state senate and very cozy with the powers at Headquarters, First District, U.S. Army. Just about everyone witnessing this arrival focused their attention on the chauffeur, a high mileage and somewhat slack goddess still capable of arresting a glance or two. Heads turned as she dropped Rafferty off at his barracks, but she departed soon after and camp activity resumed, folding the new men, including Rafferty, into its ranks.

Trouble erupted two evenings later with a bruising donnybrook behind the mess hall. The Boston crowd, all Irish, lost no time establishing themselves as pugnacious, mean fighters who tolerated no challenges. It took the senior leaders to break them up and ten recruits had to be treated at the dispensary. And that was only the beginning. Within weeks, Rafferty, who had been the organizer from the start, formed a blood brotherhood with his cronies and gained control of the informal hierarchy of all three barracks. By cleverness and craft, the brotherhood avoided challenges to the junior and senior leaders and completed all required work. But after hours it became increasingly clear who called the shots. Harwood and the civilian staff, busy with preparations for the dam builders and camp bureaucratic details, were aware of a change in attitudes, but had nothing to put their fingers on. The work was getting done, newcomer training was progressing as planned and the all-important repair of the cistern and piping for the water was on schedule. Capricious, shifting allegiances among recruits was normal and meant little in the overall scheme of things.

Only after a month went by and the hazing of the new solitary replacements by the Irish turned particularly ugly, did Harwood call Rafferty around for an explanation. Butter wouldn't melt in Rafferty's mouth as he showed great concern for the hazing, promised it would stop and couldn't he be of assistance to the Captain to be sure it didn't happen again. Harwood eyed him carefully. He was a handsome lad and while not so tall as the Celtic giant he hung around with, gave the clear impression that he could take care of himself in one way or another. The civilian leaders had pointed out with pride his mastery of every job they had assigned and how he assisted keeping the less ambitious on task. One staffer had even recommended him for temporary status as junior leader. Harwood dismissed him with the admonition that he didn't want any trouble in camp. Rafferty gave assurances and left, leaving John with the nagging thought that this young man's demeanor was perhaps a bit too helpful for the good of the camp. But Harwood had a more pressing situation in the form of an unofficial report from First District Headquarters.

Two weeks earlier Harwood had received a letter from the hapless lieutenant whom he replaced a year hence. Assigned to First District Headquarters in Boston, the young man had become chief paper-pusher, not an enviable position, but one in which few secrets escaped notice. It seemed Headquarters was growing paranoid about its CCC camp inspection system. Not wishing to be criticized by Washington, they would be revising procedure and doubling the number beginning in the spring. Harwood was not impressed, but was realistic enough to accept this as a standard and quite likely futile contortion of life in the U.S. Army. But the latter part of the letter was more ominous. A Regular Army Major by the name of Butler would be assigned to camps in the central New England area and would be quartered, at least temporarily, at Grafton. Butler, the lieutenant continued, was a high liver of some means in Boston and had a reputation for backstabbing and imperiousness to get his way. The brass at Headquarters were full of him and saw this assignment as a way to get him out of Boston and, unofficially of course, were doing everything to cut his orders immediately.

"Butler, Butler," he thought absently. "Shipped out to France with a Butler. Oh, well, a common name."

The rest of the letter dealt with the shavetail's impressions of life at the top and a few remarks thanking John for getting him out of a bind. Harwood laid the letter aside, pleased that the lieutenant had the grace to write. He gazed out across the parade area wondering how the major would fit into their primitive living arrangements.

But nothing and no one at the Grafton camp could have been prepared for Major Butler. Within a week, a flurry of communications arrived outlining his authority and expectations. As assistant to the Chief Camp Inspector, who rarely left Boston, he made it appear that he was a power unto himself. During a regular retreat, a huge Packard touring car rumbled into camp. Harwood was initially surprised by the unannounced arrival, but later became convinced that Butler had planned this to get maximum theatrical value. He interrupted the retreat, telling the recruits to stand at ease while he welcomed their visitor. That was a mistake.

A fortyish corporal with flared, slightly purple nostrils halted the machine in front of Harwood, jumped out with surprising agility and swung open the rear door, coming to attention with glazed eyes looking right through the assembled men. Butler emerged slowly with deliberate hesitation the better to savor his new moment of glory. Harwood kept his head and saluted smartly. Portly, but neat as a pin in shiny boots and razor-sharp creases in his trousers, the major touched his cap and remained on the running board, casting a long, hard look over the men standing at ease. Harwood saw the major's tongue flick out to moisten the edge of the neatly groomed mustache and heard the faint, but derisive whistle through the pursed lips.

"Is this what you call a retreat, Captain? I've seen the Boy Scouts do better."

Harwood was stung, but swallowed his annoyance.

"They're not required to master close order drill, Major. You're welcome to say something now if it pleases you."

"Carry on, Captain", Butler sighed in an exasperated voice. "And join me in your quarters in ten minutes."

Harwood did an abrupt about face and instructed the cadre to commence retreat. The major continued to look over Harwood's shoulder as the men came to attention. The bugler sounded and the flag was run down the staff. When the men were dismissed, Harwood turned to see the major and his chauffeur proceed importantly up the steps of the headquarters building. In no hurry, he followed them, wondering where the Army managed to find these nincompoops.

Harwood hadn't even gotten to the steps of his quarters when he heard the major's voice rising behind the door. He spotted the corporal rummaging about in the phaeton parked on the gravel apron near the mess hall. He went in to find a young recruit on housekeeping duty glowering anxiously beside Harwood's desk getting a royal dressing down by the new arrival.

Whirling toward Harwood, the major commenced to lecture both of them. "It's clear that your recruits don't understand basic military courtesy. When they encounter a commissioned officer, they are to salute and remain at attention until that salute is returned and "at ease" is given".

John's jaw just sagged and a fulminating rage reddened his face, souring his tongue with a taste of copper. He glared at each of them momentarily, then dismissed the recruit who snatched up his cap, twisted it violently and left, swinging the door shut behind him. The bolt had not yet clicked as Harwood planted himself squarely in front of the major.

"Let's get this straight", he began. "There is no requirement other than that of the camp commander to abide by or enforce military discipline of any kind in these camps. I have decided that recruits here will maintain normal civility but do not have to salute me or any officer who is a guest of this camp."

He hung on the word "guest".

"We have work to do here, major, and so do you, but neither of us will get much done if we spend our time interfering with each other."

He watched the major carefully for a reaction and was surprised at the response.

"Of course, you are right, captain. I must have let the old habits back in Boston get the better of me. I'm sure we'll have no further trouble, eh?"

Harwood felt the reassuring hand on his shoulder, but didn't care much for the forced smile and the dead eyes. Sooner or later a pound of flesh would be taken over this encounter. His.

The corporal entered carrying the major's uniforms and personal gear.

"This is Corporal Rust, my aide-de-camp", Butler continued in the same officious tone as before.

John grunted and nodded to the man.

"Initially, we'll need meals and quarters for three days if you will be so good to provide. Grafton will be our regular base, but we've got many camps to visit so you may expect us to come and go as needs dictate. Most importantly, we don't want to waste time here."

John bit his tongue before replying.

"Of course. There's a desk and bunk for you right through that door", he said, pointing to the adjutant's office. "Corporal Rust can join the other non-coms over in the mess hall."

The major shifted uncomfortably.

"That won't be necessary, Captain. He'll stay right here, if you'll see that an extra cot is brought in."

Harwood stared incredulously, first at Butler, then at Rust.

"I'll be needing him here to work on my reports," Butler interjected loftily.

"Suit yourself, Major", John shrugged.

"Fine. Since your camp is the first on my list, let me tell you what I expect. Mind what I said before. We don't want to bother reviewing incomplete reports or making unnecessary tours of the camp."

Corporal Rust's face bore a sickly smile.

"You'll get what you need, Major", Harwood grunted through clenched teeth.

Later that evening, Walsh ambled over to have a look at the phaeton. He'd seldom seen a vehicle of this class even in the city, let alone up here in the woods. Rust was rubbing it down like a prize racehorse, removing the bug juice and tar specks from the front chrome. Noting Walsh's interest, he launched into a spiel about how long it took to get to Boston, the size of the gas tank and horsepower. Walsh nodded, stone-faced as usual and kicked the tires gently. Rust gave a disdainful glare at this, but Walsh didn't notice and ran his finger over the license plate. Behind the shiny front surface which had seen Rust's chamois dozens of times was some webbing. Walsh pushed a finger down into the space and retrieved a large, pulsating gypsy moth pupa.

"Here's something you didn't get last time you slicked up."

Rust faced him with half-closed eyes and tight lips. "You guys have got so many bugs up here, it's no wonder one just dropped in." He grasped at the insect, but Walsh was too fast.

"No, I think we'll keep this one. Just be sure you check every nook and cranny so you don't carry any extra passengers around the northeast. Nice car, by the way."

Rust had a puzzled air as he watched Walsh return to the rec hall with his trophy.

Harwood made good on his promises. Just as he had suspected, the new regimen for inspection was simply a rehash of the old on new forms. Neither Butler nor Rust had any real experience regarding camp life, CCC or otherwise. After a perfunctory review of camp records and the mess hall, Butler had no option but to give approval. Of course, the report had to show some things as needing improvement, but Harwood made sure that these were items easily corrected. Three days later, Butler was off to his next inspection, not giving John the courtesy of a date he and Rust planned to return.

After they had departed, Harwood, Walsh and Hurlburt sat on the loggia going over the week's events, including camp adjustments to the new arrivals. Fred and John had pretty much decided that so long as they steered them clear of the work crews, there was little to worry about. Walsh, as usual, wasn't saying too much, but reminded them of a news report from Washington that high ranking Army regulars, including General MacArthur were suggesting that the CCC would be a fertile ground for building up the standing army they needed to counter future threats in Europe and Asia.

"Not much chance of that with no money in the coffers and Roosevelt and the Democrats calling the shots", John retorted.

"Maybe so, maybe so. But I seen what the regulars did to the Bonus Army down there in '32. MacArthur strutting up and down with that jumped-up aide of his, Major Eisenhower, itching for a fight, finally convincing Hoover to show some force and send in tanks and cavalry. And he let 'em go, not figuring they would overstep their orders and cross the Anacostia. With a guy named Patton in the lead, they just busted across and drove us out, men women and children, then burnt up our shacks like Sherman going through Georgia. No sir, I don't trust them regulars much."

Hurlburt and Harwood exchanged glances. Walsh had to be on a rare tear to expose this much of his past.

"I didn't even know you were a veteran, Walsh", grinned John. "What have you been up to since then, if you don't mind my asking?"

Walsh looked a bit chagrined for his confession, but continued. "Jumped me a train going south. Figured that if I wasn't going to

get me a pot to piss in, at least I'd be warm in the wi.
a tramp along with a lot of other doughboys. Spent ho
doors doing odd jobs and living on the generosity of farm
Then a bunch of us got into a dust up in the hobo jungle
of Montgomery, Alabama. Those good old boys put us all to work
on the highway shackled with 35 pounds of county chain. A year
of hauling that around cured me real good. I'd had enough and
then some. That's how you got me here."

Fred and John shifted in their chairs, not knowing what else to
say. Finally, Harwood broke the silence with a grin, telling Walsh
that he was sure glad to have him back in Tree Army.

Harwood had barely put his head to the pillow when the
telephone rang. It was Constable Snow in Newfane. He had no
small talk.

"We picked up three of your boys in Townsend. They've had
more than their share of hooch down in Brattleboro and after
thumbing a ride, their chauffer dumped them out near the West
River. That's when they got real loud and ugly, continuing to drink,
yelling dirty remarks at passing drivers and waking the folks near
the covered bridge. Now, look here, Captain, I don't want their
kind stinking up my jail, so you'd better send someone down to
collect them".

This was Snow's way of not having to book them for disorderly
conduct. Harwood, already into his shirt, told him to hang on and
someone would be right down, knowing full well who that would
be. A half hour later he was in Newfane.

The booze had worn off a bit, but Snow was right, they reeked
to high heaven. When Harwood appeared outside the cell, the
men hung their heads like bad dogs and refused to meet his eyes.
No good would come from castigating them in their condition, so
he had Snow let them loose and steered them into the back seat of
his Ford. They hadn't gone five miles when one of them yelled for
Harwood to stop.

"Sully's going to upchuck right now", came a slurred warning.
But before Harwood could even slow down and pull over, the lad

had lost everything he'd downed in the last twelve hours. His two cohorts were too groggy to be of help and the back seat fast became a ripe offal pit. Harwood slammed on the brakes and dragged Sully out into the bushes where he held his head up as the boy continued to vomit and choke. In time, Sully stopped retching, but was so weak that Harwood had to half-carry him back to the car. He piled him on top of his buddies who refused to move despite the overpowering stench.

The moon was down by the time they got back to camp. To Harwood's surprise, Walsh was waiting for them on the loggia.

"What in hell are you doing up at this hour?", John barked irritably, knowing full well that Walsh didn't sleep much.

"Heard you go out and guessed it must be some trouble. Let me have those fellows in your back seat."

"You won't like these urchins", John grunted as he held Walsh away and told the drunks to get out. But Walsh knew just what to do. With a not so gentle push, he marched them to the outdoor shower, ordered them to strip and get cleaned up, then get to their bunks quietly. He'd have more words for them in the morning.

Harwood stumbled into his office and got rid of his soiled clothing. After washing up, he looked in the mirror. The clock in his office read backwards, but anyone could see it was showing the wee hours. He considered the bags under his eyes and said to himself, "Christ, I'm too old for this job", then snapped off the lights and was in bed asleep in no time.

Walsh was up long before reveille and had dragged the three recruits from their stupor after only two hours of sleep.He led them back to the Ford which he'd parked in plain view on the edge of the parade ground and told them to get busy with soap, water and disinfectant. The floor mats came first. Luckily, they'd been thick enough to absorb most of Sully's sins. With blood-swollen eyes, half-closed in the morning light, they managed to remove the back seat entirely and, under Scooter's continued haranging, get the seat covers off. He then made them wash and disinfect every nook and cranny of the exposed frame with toothbrushes. It took them well beyond the breakfast hour and everyone in camp had a pretty good idea of what was going on, making sure not to get too close to the operation lest Walsh press them into service. As the last stains were removed, Walsh gave them a wry grin and told them to go to breakfast and enjoy their meal, then report for duty as usual.

"There'll be no time or excuses for hitting the sack until this evening and you jackasses better decide not to ruin yourselves again real soon. Captain Harwood doesn't like to miss sleep and he sure don't need shitfaces like you decorating his car." He gave each of them a withering glare which dissolved into a toothy grin. "And you better remember this. If you screw up again or decide you're going on a trip to Hell itself, you can damn well bet that the Captain will be right there arguing with Old Harry himself, fixing to snatch you back so old Scooter Walsh here can greet you."

14

Stone, feeling thoroughly soggy from the April drizzle, gazed across the camp from his seat on the headquarters building loggia. Harwood hadn't returned from the Bellows Falls, but the professor didn't mind. He'd been too long away from his beloved forests and had quite forgotten how the snows of winter could hang on in these hills. Flowers had already bloomed down in the valley just 50 odd miles south. Besides, what he'd seen of this camp so far, he liked. His eye ranged on the budding oaks and hickories, then to the balsams and scattered white pines. With this choice, surely, if the gypsies couldn't make it here, they would have a rough go anywhere else. He was pleased with his decision to locate in Grafton.

"This must be the commander," he said to himself as a car turned up the company street and came to a halt in front of the building. Harwood spotted the professor right away and came straight to the loggia to greet him.

"Hope I haven't delayed you, Dr. Stone. The roads up here are still recovering." He glanced at Stone's mud-spattered vehicle and grinned. "But I'm not telling you anything you don't know. Let's go inside where it's not so wet."

John poured a respectful shot of Scotch for the professor who took it with no hesitation.

"So what is it you want us to do for you?" Harwood got right to the point.

"My letter didn't have many details, Captain, but what we need for this research is a solid base camp and plenty of willing hands. With luck, the project will go ahead for at least two, maybe three, years during which we will gather as much information on the gypsy moth as possible. Towards the end, if things work out, we will test whatever new controls are suggested by the research."

Harwood looked across his desk at Stone. He was much more impressed than he had allowed himself. Most academics in his experience were fussy idealists, but something told him Stone was made of more solid stuff.

"A lot of what we do at the start will be tentative as we feel our way into the project. I would be lying if I told you exactly what was going to work. We'll try not to get in your way as I know you've got regular maintenance and conservation projects underway here. Your recruits will need some initial training and supervision which my assistant and I will provide. But after that, we'll be grateful for as much support as you can give."

"We'll do what we can. Hurlburt, our forestry supervisor, knows a hell of a lot more about what you need than I do, but the place is yours within reason. Of course these young men are almost all from the city and will require more training time than you may care to give. Another drink?"

Stone refused and watched as Harwood added several ounces to his empty glass.

"Pretty quick, Hurlburt will return from the ridge out back and I'll let the two of you get into the details. He runs the daily work here while I try to make the loose ends meet."

"So tell me about what's new down in Amherst," John changed the subject. "I spent some time there years ago."

"You don't say?", Stone brightened.

"I was at that private college on the south edge of town right after the Great War," John remarked with a grin. "How long have you been at Mass Aggie?"

Stone relaxed, feeling the warmth of the Scotch. "Came there about the same time as you, it seems. That makes it nearly eighteen years. What interests did you have at Amherst?"

Harwood snorted. "Oh, I wasn't much of a student. Took classics and language, but spent too much of my time trying to have some fun . . . . you know, the sorority parties and the Smithies."

"Nothing wrong with that, in moderation", Stone allowed, recalling how his sober nature had precluded that sort of thing. "I remember that you fellows held some rather fine dances at the Lord Jeffrey."

Harwood exhaled audibly, retaining a tight-lipped smile. "Yes, I met my wife there." He realized with a start that he'd unbuttoned his lip far more than intended. Better go easy on the whiskey. Yet, there was something about this old biologist that quelled his fears and the words continued to flow. "But that's over for sure. Lasted only a couple of years."

Stone was looking out the window. "You must remember the Spanish flu epidemic back then. Both my wife and I caught it somewhere . . . . could have been most anywhere, it was that common". He turned back to John, with a wry smile. "The fates granted me a recovery."

John was surprised by the professor's candor. Maybe he wasn't the only one feeling the Scotch.

"I'm sorry about your wife," he responded almost inaudibly, then continued. "Yeah, I know the time well. I lost my brother to flu at Camp Edwards. The war was finished in France and he was just trying to be the young patriot. After all the carnage, he didn't have to join up. I had already done the love of country thing in the Argonne."

The professor's eyes grew soft and dark. "Almost two decades ago. Time is such a son-of-a-bitch. Some like to gussy it up as a free-flowing river of life, but to me it either wears lead boots or comes on like an artillery barrage. About one finger more of that stuff will do," he said, eyeing the Scotch.

They continued to share some common experiences in the War and easily slipped into an unspoken, but measured camaraderie. After a while, the conversation turned desultory as they both sensed that they were easing into uncharted waters which neither was ready to test. They sat in an awkward embarrassed silence for a time, the way Yankees are apt to after sharing private thoughts. Yet, there was a mutual, if transitory respect taking root. Male resistance to further personal unburdening slowly took over as the tone became more banal. Stone sensed that there was a lot more that Harwood wanted to share, but never would. "Takes one to know one", he mused to himself, tasting the last dram of Scotch on his tongue.

The rather long silence finally was broken by Hurlburt's sharp rap and sudden entry. While a bit more skeptical than Harwood about what the camp could and could not provide, he was ready to cooperate to the full and made the professor doubly certain that Grafton was the appropriate choice for gypsy moth research.

Six weeks later, Harwood and Stone drove out to the area where trees were being banded with burlap. Despite the short preparation time, the research project was already in high gear. There were noticeable differences in the moth infestations as they approached a grove containing some valuable trees. All along the road, at Stone's direction, recruits had completed selective thinning of vulnerable host trees with apparently positive results. The oaks and maples were damaged, but had better that 60% full leaf. As they neared the banding area, the shading was even more noticeable and rarely was even an occasional tree entirely stripped. In the grove they came upon khaki figures wrapping the trunks—a length of cloth, a circle of twine, then folding the cloth over as a skirt to trap the caterpillars. Harwood stopped the truck and hailed Hurlburt. The three of them examined a few trees under attack, nodding in satisfaction. Harwood then returned to camp, leaving Stone and Fred to supervise. Ashley was very pleased with the banding process, noting that the hastily taught technique had already been improved upon by Hurlburt. But both realized that their initial success in this small area was a skirmish and holding action at best. Stone knew that the early enthusiasm would wane when the final voracious instars appeared. More training of these men was needed quickly.

"The captain tells me that you're a Belchertown native", Stone queried as they strolled beneath the maples.

"That's right. And I'd still be there except for the Great and General Court of Massachusetts deciding that they needed my farm land for the Quabbin Reservoir. Imagine, drowning all those productive acres so Boston can have a private pond. I fought them tooth and nail, but they won anyway. My share after the creditors and legal fees was title to 300 acres of mountain land in oak. Couldn't put cows on that and nobody wants to lumber it. So there it sits, useless as tits on a boar hog."

"Well, see that you hang onto it, Fred", Stone cautioned. "It may not be too long before we're neck deep in what's brewing in Europe. Even if we don't send our boys over there, both sides will need our wood."

Hurlburt searched Ashley's face for a trace of humor, but seeing none began to rub his jaw thoughtfully.

"I saw it in the last fracas", Stone continued quietly. "Bracing and duckboards were what they were after then, to shore up and bridge the quagmire. There were whole forests out there on the Flanders front, just lining the roads and the trenches." He paused to watch a pair of recruits having a bit of trouble wrapping a tree, then continued with passion. "Some waste, huh, Fred? But this time around it won't be a sapper's war. That is if you believe the armchair experts like Hart. No one will tolerate another slaughter like the Somme. My guess is they'll need small boats and aircraft more than duckboards. In time, your mountain oaks will come in mighty handy for keels and airframes".

Hurlburt grunted his assent and tried not to think about how many gypsy moth caterpillars might be munching their way through Belchertown this very instant.

Shortly after lunch John strolled out of camp down towards the new pond Merrill's engineers had created. The June day was brilliant with cumulus clouds piled high over the hill behind camp. Tiny whitecaps were already dotting the blue-green water backing up behind the earthen dam. They smacked the riprap beneath the maples shading the shore and he was surprised to note how fast the old swamp was filling. Spring had come early and was unusually dry. Even the snowmelt had not interfered with Hollis who got a lucky jump on the weather, marshalling a small battalion of construction workers and equipment. They'd finished the task in a little more than a month and moved on to another job upstate. Since their departure, it had rained nearly every day.

Harwood broke out of the maples and traversed the new dam with its cover of rough, brown earth and the beginnings of a grassy turf. The shore road continued up a knoll on which scraggly weeds had gained a foothold. John sat on this hummock for a time watching the growing waves, an indication that rain might again fall before evening. He took off his hat and let the wind blow through his hair, the unusually bright sun making him squint, its heat broiling his back so that he sought some shade in the nearby tree line. Stretching out full length and covering his face with the hat, torpor overtook him. Lulled by the breeze and the slap of waves, his cares slid away.

"So this is how our peacetime army makes the world safe for democracy", chided a strange voice. Sitting up quickly and with obvious irritation, John confronted a pair of limpid hazel eyes. "It's Captain Harwood, isn't it?", the interrupter continued. "I'm Sarah Chapman."

He would always remember her as she was this day in field jeans, ankle-high boots, and blue-flowered blouse. His irritation evaporated under the influence of the bemused smile that made her face and whole being so genuine. Here was a creature, he told himself, completely devoid of harshness and censure. John managed to pass the usual pleasantries, inwardly befuddled, but outwardly in control. He sensed that she saw through his guise. She described her role in the gypsy moth project with Professor Stone, then left him to inspect the test plots Stone had laid out beyond the dam. He watched her go, then returned slowly to the headquarters building where the usual mound of paperwork awaited.

Late in the afternoon, as he poured himself a cup of coffee, he heard several chords from the ancient piano in the rec hall. Though slightly off tune, he recognized the passages of a Schubert Impromptu and opened the window wide to hear better. That was no brush monkey on those keys, he told himself. Suddenly, the playing stopped and Sarah stepped out onto the rec hall porch. Harwood scowled, then returned to his desk. "Should have taken care of that long ago", he chuckled to himself. When next in Bellows Falls, he stopped by the only music store in town and contracted to have the piano repaired and tuned. When the tradesman declined to set a firm date, Harwood flipped an additional ten-spot on the counter with the requirement that the work be done within the week.

Most all parts of New England suffered a massive gypsy infestation in 1937. Grafton was no exception. Speculation and theories abounded trying to explain this population phenomenon—the mild winter, the early spring, the off-cycle of bird predators. Professor Stone had heard them all before, but remained unconvinced. He'd been too long in this business to fall prey to the simple answer, the easy explanation. And although his research program wasn't prepared for this onslaught, he would make the best of it, implementing as many known control methods as practicable. This meant crash training for all the CCC recruits and their leaders. He moved into the small library at the end of the rec hall and had a cot set up. There was no question, he'd be staying in camp for the rest of the summer. Sarah would come up three or four days a week to help him and would bring his mail and messages from Mass Aggie.

As summer progressed, wave after wave of caterpillars gnawed their way through the forest. First to go were the oaks and other broad-leaved trees, then the pines and hemlocks which had no way to send out a second or third generation of leaves. The camp buildings became covered with larvae desperately seeking food. The ridges behind the camp were bleak and desolate, not a green leaf in sight. The hot sun blazed down through naked twigs, scorching the previous year's leaves, leaving the soil beneath them dry and dead. In the few forest clumps untouched, the recruits labored mightily to stem the tide, coming back to camp at day's end exhausted, their hair and clothes laden with larval feces. The standard joke became, "Keep your head down and your mouth shut unless you want your Grape Nuts without milk". Frass pellets drummed incessantly night and day like an endless rain shower on the curled, desiccated duff of the forest floor.

15

John sat on the headquarters porch reading the Great Gatsby for the second time. He had nearly decided to give up in the failing light when a gray Plymouth slowly edged its way up the camp street. It stopped next to the cluster of boys who had been throwing a baseball around.

"Here's trouble," he said to himself as several hands pointed to his direction. The car progressed on and halted in the parking space next to John's Ford. A man in his sixties got out and opened the passenger door for a woman of about the same age. John was on his feet and met them at the steps. Both were dressed conservatively in dark clothes, the woman in a simple, handmade smock. Despite the poor light, John noted the man's high white collar.

"My pleasure to meet you, Captain. I am Father Mercier and this is my housekeeper, Mrs. Boisvert," he said with a slight Canuck accent. John bade them enter his office, noting that the woman cast a nervous eye towards the car.

"Nothing to worry about, these boys can be trusted," he added gently.

She glanced at the priest who smiled his approval and ushered her inside.

"Now, what can I do for you?" John said after getting them seated.

The priest cast an admiring eye towards the liquor cabinet, then began earnestly.

"We're from the Saint Boniface Church in Springfield where it is said that you have permitted local boys to join your camp."

"Several have, but none are here now. One has been transferred to Procter Piper State Park and the others have completed service and gone home. Besides, the company is at full strength right now", John lied, hoping to keep the visit short.

"Mrs. Boisvert lost her husband, Pierre, last winter to pneumonia," the priest continued with genuine sadness. "I have arranged a room for her at the rectory, but it is very cramped and suitable only for one."

John wondered what he was getting at and must have shown it for Father Mercier now leaned forward and clasped his wrinkled hands.

"The difficulty we have concerns Mrs. Boisvert's grandson who now has no place to stay. Pierre's wages and a house were provided by Mr. Atkins, a Springfield banker and farmer, in return for his and the grandson's labor. A new man with a family has now been hired at the farm leaving no room for the boy."

"How old is your grandson?", John asked the woman. She looked quickly away and said nothing.

"Please understand, Captain, the woman speaks English with great difficulty and is still upset about her husband."

"Well then, you must tell me more about the boy."

"Oh, he's a strong one and quick, too. He'll do as he's told and would make no trouble."

"How old is he?"

A growing suspicion that the pair were concealing information gnawed at John's gut. The priest didn't answer immediately, but turned to the woman and mumbled in French. John understood every word and said to both of them in French, "Just tell me everything I need to know about the boy or I can't help you."

The two snapped their attention back to John and the priest smiled, first a bit sheepishly, then with a hint of triumph.

"You know our language, Captain. That is so very good."

Turning to the woman, he said, "Go out to the car and bring Paul in to meet the Captain."

"You mean he's here with you?"

John's unease increased as it dawned on him that the couple expected to leave the boy this very night.

"There'll be a lot of paperwork to clear and I'll have to see if one of the sections needs an extra man."

Sensing an opening, the priest now played his trump.

"Mr. Atkins has assured me that he is ready to donate construction materials and equipment for your sports program."

Harwood, his dander rising, was about to level with Father Mercier when the grandmother reentered leading Paul. The boy was thin, John noted, but had a frame which would, in time, match the sturdiest in the camp. His dark, intelligent eyes met John's honestly, yet belied a sensitivity and vulnerability that could not be masked.

"Still water under the bridge," thought John as he stifled his pique with the priest and bade the boy sit down.

Ignoring the others, John asked the boy how long he had been doing a man's work on the farm. For the first time Paul averted his eyes and looked to his grandmother for help. Father Mercier came to the rescue.

"He speaks English with great difficulty, Captain."

John came out of his chair like a shot and crossed to the bookcase, clasping his hands behind him, fingers twitching slightly with anger and frustration.

"You want me to throw this boy who can't speak a word in his defense into a barracks with 50 hell-raising harps from Boston," John said evenly. Then, his voice rising out of control, "We won't get a day's work out of him in a week if he can't follow orders."

"He will have to take his chances in the barracks," the priest interjected. "As for the following orders, he will do so despite his limited language. He watches carefully and will do everything expected."

John whirled to face them and asked the boy point blank in French, "How old are you?"

"Fifteen," was the muttered answer.

"I thought so," he returned in English to the priest. "You not only want to throw the boy to the wolves, but burn me in the process. Surely you know that I am not allowed to accept anyone under the legal age of seventeen?"

At this the grandmother rose and without anger, thanked John for seeing them. She tugged at the boy's sleeve and the two of them went outside. The priest remained, his head bowed, eyes fixed on his clasped hands.

"I had hoped you could help us, Captain," he murmured.

"We had planned on saving some of the money he would send to his grandmother for his education. When he is eighteen he will be sent to Montreal to enter the seminary."

"That illiterate farm boy is going to be a priest?", John exclaimed in amazement.

Father Mercier raised his eyes and squared the slightly stooped shoulders.

"It may surprise you, Captain, that even though the boy speaks very little English and has had no formal schooling, he reads, writes and speaks French proficiently. He has been my private pupil for five years and is gifted." It was John's turn to avert his eyes. He saw the trap swinging shut.

"I meant no offense, Father, towards you or the boy."

"Do not worry about that, Captain," he said with a genuine smile. "In my profession we are taught to turn the other cheek. I think you are refusing a valuable recruit, but you have valid reasons for being cautious. Good evening, sir."

The priest extended his hand in a final farewell, but John ignored him, crossed to the door and summoned the other two. When they were again seated he told them all in French.

"Paul may stay so long as we all agree that after four weeks I will make a final decision based on how well he manages to fit into the camp."

The woman smiled warmly at John and turned to hug the boy, mumbling endearments in French. Giving Father Mercier an icy stare, Harwood let him know that he was the one responsible for pulling any strings and fixing the paperwork necessary to make Paul a "legitimate" recruit. The priest nodded as the two men stood apart, not letting their eyes meet. After an uncomfortable silence, Harwood spoke rather stiffly to Paul.

"If you have belongings with you, bring them here to the office where I'll have you meet our project leader."

The boy did as he was told and after his grandmother and Father Mercier had left, Harwood explained the rules of the camp.

"You'll be expected to do the same work as the others. Your leader will not speak French, but will give examples. Watch him carefully and do just as he shows you.

Hurlburt was summoned and determined that Paul was to be assigned to a tree thinning section and quartered in Barracks 2. He took Paul to the quartermaster shack and roused Gleason, the supply sergeant who opened the haberdashery and outfitted Paul with work clothes and boots.

"These may be a bit loose, but you'll grow into them," Hurlburt told him, forgetting he could not understand.

By the time they reached the barracks it was after ten and most of the recruits were already in bed snoring, dog tired from a day with pick and shovel. Hurlburt showed him his cot and where to put his personal belongings. By sign language he made sure that Paul knew he was to be up, dressed and ready for breakfast at 7 a.m. Hurlburt then departed leaving the boy on his own. Paul turned in quietly and lay wide-eyed in the darkness. He was very hungry, but after a silent prayer, he turned on his side and was soon asleep.

For nearly a week, Paul worked alongside the other new enrollees under the tutelage of Fred Hurlburt. As the old priest had predicted, he learned quickly and handled manual tasks with ease. Friday morning broke dismally, a hard driving rain postponing forest work. Shortly after lunch Paul was alone in his barracks waterproofing his work shoes in preparation for the afternoon when Rafferty and three cronies entered. Without a word they came straight towards Paul's bunk. He didn't like the smiles they were wearing, but bid them a heavily accented greeting whereupon all but Rafferty burst into howls of derisive laughter. Rafferty's smirk faded and his eyes burned as tiny, cruel coals. He snapped words that Paul did not understand to the largest youth who stepped forward menacingly. But Paul bounded away putting the bunk between himself and his visitors.

Rafferty chuckled mirthlessly way down in his throat.

"Now careful, Frenchie. Everyone who comes into this camp gets his initiation and that includes frogs. In fact, especially frogs. All you have to do is run bareass around the pond while we clean out your locker."

Paul understood nothing, glared at them and eyed the door. There was no way to break through as all four now closed in. But Paul, in a twinkling, leaped onto his bunk and using it as a springboard to the next cot, shot shoulder high past the groping arms. He'd have made it had he landed squarely on his feet, running for the door, but severely off balance, he saw the floor come up at him, then felt searing pain as half a dozen jagged floor splinters tore open his palms and snapped off under the flesh. The initial surprise gone, Rafferty's crew piled on him and commenced to tear off his fatigues leaving him only his briefs and shoes. While two pinned his arms in hammerlocks, the biggest Irishman grasped Paul by the back of his briefs and pushing his head down to balance, hoisted him two feet off the floor.

"Here's a frog wedgie for you Rafferty," he puffed as Paul's privates thrust out the brief front in a near perfect triangle.

"Not much there to worry the girls, would you say, boys?" More derisive laughter.

Rafferty's lips curled in a scornful smile.

"This Frenchie thinks he's so smart, let's give him a Rafferty cocktail," brayed an arm twister.

"Grab that bottle in my back pocket."

Rafferty, uninvolved as yet in the scuffle, took the bottle, unbuttoned his fly and voided into it to the halfway mark. Paul, seething with hate and indignation, nearly broke the hold on his right arm. But the big Irishman slammed him face down on the floor, a few more splinters piercing his cheek and ear.

"O.K., turn him over so he can take his medicine," jeered Rafferty triumphantly and stepped forward.

Despite his arms still being pinned, Paul knew that once he was sitting up, he had leverage. In the fraction of the second Rafferty stepped forward, Paul leaned away from the big harp and delivered a solid workshoe-clad kick to Rafferty's crotch. Rafferty uttered a sickly gasp as his eyes rolled and he doubled up, the bottle flying under the bunk, its contents gurgling away into the cracks.

Rafferty's cronies were wide-eyed in disbelief as they watched their leader writhe on the floor, groaning in agony. But they didn't release their hold. The giant grasped Paul's hair and twitched his head viciously.

"You little son-of-a-bitch," he growled. "You'll pay plenty for that."

The blows began to fall so quickly that Paul couldn't tell who was hitting where. He remembered being face down on the floor again and feeling a lot of heavy shoes buffet his ribs and face. His nose bled profusely and he barely made out Rafferty rising to a sitting position, then egging the others on to greater fury. Someone draped Paul's arm over the bed frame and he felt the unnatural pressure of someone stomping on his wrist and hand, once, twice, and yet again until something crunched. Then the buffeting stopped as Paul became aware of a huge weight on his left arm, so heavy that he became nauseous. He barely remembered his attackers running out the door as he lost consciousness.

He woke some minutes later as the trucks revved up and began pulling out with the work crews. For a moment Paul considered jumping into his clothes and dashing out, but as he slowly turned over, he knew there'd be no work for him that afternoon. His nose had clotted and now simply throbbed. Sharp pains jabbed at his ribs and back, but when he flexed, nothing got worse or failed to function except his left arm which was useless and numb. He noted with alarm the depressed bend above the wrist like the leg of that pony back on the farm that Pierre had put out of its misery with a single rifle shot. He shuddered at the memory and knew right then and there that only Grandmother Boisvert could help him.

Favoring the arm, he slid off the bloodstained briefs, made his way to the footlocker and got fresh underclothes. Then, wincing with pain and effort, he moved the arm and somehow got into the homemade trousers and shirt he'd come to camp in. He wanted to leave the Army shoes behind too, but knew that where he was going they'd be needed, and with only one good hand he'd never be able to change to his own.

No one would see his departure; he'd make sure of that. All the trucks had now gone and he waited until the cooks and camp maintenance details were engrossed for the afternoon. Slipping out as carefully as he could, holding the broken arm to his chest, Paul melted into the copse of fir. These would provide a screen nearly down to the water's edge. And had he not been spotted by a boy returning to camp for forgotten tools, his ruse would have been complete. Pausing briefly to wash some of the caked blood from his face, Paul heard a whistle across the water. He ducked back among the firs, but not fast enough. The boy continued on to camp and picked up his axe and wedges from Hurlburt.

"Say, you know that Canuck kid who arrived last week? Just saw him down near the pond. Acted strange when I hailed him. Took off into the brush."

"That so?", muttered Hurlburt absently. He had spent far more time on equipment inventory than he had planned and didn't care for this interruption. The boy departed as Hurlburt finished his tally and took it to Harwood's office for filing. Only when John asked about the new recruit did Hurlburt recall what the boy had said.

"Damn! I've got to go check on him. He must have missed the truck after lunch. Good worker that one. I can't imagine him sneaking out of responsibility. Be back shortly."

Hurlburt went directly to Barracks 2. His astute eye picked up all the evidence he needed. He wandered down by the pond where Paul had been seen, but found no one. Back in Harwood's office he expressed growing concern.

"Maybe he missed the truck and decided to walk out to the work area," John offered.

"Not in that direction. All this afternoon's work is out on the Canton road except for the thinning detail near the dam. Besides, I found these in the barracks."

Hurlburt produced a torn and bloodied fatigue shirt and the empty soda bottle.

"There's been a scuffle over there and these clothes tell me that he's involved. Normally when this happens, few if any of us hear about it. But I'm concerned this time since the boy has trouble communicating. This bottle for instance, take a whiff."

John inhaled cautiously, pulling back in disgust from the emanating odor of urine.

"That's the remains of what's called an Irish cocktail, a nasty initiation treat reserved for the most difficult new enrollees. God knows what happened, but I'll bet Boisvert got pretty well mauled and won't show up for supper."

John decided that Hurlburt's instincts were right and went himself to the pruning party near the dam to ask more questions. He learned only the direction in which Paul had disappeared, but that was enough. The lad was headed home to Springfield, which lay ten difficult miles away. He'd have to go get him, but wanted to spare him the embarrassment of a search party.

Then he remembered that Route 35 going north bisected the area. Paul would have to cross it somewhere, most likely at the junction of the tote road from camp. Harwood looked at his watch. With luck he might intercept Paul. Certainly it was well worth a try. He told Hurlburt of his plan and left camp in his Ford, making his way roundabout through Grafton. Thirty minutes later he was parked near the end of the tote road.

Half an hour passed and John had about decided his hunch was wrong when Paul emerged from the brush about 500 feet up the road, crossed the blacktop on the run and splashed into Hall Brook. The water was shallow and with little current, but the stones were slippery and impeded progress. John jumped out of the car and closed on him quickly. Paul splashed faster, the water nearly over his knees.

"Hey, wait a minute," John commanded from the water's edge.

"Come on back to camp or I'll have to report you A.W.O.L." Paul reached the shallows and turned. John winced a bit as he saw the distorted, blood-smeared face. One eye was swollen shut, but the other glared defiantly. Paul said nothing.

"You're not in very good shape. Get in my car and I'll take you back to camp where we can patch you up."

Paul continued to glare, then clutching the broken arm to his chest spat a huge, bloody clot quarter way across the stream, and, turning, skipped up the bank into the dense forest.

"Damn, stubborn mule!", muttered John as he splashed across the stream in hot pursuit.

Despite his injuries, Paul kept a good one hundred yards ahead of John and, cresting a knoll, looked down on a gentle ravine growing rank with shoulder high ferns. He'd have to get through these to the cover of the forest which began again on the reverse slope. With a bit more speed, he'd be into the trees before the captain puffed his way up the knoll. Then it would be simple to give him the slip.

Perhaps it was the swollen eye that didn't see or his eagerness to get away that made him careless. Whatever the reason, midway through the fronds, he tripped and sprawled headlong. He might still have gotten up and raced on had the broken arm not twisted under him. An excruciating pain shot through his shoulder and hung on, making him gasp. He brought the limb around and saw the bone, splintered and protruding. Tears flooded his eyes, causing the damaged one to throb, yet he did not cry out. Rather, he snaked his way fifty feet off the animal run he had been following and lay still among the clumps of fern, hoping Harwood would pass by or give up the chase.

But John had no intention of losing Paul. As soon as he had seen how beaten the boy was, he knew that medical help was needed. Otherwise he might have let Paul run all the way back to the Black River and simply cornered him at the rectory where his grandmother lived.

John crested the knoll and hesitated. There was no sound save his own labored breathing and the faint hiss of wind in the top of the forest. Nothing moved in the ravine, but scores of day biting mosquitoes rose up from its moist recesses to investigate the intrusion by perspiring, warm-blooded prey. John smacked a few out of existence and had nearly decided to plunge on to the waiting forest when he noticed the bent fronds to his left. His intuition told him to search further, and cutting into the densest growth, he almost stumbled over Paul who tried to get up then fell back in a swoon. Dozens of mosquitoes were taking turns on Paul's face and hands.

"Good God, lad, you're worse off than I thought." Paul was too sick from pain-induced nausea to resist as Harwood splinted the break with saplings and bound the arm with his Sam Browne belt. Mosquito reinforcements were arriving as John lifted Paul in his arms and, puffing with exertion, lugged him out of the ferns, down the hill and across the brook. He made him as comfortable as possible in the back seat of the Ford, then sat on the running board to catch his breath.

By the time they reached Chester and pulled up in front of the doctor's house, Paul had regained a little strength and leaning on Harwood for support, was able to walk up the steps and into the parlor the doctor used for a waiting room. Several patients stared in disbelief as Paul was hustled into the treatment room ahead of them. Paul passed out again when the physician pulled the broken bones apart to realign them. Fortunately, the protruding part was not soiled, nor was there much bleeding. Remarking that the arm might always have a slight crook, the doctor cast it in plaster then worked on the many cuts and bruises.

"He'll look like hell for a couple of weeks, Captain, but there's nothing seriously wrong. Bring him back in a week so I can check him again. I may have to recast that arm in a month or so."

"What do I owe you?", queried John.

The doctor smiled. "Forget it. You've got enough to think about over there in that camp trying to referee these dog fights."

"We appreciate your help," John said as he tipped his cap and helped Paul back to the car.

John did not start the engine immediately so as to give Paul a chance to get comfortable as possible in the back seat. He gripped the steering wheel and looked out at the heat rippling off the macadam.

"I suppose you'll be returning to your grandmother at the rectory."

Paul remained silent, licking the swollen lip. Harwood continued his wait, noting that much more time in the sun would make an oven of his Ford.

"We can't stay here and cook, you know," he tried again.

"I return to da camp wit you."

Harwood whirled in the seat, stunned by this remark.

"Now wait a minute. That's going to be impossible. Your arm will be at least six weeks healing as the doctor said. You'll need some rest after that beating you just took." He suddenly grew irritated.

"You'll be no use to anyone with work to do and hanging around camp is the last thing to think of."

Paul looked Harwood in the eye despite the swelling which was now turning an awful purple in places.

"I make myself useful for you."

"Oh, sure! We're in great need for a one-armed paperhanger", John snorted.

"I remind you, sir, dat you promise me month trial. I keep my part of da bargain."

The boy's defiance piqued him and he turned his gaze to the street once more, exhaling loudly in exasperation.

"You'll have to face those harps and they'll be after another pound of flesh." In the rearview mirror, Harwood saw the narrowed eyes and lifted chin, grimacing slightly from pain.

"O.K., dammit, be stubborn", John exploded. "But don't expect any favors. And right now we're going to the rectory to show you off to your grandmother and Father Mercier. They'll have a say so in this."

Grandmother Boisvert put on a good face, but couldn't totally hide her fear and anger as Harwood made Paul relate what happened.

"Who did this to you?", she demanded. Harwood, too, wanted his answer so that he could discharge the Irish toughs responsible. But Paul would reveal no names and was adamant about returning to camp. No amount of pleading on the old woman's part would change his mind. Father Mercier said nothing, but when the Boisverts went into the kitchen to get some cold water for Paul's face, he reminded John of their earlier conversation.

"Anything I say will have little effect on him. Remember that the boy is determined to go to the seminary and nothing will get in the way of this."

"Let's just hope that he's not being a mule. How can I press charges if he won't cooperate? Whatever did you do to make him so pig-headed?"

The priest let this challenge go by. "He needs you, Captain, more than anyone else right now."

Harwood gave him a severe look, then shook his head and, leaning toward the kitchen, announced impatiently, "C'mon, Paul. I've got to find you a safe spot to roost while that arm mends."

Harwood placed Paul on the sick roster and told the C.C.C.orderly, Rocco Donnelli, to have him stay put in the dispensary where meals would be brought in. After Harwood left, Rocco sat and gave Paul the stare.

"Say, you really got creamed. That eye looks like shit." Paul grimaced and lay back on the cot.

Rocco left a glass and a pitcher of water within Paul's reach and went to leave, but turned suddenly, opened his orderly's desk and fumbled in the bottom drawer, finally retrieving several magazines.

"Here, these may make you forget the pain for a while."

Paul grunted and closed his good eye, not noting until later that the mags were part of Rocco's girlie collection.

Rocco Donnelli had been born and brought up in New York City. This identification was renewed each time he opened his mouth, which was often. He was a bit older than the average recruit, slight of build, and clever with a refreshing sense of humor. He also had the brains to steer clear of the camp bullies, yet gained their grudging favor by quietly patching up their wounds as well as those of their victims who appeared from time to time. The camp doctor who rotated among a number of the southern Vermont camps had early taken a liking to him, especially when he found that Rocco had learned to type back in Queens. So Harwood had made him unofficial orderly at the dispensary in charge of camp medical supplies. His easy-going nature was a good influence on Paul and they got on well.

By the third day Paul looked like living hell, but he made no complaint and spent the hours reading books that Harwood had obtained from the Grafton Library. The rest of the company took little notice, but nearly everyone knew Paul was back in camp. After a week and a half, Harwood put Paul on a limited work schedule as assistant orderly to Rocco and let him take meals at the mess hall. The doctor's prediction proved true. The contusions disappeared and the arm seemed to be knitting vigorously. Except for the cumbersome cast and the maddening itch beneath, Paul was a model of health. Hurlburt found use for him as a runner and message bearer within the camp confines, tasks which put him in touch with almost every maintenance project. He learned fast and despite his language difficulty, understood nearly everything he was told or overheard.

A ten bay garage was constructed for camp trucks, but the pitch of the concrete floor was laid askew resulting in a depression at the back. In winter, water and ice would collect there and each vehicle would have to climb a slight grade to get out, defects immediately noted by the building inspector making his rounds of camp projects. In the event of fire it would be both dangerous and near impossible to roll stalled trucks out to safety. The day after the inspector left, Paul showed Hurlburt a sketch on waste wrapping paper, outlining how, with additional layers of concrete, the depression could be built up a bit higher than the level at the door. Large triangular wood wheel blocks, each with an iron ring through which was threaded a twenty foot strand of sturdy rope would secure each vehicle in place. Should a fire rip through the structure, one person could, from a distance, tug the blocks out from under the wheels and the vehicles would roll by gravity out of harm's way. Hurlburt was impressed by the boy's initiative and, with minor modifications, approved of the plan, as did the inspector on his next visit.

As reports like this trickled in, Harwood began to consider Paul in a new light. The primitive, but adequate attic room above Harwood's office was unused space and would probably never be used for its intended storage function.

"Hell, if the major can put Rust up in the Exec's office, Paul won't be any problem in the attic", he concluded to himself, smiling at the irony. Harwood could not only use the extra orderly help, but could keep a closer eye on the boy as well.

"Let's get this straight", John concluded. "You'll be here only until that arm heals. There'll be no special privileges and you'll stand with the rest of the company for all assemblies and camp functions, including clean-up details. You'll report to me first thing every morning and I will assign you work here or with Hurlburt on camp maintenance as you've been doing. Any questions?"

Paul looked at the arrangements Harwood had made for him, a bunk, a small desk and chair and a wall locker similar to what he had in the barracks.

"My book?", he asked, nodding his approval.

"Sure", John smiled, extending his hand to Paul. "I'll see that you have a bookcase for them. Now let's get your belongings over here. It's way past lunch and we have to get back to work."

The next morning Harwood came out of his quarters to find the office more neat than he was accustomed to. Paul was sitting in the loggia watching the camp wake up. Reveille would not sound for another half-hour.

"You're up early", John greeted.

"I get used to it. Have to be when da cow need milking", Paul grinned.

"I suppose that's true, but there are no cows here to worry about, thank goodness. Try to get as much sleep as you can. Some days will be very long."

"Not for me. Not now", Paul waved his cast. "Today will be a good day and I want to be at work. On rainy days, I catch up on sleep."

Harwood appreciated his good humor and decided to take him up on it. "Suppose we go inside before the bugle blows and I'll show you the ropes."

Nothing was said about Paul's earlier tidying the office as John gave him a geography lesson on where things were at.

"My job is to try to keep on top of what happens in camp and to be sure that services are provided. Once in a while there will be discipline to mete out and enforce, so I'm the court of last resort for this and other big camp problems. A lot of what I do means reports and paperwork. That's what you see here. The files in the corner contain complete accounts of our equipment and material and records of everything we do. The little file over there is for personnel records. When I'm making reports, everything on that desk is important and nothing gets moved, misplaced or lost. Everything completed goes in the file. No exceptions on this."

Paul nodded as if he understood and Harwood watched him taking stock. He got the impression that the boy missed very little.

"O.K., now off with you to reveille. Work with Hurlburt today and we'll talk again before taps."

The arrangement suited them both. Paul proved to be a quick study and never overstepped the line into seeking a special status with the company commander. He was prompt, did what he was told and never embroidered on the information he carried to and from his superiors. John began to wonder how he ever did without him, knowing full well that in eight weeks time, Paul must return to the barracks.

One Sunday afternoon Harwood asked Paul to join him on the makeshift firing range set up in the old farm's gravel pit on the far side of the orchard. John kept a Smith and Wesson .38 caliber revolver in the holster of his Sam Browne belt, using it sparingly for dress ceremonies. But when camp boredom got the best of him, he resorted to a bit of firing practice. As a younger officer, he had been known to have a good eye.

Paul lined up the glass bottles while John waited. After a couple of shots for range, Harwood picked off five of them with six shots.

"Here you go, Paul. Let's see what you can plug."

Harwood showed him the gist of operating the weapon, then reloaded and told him to shoot away. Paul's first six shots thunked into the sand two feet above the bottles.

"You're aiming too high. Hand guns always recoil up, so if you shoot right at the target you might get a lucky first hit, but the rest will go over. Aim just a little low and try again." Harwood reloaded and gave him the go-ahead. Four of the shots went wild, but two bottles disintegrated.

"Not bad, but hold steady as you can without locking up stiff. You've got a good trigger squeeze. Most people try to jerk the trigger and never hit anything."

After several reloads, Paul improved dramatically, so much so that John suggested that they increase the range. He had plenty of ammunition, courtesy of the U.S. Army. Even at longer ranges, Paul was good and by the end of the afternoon he was picking off bottles nearly as well as Harwood.

"Not bad for a one-armed soldier", John chided. Where did you learn to handle a weapon?"

"I shoot big gun", Paul replied proudly, describing the shotgun that he and his grandfather used to bring down venison. Harwood was somewhat awed that Paul had many skills which were of value to the camp and rough living and was sure that these would serve the boy well someday.

"Even if he is preparing to train for the clergy", John said to himself, shaking his head slightly. He still had trouble seeing this lad giving sermons.

16

Harwood cast a skeptical eye over the new contingent of recruits. The normal company complement of 200 was now exceeded by a dozen. He could have used the extra manpower in the fall when they were feverishly putting the camp together. Why had procurement sent so many now? If this bug project didn't pan out, Fred and the foresters would have to think up additional work just to keep these men out of trouble. He dismissed his thoughts about the obvious confusion in the system, particularly among the higher-ups who rarely, if ever, got out to the camps. Nothing he would suggest was ever going to change the bureaucracy. He'd been in the Army long enough to understand this well, only too well.

The new arrivals were a motley assemblage drawn from places beyond New England unlike earlier issues of the Irish who had come strictly from Boston. For the first time he saw some black faces. In the South, blacks were placed in special camps of their own to preclude racial trouble. He thought of putting them all on permanent duty at the mess hall where the noncoms could keep an eye on them, but discarded the idea as unfair. Anyway, he wasn't so sure that the mess hall staff would take to such an arrangement. Most reports indicated that they were good workers and often outdid the whites in endurance. That alone could spell trouble as it would feed the insecurities of the others, especially the Irish, who were sure to force their will on them. At least they were healthy-looking and could probably take any hazing the bullies might level.

After the introduction and pep talk, he dismissed them to get their gear from the quartermaster. Turning to Fred, he winked and smiled.

"These are the bodies you said you needed. Now, don't tell me you haven't got enough manpower to haul firewood for the winter."

"Thanks a bunch, Captain. We'll have the hottest damn camp in these Green Mountains. Professor Stone may even get his precious pruning work done after all."

Rafferty's giant bodyguard had watched the arrival too. He spat out the open window of Barracks B and announced to his cronies, "They wouldn't dare put them shines in here with us. There'd be nothin but grease spots in a week." He grinned diabolically.

"They got to go somewhere", someone responded. "The camp's loaded and we're probably the only barracks that has empty beds. They can't all go up to headquarters with the Frenchie." This brought guffaws from a few.

The giant glared. "Over my dead body are any coons coming in here. And if they do, they'll wish they'd never left the plantation." He looked around to catch the smirks about his clever remarks and bravado. No one challenged this as the bugler announced supper.

The newcomers finished their meal and went to their assigned quarters. The four blacks were assigned to Barracks B out of necessity and Hurlburt accompanied them to make the point that they were to be treated just like everyone else. He singled out the giant as he spoke and left the clear impression that troublemakers would have to deal with Hurlburt himself. No sooner had he departed than the giant smirked and moved towards the bunks of the blacks. Rafferty laid hold of him and steered him away.

"Not now, you jerk! Hurlburt will have you canned," he muttered under his breath. "There'll be plenty of time later to make our little welcome seem like an accident. And these black boys won't dare make a peep, mark my words."

The Irishman looked crossly at Rafferty, but said, "O.K., O.K. But I want to be the one to let them know who's boss."

Thus, the newcomers were absorbed into the life of the camp without incident. The blacks in Barracks B, although isolated by the toughs, knew enough not to provoke an incident. And as

Harwood had surmised, they proved to be hard workers who would not lay back in the harness.

This irked the Irish into a silent boil which three weeks later erupted out behind the truck garage. Hurlburt had left for the weekend as had many of the recruits. But the blacks, who really had no place to go, pretty much stuck together and were returning from an afternoon of fishing in the brook which drained Hyde Pond. Rafferty and his cronies made like they were on assignment to bring in timber for winter firewood when they suddenly appeared from the woodlot, cutting right in front of the anglers.

A short, pugnacious-looking lad named O'Neil was in the lead, struggling with a sizeable log, the other end of which was propelled by the big Irishman. At the precise moment the two groups met, O'Neil appeared to stumble and sprawled headlong, the log leaving his shoulder and rolling over his back. The first black in the file bent to help him up, placing a hand out to lift the log.

"Now, why the hell did you push my friend like that?", the giant roared, spinning the black to his feet and lifting O'Neil with his free hand.

The other blacks gathered around as the young man retreated a few paces and declared his innocence.

"Was you pushed or not, Shorty?"

O'Neil clenched his fists and thrust out his lip. "You bet I was. That one right there done it", he spat out, pointing at the accused and taking a step towards the group.

One of the more slender blacks stepped forward and touched Shorty's sleeve. "Let's wait a minute, we don't want no trouble over this. It's just a misunderstanding."

"Did you hear that, now?", the giant crowed, smirking malevolently. Shorty had elbowed the peacemaker out of the way and grabbed the shirt of the accused, popping off most of the buttons. The other blacks tried to separate them as O'Neil began to pummel his target. The whole scene was ludicrous as Shorty barely came up to the man's chin.

"Hey, let go of my little friend", yelled the giant, who then cut loose with a harsh whistle. Out of the brush emerged a score of recruits, acting for the world like they had just happened onto the altercation. The blacks looked up and got the picture instantly, taking off like lightning for the shelter of the mess hall. The Irish pursued them closely, but were too slow and all easily escaped except for the peacemaker who lost his footing before he reached the back of the garage. Three toughs piled on him pinning him fast and O'Neil unleashed a barrage of body blows. The young man fought back, but was no match for the mob.

Paul had put some tools away for Walsh and was pulling the truck garage door shut when he was nearly toppled by the fleeing blacks. He tried to grasp what was happening when he heard the fracas and giddy laughter out back. He rounded the corner to see the black getting trounced by a half-dozen mad-dog Irish, the others just standing around grinning. They had torn off his shirt and bloodied his face badly. He was beginning to groan with pain and had trouble getting to his knees. Then Shorty appeared with a stout limb in his hands. The black must have landed a few on him as his nose was bleeding profusely and his lip looked a bit large.

Paul hesitated, at first overwhelmed by what he was seeing, then remembering his own beating. Rafferty, standing back from the rest, was among those egging the others on and didn't even see Paul, who by now realized what the short Irishman was going to do with the limb. Like a shot, Paul raced to the prostrate black and threw himself over his head and shoulders. The weapon came down, catching Paul across the back. It hurt, but Shorty was so startled by this new participant that he had blunted the blow. For a moment, everything was suspended. But it didn't take long for the mob to regain their fury. Some tried to pull Paul off, but he clung like a leech. Shorty beat like crazy with the stick, connecting a few times. A blow on Paul's cast made him wince, but the plaster held.

Suddenly, the beating stopped and Paul glanced up to see Shorty more or less dangling from the end of his stick, the other end of which was firmly controlled by Captain Harwood. The mob had already split, running back into the woods. Only Rafferty and his henchman stood at the edge of the canopy to see what would happen next.

"Just what the hell is going on here?", Harwood yelled. Shorty dropped his end of the wood and tried to join the others, but John caught him by the collar and pulled him close. One look into his commander's eyes was enough to make O'Neil go limp. Harwood flung him up against the garage wall where he stayed put. As Paul rolled off the black, John gave him a ferocious look, but knelt beside the peacemaker and eased him into a sitting position.

"What's your name?", he asked as soon as he found that there were no broken bones.

"Lester Gilpin, sir. But don't blame this man, sir", the black mumbled through bloody lips. "He came to help me, but it didn't do no good."

Then, seeing the concern on Harwood's face, he continued with a wry grin. "I think I'll be all right after the hurt stops."

Harwood turned to Shorty, who was cowering nearby. "Who started this?" Shorty stayed mum and looked over the captain's shoulder at Rafferty and the giant who were now approaching.

"We can explain it, sir", said Rafferty smoothly. "Shorty and Tim here were bringing in firewood and this black and his buddies pushed Shorty down. Ain't that right, Tim?"

John was unconvinced and looked to the young black who was a bit unsteady, but now on his feet. The black looked away and said nothing. With increasing frustration, Harwood turned to Paul and for the first time noticed that his cast was cracked.

"Are you O.K.?"

"I do all right. I don't see who started fight, though."

Harwood gave withering stares, first at Lester, then at Rafferty and the giant, well aware that he wasn't going to get a straight story.

"You get those men in the woods and go to your barracks", he said evenly to Rafferty. "The lot of you are confined to quarters except for meals until reveille on Monday."

"Lester, go get your friends in the mess hall and come to my office at headquarters."

"Paul, you go find Walsh and have him tape up that cast. And tell me right away if that arm feels strange."

When the blacks stood before him, he again asked for an explanation, but none came. This was not unexpected, for he knew what the camp toughs generally did to squealers. Anyway, he knew that O'Neill was out-processing in a week. He would simply speed that up a bit with an early discharge.

"Regardless of what started the fight today, you've got to know that I'll ship anyone out of here who can't abide by the rules of civility. All of you have families who are depending on you for a little support, so next time remember them when you get riled up by troublemakers."

Still no response.

"You're all going to leave Barracks B and move permanently to Barracks A. Walsh will see that your gear is moved before supper tonight. I don't want any of you even near B Barracks any time for any reason."

Harwood looked each one in the eye while saying this. All refused to engage and concentrated on the wall behind him. Only Lester, who, while not defiant, kept his gaze steady.

"We didn't start nothin today, Captain, but things will be better in the future," he uttered distinctly despite his cracked lips.

John sized him up for a moment, then shrugged. "Well, good enough. Just stay out of trouble. Now get out of here and take care of that face of yours."

At the door, Lester turned and faced Harwood, smiling. "That Frenchie, he saved my head. Would you thank him for me?"

John grimaced. "You thank him. He's a damn fool to go mixing into a fight with a cast on." But after they had gone, he thought again about what the priest had said regarding Paul's future. The boy was stubborn, but one had to be impressed by the boy's courage and he had to admit that it was refreshing to see someone act on his convictions whatever the cost. But he knew that it wouldn't be long before Paul would see that the world needed more than boy scouts and sentimentality. Either that or the boy would crack. Harwood went to the window and caught the slanting afternoon sun on his face.

17

Harwood shut the new bulkhead to the camp cistern and brushed his trousers free of sawdust. He would have liked to spend more time in the cool interior, but he was satisfied with his inspection. At last the water supply was fully restored and the contractor had done a thorough job this time. He was confident that there would be no more freeze-ups like last winter. Too anxious to get operational in the previous fall, they had cut too many corners on the insulation.

He started down the ridge to camp when he was hailed by Professor Stone who was returning to his makeshift laboratory in the camp library.

"How's the caterpillar business?", John inquired.

"Not showing much profit, I'm afraid", the professor replied, wiping his brow. "The number of male gypsies tracking females is overwhelming, but with the leaves gone, the birds have no cover and aren't taking any prey that I can see. Of course, that doesn't mean that next year's onslaught will be the same as this." He waved a hand vaguely towards the ridge.

"Let's hope not or they'll carry all of us right out of here." John smiled and Stone brightened a bit.

"Could be. Could be. But let's not count our gypsies before they hatch. Of course, if the females are anywhere near as numerous and have successfully mated, we could be in for big trouble. I left Sarah and two of your recruits on the other side of the ridge where they're making adult counts."

John looked back up the wood tote road to the top of the ridge. He knew that the recruits had to be Paul and Rocco. They both had sharp eyes and were reliable for this kind of work.

"Think I'll go see how they do it."

"Too hot for me", Stone sighed. "Besides, I've got stuff to label in the lab. Been backlogged for more than a week." He turned and sauntered down the road while John made his way up the ridge, avoiding the scattered stones which made the tote road more of an obstacle course than a rough track.

By the time he reached the crest of the ridge, he almost wished that he had stayed with the professor. Finding even a tiny patch of shade was near impossible. But it took no time to spot the trio working as a team, Paul and Rocco observing and Sarah recording. Neither of the young men had received more than cursory instruction on the gypsy project, but were, as Harwood had surmised, diligent to the task. Rocco counted females within the quadrant that Sarah had selected, Paul doing the same a little distance away. Keeping a watchful eye on them, Sarah was busy jotting down their reports on her clipboard and didn't see Harwood approaching.

"You've all got some gumption to stay out here with these bugs", John said by way of greeting. Sarah was slightly startled by his voice and came away from her concentration.

"Just our job, Captain", she returned. "The ones deserving credit are your boys out there in the brush. But we're about done for the day." She glanced over at the recruits and hollered. "What say we call it quits for the day?" They had no trouble hearing and quickly joined them.

Sarah gave Rocco the once over. "My God, Rocco, you look like you're turning into a gypsy." They all stared at the two dozen or so male gypsies clinging to his trousers.

"They just won't leave me alone, Miss Chapman, unless I squash them and when I do more jump on board. Ever since I wiped my hands on my pants earlier this afternoon, they've ganged up on me."

"Well, you've probably got female gypsy abdomens all over you. Look at Paul, he's carrying a few males, too. Sort of supports Professor Stone's theory that the males find the females by scent alone. None of those females fly, you know, so the male has to do all the tracking and finding. Your nothing but a big, attractive female, Rocco", she laughed.

Rocco colored a bit and looked sheepish, but smiled with the others.

Changing the subject, she asked Paul how his arm felt after a full day in the field. He waved the appendage and shrugged good-naturedly. The mending was remarkably fast at his age, but the muscles were weak, wasted by inactivity. Don't forget what I said about beginning practice on your violin." She had wheedled out of him his interest in Pierre's fiddle and encouraged his playing to get strength and coordination back into his fingers and forearm.

"O.K., let's gather our markers and measure tapes and head back. You both look like you could use a dip in the pond."

Anticipating this, Paul and Rocco went on ahead like young ponies and left Sarah and Harwood walking together.

"So how are things going?", John queried.

Sarah smiled, brushing back some hair and blowing out her breath forcefully. "Ask me that after supper. This wasteland is quite unforgiving. But I feel good about my research so far and Professor Stone is a gem to work with. Doesn't always say much, but let's me know the important things and doesn't over manage. Sort of let's me figure problems for myself—until I get stuck", she added with a smile.

"Yes, I gather that you get on well just from what I've observed and heard", John continued. "But when will this seasonal work be done?"

"Oh, for this year we'll work right up til snow flies, but most tallying will be over by September when I return to regular classes. Then in the fall I'll be up here with the professor whenever he needs me."

They continued down the tote road towards camp. "By the way," Sarah interjected, "thank you for fixing up the piano."

"Oh, that's something I've been meaning to do. Just that no one showed any interest in playing until now." Shifting the subject a bit, he asked, "You were a music teacher before starting at Mass Aggie?"

She wondered momentarily how he had learned that much about her, but answered directly. "Yes, for four years after college in an

Iowa high school. I really liked that, but decided that science, especially biology, was more to my calling. My uncle, Sam Chapman, was an entomologist like Professor Stone. They knew each other years ago and when Sam—that's what everyone called him—died, I decided to leave the mid-west for good. So here I am."

"That's quite a shift. You must have some family here in New England to help ease the transition."

"No, no," she returned brightly. "Sam was the last of the Chapman line and he had no children, unless you count me." Then, seeing his face dead pan, she added, "But that's hardly a disadvantage. Let's me be myself rather than a measure stick for what others think."

"Certainly a lot of truth in that", he allowed. "But why biology and giving chase to these cursed bugs out here in the boondocks?"

Her eyes widened. "Well, first, Captain, let me correct your terminology", she replied with mock seriousness and a lilt in her voice. "Gypsies are moths, not bugs. Related to butterflies and skippers, not squash bugs and stinkbugs. Very different, you know. Don't let Professor Stone hear you making such mistakes."

John chuckled through his nose. "O.K., O.K., I'll get it straight sometime soon. It just seems like you're making a huge leap from music to insects."

"Oh, there's plenty of music among the insects, just not the usual classics, jazz and dance tunes we're used to." She grew a bit serious, then continued. "There are so many varieties of these little beasts, each with its own bizarre behavior and song amongst the cacaphony. All have a story to tell. Sam often said that even if he lived to be one hundred, he would never finish reading the wonderful life story of the insects. He loved his work and really thought of them as characters in a great, compelling and endless novel which was to be read and enjoyed every day of his life. He often shared with me how his work was endlessly refreshing. Sam was the happiest person I've ever known and some of it must have rubbed off on me." She hesitated and they walked on in silence for a while.

"Well, if you ever tire of these gypsies, I'll loan you the Victrola I've got tucked away in the office. There are a few Caruso and

McCormick records and some scratchy ones of Cab Calloway at the Cotton Club, but maybe they'll help you leap back into your former life for a few moments." His face had gone soft and she noticed.

"That's very generous of you," she said in a quiet voice.

Stone looked out the window of the library at the returning recruits piling into the barracks. Most were soaked with sweat and disheveled, longing for the dip in Hyde Pond before supper. He turned to his labels and picked up, knowing that Sarah would be back in a short while. Through the window the sun was balanced on the top of the ridge preparatory to sliding away for the night. He spotted Sarah coming through the orchard and smiled. But then he saw that Harwood was with her. His intuition had told him that they would return together, but nonetheless, a cold, dead feeling crept over his soul. He had not felt so terribly lonely in years and knew now that nothing was going to slake the need he had in the marrow of his bones.

Leaning back in his chair, John stretched his arms above his head to relieve the tension and mumbled to himself, "Damn this paperwork, anyway. Give a government agency a job to do and they make an ink and paper monster out of it."

The door opened and Sarah walked in. John turned around and greeted her, glad for the interruption.

"This is the summary of our project that you asked for," she said handing him a bound sheaf of papers. "Professor Stone will make any changes you want."

John leafed through it quickly, noting its brevity and neatness, appreciating that it most likely could be appended to his report without revision. "Looks good to me. Tell the professor thanks." He turned to the desk and retrieved a single sheet from his pile and handed it to her. "This is the camp description he was looking for. Seems that the network in Washington has got us all stuck up in their flypaper."

She folded the description in half and shaking her head in sympathy, turned to go.

"Say, I thought you were leaving early today to get ready for that trip to the Berkshires this weekend. Some new summer concert series by the Boston Symphony . . . . what's the name of that place again . . . . Tanglefoot?" he queried mischievously.

"No, it's Tanglewood, as well you know," she retorted giving him a stern look. "The trip had to be called off at the last minute. The bus driver got sick and there was no replacement. I suppose they'll try for another date later in the summer.

John put his hands behind his head, mulling his next thought. "How far did you say it was?"

She gave him a curious look. "About three or four hours travel time, allowing for stops."

"Sure makes for a long day, but I'll drive if you really want to go."

"That's most kind of you, but I thought you were behind in your reports." She gave his desk the once over.

"They'll wait. I might even absorb a little culture for a change." John shuffled some papers. "Besides," he lied, "Paul would like to go and this way I'll be able to keep an eye on him."

"That's a wonderful idea," she beamed. Then, thinking for a moment, she made a face. "But probably you'd be bored stiff by the program, a full orchestra doing some old Masters, then a quintet of lighter Romantics."

He gave her a side-wise smirk. "Oh, I've survived them before. Some of Bach's partitas are O.K. Just spare me Johann's organ music. Some Mozart and Schubert I actually like." He watched her face.

"Oh, the Austrians!!", she responded brightly. "That surprises me, Captain. I'd pegged you as liking the heavier stuff, maybe Wagner and Strauss."

Harwood shrugged.

"I'll go half the expenses . . . . ," she began.

"Now, let's not get into that," John interrupted. "Either you go as my guest or we don't go at all."

The Saturday following, Paul again sat in the rear seat of the Ford. He had been surprised at John's invitation and was very grateful to finally be able to watch classical music being performed, something he'd only heard from Father Mercier's gramophone in the rectory parlor. The trip was long, but Harwood stopped a number of times to stretch. On the Mohawk Trail, they dallied in a roadside turnout while John tinkered with the Ford's fan belt. Paul and Sarah cooled their feet in the nearby river. The water felt good and Paul basked contentedly in Sarah's company. Too soon, he thought, Harwood called out that they must continue.

They reached Lenox in plenty of time, but had to ask directions to the large estate overlooking Stockbridge Bowl. The crowd was not large on this warm afternoon, but the air was charged with expectations. The Boston Symphony Orchestra held forth in the first half of the afternoon with Bach's Concerto in C Minor for two pianos. A quintet then interpreted Schubert and Mendelssohn to end the program.

As the two pianos conversed during the rich, haunting adagio, Paul stole a glance at Sarah. Her face was serene, but the moisture on her cheeks gave away her intense enjoyment. Paul suddenly remembered a passage from Harwood's copy of The Great Gatsby he had been reading . . . . "Eyes that were made to be kissed." He wanted to tell her how happy he was, and that this was their shared moment. Harwood shifted slightly and brought him back to reality. John's face was a mask. If he was touched by the music, no one would ever know. Without fanfare, he removed a handkerchief from his trouser pocket and handed it to Sarah.

Schubert's "Trout" and the Mendelssohn were masterful, but it was the quintet's Boccherini encore ending the concert which sent Sarah back into her former life and plumbed her feelings again. The third movement minuet of the E minor Quintet resonated even with Harwood, whose head bobbed slightly in time with the melody. Sarah needed the hankie another time. After apologizing for the weepiness, she never seemed to stop smiling as they drove east, back over the mountains to the camp.

18

Two weeks later, John and Sarah were on their way to the Spofford Lake Pavilion. A swing band was ensconced there through Indian Summer, drawing the vacation crowd as well as locals. They descended the twisting road to Brattleboro and took the Keene Highway Bridge over the Connecticut, then climbed the ancient river terraces to the turn-off road by the lake. The line of thunderstorms pushing north up the river valley all day had dissipated and clean, well-washed air ushered in the final minutes of a hazy sunset.

They crested a hill and dropped down suddenly to the edge of the lake where the light was nearly gone. Before the pavilion, electric lights hove into view and they heard the music, bright and brisk. The parking lot was bursting and there was regular foot traffic to and from the darkened cars. John had to park on the grass way back by the cow pasture. They made their way between the lines of vehicles toward the blaze of the dance floor located right on the lakefront. Every table was taken.

John and Sarah pushed into the swaying crush, adroitly fox trotting among the dancers. Any former aloofness soon dissolved under the spell of the music. The touch of hands and bodies in rhythm beckoned an understanding that words would never fashion.

But not all at the pavilion were dancing. Rafferty skulked on the far side near the water, casting an experienced and wary eye over the crowd. He'd spotted Harwood and Sarah right away and was now avoiding them at all costs. He'd made a month's wages already and with luck he'd break fifty for the evening.

"Now there's another bunch of horny suckers," he said to himself, sporting a predatory grin as he slipped onto the floor where a slightly inebriated trio of locals were eyeing the skirts. As pretty girls whirled by they would smirk and punch each other on the arm. Rafferty sidled up to them and joined the game, using their same lewd remarks. He was the consummate chameleon. After a few minutes of this, in sotto voice he asked the one least in control if he'd had any tail lately. He was prepared for the nervous laugh and chuckled knowingly, to draw the noose a bit tighter.

"Seriously, I know where you can get laid within minutes of this place."

The boy's smile faded and the bleary eyes got serious. "How much money you got?" wooed Rafferty.

"About ten bucks," came the blurted answer.

"That's more than enough. Leave your buddies here and come with me. And don't tell them what you're doing."

"Gotta go take a leak," he told his companions and lurched after Rafferty. They followed a row of cars to the end of the lot and through an open gate into the cow pasture where Rafferty's Chevy stood under a huge white pine. He gave a soft whistle and a woman emerged from the back seat.

"O.K. Give me a fin and she's yours. I'll keep watch from here."

Without hesitation, the boy handed over the money which Rafferty quickly verified in the semi-darkness.

"Hey honey, come over here and give me a hug," cooed the woman.

"Queenie can take care of herself," chuckled Rafferty to himself as he made his way back to the pavilion for the next patron.

Fifteen minutes later the youth stumbled back into the pavilion. With a radiance best described as a shit-eating grin, he immediately told his companions of his conquest, as Rafferty knew he would.

" . . . . and I took her right there on the pine needles!" It was all Rafferty could do to detract attention from himself while lining up the others for the trip to the pasture.

Harwood and Sarah sat out a carioca and the intermission on the wharf. Nearby, lake fish jumped now and then for hapless insects attracted by the lights. Out beyond the last boat slip it was pitch dark. Sarah excused herself to go to the ladies lounge, so John lit a cigarette and leaned on the railing, his back to the milling crowd. Sarah returned to find him drawing slowly on his tobacco, drinking in the stars. A slight pang of sadness washed over her as she sensed that he was totally oblivious to the chatter behind him and so within himself.

"What are you thinking," she murmured, coming up beside him.

"Oh, just how fine it is to be here rather than in camp. Sometimes I can't sleep there even when I'm dog-tired. Must have something to do with all that famous Vermont conversation and commotion up there in Grafton." He laughed softly and unconvincingly.

"No. I'd say it was all that bugling and parading you people seem to enjoy so much," Sarah teased, hoping to draw out his real thoughts. "You really need to get back to civilian life and the city lights more often to see what you're missing."

In the darkness, John grunted and his mouth tightened as the suggestion conjured up Springfield and Hazel. He was not about to get into that conversation. The fog was rising on the lake and hung very low over the water. He suddenly felt lost and morose. The silence closed in again and Sarah knew intuitively that Harwood would say little more. She read his discomfort and shivered slightly, having a sudden urge to hold him and stroke the brow she knew was furrowed and hard set.

"Let's go back," she said evenly. "The band is about to begin again." He followed her without a word.

Despite Sarah's private distress, the rest of the evening went remarkably well, their dancing serving as the catalyst. It was obvious to her that John was finally enjoying himself and she knew that was enough. Her good nature soon took over and she wanted the music to play on and on.

The band was damned good and easily switched to the "sweet" sound of Guy Lombardo and gave out with "A Sailboat in the Moonlight", a very popular tune, complete with muted brass. But by one o'clock most everyone was ready to quit so the musicians concluded with "The Night is Young", then commenced to pack up while the dancers fled to the cars.

As John and Sarah sat in the Ford to wait their turn moving out onto the pavilion road, couples would pass into the circles cast by the headlights. A single woman crossed quickly and was swallowed up by the dark. John had the vague feeling he'd seen that face before, once pretty, but now a bit lined and drawn despite the makeup. He quickly dismissed the thought and turned his attention to negotiating position in the slow queue of vehicles.

Progress on the highway was glacial at first, but cars soon began to gather speed, pass and leave John and Sarah to themselves. Some turned off onto a back road that John knew was appropriately secluded for a bit of romance. And on down the hill leading to Brattleboro were the tourist cabins frequented by the less discreet. Out in back where the cabins weren't lit, the Ford's lights reflected on the chrome of a number of automobile grills poking out beside the tiny front stoops.

"Sin cabins," chuckled John as he pressed the accelerator to crest the last hill before the bridge over the Connecticut.

"Why are you so sure?" responded Sarah with a tease in her voice.

"Rumor seems to check out. The only time more than one car is there is when the pavilion books a band. And by daybreak the place will look like a ghost town."

"And do these ghosts linger?" she continued in mock seriousness.

John snorted. "Only those that return in about nine months. The rest evaporate in the heat of the night or in the light of the day."

"You mean they never come back when the moon is just right?"

John looked at her and grinned. She was lovely in the pale glow of the dash lights.

"You sure ask a lot of funny questions for a scientist."

"And you seem to have a lot of quick answers for a company commander of the Tree Army," she chided with a smile.

He shrugged. "Have to be up on all sorts of things in this job, you know." He shifted down as they descended rapidly to the bridge. In doing so, his hand slipped off the stick and brushed her knee. "Sorry," he muttered, recovering immediately and completing the gear change. She felt small jolts of electricity and couldn't stop smiling.

Rafferty had no intention of stopping at the cabins. Queenie was set up in the Tamarack Hotel in Bellows Falls and he had to drop her off, then get back to camp for a few hours sleep. It had been a good night and even after giving Queenie her cut, he would clear sixty dollars.

They cruised down Main Street. There was no one about at this hour and Rafferty parked discreetly near the side entrance.

"Can't ya come in for a drink?"

"Nothing doing, Queenie. I'm due at camp detail first thing in the morning. And speaking of guys coming in, you better watch where you keep your earnings, especially with those hot shots you've been entertaining lately."

Queenie glared at him. "Got to add to what you're giving me to live in this town."

"For Christ's sake, how much do you need? I'm paying the rent on this place for you."

"I need to be supported as fits my station."

Rafferty hooted. "Station? What station? For Christ's sake, you'd still be on your back in some South Boston alley if I hadn't set you up here."

Her eyes narrowed, but she held her tongue. He continued. "Just do as I say and we'll both be in the bucks. And another thing, use a little discretion about who you take to your room. Up here in the sticks, they don't always look the other way when strangers visit a dame alone in her lodgings."

She turned and slid out the door without acknowledgement.

"And we'll be going back to the pavilion a week from now, so be ready when I get here," he ordered harshly as she fumbled with her hotel key. He was putting the car in gear and pulled away, turning the corner at high speed to climb onto the main highway.

She stared after him. "Damn son of a bitch," she muttered under her breath. She knew from Rafferty's cronies why he was in such a hot trot to get back to Grafton. A young lass named Carrie Bush was getting more than her share of the Irishman's attention.

19

The peak gypsy moth infestation eventually passed and a few trees began to green up a bit with a sparse second crop. The camp now turned its attention from insects to extending the primitive road system and developing fire breaks. Each warm evening the tired recruits returned to supper and a quick dip in Hyde Pond prior to taking up reading or hobbies in the educational center. On evenings when Sarah stayed late, she could often be found at the piano with recruits joining her in song. As John sat in his office trying to do justice to a host of reports, he enjoyed the singing and accompaniment coming in the open window. This was punctuated by gusts of laughter as someone went off key or when Sarah added a bit of embellishment to an old favorite. She was very popular and the numbers standing by the piano or hanging back in the shadows humming her tunes were never small.

One night she turned to the group. "With all the noise we're making, there's no reason that you fellows couldn't put on your own show." Content to plant the seed, she didn't mention the idea again, but in less than a week several recruits with better voices came early to the rec hall.

"We liked your idea about a show, Miss Chapman. Would you be willing to help us put it together? We're not very good, but we know some of the old songs and could probably learn a few new ones.

Inwardly excited, Sarah agreed to this with mock reservation. Instead of impromptu sessions, she gathered the better singers together and worked with them, never controlling, and all the while drawing the less courageous and less able into the chorus, pulling out of them their favorite songs and best voice. As the project grew, so did the repertoire. She kept telling them, "I'm not in charge of this thing. If you really want a show, you've got to be responsible." A variety show of comedy routines, a passable jug band performing a slow version of "Soldier Boy Blues", some solos and the backbone of group singing began to take shape.

Watching the activity from the periphery were the black recruits recently arrived in camp. Lester, the youth from New York, was accepted by all, save the Irish, but since the dust-up behind the garage, opted to be a loner who stayed close to his own kind. The organizers of the show did invite him into the rehearsals, but he showed up late and hung back joining the chorus with only a murmur. But that was enough for Sarah. Her trained ear soon picked out the richness of that black voice amid the others and as the group disbanded to go off to their bunks, she asked him to stay awhile and hum some tunes. Not by accident, she moved into some Negro spirituals and without taking her eyes from the keys, felt him relax a bit and begin to hum confidently. At the end of a chord, Sarah suddenly stopped. "You can sing well, you know. I'd like to hear a little more of your voice."

"Oh, mam," he replied, a little shame-faced, glancing warily, "I don't want to sing too loud."

"You don't have to. Just sing what suits you and I'll play softly."

So he began to sing a well-known spiritual and after the first few bars, poured out some of the emotion he had so carefully hidden. He knew every word and when they had finished, Sarah sat quietly, looking at her hands folded in her lap. Turning to him slowly, she said, "That was fine music. Your voice teacher must be very proud."

He looked at the floor and shoved his hands in his pockets, finally admitting that he had sung in the church choir. Without raising her voice, Sarah said, "I would like you to do a solo in the show. Do you know "Old Man River" from *Show Boat*?"

He looked her squarely in the eye. "I've heard it, but don't know all the words."

"Do you know who sings that better than anyone?" He shook his head. "I'll tell you," she continued, "Paul Robeson. That man's talent is the envy of many and when you sing I am reminded of him." After a pause, she added, "Won't you help us out?"

"Well, I don't know, mam. Maybe some of the other boys should do this. You see, I'm very new here and . . . Well, maybe they wouldn't like me to sing it."

"Nonsense. They wouldn't have asked you here tonight if they felt that way. And they've said they've heard you humming and singing out on the job. Don't let them be disappointed." She paused, "If not for them, would you do it for me?"

"Well . . . O.K. mam. If it pleases you."

She rose and clasped his hands in hers, saying, "Thank you, Lester. It is Lester, isn't it?"

At a loss for words, Lester nodded his head, but kept his eyes on his feet.

After they went out, Rafferty dropped the newspaper he had been reading and kicked the foot of the young man next to him. With grimaced face, he chortled, "Thank you, Lester. Be sure you get your black ass onto that stage and sing, Lester. Good Christ, Patty, I thought that nigger-lover was never going to stop. And you know that coon Robeson she mentioned? My father was saying a few weeks ago that he's the guy everyone is calling a God-damned Red."

"That's a good one! A red nigger," the other boy chuckled.

"Yeh," Rafferty continued with vehemence, "the cops oughta shove him right off the stage when he starts to crow. Mark my words, he'll get his one of these days."

Sarah crossed the review area to get to her car. Practice for the show on top of her long day in the field had been exhausting and she still had the two-hour drive back to Amherst. She was about to open the door when McGarry appeared, limping his way over to the mess hall for some coffee and conversation, having arrived from parts unknown a week earlier.

"See you next week, Sarah, for some more of that sweet whorehouse music," he chuckled.

She whirled and confronted him. "Now, I'll just bet you know quite a bit about brothels, Captain," emphasizing his rank with mock sneer. "An officer and a gentleman by act of Congress. Hah!!"

Caught off guard, McGarry paused and searched her face for anger. But there was none as she continued the bantering tone. "A guardian of the bordello, now that has a fine ring to it." McGarry's jaw, already slack, sagged further.

"But regardless of your official duties, you do seem to have a fine voice. How about joining us in the show?"

Before he could think twice, McGarry had signed on and had even promised to dragoon Harwood into a poetry reading. As Sarah drove away, he hobbled up the mess hall steps, wondering what he'd just done. Two cups of coffee later he laughed like hell as he told Harwood to brush up on his verse.

At first, the show was to be strictly a camp affair, but as practice continued and talents began to shine, enthusiasm for something bigger grew. By September they had perfected the show and performed it for the assembled company. It was a big hit since Rafferty and his cronies managed not to be around to carp and criticize. Harwood had done his best to book the Bellows Falls movie theater for the two hour Sunday matinee, but was unsuccessful. Just when matters seemed worst, he got a call from the theater manager who, in thrifty Yankee fashion, struck a deal. In place of his usual fee, the boys would be required to clean up after the Saturday night show as well as their own.

Sarah and the troupe jumped at this opportunity, their enthusiasm and confidence now running at fever pitch. Harwood put notice in the local paper several weeks running before the show and the camp art class did their best to pepper Bellows Falls and the countryside with clever broadsides.

When the appointed Sunday rolled around, Sarah and her group knew they were ready, their talents honed as best they could. The CCC trucks appeared right after nine o'clock church and the props were loaded. With yeoman teamwork, the troupe was ready to go by one o'clock. Even before this, the audience began to drift in, curious to see what the boys were about. The theater manager tried to stay out of the way, but kept a sharp eye on his property. Learning that he used to provide piano accompaniment for the silent movies, Sarah managed to press him into his old service.

By curtain time the house was at overflow. Then the curtain rose and they were launched. Sarah was everywhere, checking, encouraging, and making sure that no one missed a cue. A series of comedy routines followed the opening number sung by the full cast. With manager on the piano, McGarry gave a near-perfect imitation of Harry Lauder's "Roamin in the Gloamin". Then, Sarah and McGarry sang a Sigmund Romberg duet, slipping smoothly into a rollicking version of "You'd Be Surprised". Their final verses were more energetic than any practice and at the final notes they flopped together into a Morris chair right onstage in mock exhaustion. The crowd, wild with delight, could barely be contained.

Opening the second half of the program were more comedy routines and the jug band, followed by "Shine on Harvest Moon" with the full chorus. The stage then darkened except for a spot on Harwood cutting quite a figure in full dress uniform. He began reciting Service's "Cremation of Sam McGee" quietly, carefully enunciating his lines so all could hear. His volume grew, as did the laughter. He cut the end cleanly, bowed once to applause and made his exit.

While scenery was being shifted, Sarah and Paul appeared at the other end of the stage with piano and violin. They tore into a French-Canadian reel and soon had everyone clapping in time. Then the entire cast was back in front of a Mississippi Bayou scene for a medley of Jerome Kern tunes which included Lester's solo.

Sarah watched from the wings as the house manager beat out some introductory themes of *Show Boat* on his piano. The andante faded and Lester began, building slowly and surely, his confidence growing as the song rolled out. He could have stepped right off the Cotton Blossom. A hushed audience riveted their eyes on the black face as Lester poured out "Old Man River" heart and soul. Even the accompanist looked up from his music, face incredulous. All the aches and injustices of Lester's race seemed to float out over the heads of the throng to the farthest reaches of the theater. He finished with gusto and the silence was so dense one could hear a rat piss on cotton.

Finally, some weak applause began, then rolled up like a Fundy tide with the entire audience clapping and standing. Sarah's eyes were moist with tears, but she had the presence of mind to signal the drawing of the curtain. Still the clapping went on and on, punctuated by roars of "More" and "Encore" from the patrons. After three curtain calls and continued ovation, Sarah walked out and called Lester from backstage. He looked extremely uncomfortable, but she held his hand and whispered in his ear. He made several stiff bows before retreating back to his place among the assembled singers. Sarah curtsied and the curtain closed for the final time.

The show's success was soon trumpeted throughout the river valley. Requests for reruns and special engagements were many and parts of it were given for civic groups. But it was never again done in its entirety. Many of the recruits were soon reassigned to other camps or were discharged and the magic of that fall afternoon dimmed. Yet some memories and a bit of pride in this adventure would remain forever in these young men. Even Walsh was impressed, remarking that their music sure helped shovel a little shit out of life.

20

Paul continued to rise early each morning throughout the fall and was off exploring the periphery of the camp while the rest of the contingent was asleep. The pre-dawn perambulations had fixed camp layout and function clearly in his mind, giving him a decided edge on recruits who might better comprehend the language, but remain ignorant of the territory.

At sunrise in mid-October, he stood in a copse of maples on the little hillock just beyond the orchard. The maples made a tonsure of this mound, the pate of which was a smooth granite outcrop. A hard frost had stolen across all of southern Vermont and at this hour the orchard and camp lay hushed and golden in the frigid air. Not so much as a twig moved in the still, yellow light, made more luteous by the nearly full-turned foliage. Then, as if by some mute and secret signal, the strengthening sun began to melt the delicate icy fretwork clinging to the maples. One, then another, followed by several and soon scores of leaves fell in brilliant flashes. Released from their abscission by the weight of melted water accumulating at their tips, they sailed lightly among their neighbors, tap tapping on twigs and sounding much like the patter of rain.

Paul marveled that not a puff of wind had stirred this gentle avalanche and he was loath to budge for fear of breaking the spell of this delicate music. He felt the sun's warmth mellowing his own fretwork of arms, legs and torso as something omnipotent and grand broke loose within him, like ice going out of spring ponds. A happy turbulence he had felt even as a small child began seeping and flowing into what was real and right, a love affair with the land, this land.

His eye moved up the ridge behind the camp. Had something moved there by those scattered stones? He could not be sure. Only a cluster of white pine sheltered by a misshapen, old giant in whose bare and splintered top perhaps a hawk had stretched wings to the new day. In an unsettling way that Paul did not comprehend, he felt his spirit bound to this broken, hardscrabble farm by cordage, which seemed to stretch far back before his birth or even his grandmere's time. Something, a presence, was very close and palpable here, which he could neither see nor touch.

Mary Grout was furious. In her nine years as public health nurse in Southern Vermont she hadn't been prepared for this. She knew that the Bush clan was slack, but never suspected anything like what she was hearing. The girl seated across from her at the kitchen table was only 15, but she could have passed for 21. Carrie Bush, by some random toss of genetic dice, was a comely young woman; a child trapped by nature too-soon a blooming. "By God, I'd have given my eyeteeth for that face and figure", Mary thought to herself, then considered Carrie through narrowed eyes. "But, she could be devious. Children wanting attention often were."

"Now, don't embroider anything and tell me the facts straight," Mary demanded sharply.

Carrie had been looking after her older sister's children at the Pervis family farmhouse over on the Green Pond Road. The sister and her husband had left early before chores to go dancing for the evening. Carrie prepared supper and fed the tots. After chores, old Henry Pervis and the hired hand ate, then listened to the radio, as was their custom while Carrie entertained the children until bedtime with stories and quiet games. The two men turned in by 10 o'clock, as they would be up long before dawn for the morning chores. Carrie waited up late, then went to bed wondering why the dancers were so late.

She was up at dawn preparing breakfast. Old Henry was mad as hell coming in from the barn. "Where was his son when he needed him?" Carrie had no answer and the old man swore, choked down his bacon and eggs, then departed with his helper to mend fences. By mid-morning Carrie decided to walk the children the mile up the road to the ramshackle frame house rented by her sister and brother-in-law, thinking that they may have come home so late they didn't want to disturb the children. The house was set back nearly out of sight from the road, its weathered exterior needing serious mending. Uncle Cyrus' battered car was in the drive. Carrie left the children in the shade of some overgrown lilacs and climbed the steps. The door was ajar and she was about to enter when sounds from within made her freeze at the threshold. Pushing the door open a bit wider, she saw her sister and a slovenly woman Carrie had never met lolling on the living room floor with Bush amidst discarded whiskey bottles. All were partially clad and emitting giddy, empty-headed laughter for no reason. The women alternately pinched and bit Bush's near naked body. He, in turn, responded with lascivious pats and kisses. On the far side of the room, facedown on a vomit-stained couch lay her sister's husband, unconscious.

Carrie caught the acrid smell of human sickness that almost turned her stomach. She stepped back onto the porch, but not before Bush had spotted her.

"I'll be damned." He muttered as he arose, wrapping his loins in one of the women's petticoats. As he staggered to the door, Carrie was down the steps, shooing the children in front of her like chickens.

From the doorway Bush roared, "Why the hell did you bring those kids here?"

Carrie was too terrified to answer, but told the children to start down the drive. Bush came out on the porch, his face changing slowly into a malevolent smile.

"Maybe you ought to tell those kids to go play while you come in here and join us. Isn't that what you really come up here for?"

He lunged for her, but Carrie nimbly descended the remaining stairs and ran for the children. Bush had missed the top step and sprawled headlong in the weeds, losing his garment and striking his head on some scrap metal carelessly thrown next to the porch. Carrie paused by Bush's car, keeping the children behind her.

"Where's mommy, Carrie?", one of them asked with eyes of fear. Carrie paid them no mind as she watched Bush, buck-naked, rise to his hands and knees in the weeds. A cut on his forehead streamed blood into his hair and eyes. Cackles of drunken laughter emerged from the house as the women tried to find Bush. Pushing the children quickly before her, Carrie sought the safety of greater distance. Just as she reached the end of the drive, Bush yelled something incomprehensible, but rude at her.

"So that's all that happened?", Mary swallowed her anger and held the girl against her chest. All she got were tears.

"O.K., O.K., then. Just you stay away from your uncle and never again let yourself be alone with him. You hear me? Never, never!!"

21

Stone formed the men in two ranks, 25 to a rank, and gave instructions. "Now this is going to seem elementary, but you've got to maintain these ranks. Each of you are two feet apart and the second rank is eight feet behind the first. You in rank one are spotters. Whenever you see a gypsy moth egg cluster, you stop and inform the man behind you. Each of you in rank two will have a paint pail of creosote and a brush. When you get the word, step forward and thoroughly soak the egg cluster and any others you may see. Don't try to go too fast. We want to find and destroy every cluster possible. And keep your lines straight. If you break ranks, you'll be bobbing and weaving all over the woods and not giving lateral support to those on your right and left. Remember, we're looking for uniform coverage. Any questions?"

Seeing no hands, Stone continued. "The areas you'll be treating are already mapped out and senior leaders will be responsible for keeping records. Junior leaders will see that everyone has enough creosote and will wear climbing spurs to treat egg masses in trees out of reach. My assistant, Miss Chapman, and I will be around if you have any questions. And please ask if you are in doubt about anything. We want the hatching data next spring to be as accurate as possible."

The two lines started forward over the rough and frosty ground and Stone and Sarah kept a close eye on them as they inched their way. The ranks became staggered and drunken as dense pockets of egg masses alternately slowed up some of the creosote painters. Those spotters finding few egg masses were impatient to continue. In time, a signal system evolved. A spotter would yell out, "BUG", when a find was made and the entire rank would pause until the creosote treatment was made, then lumber slowly on until the next signal. It was plodding, tedious work, but at least the lines remained even. The signal soon became a joke to relieve the boredom of it all and cries of "BUGGLE" could be heard up and down the ranks followed by hoots of laughter. The senior leaders tried to dampen the frivolity, but Stone good-naturedly intervened and let it go on, knowing his plan was in no jeopardy. Soon a pattern, almost a cadence, developed among the spotters. "BUGGLE LOW", for egg masses within reach. "BUGGLE HIGH", for those up in the trees, whereupon a recruit would dash forward from behind, scale the tree and paint away.

The egg mass painting went on for a week before Sarah discovered its futility. Actually it was brought to her attention by a spotter who, crossing one of the many stone walls running throughout the forest, accidentally knocked a portion down, revealing large caches of hidden eggs. Sarah then had the ranks tear down ten-foot sections of several walls and found each one rife with dead females and their eggs. The gypsies had figured out the protective sanctuaries of tumbled stone walls long before the CCC had arrived.

Hoping to convince Ashley of the project's futility, Sarah showed him her ledger in which she had computed the average number of egg masses per ten feet of wall.

"Probably should have thought of that." His eyes crinkled at the corners as he realized that she was waiting for his next move.

She thought to herself. "My God, a lot of people would throw up their hands in frustration, but he really loves the challenge!!"

"Oh, we'll just continue as planned. The negative data, if that's what turns up, will be nearly as valuable as support for our hypothesis, don't you think?"

She considered this, saying nothing out loud, but wondering, "Is he just trying to cover up a false start or is he just hide-bound-set in his ways to not change even when the obvious appears?"

His next words snapped her back and she realized how much she had underestimated Stone's acumen. "We'll do line transects through these areas early next summer to determine hatch rates and first instar infestations, then compare readings adjacent to and distant from the walls. That way we'll get another set of data without modifying our experimental design."

He ignored her sheepish looks and continued. "If they hole up in those walls, where else do you suppose they go and how?" She could read his mind running over the possibilities, but he was waiting for her answer. She grinned and shook her head. "You're telling me I've got some more work to do." He nodded and smiled, radiating his confidence in her the way he often did since they had begun working together in Vermont. She suddenly remembered the simple, framed document on the wall of his office, "Happy is he who has found his work."

"So what do you think we've seen this summer, Sarah, that might predict what next year will bring?"

"Right now, I'd say we won't have many gypsies survive, as the food is mostly gone. Of course, if we get a really wet spring the trees may recover and set more foliage than we think."

"Not a bad hypothesis, but do you remember that oak grove on the other side of the ridge that wasn't attacked? Our data is showing that for some reason the caterpillars never got there to do much damage. Maybe all the banding the boys did out that way helped. But even when we put those starved larvae from the high-density areas into the grove, they decreased their population size at the same rate as those from which they came even though the food supply was plentiful for them. I wonder why the two populations declined similarly."

"Maybe the weather was responsible. That was the only common factor affecting them that I can think of. With all the leaves gone off the trees, the forest floor must have been at least 10 degrees hotter than normal." She thought for a moment. "Of course, that wouldn't account for the decline in the oak grove, would it?"

"Well, take a look at these weather records I dug up. I can't find any links in past years between the weather conditions and what seem to be population cycles. Even in some of the higher elevations where there are large variations in temperature and rainfall, the gypsies seem to have the same high and low population cycles."

"But I thought I read that gypsies were intolerant of very low temperatures. They haven't been found near the Canadian border yet. Maybe the winters are just too cold."

He nodded and smiled. She had begun to challenge and weigh the evidence he presented. "That's possible. Why don't you set up a few lab tests on temperature with some eggs to see how they survive?" Glancing out the window, he continued. "But what else is out there checking the population? Birds are very picky and don't seem to like the caterpillars as food, at least not the big, hairy ones that do the most damage. Other predators are remarkably shy except for ground beetles, which never seem to occur in large enough numbers to be a threat. I've seen wood mice tackling a larva or two, but the anecdotal evidence is not impressive. Parasites hold them down in Europe, according to some researchers there, but here the gypsies have no serious contenders. Sickness, disease maybe. Back in 1903, Davis developed a hypothesis along these lines." He shook his head. "But we're fast running out of possibilities, Sarah. Maybe some combination of checks is doing it and we just haven't seen the connection."

She knew he was musing more than talking to her. That was his way of putting things straight in his mind. Stone showed a curiosity and passion for knowing that even exceeded Sam's. Earlier on she had thought Stone a kindly old pedantic, but the passion often caught her off guard. He would churn hypotheses, wild guesses and snippets of data together, then sort it out with a fresh insight or two. Like a skilled tradesman with an elegant tool, he isolated problems, defined them precisely, then looked for missing data which might suggest solution, never getting lost in the welter of confusing detail. Later, next week or even next month he would seize upon something and run to earth, always looking for patterns behind the accumulating facts.

Watching him now, it suddenly dawned on her that she was more than just his graduate student. She'd become part of his tool kit, his sounding board, his alter ego.

22

Fall came, then went suddenly as an inch of snow blew in on Armistice Day, melting quickly but turning the camp roads to muck. They saw less and less of Butler and Rust as the freeze descended and more snow fell, piling up this time. It was rumored that the two of them often stayed in Bellows Falls in a hotel.

"Very likely at government expense," Harwood thought privately. In just a matter of time, he knew they would return, however, and the threat of failing one of the inspections for frivolous reasons was always there.

The second Thursday of the month was medical inspection. An Army doctor assigned as a circuit rider would arrive Wednesday night, conduct a site inspection and refurbish the dispensary, then see anyone who was ailing on Thursday morning. By noon, unless there were problem illnesses or injuries, the doctor packed up and left for the next camp on his list. An on-call system provided for emergencies, except in the very isolated camps where a doctor was permanently assigned or shared among adjacent camps.

Harwood looked forward to these visits as most Army medical personnel shared his disdain of ostentatious military decorum and were a window on the outside world. Captain Enrico Porcini, U.S. Army Medical Corps Reserve, was no exception.

He and John had understood each other at once. Their mutual interest in baseball meant that they often found themselves on opposite sides of camp pick-up ball games on evenings when good weather permitted. Harwood was hard-pressed to even tie a Porcini team, which seemed to draw inspiration and energy from his flamboyant coaching and Italian-American expressions. "Dr. DiMaggio", as he was soon tagged, assured a lot of biting banter and high amusement.

Porcini finished his regular check-ups on Thursday morning and was getting into his car when John came across the parade area.

"Well, doctor, are we up to your standards?"

"As usual, your dispensary is about the best I've seen out here in the wild and I can't say any of these fellows are starving. But I hate to look in the mouths of some, especially your backwoods boys. Their teeth are full of rot for lack of food and care when they were young. I'm going to request that a dentist come up here to fix what he can and pull out some of the garbage. With luck, they may have a few teeth left by the time they're thirty."

"Yeah, I know what you mean," John responded shaking his head, "I get quite a few toothless grins in the mess hall. Wish there was more we could do."

"It's beyond us to do more than raise hell and shame them into better habits. Maybe that'll be one of the lasting benefits of Roosevelt's Tree Army and if any of the learning sticks, at least their kids will have some choppers."

"And another thing," Porcini continued, "a number of men are scratching a lot. Looks like jock itch or maybe ringworm. I can't tell for sure. Better enforce your towel discipline and don't let them go too long without a change of underclothes, especially as this winter weather sets in. I'll check them again next time I'm in camp."

Harwood watched the doctor's sedan disappear down the company street and wished his other inspections were as honest. He scowled, remembering that Major Butler was due in again the following day.

"What a jerk!" He spat out under his breath. "And that goes for his weasel batman, too."

The major decided to stay through the weekend and into the next week, claiming that there were a number of inconsistencies in Harwood's reports to investigate. John concluded that the real reason was the special treatment Butler got at the mess hall. The major's chief claim to fame was his ability to put away prodigious quantities of food.

"Hell," thought John, "if that's what it takes to keep him happy and off my back, so be it."

Smack in the middle of Butler's visit, John got a call from Porcini.

"I've been thinking about that itch I mentioned to you and remember where I've seen it before. Right after I finished medical school, I was sent to an Army post near St. Louis as part of my internship. Found the worst case of crabs there."

"Crabs?", echoed Harwood, sounding vague.

"Yeah, pubic lice!", Porcini came loudly over the phone. "I want to look at some of your boys again and will stop by on Sunday afternoon."

"That's not the best time," Harwood stalled, thinking about Butler. "A lot of boys leave for the weekend."

"Doesn't matter. The names of those who have complained are in the medical files in the dispensary. Just find me one who will be there and I'll examine him. If no one is available, I'll stay over Monday. You don't want these things spreading. Most people think that a roll in the hay is the only way to pass them around, but let me tell you different. Camp life with people sharing clothes and God knows what else lets these little beasts in for a field day. All it takes is an infested body."

Harwood felt trapped.

"Look, the good major is here right now and I don't want him to get wind of this."

Porcini hooted over the phone.

"You must mean Major Hoople. Look, John, I understand. Trust me to keep the lid on. But I do think we'd better not let this thing get out of hand. Actually, the crabs are not the big problem, but where they are, VD is not far behind and that can be real serious."

"O.K., O.K.," John relented. "I'll have a body ready for you."

"Good. See you Sunday." Porcini hung up.

Harwood cast his eyes over the young men of B barracks. They consisted of Boston area boys, mostly Irish, many of whom Harwood knew made up Rafferty's coterie. He noted from the roster Walsh carried that two of them, O'Leary and Galvin were on Porcini's report. At the end of the inspection, he told Walsh to have the two of them in his office right after church services on Sunday.

Porcini and Harwood were waiting as Walsh and the young men entered. John shut the door and turned them over to the doctor.

"Just wanted to run another check on your complaints about that itch. Is it still bothering you?"

The two lads looked at each other a bit uncomfortably, then one exclaimed, "Yeah, if anything, it's worse."

"Then let's see what the problem is. Drop your pants and shorts."

After a brief examination, Porcini asked Harwood to hand him a piece of transparent tape and a microscope slide. Just then there was a knock at the door. John shifted off his desk to open it, but before he reached it, Rust walked in.

"Don't you have any respect for a private meeting?" John hissed irritably.

Rust looked at the bare backsides of the men and Porcini trying to collect specimens with the tape and a fine comb, his drooping eyes widening.

"What's the matter, Corporal? You've never seen a short arm inspection before?" Porcini thundered.

The doctor rose and stood right in front of Rust.

"I ordered this inspection as a follow-up on a problem noted last week. Captain Harwood has cooperated marvelously to assure the health of these men. That's . . . ."

He stopped in mid-sentence and stared hard at Rust's forehead. The same type of bluish welts he'd seen on the pubic areas of the young men rose sporadically along the margins of the corporal's eyebrows. Rust quickly looked away from the doctor, then rubbed his eyebrow furiously.

"I'll be damned," said Porcini a bit breathlessly. "John, hand me some more tape and a new slide."

Rust turned to leave, but Porcini caught his shoulder and whirled him around.

"Stay right here, Corporal. I'll need a sample from you, too." He pressed the tape onto Rust's eyebrow, removed it with a jerk and applied it sticky side down on the slide.

"While you're here you might want to drop those trousers as these men have done."

Rust hesitated.

"Now!" barked Porcini.

The pants and shorts came off slowly as Walsh and Harwood looked on incredulously. Porcini inspected the man quickly.

"O.K., pull 'em up," he directed and turned back to O'Leary and Galvin.

Rust snatched up his pants, buckled his belt and bolted from the room.

"This is quite a place," Porcini smiled slyly, looking at Harwood and Walsh. "Maybe I ought to check you two out for the possibility of a full house. Later, perhaps," he chuckled and turned again to the young men.

"Any trouble urinating? Burning or painful sensations? Any discharge that you don't normally have?"

The boys shook their heads, reddening and looking down at the floor. Porcini finished his collections, putting the hair and debris collected on the comb in small vials of alcohol.

"Get dressed," he ordered as he labeled his specimens. Then he sat on the other side of Harwood's desk and looked at them.

"Where have you been to get infested?"

O'Leary and Galvin exchanged glances, then reexamined the floor. Porcini sensed he would get nothing from them and took a different tact.

"Any of your friends have the clap?"

Still no answer as they shifted from one foot to the other.

"C'mon you two. You know what we're asking," Harwood cut in. "If we get VD in this camp, you and all your friends will be susceptible unless we find the carrier . . . . male or female," he added. "We can't treat VD here and you'll be discharged immediately for bad conduct, do you understand?"

One of the boys looked up.

"No sir, ain't no one in our barracks got the clap; but quite a few are scratching like us."

"Did you all get the crabs at the same place?" Porcini asked.

Again no answer.

"O.K., listen to me carefully because in two weeks I'm coming back here and I don't want to find any more problems. You stay away from wherever you got these things. Get everybody who's itching to wash everything they wear or sleep in. Do each wash separately this very afternoon. I'm sure that Walsh, your senior leader here, will get you whatever you need. And if anyone comes down with a fever or any of the afflictions I asked you about, report them at once to Walsh who'll let Captain Harwood and me know. Now, have you got that? I want no mistakes and no cover-ups."

The pair nodded and Harwood dismissed them.

"I think you're lucky, Harwood. Other than these crotch cooties, there's probably little to worry about if these boys were telling the truth. Say, I'd like to confirm what I have here with that entomologist running your bug program. Is he here today?"

"Was this morning in the library where he's got a little office lab set up."

He nodded at Walsh.

"See if he'll let us use his microscope. We'll be there in ten minutes," added Porcini.

Walsh left and Harwood stared out the window.

"What do you make of Corporal Rust?", he asked eventually.

"Oh, him!" Porcini chuckled, then scowled. "He could be the whole problem. I've only read about crabs getting so thick as to infest the beard and face, but here was living evidence. And the man's crotch was blue enough to pass for Old Glory."

"But he doesn't get near the barracks or the men."

"Then he's either into something different or hanging around the same place as these boys. Any farmer's daughter doing business in the vicinity?"

John rubbed his chin thoughtfully.

"Not that I know of, but Rust does spend a bit of time on the Major's errands in Bellows Falls. As a matter of fact, the Major goes with him at times, but who knows, they both hop from place to place on their foolish inspections."

"What are you going to do about him?" Porcini asked with raised eyebrows.

"I thought you'd ask that," John smiled grimly. "If you're absolutely sure of what you've seen, I've got to confront both Rust and Butler. As far as I'm concerned, Rust will do the same as the recruits. Fortunately, both he and the Major leave late today and take most of their parasites with them. Their quarters will be thoroughly scrubbed after they go."

"Let's hold that for a while, John, and go see if that bug chaser knows anything about what he preaches."

Stone welcomed them into the small room that served as his makeshift field laboratory. The place smelled of KAAD mixture and naphthalene. Three microscopes were lined up on a side bench and a collection of beakers, killing jars and boxes littered a corner. Two soiled collection nets were stacked by the door. Beside one of the microscopes was an opened ledger with neatly written test and tallies of figures forming straight, even rows.

"What can I do for you?" He asked softly, looking at them over his tiny glasses.

"Professor, you've met Doctor Porcini here, who gives us medical support. He needs some positive identification of what may be pubic lice," Harwood began.

"*Pthirus pubis?* Here in Grafton?" Stone muttered in surprise.

"Could be," interjected Porcini. "It's kind of important to be sure. Could you look at some specimens I have?"

"Certainly, certainly. Come over here to this microscope and let's have a look."

Porcini laid his slides down and placed the small vials beside them. Stone puttered and squinted over the scope, adjusting the light and shifting the slides, one by one, across the stage.

"You are absolutely right," he said finally. "Take a look here. There are hardly any other choices once you see the squat, tuberculated body and those very obvious claw-like legs."

Porcini, then Harwood, peered through the scope.

"Are you sure these are from this camp, these boys?" Stone queried a bit suspiciously.

"They were just taken off two men from B barracks." Harwood answered, waiting for Porcini's reaction. But the doctor was engrossed in the objects under the microscope.

"So, on to the next step," Porcini muttered without enthusiasm. He straightened up and continued thoughtfully, "Tell you what. I'll handle Rust and the Major. Doctors have some privileges that you company commanders can't invoke. This will never see the light of day in the Major's report."

Harwood was not so sure, but Stone had pretty much sized things up.

"Let him handle it, Captain. I know from experience how popinjays like that Major react to medical evidence. They never want a fire in their own barn. Now what are you doing to rid the men of this?"

Porcini went over what he had told O'Leary and Galvin.

"May I suggest that anything they've used for clothing, toilet or sleeping be washed in water at a rolling boil to get at the nits," Stone said, matter-of-factly. "And have the men use rotenone dust after every body washing. If you keep that up for at least two weeks you'll get all of the new hatch. Use a little mercuric oxide on the welts to heal and prevent infection from scratching. And if all else fails, everyone will have to shave his crotch and start over."

Porcini's eyes widened.

"Do just as he says, John, and they'll be fine. Thanks for all your help, Professor," Porcini said respectfully, shaking Stone's hand. "I'll write this down for Nurse Grout so she can do any follow-up needed. Oh, did I tell you, she'll be my replacement on this circuit? Headquarters has moved me up country to the Waterbury Dam project, so I may not be back for a while. From what I've heard about her, these boys will really toe the mark from now on!!" In the doctor's mind the louse problem was settled.

Harwood would miss the doctor regardless of his replacement, but that was far from his mind. There were too many loose ends for all of this to be mere coincidence. Someone or several persons outside of the camp were involved and, by God, he was going to find out who they were.

Both Rust and the Major avoided him for the rest of the afternoon. Just before supper, Major Butler knocked on Harwood's door and stepped in.

"We'll be leaving a little earlier than planned and will not be eating supper with you. I'll expect your response to my findings on the supplies discrepancy this week. Send it to the usual address. I'll be back on the 25th of next month."

Harwood regarded him thoughtfully before acknowledging. Perhaps Rust had not spilled anything to Butler yet. Anyway, the sooner these two were out of camp the better. But their missing supper was hardly like them.

"As you say, sir," John responded. "Have a good trip." He saluted and saw the Major out. Rust was already packing their duffel in the car.

Returning to his office, Harwood decided immediately to skip supper, too. His curiosity about where the Major was going had gotten the better of him. A few minutes after the big Packard had left, he donned civilian clothes, borrowed Stone's auto and pulled out of camp. He'd given Stone a story that his Ford was not running properly and that he had to make a run into town. Stone gladly obliged.

He had little trouble tailing the phaeton. It was a dinosaur with few kin in southern Vermont. After getting them in sight, Harwood eased back and followed at a discreet distance. Rust stayed on the tarred road to Route 5, then turned south to downtown Bellows Falls. Harwood nearly lost them in traffic, but after several passes up and down Main Street, he spotted the touring car parked carefully out of the way behind the Tamarack Hotel.

"Not the fanciest digs hereabouts, unless they plan to stay for a while," Harwood mused as he brought Stone's vehicle to a halt a block away from the Tamarack.

"Dinner, sir?" Harwood was greeted by a short man in what looked like a second-hand suit. The dining room off to the left in one of the wings was beginning to fill with hotel guests and walk-ins.

"No, not just yet. I'm waiting for two other gentlemen who may have already arrived. I think that's their touring car out back."

"You must mean the National Guard officer and his aide. The Major is in the dining room now. The other chap has taken some luggage upstairs." The clerk suddenly looked a bit uncomfortable, as if he'd revealed something more than he had wished.

"Well, maybe I can find him in then. What number?" John asked smoothly, holding his composure. "Don't worry about the Major. We'll both join him shortly."

The man hesitated and looked toward the dining room, then up the staircase. He went around to his desk and ran a finger down some numbers.

"Try 249," the clerk said quickly and hurried off towards the kitchen.

Harwood went up the stairs and entered a long corridor to the back. Room 249 was at the end, next to another stairway from a small side entrance. He stopped before the door and listened. Voices, slightly raised, came from within. They stopped when he knocked softly and he could hear some muffled movement. After a little while the door opened. Harwood looked into Queenie's face and knew immediately where he'd seen her before.

"What do you want?", she asked sourly. Harwood could see the interior over her shoulder. The door to the lavatory was slowly closing. He smiled and sidestepped over the sill so that she couldn't slam the door. The room was disheveled and smelled strongly of smoke and cheap liquor. The bed was unmade and dog-eared magazines littered the floor. Through it all was a faint odor of harsh perfume.

"God," thought Harwood, "does every slattern use the same stuff?" Queenie looked him over; and liking what she saw put on her best predatory smile.

"Tell you what, come back later. I'm busy right now," she cooed.

"Oh, that's O.K. I think we've got to talk and you can include that chap in the bathroom if you'd like."

Queenie suddenly looked a little ill, but pulled him inside and closed the door after quickly glancing up and down the corridor.

"Say, are you from the constable's office or somethin? Corporal Rust and I ain't done nothin wrong." She gave him a vicious look, then added, "You know him and Major Butler?" She put heavy emphasis on the "Major", hoping to extract some authority or negotiation from the name drop. Harwood smiled again. He was learning more than he had expected.

"I know them better than I want to," John said evenly.

Queenie pushed the door lock into place and went over to the lavatory.

"Hey, Rust. Some guy here wants to talk to us." She pushed the door open and there stood the corporal, a whiskey in his hand, his mouth wide open.

"Now, let's get acquainted. Rust and I have already met. Who are you?"

Ten minutes later, Harwood had all the information he needed. Rust vacillated between fear and rage, glaring first at Harwood, then at Queenie. In his bluster, he threatened, then pleaded, with Queenie to button her lip, but she was having none of that.

"You come back here, tellin' about how you got those crabs from me. How do I know where else you been. You and that peepin Major who never wants to come in here, but likes to watch you and me through that hole in the wall."

John had trouble believing his ears, but then Queenie strutted over and pushed aside a picture on the wall separating Rooms 249 and 247. Big as life, there was a spot about the size of a half-dollar. She pushed her finger through to emphasize her point. Rust was holding his head in his hands.

Like a cornered dog, Rust suddenly turned vicious. "You say anything about the Major or me and Butler will fix your wagon just like he did when you took them boys to slaughter in the Argonne."

John whirled and faced Rust who now leaned pugnaciously on the bathroom doorjamb. "What happened in France, Rust?" Harwood demanded angrily. Rust glowered and edged toward the door to the corridor. John crossed the room in a flash and grasped the corporal by the shirt collar with both hands and squeezed.

Queenie's eyes turned glinty with fear, but she couldn't suppress a smile. She hadn't seen a good brawl in months. Harwood added some pressure and Rust's face flushed, his eyes bulging wildly in their sockets.

"Tell me!", croaked John and applied more muscle.

The corporal, panic stricken, began to nod rapidly and John released him with a shove that sent Rust sprawling into a stack of old newspapers. He got up, clenching his throat, but had no trouble talking.

"It was like this," he began. "Butler was the new battalion Exec. Messages from intelligence had warned us of ambush by the German rear guard, especially for those platoons on rapid advance. Wanting to make the battalion look good, he never passed the information on to company level. When you got trapped out there, he panicked, and decided to cover up by quickly sending runners with the information to engaged units. You were made the scapegoat when he told the battalion commander that you were over—zealous and irresponsible, refusing to heed the information from intelligence."

Harwood's mouth had dropped wide open as he glared at Rust in stunned silence. Rust rubbed his neck and nervously made ready to dash if Harwood came at him again.

His rage had not slackened, but Harwood was composed as he told Rust to get Queenie packed and pay her hotel bill, then go join Butler for dinner. Despite the contempt he felt for Rust, he knew that he was but a toady. He also guessed that there was little chance that Rust would be up to relating what Harwood now knew or that the Major would have the guts to confront him if he did. Oddly, Queenie had few misgivings about being uprooted. She had that "fish out of water" look in her eyes and openly cursed her excursion to the Green Mountains. When Rust had left, she unloaded her feelings on Harwood. The import of Rust's confession had not even registered.

"Damn glad to get out of this hellhole before I freeze solid. Nice place in the summer, but give me the big city when snow flies."

They exited from the side entrance and piled her things into Stone's car. On the way to the bus station, John got more details on her connections with Rafferty. She took pleasure in exposing his operations, his setting her up in his employ at the Tamarack, her dropping him off at the camp, then hiding his car until he could pick it up, the weekly Spofford Lake arrangement. He had to shut her up and tell her to take her bags into the bus station.

"When you get home, be sure to clean yourself up," he admonished, handing her the one-way ticket to Boston.

Defiant to the end, she retorted, "I ain't had the crabs. Rust got 'em somewhere else. And those CCC boys never take baths, I been told. Probably brought them from home."

Harwood threw up his hands and left her waiting for the bus, hoping that she had not dropped a specimen or two in the car for Stone.

When he got back to camp, he had Rafferty brought to his office. The young Irishman admitted nothing, so Harwood had the infested men join them. In short order, under pain of immediate discharge, they pleaded with Rafferty to own up. He remained sullen until Harwood asked, "Where did you hide the car? Queenie said you had transportation and I know that she didn't walk to Spofford Lake and back."

Silence.

"O.K. I'll let your friends here go find it with Hurlburt. If it's not yours we'll impound it until someone makes a claim."

John observed the slow transformation on the handsome face of feigned innocence to a loathsome sneer.

"You think you're pretty smart, don't you, Captain?" O'Leary and Galvin looked at Rafferty in pure dismay. "The car is over in Templeton's hay barn. There's nothing illegal about it or even against camp rules. So what are you going to do to us?"

Harwood gave him a riveting stare, then rose and stood, looking squarely into the insubordinate eyes. He recalled Rafferty's first visit concerning the hazing and cursed himself that he'd not seen through the duplicity then.

"You're lucky you have a car, Rafferty," John began quietly, "because you're going to be in it on your way back to Boston in the morning. I should have put you on the bus with your friend Queenie, and let her go at you for a while, but as I said, you're lucky. Your friends here have made a mistake, but will stay in the Corps and in this camp because they need to send their pittance home each month. Once you're gone, they'll have a chance to redeem themselves. But you don't show me any reason to stay with us and I doubt that your monthly allotment is of any concern. Your family won't have to go back to living on murphies with the political connections your father has."

Rafferty's face remained calm as he spoke. "My father could have your bars faster than you can say Jack Robinson." O'Leary and Galvin began to inch towards the door.

Harwood came round his desk and put his face near Rafferty's. "Your pimping days are done, Rafferty. Nobody wants a grifter around, especially at a camp like this. You can pick up your discharge right after breakfast. Now get the hell out of here."

Hurlburt hustled the trio quickly out of the office as John threw his cap across the room and sat down. "We'll see how much of all this the major wants to put in his bloody reports," he sighed with exasperation. He went around to the bottom drawer of his desk and found the bottle of scotch, poured a stiff one and sipped it slowly, eyes closed.

23

The massive 1937 forest defoliation was a black eye for everyone. Early on, the USDA had, over Stone's objections, trumpeted its Vermont research project as a broad attack on the gypsy moth, certain to roll back the pest once and for all. This despite preliminary evidence that a big hatch was imminent and, barring some natural catastrophe, nothing was going to stop the hungry caterpillars. Of course, no one had wanted to hear that and now with the criticism and finger-wagging reaching a crescendo, USDA bureaucrats feared heads were about to roll. Stone knew that this was the real reason for the hastily called Washington meeting.

He glanced out the window at the dull, winter afternoon and the traffic shuttling around the mall beyond the leafless trees. He had just spent the last hour explaining the cyclical nature of moth populations, what the summer project had shown them and how that would lead to a much better understanding of the pest. But the glazed eyes told him that the bureaucrats were buying none of it. They wanted some showy results, but he honestly could not predict or promise how much actual control to expect in the coming summer. He was uncomfortably aware that had the chairman of this committee of paper pushers not come out on his side, he would have lost his grant entirely. It was that close. The shadow of the good senator from Vermont was all over this group.

The discussion turned to future operations and again Stone made the case for thorough, patient research, but they would have none of this. Something dramatic was needed to justify their continued support. Out of the blue someone brought up the example of insect control by dumping insecticides out of airplanes. Stone was vaguely familiar with the scattered reports in the research journals. Used mainly as dusts on closely confined herbaceous crops like cotton in the South, the results had not been definitive. But it didn't take a genius to see where this group was headed. Stone knew that the best he would get was a compromise, so while voicing strong reservations about widespread poisoning of forest life, he did agree to a scheme using aircraft to treat a limited part of the Grafton test site. The chairman clinched the deal by giving Stone full support for his basic research on gypsy cycles.

On the long train ride back to Amherst, Stone endlessly mulled over the meeting, finally concluding that the changes they required of him really would not modify the project very much. His and Sarah's studies on the biology of the gypsy remained secure. In the library at Mass Aggie he would again read those scientific reports on aircraft use and make his usual thorough plans. Conceptually, he knew what was required, but the technology of application was beyond him. To deliver on his plan, he would have to find an airplane . . . . and a pilot.

Sarah and the professor laid out plans for more fieldwork on the gypsies. They had many thoughts in common and the give and take was easy for both of them.

"But our samples from last year don't show any infestation up on those ridges." Sarah was pointing to the topographic map on Stone's office wall. "No females, no eggs, not even any males were taken. So how come that stand of oak is now loaded with first instar larvae? They're much too delicate to crawl up there."

Stone shrugged his shoulders. "We might just have missed them. A sample is only a sample, you know. The important thing is that you found them, Sarah." His eyes had already moved to another area of the map. "Let's look for another site for our control plot. With all this aerial application we can't be too careful."

He thought little of their chat until a week later when she announced that she was setting sticky traps up and down the ledges. "I know from my field notes that most gypsy moth eggs hatch about 8 to 10 in the morning and as the day warms they crawl to the tips of branches. What I don't know is where and how far they go from there or what percent of them actually make it. I must do a mark-recapture study on their migration patterns."

"That will be a chore with the little ones, Sarah, but give it a try." He made no secret that he admired her thoroughness and perseverance.

"Good weather continued for the week and assisted by two recruits, she was out every morning early by the stone walls capturing hatching gypsies, marking them with a speck of fingernail polish and releasing them at the base of the crags. In the afternoons, they placed a series of square foot traps coated with fly goo at the bottom, top and several mid-intervals of the ledges. It was hot, fussy work, but the recruits preferred it to the road maintenance detail.

One day, around noon she paused from the marking to look up at the ridge, then at the oaks to her right and left. Hanging down on their fragile silk were scores of barely visible larvae. She had seen them before, but this time was different. Every breeze moving through the forest caused the insects to bounce on the end of their lines while the hot mid-day updrafts from the forest floor would lift them up and out of sight. She watched this for a time without thinking, then patted her check in disbelief.

"Of course," she said out loud, "they're ballooning! It's old Aeolus doing his tricks!!"

The two men looked at each other, but remained silent.

"Doesn't it make sense? They are so light that they are being airlifted up to those ledges." She turned to get their answer, but was met with blank stares.

Finally, one responded. "I guess so, if you say so, Miss Chapman."

And it did. The sticky traps collected all sorts of beetles, flies and confusing debris. The cleaning; sorting and identifying the catch was painfully slow and messy. They re-caught only a small fraction of the marked larvae, but enough to show the pattern of wind dispersal. She enlarged her study and built platforms up in the canopy of a number of the taller trees, then sampled from there. As the data were tallied, both the method and the timing of the migrations began to show. Stone immediately grasped the significance of this evidence which suggested that barriers to the gypsy were of little value and why a lot of the work in earlier decades by timber crews had been for naught. He suggested that Sarah publish her information at once and that his name appear as the junior contributor only so that other entomologists might recognize a familiar name in the literature. The credit for this finding was to be totally hers.

"She's a shabby old streetwalker," Harwood sighed.

"But there are possibilities . . . possibilities," responded McGarry slowly, his eyes flickering over the splotched and faded canvas.

McGarry had found the DeHaviland in a little used hangar at the Northampton airport. The biplane had definitely seen better days, but, as McGarry had surmised, the owner was ready to sell and had even agreed to refurbish.

"It must have a name," Harwood continued a bit wearily. He had to admit that the dowdy old craft looked durable

"It's a DH4, one of the JN series, often called the "Canuck" for reasons beyond me. See those ailerons on both top and bottom wings? Most DH's have only one set. The double set gives a pilot much tighter control of his craft when turning or rolling. This one must have been a barnstormer."

He peered into the cockpit. "I've never been too keen on where they put the gas tank. Sits right over the family jewels. No wonder they call them blazing coffins," he added with a wry grin.

"Looks like one of those old Liberty engines under that screen," John offered.

"Yeah, they never quit. See any oil on the under side?"

John rubbed his hand under the lowest point of the engine, brushing away some years of accumulated dark brown goo. He smelled his fingers and caught the sharp odor of castor oil, but found no fluid.

"Not a drop, assuming the engine's not dry."

"Good. Then I'll get them to roll this old girl out into the light and really see what she's like. Leave me here for a few days and I'll give you a call if I need a lift back to Grafton."

A week later the camp was startled by McGarry cruising over them at treetop level. He couldn't resist showing off and on the next pass executed a perfect four-point roll, then put the Canuck into a steep climb nearly to ceiling, then side-slipping and corkscrew spinning down, leveling out just above the flagpole. As he zoomed away they all caught the sharp odor of castor oil thrown off by the laboring engine.

Hurlburt chuckled. "You smell that, boys? It's the same stuff your mother gives you to loosen your bowels."

Shooting out over the pond, McGarry barrel-rolled, finishing up in a neatly executed Immelman turn before buzzing back across camp, waggling his wings to the acclaim of the audience assembled on the parade ground.

John shaded his eyes and followed the biplane as it disappeared over the hill, saying to himself with a smile, "That damned McGarry never has to worry about his bowels!" Turning to Walsh, Harwood threw him the keys to the Ford. "Go pick him up at the Tater Hill strip when he comes down. We'll give him an early supper so he can handle the week's worth of questions he's going to get from this bunch.

Stone went over the plans for aerial application of insecticide for the umpteenth time. Highly suspect of unknown or untested chemicals and their effects on wildlife, he would use only an old standard, lead arsenate. Even this, a powerful stomach poison selective for chewing insects, did not sit easy with him. At least, he reasoned, there would be less chance of harm to the gypsy's natural controls. Modifications of the DeHaviland would be needed to fit the aircraft for its new role. Stone had ruled out dusting after reading what happened in Ohio where it had been used in attempts to control the catalpa sphinx moth. The tiny particles of lead arsenate dust tended to drift capriciously in the wind tunnels of the forest. Even the slightest draft would blow them hither and yon, rendering their adherence to foliage practically nil. But aircraft application of a spray was more complicated and would require the Canuck to carry both tanks and pumps powered by small, gas-driven engines.

A fairly accurate dispersal was assured so long as warm updraft convection currents from the forest was near zero. For this reason, spray applications were timed for sunrise and the twilight hours when the air near the ground was cooler and heavier than that above the trees.

The thorniest problem was how to formulate the spray. Lead arsenate poison, while remaining in fluid suspension, is notoriously insoluble in water and fish oil had to be added as an emulsifier. This would disperse the poison throughout the mixture and promote a uniform application. Fortunately, the emulsion produced was of the quick-breaking type which upon contact with the foliage, broke to release the poison. The fish oil also acted as a sticker so that the poison didn't slide off the leaf surface so easily. He finally figured that eight pounds of lead arsenate and a pint of fish oil added to each 100 gallons of water would do the trick.

Stone and McGarry had worked for several weeks with a ground-based mock-up of the power sprayer, testing pressures, adjusting dosages, volumes and emulsions until they were sure that the spray would go where it would be effective and do what it was supposed to do. Paul looked over their shoulders and did fetch and carry as needed. The most difficult part was keeping an agitator going in the tanks so the emulsion would not settle out. Then there was the little matter of how this ugly duckling could be safely attached to the aircraft. Fortunately, the small, 2-cycle engines and pumps fit nicely onto the sides of the fuselage and were bolted snugly into place right beside the spray tanks. The beauty of the biplane was not improved by these additions. In fact, it looked even more like a gasoline alley contraption, but air drag was minimal and the extra weight seemed no challenge for the plucky Liberty engine.

Once assembled, McGarry took off fully loaded, sans fluids, and easily put the Canuck through tough maneuvers he knew he would never use in delivering the poison. Passing low over the camp, he gave Stone the thumbs-up. The final test was to fly loaded with liquid, first plain water, then the emulsion of lead arsenate. These, too, were successful and they were ready to commence spraying. The remote area selected for test plots was far removed from the camp and Hyde Pond. Stone wanted no part in a contamination of human haunts. He individually trained the small group of recruits who would serve as spotters to mark the boundaries of the plots, emphasizing personal protective measures and essential decontamination should they come in contact with the poison.

After surveying the forest research plots for a final time, McGarry turned back to Tater Hill. The gas gauge told him that he had more than three more hours of flying time. The DeHaviland purred like a contented cat as he climbed steadily. The day was bright with cumulus packing an otherwise azure sky. There was no wind up here, unlike the occasional side gusts and up drafts buffeting the woodlands below. He climbed still higher and entering a cloud felt the cool moisture on his face, like a good aftershave. Putting the biplane in a dive, he sought the protection of the windscreen. More reckless fliers had landed with frostbitten cheeks and noses or worse.

They heard him coming down and started for the edge of the strip, Donnelli in the lead.

"He must be breaking 200 miles per hour!" Donnelli yelped excitedly, looking up with his hands shielding his eyes. The others nodded in agreement and waited for McGarry to pull out and land. The DeHaviland leveled off and came over the woods, plunking down like cotton candy and rolling to a stop not 25 feet from where they were assembled. McGarry did not kill the engine. As usual, Donnelli was the first to reach the plane and McGarry couldn't miss his enthusiasm as he patted the side of the fuselage. McGarry removed his goggles and boomed over the idling engine.

"Jump in and we'll take a ride."

Donnelli eagerly clambered up into the front cockpit and McGarry ensured that he properly donned the flying helmet. Before gunning the engine for take-off, he yelled to the others standing on the grassy strip.

"We'll be back in about an hour. Going down to Massachusetts to see the French King Gorge", the wash of the propeller rendering his last words indistinct. He turned up the power and the biplane bumped down the field into a perfect take-off.

"What did he say . . . some French King?" Mumbled one of the recruits, cursing his luck for not having beaten Donnelli to the plane. "I thought he was looking for George somebody," came the answer.

McGarry and Donnelli passed once over the strip, the DeHaviland's wings waggling, then turned southeast for the Massachusetts border. Soon they caught sight of the Connecticut River, a silver ribbon running due south between swards of checkerboard green. Over to the left they could see Spofford Lake, and then Brattleboro slipped under the wings. On to the south the river crossed the state line threading like a lazy snake through farmland cultivated right up to the water's edge. Only an arrow-straight run through a wooded cut altered this pattern. At the end of the cut the stream ran head on into resistant rock and executed a smart right turn, flowing nearly northwest to Turners Falls before once more resuming its languorous journey south.

Donnelli noticed that they were losing altitude. McGarry's hand tapping on his helmet and finger jabbing towards the cut told him they were about to meet the French King.

The French King Gorge is the result of a geologic coincidence. As the old glacial lake drained the Connecticut Valley thousands of years ago, the river cut deep into the soft rock on one side of the fault line, but more than met its match on the other side. The result was a narrow, steep-sided water gap through which the chilled waters surged, dropping 45 feet in a distance of less than two miles. The rapids formed here were called the Horse Race by early settlers and was a natural obstacle on their direct route to Boston. Seasonal ice and the battering and scouring by boulders over the millennia made no appreciable impression on the narrows which remained the single escape route for the restless river.

A few years before the Grafton Camp was established, a magnificent bridge was built across the most constricted part of the gorge, cutting time for travel on the Mohawk Trail by a significant margin and allowing easy access, finally, for Boston city-folk to their Berkshire vacations in northwest Massachusetts. Standing 140 feet above the river, it was one of the engineering marvels of the Great Depression.

McGarry circled the cut twice giving Donnelli a panoramic view of the gorge and bridge which, at just under 1000 feet, appeared as a tinker toy. They ran a leg north to Mount Herman, and then McGarry was tapping on the boy's head again. Donnelli turned around to see a finger gesturing down and a broad smile. Donnelli nodded and smiled back, then looked below unsure of McGarry's meaning. The plane began a slow turn, then dropped suddenly, leaving Donnelli's maw floating somewhere in the space above.

McGarry leveled off at 200 feet and pointed the nose of the DeHaviland south, right into the gorge. The noise of the engine became deafening as it ricocheted off the walls of the gorge. They were quarter way through when Donnelli saw the bridge, no plaything now, but more a huge steel trap. McGarry dropped the plane even lower so they were but 30 feet above the river and poured on the gas. Donnelli turned to look at the pilot, but saw only a maniac with goggles, lips compressed into a stiff, straight line. A huge boulder in the middle of the stream loomed up very fast, but McGarry ignored it, the wheels of the biplane clearing it by only a whisker. The arched steel spider's web was now right on them. McGarry increased power and aimed for the hemisphere of light at the center. Donnelli was petrified, his ears rendered useless by the roar. He clutched desperately at his scapula, murmuring hysterically to Jesus, Mary and Joseph, and involuntarily ducked, slipping out of sight into the recesses of the cockpit. The last thing he saw were the under girders of the French King Bridge flashing over his head.

The DeHaviland threaded the eye of the needle perfectly, but shooting out from under the bridge was caught in the crosswind from the right where the river makes its turn. The craft shuddered and threatened to kick over on its side into the trees lining the riverbank. But McGarry was ready and leveled the plane while pulling back on the stick. The biplane responded bravely and shot up and out of the gorge.

McGarry looked for Donnelli and nearly panicked when he saw the empty cockpit. Then a hand came up and grasped the windscreen. Slowly the helmet eased into view. Donnelli didn't look back and McGarry made no attempt to stifle his laughter after tapping the boy twice on the head. A half-hour later they were circling Tater Hill. They taxied to a halt a short distance from the shack and McGarry killed the engine. The others had left, but Walsh ambled out to meet them as McGarry jumped down, removing his helmet.

"You can come out now, Rocco," he said good-naturedly. Donnelli scowled silently and looked at him over the cowling. "Oh, come on. That's no way to show gratitude." Pel leaned against the fuselage ready to offer a hand.

A rank odor of urine and fresh feces wafted up out of the cockpit, but McGarry didn't bat an eye.

"I can't get out like this." Donnelli mumbled. Then louder he said crossly, "I crapped my pants under the bridge, you know."

McGarry never cracked a smile. "That's par for the course, Rocco. If I had a nickel for every time I shit mine, I'd be a rich bastard." Donnelli brightened. "No kidding, sir?"

"No kidding. Now get out of there and clean up a bit in the shack while Walsh and I tie this old whore down."

I suppose everybody will hear about this, won't they?" Donnelli asked glumly.

"Not from me they won't," he reassured.

24

Stone bore a puzzled look as he glanced again at the note on his desk. The Dean had not spoken to him in nearly a year and yet he was asking him to make an appointment before the day was out. The professor's inclination was to stay out of the way of college administrators of any stripe, but this, he knew, was one that couldn't be avoided. All his grant budgets and even his academic appointment hinged on at least tolerable relations with this man. Not that he worried much, having tenure and all, but there was certainly no profit in denying such a request. He lifted the phone and called the secretary to the academic dean.

In twenty minutes he was sitting in a rather sumptuous chair waiting for the dean to begin. He didn't like the man's discomfort at all. While they both recognized that they were of different camps, he had come to appreciate and even respect what a dean must do to keep the institution on an even keel.

"Ashley," the dean finally began, "I understand that your gypsy project up in Vermont is going well?" Stone thought for a moment, trying to figure out what the man was getting at. It seemed like a strange statement framed as a question right out of the blue.

"Yes, I would say remarkably well, even after the difficulties of last summer. The USDA has agreed to continue the funding and we've developed plans to expand the control side of the project." He knew that the dean already had this information. Something else had prompted this opening.

The dean looked out the open window for a time and they both could hear the R.O.T.C. cadet sergeants counting cadence out near the pond. The dean suddenly stood up, went to the window and closed it, and almost angrily whirled around to look Stone in the eye.

"Let me get to the point, Ashley." His voice belied his body language and Stone knew that whatever was coming had nothing to do with his research. "I received a call this morning from the president who had just come from Boston. Seems that he had a conversation with Rafferty, the Senate President in Boston. I'm sure you know that Rafferty controls the budget of just about everything we do here. "Well, it appears that his son has gotten into some trouble," he hesitated, then went on, "actually quite a bit of trouble—involves some stolen cars, maybe something else."

Stone said nothing and kept his eyes level. The dean continued. "To be brief, Rafferty has asked us to arrange his son's return to the CCC camp up there. He got kicked out last year as I think you know. The boy now needs to leave the state for a while until his father gets the charges cleared up. You know the commander in the camp well and we thought that you might put in a word?" The dean's voice dropped low at the question and he looked out the window again. "God dammit, Ashley, do you know how I hate this shit?"

Ashley knew, but that's what deans were for. If it bothered him so much, why the hell didn't he return to the classroom? In earlier years the dean had been an up and coming academic who saw the deanship as a stepping stone for his ambitions. He kept staring at the dean and didn't say a word. The man was clearly not at his best.

"Rafferty put the squeeze on the president. Threatened to take back some of our appropriation if the son doesn't return to Vermont." The dean turned to meet Stone's gaze. "There was even the mention of cutting some of your state grants. That might affect your research and the number of graduate students you have."

"So that's it, the old political squeezing of the balls!" Ashley muttered, trying to contain his outrage.

"Now, Ashley," the dean looked alarmed. "Let's put this into perspective."

Stone relaxed and actually grinned. "No need, I get the drift. I scratch your backside and talk to Harwood and you and the president get your money."

"And you keep your grants." The dean had a sly smile that Stone didn't particularly appreciate, but he kept his thoughts to himself.

"I'm not so sure Captain Harwood will take him back. That blackguard is a troublemaker wherever he goes. But I'll talk with Harwood."

The dean came around the desk with a triumphant look. "That's just fine. Both the President and I are in your debt." Stone glanced at the outstretched hand and ignored it. "Don't mention it," he muttered as he made his way to the door.

Harwood stared at the professor, not believing his ears. "You saw what that bounder did to this camp last fall. I tell you he's poison and needs time behind bars, not a vacation in Vermont."

"I know, I know," Stone was holding up his hands as if to try to calm the waters. "But if I'm to finish this project and get out of your hair, I need that research money."

Harwood crossed his arms and exhaled audibly. "And if I refuse, you'll have to shut it down anyway and be gone that much sooner."

Stone fidgeted with his collar and felt his neck. The little fire behind his breast bone had just crackled. It was time to play his ace.

"I'd like to see Sarah finish her dissertation research up here. If she doesn't, her degree will be delayed at least a year. Without the grants, she falls between the cracks." He said this almost in a mumble, but he knew Harwood was listening and he watched the captain's face for a reaction.

Harwood eyed him coolly for a time. "You high-minded academics are like the rest of us, Stone. Put your most treasured captive on the block when the time is ripe. I think you'd sell your mother if the opportunity arose. What makes you think that I believe you? If you really want to help Sarah, you'll find a way. Now get out of here. I've got some work to do." He started to shift some papers into the file. Stone got up and made for the door, his lips grimly pursed, but his mind relieved. The old ball twisting in Boston had worked just as it always did.

25

"If you're not busy, could you come down to Burkett for the fireworks?" John asked casually as he dropped Sarah off at Mass Aggie. Stone had returned to the college in mid-week, leaving Sarah to tend the gypsy counts and close up the field lab. Hearing that Harwood was going home for the weekend, she had hitched a ride. "In fact, why don't you stay at our place over Sunday, if you want to? You'd be welcome company for my mother. Her constant waiting on an ungrateful son can be a trial. What say?"

Sarah hesitated, not wanting to appear too forward. "I'll take that as a yes. Pick you up here tomorrow afternoon. We'll have a quick supper and find a good spot for viewing the show."

"Sounds good," she smiled, grateful for the invitation. Facing the 4th of July holiday on the nearly deserted Mass Aggie campus had nothing positive to recommend it. Of course, meeting and enduring the expected scrutiny from Mother Harwood was daunting, but she decided that would have to take care of itself.

If John's mother had any reservations about Sarah as a companion for her married son, she never showed them. Gracious and thankful for a fresh face in the old house, she and Sarah were immediately on the best of terms. So much so that John began to wonder if his mother had forgotten about his wife fifty miles down the valley. And he was truly awed by her enjoyment of the fireworks, something he had not seen for years. Later, they retired to the back porch and played cribbage until midnight.

On Sunday morning they all went to church. John and Sarah weren't so sure about being exposed to the beady eyes of the elders, but Mother Harwood would hear none of that and insisted that as their guest, Sarah was part of the community.

After Sunday evening dinner they strolled out across the broad west lawn. The sun had nearly disappeared behind the mountain across the river two miles distant, but dark would wait at this season. At the far end of the lawn was a wooden fence behind which the land dipped down sharply to Bailey's Brook. A dairy herd pastured here and the meandering stream had created a swimming hole which John and his brother, indeed the whole family, had used for generations. The cattle were there now, drinking and trying to decide where to lie down for the night. Their sloshing about and conversational lowing heightened the tranquility of the evening. A cool, moist breeze bearing the slight tang of decomposition from the adjacent swale swung up the hill to where John and Sarah leaned on the fence rails.

"This is such a charming place, John," Sarah said softly. "How can you bear to leave it?" Her eyes focused across the field to another small hill, its top crowned by a small stonewall enclosure.

"That's the family plot over there where Dad and my brother rest", he muttered, reading her.

She bit her tongue, remembering what Ashley had told her about the brother. She took a deep breath and looked out over the swamp.

"Why don't we walk a bit down by the water before the light leaves?"

"O.K., just watch your step. The cows have used that path over there for more than a stroll," he chuckled taking her arm.

It was surprisingly cool near the water. Sarah hunched her shoulders slightly as John slipped his jacket over her. The light was fading fast and the stars had punched through. The moon would be late rising.

"Better let me go first," suggested Harwood. "In some places the path goes right to the water's edge." He lead the way to the swimming hole, carefully skirting areas where spring floods had undercut the stream bank and the alders were encroaching. But the ground gave way suddenly, pitching him headlong into the pool. Fortunately, no snags reached out for him and he surfaced quickly, splashing his way to a shoal about midway of the stream.

"Are you all right?" Sarah shouted, her voice halfway between humor and concern.

"Nothing more than wet clothes and lost dignity," he laughed, stumbling into the shallower water. "You ought to try it sometime." He stood in the pebbles, his feet squishing and contemplated the best course back to where Sarah waited. It was so dark now that he couldn't see her clearly, so he decided to walk down the shoal and cross where the stream was wider and less swift.

"Stay where you are and I'll go around to where it's easier," he tossed over his shoulder the same time he heard the smack of water on flesh. Sarah surfaced in the middle of the pool.

"Hey, I wasn't serious," he muttered in amazement.

"No, I'm sure you weren't," she chided in mock tones. "But if you're going to swim, so am I. Take off those clothes and get in here." Harwood was nonplussed, but did as he was told. They met in mid-channel and held each other's shoulders for balance.

"Now, don't get any ideas about this," she warned. "All we need is a dip to float away some of that past that keeps eating at you."

She struck out effortlessly upstream to the dark side of the pool. He followed her at a distance, still befuddled. After ten minutes she asked him to get her clothes and meet her by the fallen tree which afforded an easy exit. He did so and with appropriate demeanor called her to come out. In the dark he convinced himself that only a scoundrel would cast an uninvited leer, but was stunned when Sarah's naked form swelled up next to him under the fallen elm.

She had emerged with no sense of false modesty. Her firm, elevated breasts and appealing derriere observed through the dim lens of starlight drove darts of desire to the quick, but Harwood contained himself and she paid him no attention. They dressed in silence and walked back, avoiding the cave-in. Night creatures were calling, a few toads as trilling tenors, and the bullfrogs muttering their bass cacophony. Cresting the hill, the pasture now lay behind them, the sky a black canvass lit here, there, most everywhere by fireflies. Several alighted on John's shirt and he flicked them off remarking casually that they were after the wrong animal.

Sarah laughed brightly and leaned on his arm saying nothing at first, then drawing him closer whispered gaily in his ear. "The lightening bug is a wondrous sight, but you'd think it had no mind. It pumps around in the darkest night with headlights on behind."

"I like that," he said with a chuckle.

A little later they crossed the lawn and went in. While John changed to dry clothes, Sarah chatted with Mother Harwood, laughingly describing her son's tumble into Bailey Brook. After the late evening news and bidding ritual goodnights, they all went to their separate rooms. Harwood slipped off his clothes and clicked on the radio, the volume way down low. He opened the window and let in the night sounds of moving leaves, the clack of the train moving up through the valley, the distant lowing of a cow in heat. The air moving up from the slough was slightly musty. He sat naked near the darkened window for a very long time gazing at the flashing pinpricks, brief presences of life on the lawn, up in the trees, out in the obsidian sky. In Sarah, he saw the chance for a new life, a different tack into an unknown future. But still he hesitated, unsure, in fear of giving up the progress he'd made since leaving Springfield. He could handle the day to day stuff up in Vermont, but this was too close to the bone. He'd been living a winter of despair for too long and was loath to think that true change was in the air. A bad case of the collywobbles tweaked his confidence, leaving him clammy, irresolute.

Shortly after midnight the moon rose, scattering the dancing lamps. They had begun to wane earlier, but in half and hour they were all gone and the wash of light brought out familiar trees and the long swath of grass. He lit a cigarette and slowly exhaled.

"What was he doing here alone with the moon, with an intriguing woman under his eaves?" From the radio on his dresser, some JellyRoll Morton was throbbing out of a station in New York. He'd played the mating game too many times to wade into a heady affair with this earnest, yet naive creature. While he felt drawn to her and yearned for intimacy, there were boundaries he must keep. Summer may be in the air, but the ice was not yet out of the pond. As the first gray fingers of dawn thrust out, he knew that she must remain a friend, a companion and nothing more. Of course, he didn't have a clue as to how he would handle such an arrangement.

26

Paul hammered the last plank of the tent platform into place and spiked it. Satisfied with his work, he stood up, stretching in the Indian Summer sun. The rest of the detail assigned to build the recreation area on Johnnycake Hill had departed for Grafton at noon leaving him to finish the rough carpentry. He would watch over the lumber and supplies until Monday when a truck would be sent to clear the site.

Paul sat on the platform and admired the structures they had built, six tent platforms, three lean-tos and a pavilion to shelter picnic parties of fifty, complete with tables and central fireplace. The recreation area was set just below the brow of a large drumlin and one could look south and east over the Saxton's River Valley to count a score of farms surrounded by their squares of wood lots and fields. Following the winding road to the river, the eye caught the steeple of the Congregational Church in Salem with its white clapboard base and the string of homes leading out from the common before being swallowed up by the fields and forest.

As he put away his tools, Paul became acutely aware of the crisp odor of exposed wood newly cut. Resinous and clean, the pavilion gleamed in its newness and he felt proud and strong to have been part of it. He went to the spring up behind the pavilion and brought back a jug of water, which he placed on one of the rough-hewn picnic tables. He filled his cup, drank it all and filled the cup again. Leaning back, he rested against one of the roof supports, a length of oak, which had been hand trimmed and barked, but otherwise unmilled. He ran his fingers over the familiar surface, feeling the grain and lumpy knots where branches had been. A great calm came over him and he was thankful to be here on his own for the weekend and not on camp detail. Soon he would make his supper over the fireplace outside the lean-to which served as his home base. His meat and milk were right now cooling in the little rock cavern he had constructed in a pool of cold water leading from the spring. He would turn in early tonight for he had worked hard to make the site presentable for Hurlburt's inevitable inspection.

Paul finished his supper and renewed his water jug in the spring. The twilight would linger for another hour, but he sprawled, fully clothed on his cot savoring the lingering warmth and the clear sky. He fell asleep almost at once and would have not stirred until dawn's first light, but for an unnatural sound which reached down into his slumber. His eyes flickered open and drank in the darkness, pierced only by myriads of bright stars. He shivered slightly in the cool drought rolling down the drumlin into the valley below. There it was again. He recognized the drone of an automobile engine gradually increasing, and judging from its laboring whine was climbing Johnnycake Hill and would soon be right in camp. Paul felt vaguely uneasy and decided it best not to be caught in bed. He rolled up his blankets and kicked them into the corner, then ducked across the clearing and sought refuge in a clump of young hemlocks. If this were trouble, there was little he alone could do and he did not relish the idea of having to confront midnight visitors bent on theft or destruction.

The vehicle swung around the last curve and approached the recreation area cautiously throwing its headlamp beams between the trees and onto the recently completed structures. It continued slowly right past Paul who lay flat in the copse of hemlock, and on up the dirt road carved out of dense laurel years before by loggers. Just over the crest of the knoll lay a hillside hay meadow recently mowed for rowan. The car pulled off the road into the field, the driver cutting both lights and engine abruptly. Paul could hear the doors slam and voices talking low. Leaving his concealment in the firs, he moved quietly up the road until he could make out four figures against the sky. He heard hacking of a throat and expectoration followed by a raised voice.

"Well, if we don't get nothing up here in this deeryard tonight, I'm through for the summer, Cy. Gettin' sick of all your damn fool

mistakes." The voice Paul did not recognize, but he heard the loud
click of ammunition being rammed home in the chamber of a
shotgun and knew what that meant

"We can't miss with all this new cut rowan. Draws deer like
sailors to a hot woman." The new voice ended in a chuckle then
issued a loud warning.

"Be sure you stay on this side of the road, Porter, or one of us
will pepper your tail with buckshot."

Paul heard a whinny voice mumble something in return. The
other three guffawed at this.

Suddenly Paul realized that two of the men were coming his
way. He froze momentarily, then beat a stealthy but hasty retreat
into the brush, taking cover behind an oak. The two men passed
him by nearly within touching distance. The poachers foul purpose
was now abundantly clear to Paul. Strung out along the road they
would be able to catch anything trying to move into the field in a
crossfire. The loud man stayed near the car while the fourth headed
for a point just over the hill. The two closest to Paul continued for
only a little way and took up positions in the roadside ditch. Paul
was now blocked on two sides. He dared not back into the woods
for fear of breaking branches and giving himself away. Silence
descended as the hunters began their waiting game. Paul's legs
were stiff with inactivity when he first heard the furtive crackle
across the road, then the soft tamp of hooves along the shoulder.
The poachers heard it too, but held their fire. Just as the arrival
crested the knoll and turned to go into the field, the auto headlights
flicked on illuminating a big doe that stood transfixed in the pools
of unnatural light. Two shots rang out and the deer collapsed. The
man near the car let out a whoop.

"Looks like you got her, boys. Slit her throat before she gets
up!"

The two who had fired hurried to the thrashing deer to finish
their bloody business. As they entered the circle of light, Paul's
suspicions were confirmed. He recognized both the bearded giant
Cy Bush and Porter a surly Springfield youth whom Paul had seen
squiring Carrie Bush to camp sporting events. Porter flicked out

his knife, bent over the badly bleeding animal and viciously dispatched her. After a short spell of vigorous work, the poachers had gutted the doe and slung the carcass over the boot of the car, throwing the offal far back into the laurel. They had barely finished when a fawn, perhaps rattled by the kill or seeking its mother, pranced out of the brush into the field, stopping suddenly to gaze balefully at the headlights. Porter swung his weapon around and shot point blank, lifting the fawn off its feet, sprawling its mangled body into a small stack of rowan.

"Why'd you waste a shot on a little shit like that?" Bush bellowed out in consternation.

Porter crossed the light beams and ejected the shell casing over the motionless body. He looked down in disdain and kicked the carcass.

Ears still ringing from the shot, Paul felt the bile of anger and revulsion well into his mouth. With the poachers now focused on the new kill, he seized the opportunity to flee this barbarity. He backed into the brush as quietly as he could, but in so doing dislodged some loose stones which tumbled into the dry leaves of the ditch. Paul froze, but one of the men swung about.

"Hey Bush, I think there's somebody else up here with us."

Paul dared not move and squatted lower behind the oak. The car lights were snuffed out and Paul knew they were closing in. Out of the dark silence a strong hand grasped his shoulder and spun him around so that he toppled into the road.

"Stay right where you are," a harsh voice commanded.

The lights flashed on again and Paul was lifted and roughly propelled into the circle of light.

"What the hell is going on here anyway?" growled Bush as the poachers formed a tight circle around Paul. Bush produced a flashlight and shone it in Paul's face, momentarily blinding him, but not before he saw the sneer on Porter's face.

"Looks like a CCC kid from the Grafton camp. Must be working on them picnic grounds down the hill." Paul's captor muttered.

Bush said nothing, but continued to glare at Paul. Out of the dark behind him, Paul heard a chuckle.

"You'd never know this fella, would you Bush?" More tittering.

Bush still made no response, but narrowed his eyes, finally demanding sarcastically, "What are you doing out here, kid?"

Paul said nothing.

"I'm talking to you, Frenchie," Bush yelled and shoved Paul into the ditch.

Paul found his tongue as he brushed off leaves and dirt with a skinned hand.

"Supposed to be here. I'm guarding the buildings we just put up."

"Oh you are, huh? Well now, it seems that they're down the road a bit, ain't they? What are you doing up here checking on us?"

"No reason. Just had to make sure no one was coming in to take government lumber."

"What do you think we are Frenchie, a bunch of crooks?"

Paul said nothing and hung his head. By now the fourth man had come up from behind the hill.

"Well, I'll be damned if it isn't that little tongue-tied Canuck from Springfield."

Bush flinched slightly. The two poachers smirked and exchanged glances. Porter just glared.

"What you gonna do about this, Bush?" The newly arrived man chuckled.

Bush glowered, then said, "Not going to do a damn thing. You haven't seen anyone up here tonight, have you, Frenchie?"

Paul said nothing. The glare of the headlights hurt his eyes and he tried to edge his way out of their direct line.

Bush grabbed his shoulders and spun him back into the center of the light.

"What's the matter, cat got your tongue again?"

Bush's face was purple with rage.

"If I ever find out that you talk anything to anybody about us, you'll wish you never left that old woman of yours."

Paul didn't know what this meant, but kept his mouth shut and stared defiantly back at the huge man whose contracted face nearly touched his. A hate rose within him so spontaneously and strong that he clenched his fists and sucked in his breath in agitation. He had never felt such malevolence for anyone before and the humiliating face glaring down on him represented all the shades of evil Paul could imagine.

Suddenly Bush released him and turned away leaving Paul drained and quaking inside. The lights were cut and blackness enveloped them all.

Bush grunted a single word, "Git!"

Paul took a deep breath, turned his back to them and stumbled down the road in the direction of the recreation area, his feet not his own. He heard the motor start behind him and the car swept down the hill, forcing him into the ditch. As it passed him, Bush roared out the window, "You remember what I told ya."

He tried to sleep, but no sooner dozed than images of Bush and his cronies would jerk him awake. Long before the sun, he had arisen for the day and assembled his tools for some final touches needed at the site. He savored the morning star and rosy dawn, but knew the day would be a scorcher. He must dig out and gather rock early, leaving the sanding of the picnic tables for late in the shade of the pavilion. He prepared a breakfast of bacon and eggs at one of the fireplaces and washed these and a chunk of bread down with cool spring water. Grappling and splitting rocks, he worked steadily in the increasing heat, but had little heart for the task. Full of turmoil and repressed anger, he harrowed himself, mulling over Bush's too familiar sarcasm and the knowing smirks of the other poachers. What did they know about him? What forgotten deeds had he committed to draw their scorn? He might be different from the other CCC men, but why an outcast? Nothing was resolved when he quit for lunch. Just as he pulled his milk and meat from the spring, he heard another vehicle climbing Johnnycake Hill.

"Put that stuff away, Frenchie," yelled McGarry as he hopped out of John's Ford. "We got better grub. Hamburgers, salad, biere, vin! We having a pique-nique, boy!"

McGarry had more than sampled the wine. Paul never failed

to get a good laugh out of the officer's fractured French. Despite the endless ribbing, it was always good to see McGarry.

Sarah came around the back of the car carrying a picnic basket and a blanket, while Harwood rummaged in the trunk, finally emerging with a hand-cranked Victrola which he placed on a table under the pavilion.

"So how has your vacation been up here in the wilderness," John inquired, putting his hand on Paul's shoulder. Paul thought that Harwood looked better today than he had for months.

"Just fine. O.K.," Paul responded with a nod. He wasn't about to mention his trial of the night before.

"Take a break, Paul," Harwood continued. "Hurlburt won't be up here to check out this work until next week. By that time, you'll be back in camp on another project he's cooked up. We'll take you back to Grafton with us today."

Sarah had laid out the food and drinks in the pavilion and was sitting on the blanket at the edge of the platform. The sun, dappled by leaves overhead, was in her hair. Paul noticed the way it moved across her brow in the occasional breeze. She spoke.

"There is some root beer in the basket, Paul, in case you don't want to associate with these two patriots I've brought along."

McGarry didn't let that go by. "Now wait a minute. You mean we spent our money for this vin in Frenchie's honor and here you're trying to put him on the wagon?"

Paul grinned sheepishly.

"You mean you've really saved some for him, Pel?" She laughed. "And I thought that it had all evaporated on the way up here."

"Nope." He responded, holding up a full bottle. "Now just a small glass for the Frenchman, then I'll crank up the music." He poured wine for all and toasted Paul and the new recreation area, tossing down his glass in one quaff, then ambled over to the Victrola, cranked it a few times and put on a record.

"Music, let's have music! Oh, here we are. What did old Omar say? A loaf of bread, a jug of wine and thee in the wilderness." He glanced at Sarah as a crooner cooed his verses in a tinny voice.

"Shall we dance, Miss?" He took Sarah in his arms and they began to circle the pavilion.

"What do you make of this Paul?" Harwood was in a very good humor as he watched the dancers.

"I think the Captain is funny, very funny." Paul beamed. His heart was gay. He had quite forgotten his earlier mood as he sipped the wine in the shade of the pavilion overhang.

"My turn, Pel," John announced as the record ended.

"Oh, if music be the food of love, play on," mumbled McGarry as he released Sarah, put on a record and leaned casually against the wall, contemplating his glass.

The sensual tempo of the tango rather startled John and Sarah but, after a brief scowl in McGarry's direction, they decided to go along and soon were parading stiffly up and down, their bodies closely pressed. Paul had never seen such expressive dancing. McGarry had all he could do to keep from doubling up.

Several records later, after a break for a bite of food, Harwood called Paul over.

"Now Sarah, here, is no ordinary taxi dancer, Paul, so listen up and she'll teach you a few steps."

McGarry let out a chuckle over in the corner. Paul looked away, slightly abashed, but Sarah took his hand.

"Don't listen to either of them. That's the wine making them foolish." She shot a glance in McGarry's direction and directed Harwood to put on a slow waltz. She gripped his shoulder and waist, urging him to do the same, and talked him through the basics. Picking up on the tempo, they moved, furtively at first, then with more confidence.

"That's right, Paul," she encouraged. "Keep in time with the music. You're picking this up rather fast. I'd say that you were a natural. Are you sure someone hasn't danced with your before?"

He ignored the question and wouldn't look at her. They whirled and gathered speed in near perfect synchrony. She was light and adroit in his grasp. When the record ended she put on a foxtrot.

John and McGarry moved out among the trees with drinks in

hand to chat. McGarry disappeared for a while, off in a dense thicket to relieve himself.

Sarah's smile broadened with each new mastery of footwork. After a time, she put on a Lehar waltz and they moved, almost as if by habit, closer in each other's arms. For Paul, the two officers had disappeared from the face of the earth, so complete was his focus on Sarah. Her right shoulder slipped closer and he put his chin on her forehead, smelling her hair and perspiration, a slight tang barely masked by her perfume. The music enveloped him and he suddenly held her at arm's length, gazing into her eyes.

McGarry stirred slightly as he glanced towards the pavilion.

"I do believe those are cow eyes on Frenchie. He must have sipped too much wine or is about to be pussy-whipped," he chortled.

John looked at the dancers, but said nothing. After an uncomfortable silence, McGarry kicked at a stump with his boot.

"I shouldn't have said that, Harwood. I'm sorry. A woman like that isn't the kind for cheap talk."

Harwood grunted but did not take his eyes off the pavilion.

"Dammit, Harwood, you should be busting my chops for that remark!! What makes you such a fatuous bastard, anyway? She's just what you need to get you unstuck from that fly paper you're wrapped in !!" McGarry turned and savagely punched the tree next to him, then screwed up his face in pain. "I'd ruin her in less than a year, but she'd be everything to you and maybe get you over what you can't seem to change!" He stomped off looking for his bottle, rubbing the hurt hand.

Sarah returned Paul's gaze with a smile, but realized in a rush that he was expressing something to her far beyond the pleasure of the dancing.

"God, what have I gone and done," she wondered.

She certainly hadn't intended to lead him on. That was furthest from her mind. He was naive and decent. Better to keep smiling and cushion his innocence from any hard landings.

"Oh, that music just gets inside, doesn't it? Makes the feet and heart really move together," she said lightly, but with fear inside. She let go his waist gently and extended her arm to get some distance.

The record had nearly ended when John stepped between them.

"You're doing well, Paul, but now it's my turn," he remarked with a smile and whisked Sarah away.

He watched her go, the bubble broken, and felt a little ashamed. But his eyes remained on her lithe body, swaying and turning to the remains of the waltz.

27

Paul's section had been assigned the afternoon project to repair the siding and fix the roof of the infirmary. It was hot and the men had worked hard mowing the parade area and filling in potholes in the parking areas. Hurlburt had trouble rounding up his charges and it was two-thirty, after much haranguing and badgering, before the boys were ready to commence work.

"I shouldn't have to deliver special invitations to you every time there's maintenance to be done," Fred said heatedly. "When your other work is finished, you come where I am. Now, several of you grab that old tarpaper and rip it off. You four there, take out the old nails. Marvin, you and Paul unroll the new paper while Jim and I tack. And don't forget to overlap it so the rain doesn't get in on Miss Grout.

"She's all wet anyway," said a voice from among the group ripping away at the old siding with claw hammers." "Yeh, and colder than a pump handle in January," quipped another, followed by tittering.

"Whoever said that is lucky Miss Grout left for town early today," Hurlburt retorted. "She'd tell you in no uncertain terms where the bear shits in the buckwheat!"

"Do you suppose she's ever had it, Fred?" Chimed in another voice amidst the scraping and clatter.

"Had what, for crying out loud?" Hurlburt returned with mock seriousness.

"Aw, you know, Mr. Hurlburt," drawled off the voice, now embarrassed and hastening to be formal.

"I'll tell you this. She knows a lot more about what you are imagining than most of you will find out in a lifetime."

"Where'd she find out?" Another voice, immature, vaguely derisive, but shy and with an edge of honest curiosity.

"Well, for one thing, she's a nurse. They've got to know about such things to straighten out the girls who the likes of you try to get in trouble."

More laughter.

"For another thing, Miss Grout doesn't miss much. She's talked to lots of people with lots of different problems. People who do that usually have things figured out pretty well."

"You think we're all after one thing with the girls, don't you?" A challenge. This was Marvin who tended toward sullenness.

"Yes I do, if you're healthy." He looked the boy squarely in the eye. "But don't think you're the first to stumble over this revelation or that you're free to pant over those town girls like some farm stud. Oh, they'll flirt and act like you're the prize bull. That's what they've learned to do from their mothers and sisters. But when the chips are down, they want a man, not a piece of beef. They don't always understand what they need and less often talk about it, but down there in their guts—leave the heart out of it— they want some protection and dignity, some way of knowing that their babies will have a father who comes home to them, a mate who cares enough to be their best friend. You'll get all you want if you're willing to give them this and a good helping of hope."

Hurlburt paused and realized a little sheepishly that everyone had stopped working to listen.

"Now, let's cut the talk and get this job done," he said as much to himself as to his section.

Paul held the paper so Hurlburt could drive a few more nails home. After a respectful silence, he asked quietly so that only Jim and Marvin could hear, "Are all girls like that, Mr. Hurlburt?"

Fred looked at him sharply, then softened and said, "Well, most of them, Paul."

They made good progress and by late afternoon had completed the project.

Hurlburt dismissed them early as a reward and with a hoot they all ran down to the pond for a cool dip before supper. Hurlburt gathered the tools into his box and was about to take them to the garage when Mary Grout opened the infirmary door and stepped out. Hurlburt's face dropped and reddened to the tips of his ears as he nodded more than spoke his "Hi, Mary," before striding purposefully away towards the garage. Mary watched him go, a slight smile playing about her lips. Now that her reports were done she could finally leave for town.

28

So it was settled. Paul and McGarry would leave early Friday morning for Belchertown and the motorcycle hill climbing competition at Dana. Harwood called the CCC camp outside of Belchertown to reserve weekend accommodations for the two. When Hurlburt heard of the trip he became unusually interested and passed the remark to Harwood that he wished he were twenty years younger.

"We both do, Fred," John laughed. "Why don't you take some leave and go along?"

"Oh, no. Not me on the back of that machine. Besides, there's too much going on here right now. I'll try for a week in late fall."

That evening Fred cornered Paul on the way back from the mess hall.

"You'll be going down to Massachusetts this weekend, I hear." Paul nodded.

"Maybe you could check out how that Quabbin project is going. That's still my neck of the woods, you know, even if the state with their damned MDC is running roughshod over it."

"I'll find out what I can for you, Fred," Paul offered.

"And if you get a chance . . . . ," Hurlburt's voice trailed off and he turned to look out at the pond. Paul waited, realizing that Fred was having a little difficulty getting something off his chest. When he continued, his tone was mild, the excitement gone.

"Not too far down Route 9, just east of where that CCC camp ought to be, is a dirt road which cuts to the left and climbs the height of land east of the Quabbin project. At the crest you can see the entire Swift River watershed and if you were to face directly west you'd see twin hills lying like the breasts of a maiden in the folds of the valley. The land you stand on there is mine, rocky and poor as it is. I've seen those hills in all seasons since I was old enough to hang onto my father's back. He told me to never sell that height of land and to take my children there whenever I could." He paused, then went on barely above a whisper.

"Never having any children, I won't share that peace of spirit the same way he did, but I want you to see it lad, and to savor it before those cusses tear it up."

Paul remained silent, hanging on the meaning of these words, looking off at the shadows thrown by the hump-backed hills up behind the pond. He expected Hurlburt to say more, but when he turned, his leader was walking away.

They made good time traveling south. The Indian Summer languished over the land, bringing cool nights but gloriously bright days, each new one more impeccable than the last. McGarry was in high spirits as they turned east towards Belchertown and it wasn't until they hit the outskirts of the village that he realized it was fair time. Heavy traffic slowed them to a crawl around the common and down the hill to the fairgrounds.

"After some supper at camp and a change of clothes, we'll come back to see the sights," McGarry announced over his shoulder. "Ever been to a fair, kid?" Paul mumbled that he hadn't and McGarry continued.

"This one has a little of everything, if you know what I mean." He couldn't see Paul's uncomprehending face.

They pulled into the Belchertown camp just in time for supper. McGarry parked his machine and went into the commandant's office, leaving Paul to satisfy the questions of the growing knot of envious boys who poured out of the barracks to see the latest arrival. As the newness wore off and the crowd began to drift away, Paul learned that Belchertown was a "bug camp" very much like Grafton, but that many boys pulled periodic duty on the nearby Quabbin project. Two chaps had just agreed to take him to the construction the next day when McGarry came out with the camp commander.

He gave Paul a warm welcome and announced, "Better get your gear over to A barracks son, and jump into their shower before supper. McGarry, are you and the lad going to ride that contraption back to the fair this evening or do you want a lift in one of the camp trucks?"

"I guess our butts can take a bit more punishment. What do you say, Paul?"

Paul grinned sheepishly. McGarry laughed and punched Paul's shoulder.

"These frogs are born to ride bikes, Jim. He's my mechanic and substitute for the hill climb on Sunday."

Paul self-consciously unstrapped his gear, quietly elated with McGarry's praise.

"Well, good luck to both of you. I'll take four wheels under me any day. Supper is in half an hour.

With their bellies full and in fresh clothing, they entered the fairgrounds at sunset. A number of boys from the camp had already arrived and were milling around in small groups, gawking at the cattle exhibits and beginning to work the midway. Several had won stuffed animals by knocking over milk bottles with baseballs. A spirited session at the coin toss was in progress. Paul spotted his two recent acquaintances waiting in line at the ferris wheel.

"Want to join us on this thing?", one of them invited.

Paul's stomach quaked a little as he watched children squealing in their seats as the big wheel picked up speed so he declined, saying that he preferred to watch.

"Well, hang around til we're off then. The horse drawing starts in fifteen minutes over in the show ring."

McGarry urged him to join the two for the evening and after arranging to meet at closing time near the main gate, departed on his own.

There was a huge crowd at the draw, the main event of the evening. The winner would take home one hundred dollars, so competition was keen. Farmers from up and down the valley and as far away as the Berkshires, paraded their teams of draft animals proudly around the ring before hitching to the stone boat laden with concrete slabs. Spotted Percherons and dapper Clydesdales with their white fetlocks and pasterns made up most of the entries, but a fair number of drab Belgians were represented. After each round of draws, several more slabs were added to the sled, the ringmaster booming out the new total weight. Teams gradually became eliminated as the more prudent farmers declined to put their animals to the test. It soon developed that two teams were going to be finalists, a handsome pair of Clydesdales driven by a beefy fellow with a braggart's look about him and a lackluster team of Belgians owned by a small, somber man who, unlike his competitor, rarely used the whip. Paul was struck by how very much the horses and drivers resembled each other.

The tension grew as more slabs were hoisted onto the sled. Each team had drawn several successive increments and the load now looked formidable. The Clydesdales were first and the big man smiled confidently as he hitched up. But when commanded to pull, the Clydesdales faltered and began to stomp in place. The driver's face became clouded and the whip flicked out, not touching the animals, but snapping viciously about their heads. Their huge muscles tensed and rippled as the team leaned to the task, heads down at the ends of their rigidly arched necks, front legs unyielding as columns, hind quarters straining and falling. The sled didn't move an inch.

Five hundred pairs of eyes flickered from the team to the driver's face, now flushed and angry. Paul closed his eyes, knowing full well what was coming next. Pierre had told him about men who used the lash. And most harshly did the strokes fall, welting flanks and backs. A string of angry, shouted obscenities seemed to make each crack of the whip more painful until a low groan issued from the crowd. One of the Clydesdales broke wind violently under the strain and the other lurched haphazardly, fell to its knees and pawed the earth desperately then rose and leaned back in the harness, trembling. A woman in the throng finally shouted, "Stop it. For shame!"

The ringmaster, ousted from his lethargy, guiltily signaled the driver to unhitch. Red-faced with shame and anger, the beefy farmer led his animals away still cursing their performance. Paul noted that one of them had a limp.

The slight man now brought his Belgians around and hitched up. Without fanfare, he stroked his animals' faces and cooed to them in low tones. Then, standing off to one side of the sled, he gently slapped their rumps with the reins and uttered a nearly inaudible, "Giddap, you!" The Belgians arched their necks and strained, their leg and back muscles popping so that they appeared to increase in size. Breathing heavily, the team stomped loudly in near unison on the worn turf ring and, by inches at first, eased the load forward. Finding their common ground through the pressures of the harness, they surged forward more than the required stone boat length, throwing bits of turf at the ecstatic spectators. The driver relaxed the reins and, ignoring the bellowing ringmaster, went immediately to his team and hugged their faces, cooing again in that strange way. Paul and his companions joined the cheers of the enthusiastic crowd as they watched the small driver, unsmiling as ever, saunter to the judges' stand for his prize money.

The boys returned to the midway, stopping to take a few small prizes. Paul was singularly unsuccessful despite the many tips offered by his compatriots. But the evening was jolly on the whole and time passed swiftly. Paul began to notice as the hour drew late that the women and young families had drifted away and that loud men began to congregate at the sideshows with expectant or lascivious looks on their faces. His companions halted outside a tent from which tinny music was emanating. A small sign on the barker's booth reading "Lola—Modern Dancer" was overwhelmed by a painting of a woman in tights wearing an enigmatic smile.

"Here we are," announced one of the boys. "How much money you got left, Paul?" Paul shrugged and brought out his change.

"Just enough for the three of us," the boy laughed as he helped himself to the coins.

"You sure we got time?" Paul mumbled dubiously, hanging back and glancing at the painted lady. The boy with the coins winked at the other.

"Now, c'mon, Paul. Lola's not Sally Keith, but she won't bite."

"Who's Sally Keith?" Paul asked innocently. The Boston lads looked at each other and grinned broadly.

"I guess you've never been to the Crawford House in Scolley Square," answered one of them as they pushed Paul toward the ticket booth.

Inside the tent it was incredibly hot. Most of the seats around a small, raised stage were already filled with sweaty men talking and laughing clamorously. A rope barrier separated the audience from the stage and a three-piece band was playing "Yes Sir, That's My Baby" to the right of the platform. Suddenly, the music stopped and the players wiped their brows. After a short intermission, they began again with a blues tempo. The crowd suddenly hushed as the curtain twitched at the rear of the stage and Lola emerged. Clad in a filmy red gown, she proceeded to traipse around the edge of the platform, head tilted back and arms launched, one in front, one behind. The mob clapped and stamped their approval as she glided up and down the stage, swirling the gown so that ample portions of leg winked out ever so briefly. Paul's eyes opened wide with embarrassment as he tried to concentrate on her face, the heavy make-up, the hair piled high and the brilliant red gash of cosmetic on the unsmiling lips.

The band broke into "Love For Sale" and Lola began her shimmy. Eyes bulged from sunburned faces as she caressed her hips and thighs, quivering with energy. She closed her eyes and with her arms behind her head, spread her legs and gyrated. Whoops and whistles brought a plastic smile to the painted, pouted lips. She was getting in the groove. The gown fell from her shoulders to reveal a near perfect set of breasts supported by a tiny sequin halter. The lights dimmed and the band reverted to the blues, the saxophone player blowing goggle-eyed. Lola now shed the gown completely and kicked it to the rear of the stage. The briefs matched the halter in size and sparkle and several farmers leaped to their feet for a better view, but were dragged down by those behind who couldn't see. Lola shook her shoulders so the breasts fairly danced by themselves, and then she lifted them with her hands and pointed one, then the other, at the men closest to the stage. Unable to contain themselves, the shouters began.

"Take it off, Lola. Show us what you got."

Paul shrank back a bit in his seat and was thankful for the dim lighting. No one could see his scarlet ears that way. He had trouble breathing in the close, cigar and whiskey-scented air. A number of men near the ropes openly refreshed themselves from a hip flask. These were Curley's Boston men from the Quabbin project, their citified faces flaccid and gone with drink.

Lola really got down to business by pulling the front of her briefs out like a kangaroo pouch and yelling, "Fill it up, boys," in an incongruously musical voice.

The coins soon began to sail over the rope and onto the stage. Lola caught quite a few of them and her knickers were soon overflowing. Still they came, jingling across the planks. Somebody hard-pitched a half-dollar from the back rows and zinged her slightly below the navel. She recoiled from the sting, looked up and yelled.

"Hey, you son-of-a-bitch, that hurt."

A roar of laughter swept the throng, but the coins kept flying as she resumed her collection. The band played on.

Paul caught sight of McGarry near the ropes grinning broadly behind a cigar. He held high for Lola to see a dollar bill rolled into a cylinder and, as if on cue, the lights dimmed further and the music became muted as she removed the sequin halter and took the combs from her hair sending brunette billows cascading down her back. Stepping out of her panties, she tied her loot into a little sequin sack.

Completely bare, she did a slow walk around the stage to a hushed audience. Paul averted his eyes, trying not to be obvious about it. None of the scantily clad cuties in Rocco's library collection had prepared him for this. Pierre, in a thoroughly innocent way, had taught the boy to be a fair judge of good breeding stock and he was seeing enough now to know that here was an exceedingly well-proportioned woman. The nipples at the ends of firm, grapefruit breasts jiggled to a halt before McGarry who stood poised with his dollar. She turned and bending at the waist, thrust her tight derriere towards the flyer who reached across the ropes and planted the bill between her buttocks. Swiftly straightening, she plucked the bill from his hand and shimmied away, deftly retrieving the money and holding it high over her head. The crowd gave off a thunderous roar as she pranced suggestively back to McGarry for a rerun. McGarry puffed his cigar and feigned refusal, offering his place to surrounding men. He was nearly trampled in the frenzied rush as twenty panting faces lurched forward, led by the Clydesdale driver. The strain on the rope was too great and the entire phalanx went down in the dust under the stage, a writhing mass of arms and legs. McGarry and the others whooped in spasms of laughter as Lola shook her head and took up a position on the other side of the stage. She was soon collecting dollar bills faster than picking bush beans and called it quits only when the band, in desperation, blew their final stanza of the Dogtown Blues.

Lola flashed a big smile to the audience and threw them kisses, then grabbed her money and disappeared behind the curtain to loud catcalls and stamping. The lights came up and a skinny man appeared on stage and began sweeping up the scattered coins as Paul eased himself towards the back of the tent followed by his two companions. McGarry was nowhere to be seen.

"That show was hotter than Dutch love, huh, Paul," panted one of the boys. "What a rack on that dame!" Paul wondered what that meant and walked a little faster out into the cool, refreshing night. He couldn't control the hot, hard rise he felt in his pants. It just stayed and stayed and he was having trouble with his hand in his pocket to keep his swollen member from showing. A furtive glance at the crotches of his cronies assured him that he was not alone.

Most tents on the midway were shut up for the night causing the CCC boys to drift back to the trucks. Paul searched in vain for the motorcycle near the main gate. Just as the boys began to board, he heard the growl of a machine coming from the sideshow area. Soon McGarry hove into view and rumbled to a stop by the trucks. On the seat behind him was Lola, clinging to his waist, wrapped in slacks and a jacket, her hair carefully held in place by a bandana. The boys gawked while McGarry asked Paul if he'd mind riding back to camp in a truck. He mumbled his assent and looked hard at Lola who was close enough to touch. Despite the sharpness of the night, her perfume, not at all unpleasant or cheap, pervaded his nostrils. She stared back smiling slightly, no plastic or coarseness now, and kissing her finger, planted it on Paul's lips. He looked down, but before the other boys could see his embarrassment, McGarry engaged the machine and shot forward causing Lola to squeal and hug him for dear life. His taillight disappeared in the cloud of dust at the end of the parking lot. Paul hauled himself into the dark recess of the last truck in the line, assisted by a small knot of envious boys. He said nothing and shrugged off their remarks. When the truck slowed to turn onto the highway, Paul could hear the motorcycle roar as it crested a hill somewhere in the distance, then descend to a hum and finally die.

Lola was shimmying towards him in a dream when a hand shook him awake the next morning.

"Hey, Paul, if we're ever going to get to the Quabbin dam, we'd better get some chow and move."

Paul felt both a little cheated and red-faced as he stretched and felt the stiffness in his hips from the previous day's ride. The other boys were already dressed and preparing to leave for the mess hall.

"I'll join you in a minute," he said, pulling on his shirt and pants. He washed quickly and wetted his hair in place. Crossing the review area on his way to the mess, he spotted McGarry's motorcycle parked beside the headquarters building. He thought he'd heard a rumble sometime in the early morning, but had been too asleep for it to even register.

After breakfast, he and his two new friends walked the half mile through the forest and climbed the earthen dam rearing like a mammoth nearly 170 feet over the river channel. Four million cubic yards of fill laid 2,640 feet long now plugged the Swift River gap. Tunnels drained water below the dam until construction was complete, then they would be shut causing the watershed to flood for eighteen miles to the north. Paul was stunned by the totality of the destruction going on in the bowl of the reservoir. A steady stream of trucks moved wood and rubble out of the valley while

the smoke of a score of brush fires cast a funereal pall over the
scene. In the distance, occasional bursts of dynamite boomed,
destroying, he was told, the remaining bridges of Greenwich and
Prescott. In all, four towns would disappear. The residents, although
compensated, would be shifted, taking with them to higher ground
only their movable possessions and the remains of their ancestors.
It was hard to imagine that the wretched landscape would one day
be covered over with a hundred feet of water and Paul began to
sense Fred's anger and frustration.

"Let's go back by the spillway and get cooled off in the river
before heading back for camp," suggested one of the boys.

The spillway was an engineering marvel and Paul was glad to
be rid of the moaning cacophony of the dozens of bulldozers working
the reservoir like giant dung beetles. A little way beyond the dam
a narrow gap had been neatly cut with dynamite out of thirty feet
of granite. A concrete weir had been laid in the cut at the
appropriate height so when the reservoir was full, any excess water
would drain away through the gap down into the peaceful valley
below. A stone bridge was being built across the gap making a
tunnel which when viewed from the north, framed as idyllic a
scene as might be found anywhere in New England. Below the
bridge, the water was to fall away nearly two hundred feet through
a rocky gorge and meadow before linking up again with the Swift
River a half mile distant.

They picked their way carefully down the steep slope and
eventually reached the riverbank.

"Last one in eats cow pies," yelled the more talkative companion
and they all shed their clothing except shorts and dove into the
cold, green water. The shock took Paul's breath away, but it was
indeed refreshing. Later, he was glad to come out and sprawl in
the sun among the buttercups.

The lunch hour had come and gone. McGarry still had not
stirred, so Paul tinkered with the machine, wiping it clean and
checking the electrical system. About one thirty McGarry came
out and stood on the porch, blinking in the sunlight. He stretched
like a tomcat and a self-satisfied smile rode his face.

"What's for lunch, Paul?"

"Egg salad sandwiches."

"Sounds good to me," he chuckled knowingly.

"Here, take some money and go down to the nearest gas station and fill up. Nothing will be open tomorrow and we'll need plenty for the trip to Dana and the hill climb. And if you see any police, play dumb. Get off and push the damn thing so they won't haul you in for operating without a license."

Paul ripped down the road towards Ware, exhilarated with the power between his legs. After filling up several miles outside of the village, he headed back to camp recalling Fred's directions. Rounding a bend, he spotted the country road just where Fred said it would be and pulled off into the pines. He slowed as the road became rough and strewn with small boulders. Grass grew between the wheel ruts and the track angled sharply around the edges of bogs and rock outcrops. The air was close to unmoving. He'd gone about three miles without seeing so much as a cowshed and nearly had decided he'd taken the wrong road. Suddenly, he started to climb the face of a hill in crisscross fashion and entered a copse of tall hardwoods, their thick canopy covering the road. He continued for another mile and broke out of a dense stand of oaks at the crest of the hill. Off to his left spread the panorama of the Swift River valley, capped by the haze of burning brush. He knew he'd found Fred's property.

Paul stopped the machine, laid it against a tree and climbed some boulders to get a better view. A cool wind blew up from the valley bringing with it the tang of wood smoke. Off to the west, as Hurlburt had described, were two small mounds nearly obscured by haze. Their bases had been clear cut up more than half way and the surrounding desolate valley was one long brown scar. He shut his eyes and tried to see them as Fred had, smooth and forested, but all that came to mind was Lola. He felt twinges of guilt and regret that he could not share Fred's vision.

"Someday, perhaps," he thought, "when the healing has taken place and the water runs clean, I'll return."

He sat down on the rocks and observed the other side of Fred's hill. Removed from human ravage, it grew lush and strong. Just beyond the ledges lay evidence of deer sign and in the deep woods a thrush piped. Far to the east another hill rose, on whose grassy slope Paul could see scattered puffs of grazing sheep and it became clear in that instant why Fred and his father had found solace there.

29

The hill climb required negotiating 200 feet of twenty-percent slope at the end of a sand and gravel pit. Like other Swift River valley towns, much of Dana had been swallowed up in the Quabbin project. But this peripheral piece of land remained unscathed except to provide till for concrete footings. The air was dead in this depression and the afternoon heat brought out the mosquitoes. Frenzied by the smell of warm blood, they rose in small clouds from the vegetation where they had been resting. Paul and McGarry, along with fifty odd spectators slapped at them vigorously as one after another the cycles angrily clawed their way to the top of the pit, first in the trials, then for official times.

Each street-legal machine was refitted with an oversized rear wheel sprocket onto which was fed a heavy-duty drive chain. Rear tire chains were added to give maximum bite. Paul taped the lights and removed the fenders. Regular gasoline was siphoned out of the tank and replaced with alcohol for better combustion. Castor oil, which holds its consistency better under the increased stress, was added to the crankcase to reduce friction on the cams and rods.

The referee stood at the top of the bank with a stop watch, keeping a sharp eye out for the starter's red flag and as the rear wheel of each contestant shot past the lip of pit, he logged in the times. Two spotters held position halfway up the slope. At the drop of the flag, motorcycle and rider would lurch up the thirty-foot launch track, often with only the rear wheel in contact, the rider leaning forward to balance, and dirt flying out in a plume behind. Real skill and precise timing was required just to remain mounted on the incline. Many a rider flipped backwards if his balance was off or upon cresting the hill, would be thrown off as the machine's center of gravity abruptly changed. This was often the most difficult part of the maneuver for to cut power too soon to get greater control might result in a poorer time or a sudden spill.

McGarry had made three trial runs, successively reducing his time, but not enough to best a young chap riding an Indian Chief, a sleek, well-balanced and powerful machine. Paul had put in new plugs after the first trial and now in a desperate attempt to reduce weight, he helped McGarry remove the seat and siphon out all but a small quantity of the alcohol. Paul looked dubiously at McGarry as they tipped the cycle to get a better siphon.

"Don't worry, kid. She won't die on the way up. This engine is a triple-nine knucklehead with pressurized oil. It'll beat the ass of that Indian any day."

Now it was his turn. The Indian had scored its best time so far in the official run and, not to be outdone, McGarry, the old aviator showing, tore into the track as if he were contemplating take-off. The Harley wailed like a banshee as it skittered up the slope, the chains throwing sand high. Paul kept his eyes glued on McGarry's watch, waiting for the sound of throttling back to tell him that the vehicle was at the top. Suddenly, the Harley screamed. McGarry became airborne as he overshot the lip. He'd never let up on the accelerator and now had to pay the price. Man and machine went down heavily out of sight of those below and the engine noise abruptly ceased. The referee disappeared momentarily, then reappeared, gesticulating wildly for help. Before Paul could charge up the hill, he heard an anxious voice in his ear.

"Oh, is he all right? Let him be all right."

He hadn't noticed Lola before, but here she was swatting mosquitoes with the rest of them. She looked cool and lovely in a sundress and wide straw hat. Their eyes met and Paul blurted, "I'll check," then ran as if his life depended on it, propelled by forces equally strong, ahead and behind.

McGarry was up rubbing his bad leg when Paul arrived ahead of the others. The Harley lay twisted in a heap. Fortunately, the impact with the ground had thrown McGarry off into a clump of pines. The machine had traveled on for fifty feet before sideswiping a big maple and coming to rest in a pile of sand.

"I'm O.K., Paul," McGarry winced. "How was my time?"

Paul said nothing, offering his shoulder to McGarry for support and passing him his canteen of water.

"Thanks, kid."

The referee chatted with the spotters, then came over.

"Looks like you wrecked your machine and nearly broke your damned neck, but if it's any consolation, you had the best time."

"Then that's all that counts," McGarry said softly.

The referee shook his head and eyed him.

"You sure you're O.K.?"

"Yeah, yeah! Let's look at the Harley, Paul."

Although severely banged up and scratched, the motorcycle had no serious damage and after pulling the twisted spokes back into place and reshaping the handlebars, Paul pushed it back down the incline to the sandpit where their gear was stowed. The spectators gave the limping McGarry a rousing cheer while Lola ran forward to hug the aviator, losing her hat in the process. Paul stared straight ahead and kept pushing the machine to the waiting gas can. He removed the climbing gear and chains and after filling the tank and tinkering with the throttle, jumped on and kicked it over. The engine roared to life like the legendary phoenix from the ashes. He drove it a few feet to test the steering and the brakes. Except for some stiffness at the end of sharp left turns, the machine ran well. He idled to a stop in the shade of one of the scant trees and, seeing Lola and McGarry approaching, busied himself with the fenders and tail light.

"Lola, I want you to meet my handyman, Paul Boisvert, one of the best damn motorcycle mechanics in the CCC," McGarry announced expansively.

Paul glanced up at the lovely features and amused eyes.

"I think I already have Pel," she laughed good-naturedly. Paul heard again the sweet music, but he reddened anyway and turned quickly toward his task.

"Very good to see you again, Paul," she continued and, seeing his discomfort, turned to McGarry and asked how long he would stay in Belchertown.

"Well," grinned the aviator, "Paul and I are due back in Vermont so he can report for duty tomorrow morning. And none too soon either. Judging from those red ears of his, I'd say that this Massachusetts sun was getting to him."

"Pel, you really are a pain!" She chided and turned to Paul again.

"Do you have relatives in Holyoke? I know your name from somewhere."

Paul looked up, his face set like a stone, eyes unwavering.

"No, mademoiselle," he retorted, a bit loftily. McGarry broke up.

"*Mademoiselle*," he hooted. "God, that's good!"

"Oh, be still you cad," Lola commanded sharply, but her eyes flickered ever so slightly under Paul's steady gaze, then became thoughtful.

"Don't let yourself be ruined by this fellow. He means well, but his addled brain won't let him pass up a challenge, even when he knows he should run the other way. Bad luck for me, I find him interesting, but never know where or when he'll show up next." She glanced briefly at McGarry who paid no attention as he massaged his damaged leg. When Paul caught her eye again, the isinglass curtains were drawn shut.

She didn't give McGarry so much as a pat as she turned on her heel and strode to her car parked by the entrance to the sandpit. McGarry noticed that Paul continued to look in her direction and muttered in a low voice.

"Everything she's got is real, boy. But it's available to just about anybody."

Paul studied the sand at his feet, embarrassed. They packed their gear and made to leave when the referee shouted over to them.

"Hey, don't forget your trophy here."

"Give it to that dame getting into her car over there," McGarry shot back, gesticulating towards Lola.

The pain in McGarry's leg was so bad that Paul drove all the way back to Vermont.

The aviator eventually needed more surgery and returned to Massachusetts for treatment. Harwood drove him and the Harley to Springfield in one of the camp's ton and a half trucks where Gladys met them and immediately confined McGarry to her flat.

"Don't worry, John, I'll see that this tomcat recuperates properly," she said cheerily, helping her patient out of the cab.

McGarry gave Harwood a broad wink and hobbled up the steps. John rolled the Harley off the flatbed and into Gladys's garage. He considered a visit to Hazel, but shook his head at the turn off and stepped on the gas, pushing his way up Route 5 to Vermont.

30

Harwood went over Hurlburt's recreation hall want list, then glanced at his watch.

"This looks fine, Fred, but don't add anything more."

He smiled wryly. "And I'll pick up the new man . . . what's his name? . . . Liebowitz? He's due on the 4 o'clock train and probably has no idea what he's getting into. Be sure that someone makes the Exec's area presentable for him."

It took John about an hour to pick up Hurlburt's things and complete his errands in Bellows Falls. He pulled into the railway depot with ten minutes to spare, got out and crossed the dirt parking area to the platform. The depot was deserted except for the pig-eyed clerk in his cage and a tired looking baggage handler leaning on a hand truck, his manner suggesting he would just as soon not use it ever again. Harwood found some shade and recalled his earlier visit to the station with the hapless shavetail lieutenant.

The train pulled in slowly and came to a halt some distance from where John stood. A few cartons were thrown onto the platform from the baggage car, causing the handler to spring to life rather unexpectedly and heave them onto his conveyance. He trucked them away to storage, disappearing around the edge of the overhang.

No one emerged from the coaches and John again checked his watch. "Right on time, dammit. Maybe I got the wrong train?" He waited until the locomotive lurched forward, then turned to go. He hadn't noticed the slim, short man standing at the far end of the platform before, but had the funny feeling that this person had been eyeing him for some time. He paused and nodded to the stranger who still did not move. Then, as Harwood took a step forward, the man turned and picked up a small, battered suitcase.

227

"If you're Mr. Liebowitz, I'm your transportation to the CCC camp. The name is John Harwood."

Liebowitz gave the uniform and the two silver shoulder bars a fleeting glance, then put out a pale palm which grasped Harwood's with surprising strength.

"Joshua Liebowitz," he announced simply, the accent giving away his Queens upbringing. He looked across the lot to the only vehicle, John's, and stepped off clutching his meager belongings.

"Christ," thought John, following a few steps behind and sizing him up, "those brush monkeys will have him for breakfast. Right out of the city, no small talk, a Hebrew and a runt to boot. Wonder how we got to host a resident counselor? Most camps have circuit riders who come in for evenings, do their teaching and back patting, then go home. I'll wager this one will be on the return train about this time next week."

They got in and John started the engine.

"We'll take care of most of your basic needs in camp, but do you want anything here in town before we head upcountry?" John inquired.

"No thank you, Captain. I'm quite accustomed to living with what I have."

John grunted and turned up the hill road away from the river.

"How was the trip up here?" Harwood could see that the little Jew was not going to be much of a talker.

"Fine, but a little slow."

Harwood waited for him to continue, but the silence lengthened and he knew that was all he was going to get. Resigned, John commenced a monologue on Grafton and camp life, expecting at least a couple of questions from Liebowitz on the job of educational advisor. But none came and the too long silences hung between them.

"Damn," thought Harwood with mild irritation, "if he's like this all the time, we'll have to hang a bell on him."

Long before they reached camp, John had decided to count his blessings. At least he wouldn't have to share space with some garrulous academic wanting to play one up-man-ship at every turn.

They arrived back in time for supper and after showing Liebowitz his quarters and where to draw extra clothing, Harwood left him alone to freshen up. He reappeared shortly in Harwood's office and the two of them crossed the parade ground to the mess hall.

"That's the library over there," John pointed to a barracks-like structure near the mess hall.

"It's got space for meeting a dozen boys there, but larger groups will have to assemble in the rec hall over here to our right." Harwood nodded at a longer, but identical tarpaper building and added, "Nothing's very fancy here. We have a few books, mainly popular classics and recent novels, and plenty of old magazines which the lads read from cover to cover. Textbooks and technical works are non-existent and you'll have to improvise. Miss Pyle runs the lending library down in Grafton and has been very generous to us. Quite a few of us pick up a week's reading there."

Liebowitz said nothing, as usual, and they went in to eat.

John purposely steered him to the table where Paul and the bunch from barracks B had gathered. After introducing Liebowitz, he withdrew from the conversation and concentrated on his dinner.

"This guy is on his own from here—sink or swim.", he concluded to himself.

To his surprise, the newcomer handled the group with aplomb, showing sincere interest in the boys by asking questions, which let them reveal themselves and their aspirations without awkwardness. John observed, too, that Liebowitz was mentally recording everything they told him, yet never once let anything slip about himself.

On a Sunday, two weeks later, Hurlburt tromped into headquarters, shutting the door loudly behind him. "God Almighty!" He muttered under his breath.

Harwood was reading near the fireplace and looked up. "What's the problem now, Fred?"

"Oh, nothing much. I passed the recreation hall this afternoon and caught the end of that fella Coughlin's weekly lecture. You don't know how I wish the power would fail every Sunday at 4 o'clock so we wouldn't have to suffer those diatribes. It's hard to figure who gets the worst of it, Roosevelt or the Jews."

"I hear you, Fred, but he's got one hell of a following. Sort of proves what J.P. Barnum said about circus lovers."

"Yeah, but those Boston bogtrotters don't miss a word and tune in as if it was the start of the Second Coming."

Maybe they're just using him as a substitute," John offered. "When the weather's bad, not many of them make it over to Chester for Mass."

Hurlburt remained thoughtful for a moment. "I feel embarrassed for Liebowitz. Not that his cocky ass doesn't need a whipping now and then, but the stuff that priest spews out is the worst heifer dust I've had shot my way."

"Demagoguery!!" John corrected. "Those with a cause have to look for scapegoats to make their purple prose believable. And who's to argue with a heavenly cause? If Pel were here, he'd add a footnote or two from his Spanish adventures."

"You're right there, Captain." Hurlburt cracked a grin. Then they both fell silent, neither wishing to pursue the matter further.

Liebowitz took to the job of educational advisor with a passion. Inside of a month, he had doubled the size of the library by scouring the attics of surrounding schools for disused materials. He scrounged anything, primers, dictionaries, encyclopedias, dog-eared and scribbled-on novels and biographies. He pored over recruit records to find out their backgrounds, the levels of schooling each had attained and talked with them at supper, a different table each night, all the while sizing up each individual's potential for learning. But most of all he watched and listened, learning the dynamics of the camp, what the recruits were reading, what they did with their free time. Early on he noted that Sarah was a gifted teacher. While he didn't know the first thing about insects, he was in her classes, watching for process and how the recruits learned best.

By the middle of September he was ready to establish a program in remedial high school subjects. Some of the boys who had quit

school in the primary grades would have to strain, but he had
coaxed a few of the high school graduates to become tutors and
took the bold step of asking Sarah to be their mentor. On three
evenings each week, he would teach basic subjects, alternating in
three areas. On Thursdays, a summary of their progress would be
given and the tutors would take over, providing help to their
charges. Sarah stayed in camp Thursday nights coaching wherever
needed. A few recruits were ready for advanced subjects and
Liebowitz even arranged for a high school teacher who came in
two nights a week. Harwood panhandled the Grafton School
principal for several more old blackboards and paper and pencils.

Classes commenced and everything seemed to fall into place
nicely until Liebowitz got to Civics and Democracy. When trouble
came it was not from within the classroom, but from the outside.
Rafferty and the Boston toughs had never been interested in
Liebowitz's program, but its popularity and the little Jew's apparent
tepid and easy style was an inviting target for them to exercise
their dwindling power.

As the class developed, Liebowitz had presented a rather benign
and conventional analysis of U.S. government, but had painted
the alleged great benefits to society of capitalism in less than bold
colors. Mention of this to Rafferty started the wheels turning and
before long he had the others thinking that Liebowitz was preaching
socialism. The successful gutter fighter and mob rule tactics of
Boston politics had not been lost on the lad. Questions began
to be asked of Liebowitz in and out of class, but with caution
and skillful parrying, he had deflected their discussion away
from himself back to the topic at hand. When Rafferty saw
that innuendo was not doing its job, he tried the more direct
route of getting a contingent of cronies to sit in the back of the
next class.

Liebowitz was cordial and welcomed them, but was soon
challenged with commotion and uninvited questions.

"I must ask that you not disturb the class, as we have a lot to
cover tonight." Liebowitz began to see the trap and moved to silence
the visitors.

"What, so you can feed them some more of that socialist crap they've been getting?" It was Rafferty.

A heavy silence followed as all eyes went to Liebowitz.

The little Jew's eyes were cold steel as he met Rafferty's and Rafferty blinked before continuing. "This is America and a free country," the handsome youth went on. "We don't like the state telling us what to do, where to go and making off with our hard-earned tax dollars."

The Irish gang clapped, hooted and stamped their feet. "Oh," Liebowitz responded when the din had subsided. He spoke in a calm, even gentle voice that carried throughout the room. "Then tell me if you would what the term "Nazi" means."

Rafferty hesitated, then mumbled something no one could hear.

"Come, come, young man, that literature you and your friends read from Father Coughlin and Camp Siegfried should tell you." A slight gasp went up from the students. "Perhaps you have a friend down there on Long Island who is training to be a Nazi and could help you out." Rafferty's mouth hung open a bit as Liebowitz continued. "Well, since you don't know, I'll tell you. Nazi is short for the National Socialist German Workers' Party, which swept your friend Hitler into power. Now there's a social reformer for you who's managed to beat the tar out of anyone who disagrees with him and to banish those whose pedigree doesn't seem right. As for making off with tax money, I'll leave that explanation to your father. He's in the Massachusetts Senate, I believe?"

Liebowitz hesitated, realizing that he'd way overstepped his bounds. Stunned, Rafferty tried to come back with something, but his voice was weak and whiney. "You're just a lousy Commie," he screeched, but the class now turned on him and his cohorts, hissing and telling them to get out. They left with their tails between their legs and the class resumed. Liebowitz had won a brief skirmish and retained the loyalty of his students, but he knew better than anyone that the war was not over yet.

The next day was Thursday and Liebowitz went to his quarters right after supper. The tutor sessions were going well and Sarah was backing up the learning. He'd thought about his treatment of Rafferty all day, but no one had come near him, least of all any of the Irish toughs. He guessed they were quietly licking their wounds, trying to decide how to regain some of their dignity. As brutal as he'd been, maybe it was a good lesson for both Rafferty and the class.

The knock at the door startled him and he instinctively covered his shoulders with his shirt. He opened the door a crack and saw Harwood standing there.

"We need to talk. I'll meet you in my office in five minutes."

When Liebowitz arrived, Harwood was bent over a report, but he put down the pencil immediately.

"I'll get to the point. Talk has it that you trimmed Rafferty's sails last night over some question about socialism."

Liebowitz assumed the aloof approach. "Who told you that, Captain? There was no disturbance and the class finished as planned."

"Come off it, Liebowitz. You've done pretty well with your program, but I want to know what you are up to. Paul Boisvert told me about it after he'd heard it from one of your students, so I know it's reliable."

Liebowitz nodded in agreement. "All right. We did have some words and I may have embarrassed him, but I think more good was done than harm."

"What I want to know is what sort of politics you're teaching over there." John's ire was rising.

"If you are referring to propaganda, Captain, you've got it very wrong. I was being accused of promoting a socialist doctrine, which I'm not, and I merely made the point that names and labels have a way of being twisted to the user's advantage."

John's eyes narrowed. "Would you care to explain to me how you got that load of buckshot buried in your back? You seem to take great care never to show your backside to anyone, not that we're all that interested, but Hurlburt saw you down at the pond the other day and remarked that your tender hide was the mirror image of an old hunting injury he'd seen. The hunting opportunities must be pretty slim back in Queens!"

The little Jew's mouth went dry, but he never wavered.

"You may as well know," Liebowitz finally said with resignation. "I had a bit of trouble before I came here."

John perked up. "What kind of trouble?"

Liebowitz told everything while Harwood's incredulity ran off the scale.

"So, you are a goddamn Red, I just knew it! How do I get these people?" John said to the wall and sprang out of his chair to pace the floor.

"Do you really want an answer to a question like that?", retorted Liebowitz a bit jubilantly.

Harwood just glared at him.

"Let me tell you Captain. There are lots of people like me, maybe not in your circles, but where I've been, who feel that they've been screwed long enough. This Depression wasn't of their making and now with even the "old money" hurting, the gods of greed are really thirsty. Old money, new money, it doesn't make much difference. Capitalism doesn't work unless someone somewhere is being exploited. The point is to take it out of the hides of those who can least afford it and have no voice to protest."

"So you really want to protect the common folk, eh?" John parried with sarcasm. "I suppose that's why you use down home, apple pie unfortunates like Mother Bloor to do your public events, but pay your party hacks and rabble-rousers from Soviet coffers. I wonder if the protesters Stalin is sending to Siberia or dispatching by firing squad would agree with you. And maybe those lucky collective farmers in the Ukraine living on turnip soup enjoy sending you their cash."

Liebowitz warmed to the fray. He squared his tiny shoulders and threw out his chin, ready to counter whatever Harwood had. John looked him up and down and saw a bantam rooster strutting his stuff, or maybe it was Jimmy Cagney.

"Mother Bloor is a wonderful person who is mature enough to see through the many injustices of our class system and has the courage to speak out against it. She saw the effects of jingoism and propaganda, which sent away and failed to bring back so many young men in the Great War. And for what? To keep the power brokers and their capital right where they wanted to be—in control. And what did they give the rest of us? This Depression we've got didn't start in 1929 with the crash, it was built into the system long ago by you old money people who never figured it would be this bad."

He hesitated, then with a barely discernable smile, exhaled in resignation, letting John fill in the blanks.

Harwood put Liebowitz in the crosshairs and continued in a low voice.

"It seems there are some who would put your own people right at the heart of what you would bring down. I'm talking Jewish bankers here."

He waited for the explosion, but the little Jew retaliated coolly.

"Just what your kind would have us all believe. 'America for Americans', but let's be choosy who fits the bill. And above all be quiet about this. The Father Coughlins and Pastor Smiths will do all the dirty work braying about bogus social justice under the guise of religion while the rest of you sit tight and not so much as raise a finger. Good time to stay on the sidelines while everyone is diverted, rushing to join the fray, blaming and hating the wrong people for society's misfortune. That way you capitalists have a smokescreen to hide under and go right on as before, not worrying about real justice being done or any of those other lofty things like getting bread on the table or medicine for the kids."

In spite of the sophomoric melodrama, he was impressed by the Jew's analysis and composure.

"You're incredibly naive, Liebowitz. Not all people with a little money or property are rouges. Sure, we've got our demagogues, but we don't muzzle them just because they are disagreeable. That's more Uncle Joe Stalin's style. There's not much difference between Hitler, your fascist social reformer, and Stalin, the way I see it. They both want anyone who disagrees to go away and if they don't, a quiet disappearance or trial by kangaroo court will amount to the same thing."

"You may not like the Soviet trials, Captain, but you have to admit that they do identify and punish in a court of law those enemies of the people who would concentrate power and riches to themselves while oppressing the rest."

"Oh, 'enemies of the people', is it? Now there is a good phrase, Liebowitz! That sounds about as holy as the scripture you accuse others of bastardizing. It's been used for centuries to get rid of people just like you! Those forced confessions engineered by your Uncle Joe make it all sound legitimate for the gullible pawns." He crossed his arms and stood for a moment shaking his head in derision.

"When they come looking for you, Liebowitz, what do you think the rest of us are going to look like?"

Liebowitz regarded him with a tilt of the head. "Oh, so that's the problem, Captain. Your image! From what I've seen in this camp, I wouldn't have thought that of you, but I suppose it's part of the job. Never fear. I shall be packed and gone tomorrow. You can report that my services were unsatisfactory. That should cover you. I only ask that you give me enough time to get back to the city."

As Liebowitz turned to go, Harwood came around the edge of the desk and stood in front of the door.

"Liebowitz, I don't give a fiddler's fart for your politics or whatever kind of mischief you may have stirred up in Chicago. That's on your conscience, not mine. What I do here is just a job, not a springboard to glory, and jobs are not what we'd call plentiful here or anywhere. Neither of us can afford to bugger what we've got. I want you to get back in that classroom and do what you've set out to do. Just don't go parading around any of your personal preferences on politics, especially in front of the Irish, for God's sake."

The little Jew's eyes lost their piercing quality and the face softened.

"You're right, of course, Captain. You have my word that what happens in my program will be education, not indoctrination."

John relaxed and a half grin showed. "Then your Chicago story goes no further than this room. But when the authorities show up for your pelt, I won't know who the hell you are!"

For the first time, Liebowitz cracked a smile.

"Then that's settled," John continued. "Now I've got a special assignment for you."

It was Liebowitz's turn to raise an eyebrow.

"We need a newspaper in this camp for lots of reasons, but mostly as entertainment and to keep our recruits from getting bored and into trouble nights and weekends. Rocco, over at the dispensary, has a funny bone and is a quick study while Paul Boisvert sure needs to polish his English. Headed in the right direction, even some of the Irish may surprise us with a phrase or two. I'll find a way to get the equipment you'll need. What say, can you help us out here?" Harwood could see the wheels turning as Liebowitz mulled things over, but he knew the Jew would do it before he so much as opened his mouth.

A make-shift "composing room" was organized in the corner of the library. With the help of his mother, Harwood was able to scrounge an old typewriter and a broken hectograph from Burkett College. Paul and Rocco tinkered with the hectograph for a while and managed to get acceptable blue and white copy. Under Liebowitz's discerning eye, they thought they'd get the first issue out by the middle of October, but Mother Nature had other ideas.

31

A low-pressure trough had hung over western New England for three days squeezing out a steady warm autumn rain. Most forest activity had been curtailed and the sections were assigned to interior camp renovations and preparations for winter. No one had much enthusiasm for these tasks and knew that until the rain let up, most projects were only make-work. September 21 promised to be just as murky and after morning assignments and lunch were done many went to the library to catch up on a little reading or to their bunks for a quick nap.

By two o'clock there was a strange stillness in the air. The rain had stopped, but low clouds pressed in over the pond from a dark mass in the south.

"Looks like we'll get more again later this afternoon," grumbled Walsh as he made his way back to the barracks with Paul. Paul glanced out over the water. His ears felt funny, as if something was pressing to get inside—or out.

"I never seen a day like this. If the air get any heavier we could slice it. Look at that tree. Not a twig moving, but that tumble of cloud out there she boiling in on us."

Walsh grimaced and said, "Once down on the Maine coast I saw a northeaster act like this. All growl and no teeth."

Walsh turned in and almost immediately began snoring. Paul collected his books and went out, heading for the library.

Still no rain, but the sky was packed now with nimbostratus and slowly filling with a lemon light. A strange purple glow hung in the south, then after ten tumultuous minutes gradually lightened up to gray, then yellow. Just as the promise of sun seemed greatest, sudden gusts of wind would bring a scudding rain in low over the trees. Inured by the previous several days' weather, all but Hurlburt remained oblivious to these events.

At about 4 o'clock Hurlburt squished his way up the company street to headquarters. In the orderly room John was bent over his company fitness report. He looked up, glad for the interruption, as Hurlburt stepped inside and removed his army-issue poncho.

"Just thought I'd check that barometer again. Sorry about the drips."

"You're more nervous than a mother cat, Fred," John said good humouredly.

Fred squinted at the instrument for a minute then removed a pad and pencil from his pocket, squinted again and scratched some numbers.

"Look at this, Captain," he said sotto voice. "In the last hour the pressure has dropped nearly an inch. Doesn't do that unless something big is coming in. I can't ever remember seeing that happen before."

"We've had all kinds of crazy weather this summer, Fred. Remember that rain in July when we nearly floated out of here?"

Hurlburt went to the window to view the sky now showing green along the edges of the ridge, then grunted and said, "Have you heard anything on the radio?"

"About an hour ago I picked up Boston and the forecast was for more drizzle and some gusting. Funny, I couldn't get Hartford because of the static."

"Well, let me know if any big news breaks. I'm going to have all the doors and windows secured just to be sure. I don't like the looks of that brassy sky."

Fred left in a violent gust of wind followed by another sudden calm. John stepped out on the veranda and listened. Small gusts flapped the forest edge. Then he heard it, a mighty wind starting as a queer roaring way up in the sky. Gray, almost black clouds rolled in and a deluge burst upon the camp. John hurriedly retreated inside and snapped on the radio.

The sky darkened so quickly that those reading in the library shut their books and lined the windows talking in low tones. The wind grew less erratic and commenced a mournful howl as its power grew. Small saplings swayed nearly to the ground as if great hands were pushing them. The first tree went down behind the infirmary at 4:45 p.m.

Walsh woke up about 15 minutes later and had to relieve himself. Mumbling, he pulled on his trousers and boots and left for the privy. Paul and the others at the library windows saw him charging against the gusts. As he went by, he tossed their amused faces a sour look and entered the outhouse. Several trees along the exposed lakefront blew down with a roar and strips of tar paper peeled off the roofs of barracks B and D like Christmas wrapping. Walsh, perhaps indisposed, spent a long time in the privy. The boys had nearly forgotten about him when a tremendous gust uprooted the nearby maple, its top pushing the outhouse completely over so it landed with its door pressed to the ground. Aghast, someone shouted, "We'd better see if Scooter is O.K." But before they could turn away from the window to help, Walsh had crawled, wild-eyed, out of the bottom of the privy, bare from the waist down. Member flapping in the wind, he dashed for the barracks, misjudged the slippery steps in the blinding rain and rolled in the mud of the company street. In a flash, he was back on his feet and inside the building. Paul and the others were doubled up, weeping from laughter, hardly believing what they had seen.

"I guess old Scooter will think twice before using the crapper again in a thunderstorm," howled Donnelli.

But the others had returned to the window. Four maples crashed down in quick succession, cutting short their mirth. The howling wind began to sound like a passing freight train. Just then the door burst open revealing Hurlburt and Harwood soaked to the gills. John spoke first.

"You fellows get those extra cots stored in the rec hall set up in here immediately. Everyone from Barracks B and D will be sleeping here tonight. This blow is a killer and we may have trees across those buildings by morning. After you're done, go directly to the mess hall and do what you can to keep things dry. You'll be safe riding out the storm there."

"Fred, you have Walsh get a party together and prepare those kerosene lamps for the mess hall." Donnelli smirked at this, but Harwood did not notice and went on. "We're sure to lose power tonight and each sleeping area will need light. Check out the auxiliary generator too, so we can have power for the cooks and their equipment. I'm going to rouse everyone and get them into the mess hall for an early supper while there's still some daylight. I'll see you there."

He ducked out into the gale again, the door very nearly leaving its hinges. Hurlburt eyed the stunned group. "Better get moving. We'll have to give the cooks a hand with supper."

Their meal was finished in silence with the storm showing no signs of abating. The pitch black gloom was broken only by the mess hall lights kept burning by Fred's coaxing of the gas generator.

Harwood rapped for attention.

"You all probably guessed by now that this blow is an errant hurricane. It's not supposed to be in New England and we've no idea how long it well stay around, but since we're fairly safe here, we'll stay put. Assuming it's moving over us, the eye or calm of the storm should be here in an hour or so. Those who bunk in barracks 1 and 2 will spend the night in the library. You go directly to your barracks as the eye passes and pick up what you need, but get back to the library and stay there. When the other half of the blow hits us it will be a repeat of what we have now. By midnight the winds should die down."

A clattering roar cut him short and he looked apprehensively at the cooks, one of whom piped up, "That was the stack of milk cans on the loading dock. Don't stub your toe on them when you go out." This crack generated some smiles and reinforced John's perception that the men were handling things well.

"We'll have one hell of a clean up tomorrow, so get as much sleep as you can," he concluded.

Harwood's assessment was on target. The night passed wildly, but uneventfully and by daybreak the storm, sapped of its vitality, was whimpering off up the St. Lawrence valley. The sun rose clear and bright over Hyde Pond, revealing a colossal tangle of broken and uprooted trees. The usual morning cacophony of bird songs was replaced by an eerie silence.

Long before sunup and reveille nearly everyone was out at sunup surveying the aftermath. Barracks 2 and 3 had taken some hits from flying timber and debris. Limbs and tarpaper roofing were everywhere.

On the way to the mess hall Donnelli nudged Paul. "What do you suppose happened to all the birds last night?"

Paul looked at him askance.

"I really don't know, but they are probably scared shitless and blown to hell and gone." He rather enjoyed using the slang he learned from the work gang.

"I know one that wasn't. After breakfast you and I are going out behind number 4 barracks where I'll show you something. There's a big, weird bird out there in the shrubs with a bum wing. Never saw anything like it. Together we can run it down."

Paul was interested.

"Let's look now and still get back in time for Blantin's poison."

"O.K."

They scuttled to the spot where Donnelli had seen the bird. It lay quietly but in great pain. Its tiny webbed feet mud-caked. The peculiar bill, bent downward at the tip, was bloodied from crashing into heavy timber.

"What the heck do we have here?" mumbled Paul, amazed by the stranger.

"Damned if I know, but let's see if we can get it into an orange crate. After chow we'll give it to Doc Stone. He'll know what to call it."

The professor was very excited by their find. "You've got a frigate bird there, boys." Donnelli began to titter at this near allusion to the copulatory process, but Stone stopped him short with a good natured glare. "The storm must have brought him all the way up from Cape Hatteras. Look at that bill and the forked tail. Yes, I'm sure of it. That's really quite a find up here in Vermont. They're usually miles out in the ocean. The poor thing can't figure out what hit him or how to make those tiny feet work on land. Here, hold the crate while I look at that wing."

Stone examined the bird carefully, getting pecked soundly a number of times. He bent the wing gently forward a few times and exclaimed, "it's not broken, just dislocated. Probably was blown against the wall of the barracks last night. I think the bone is back into the socket now." He stood back and eyed the bird. "Why don't you keep him caged for a few days and feed him up on raw meat scraps? Next week we'll take him out into the pond, release him and see if he can take off without running into something."

"How'll he know how to get back to sea?"

"He may not ever make it, but so long as his wings are strong he has a better than average chance. Men-o-war frigates are used to covering huge distances and riding out foul weather."

Just then the bugle blew so the boys hastily thrust the bird in a tool storage bin and barely made roll call.

True to form, Harwood already had a plan of action for the clean up. He had sent Hurlburt and Walsh down to Grafton as soon as there was light enough to travel. They'd returned at breakfast with a tale of incredible damage. Both of Grafton's bridges had been taken away by high water, effectively isolating the town from outside help. A score or more of downed trees blocked all traffic movement. Miraculously, only four houses had tree damage and no one had been injured in the blow.

When the company formed up on the camp street, Harwood assigned half the group led by Walsh and senior leaders to clear the camp and access roads. The rest he and Hurlburt put on the road to Grafton, equipped with shovels, saws and axes. They skirted dozens of blow-downs that would have to be dispatched on their return.

The townfolk were out surveying their loss and scratching their heads in frustration when the CCC column, one hundred strong with Harwood and Hurlburt at the head, swung smartly into view. Harwood stopped them in front of the library and gave them at ease while he sought out Constable Snow, the head of the selectmen, and Wade the tree warden.

He found them commiserating in the general store, but they brightened perceptibly when John offered them the services of his men. Inside of two hours, most of the town center had been cleared of trees and limbs and some of the larger logs were already being skidded toward the river to make temporary bridges.

At noon, hundreds of sandwiches and gallons of lemonade appeared, the womenfolk and young girls making grateful distribution to the men. The men of Grafton pitched in where they could, but spent considerable amounts of time mumbling to each other, scratching their faces and getting out of the way.

Miss Pyle opened the library for use as a command post during the operation, retiring to her tiny office, busy with the circulation records, but not missing a thing that happened or was said inside or outside. At two o'clock the first vehicle crossed the raging Saxtons River on the makeshift bridge. John and Fred were everywhere directing things, heaving brush into piles and passing words of encouragement. Finally, dog-tired, they returned to the library in late afternoon to assemble the equally tired boys for the hike back to camp. They left as suddenly as they appeared, but not before assembled townspeople gave them a spirited ovation.

As their footsteps and the occasional clink of a shovel blade on wood were swallowed up by distance and the forest, Miss Pyle went to Constable Snow and asked impishly, "And what do you think of the Tree Army now, Horace?" Snow turned to her. His face was a mask, but the ancient chin trembled with emotion.

"I ain't gonna say its good and I ain't gonna say its bad. I just wish Hoover had recruited them fellows instead of that damned Roosevelt." His eyes were twinkling and steady, the splotch of tobacco juice drooling down his chin from the corner of his mouth giving him the appearance of a healthy grasshopper.

The '38 Hurricane in New England caused upwards of 600 deaths, made more than 20,000 people homeless and cost untold millions of dollars in property damage and lost forest resources, effectively rearranging the landscape for years to come. Despite the havoc and the massive new work challenges for Camp Grafton, there remained among the recruits aroused interest in the camp paper. Liebowitz coached Paul to produce grammatically correct articles and encouraged joint pieces with Rocco who had a flair for short, humorous stories. Soon Paul was writing nearly as good copy as Rocco.

The name of the weekly was determined by acclamation and sprung from Scooter Walsh's repeated harrangings of recruits for their resistance to work. "Damn jackass!!" was one of his favorite expletives and Rocco quickly seized on it as the appropriate masthead. After one colorful Walsh dressing down, a Vermont recruit straight off the farm and with a droll sense of humor had whittled a foot high, rough carving of a seated mule with its teeth bared and ears laid back. This icon had a special place in the library where other crafts were displayed. Rocco's sketch of the carving as a graphic for the proposed masthead caught the mood of the entire camp and was a shoo-in. Even Walsh cracked a grin or two, but Harwood, reluctantly, had the name over the sketch toned down a bit to "The Grafton Mule" knowing that the stiff-necks up the chain of command would never permit such high jinks.

32

Sarah drew her scarf up around her ears to fend off a biting November wind as she crossed to the mess hall for a cup of coffee. Sergeant Blantin hailed her when she entered and shuffled to the urn to draw her a mug.

"The regular," she said gratefully and removed her wraps. Mary Grout was reading a paper in the corner alcove where the sun was strongest. When Sarah came over to sit with her, she folded it and put it beneath her handbag.

"Don't stop your paper because of me. I'm surprised that you're still here."

"Usually do get back to town before lunch, but I've been waiting to talk with you."

Sarah was surprised. "Me? Now, what have I done?" She gave a slight shake of the head in amusement.

Mary beamed. "You've done nothing that I wouldn't have done at your age." The two of them had always been close despite Mary's rough-hewn way, a directness that Sarah always found refreshing. As she settled into a wicker chair, she reflected on how much the Vermont veneer was rubbing off on her.

Mary came right to the point. "I know it's none of my business, but I'm concerned about you and the Captain. There's the wife, you know."

Sarah reddened slightly, but kept her eyes level with Mary's and sipped her coffee. Mary laid a huge paw on her arm.

"Oh, don't misunderstand me, please Sarah." It wasn't like her, but Mary was agitated. "What you and he do are no one's concern but yours, regardless what the gossips think or what rumors those pompous asses in town may be spreading." She paused in a long silence and Sarah, with relief thought she was going to change the subject.

"Probably his wife is not so big a problem." Mary spoke slowly and seemed preoccupied with the wind whipping the leafless trees outside the window. "But there's something not free inside the man. I saw that look in France in the Great War." Mary was reaching back, way back. "Never really understood it then," she smiled. "God, I was young and tender. Only partly grasp it now," she continued absently.

Sarah would have sworn that Mary, progeny of tough hill folk, had never been out of the Green Mountains. Her involvement in the war was a big surprise. But then Mary was not one to disclose much of herself.

"Can't imagine me as an Army nurse?" Mary read Sarah's face and laughed. "Well, as a young heifer, I didn't know much, but there I was full of pep and vinegar. Our boys weren't into it yet, but we were rushed right into service backing up the Canadians. Some of those young men had been in the trenches for months. Our work wasn't pretty, as the shelling in our sector was especially bad. Gas, you know. The lucky ones with minor or self-inflicted wounds would come out relieved and smiling, knowing full well they had a ticket home. Blighties, they called them." The crow's feet around Mary's eyes softened.

"But once in a while we'd get a quiet one who had but a single urge, to repair and return to the carnage from whence he came. Poor souls. Rarely talked about anything except duty and getting back to support the lads. They were lying, of course, using smokescreens to hide the emptiness in their hearts, a void so large and terrible that nothing they would ever see or hear again would fill it. The newspapers and politicians called them heroes so they could goad others back to the front. These young men loathed and scorned the war-mongers who mouthed king and country, but were like sheep obeying some superhuman presence found only in the shell holes, barbed wire and mud. It bound their souls in an unholy alliance, a hellish affliction beyond our knowing. After the war, they took this monster home with them, silent but alive, turning over in their guts like a great worm. Many tried to kill it with daring-do, drink or deprivation." Mary's mouth was drawn into a bloodless line.

"Rather than waste away in the rot of self-loathing, some of them faced their ghosts head on. Chance events turned them into zealots and they took on causes which they thought might make humans rise above their animal meanness in another hour of crisis." Mary paused for a moment while Sarah caught her breath, trying to grasp the significance of all she was hearing.

"John is one of those, I'm sure," she began again. The CCC has given him a reason for living and anyone can see that he excels at what he does. Mary swallowed some coffee, then looked steadily at Sarah. "Just don't be disappointed in him, girl. You may never possess him." The words came out with a gentleness Mary seldom revealed.

"But I'm not looking to gain some hold over John or control his life," Sarah returned firmly.

Mary eyed her severely and continued. "We females never do at the start when romance is enough. We mouth care, commitment and sacrifice, but as the ties mount and our souls become exposed, it's only natural to lay as many claims on the body as the traffic will bear. And we want the same from our men. But their love is different. They hedge their bets, figuring that the skirts who get away are the very ones they're most entitled to. Only a precious few have the knack to share right up to the hilt. Most stop somewhere short and when they do, we try our damnedest to bring them along. Something down deep, like birds nesting, comes over us and we become demanding, bitchy and fearful. Fortunately, most men eventually fall into place, however reluctant or ungrateful. Some never do and make our lives pure hell."

Mary watched Sarah's face and knew it was time to quit. There was no anger or resentment, just a stout endurance which did not surprise her. Mary smiled. "Well, I've had my say. How about another cup of Blantin's brew?" Sarah agreed and the rest of their chat progressed as if neither could recall what had been said.

Thanksgiving came and went without incident, but by Christmas Grafton was under a foot of snow. After digging out, most of the recruits took leave for the holidays and some, their enlistments up, were permanently discharged. Sarah finished up her courses at Mass Aggie and returned to Iowa for Christmas with friends. Stone had provided some support for her trip on the condition that, he mischievously added, "she not forget to come back!" In the new year, life at camp slowly returned as new recruits arrived and routines were reestablished.

Harwood pulled fire drill at midnight. Bodies tumbled out of the barracks, nearly all of them incredulous, mumbling their complaints about the bitter cold. And with good reason. The thermometer stood at—15 degrees Fahrenheit. But there was Harwood, stomping about in the frigid air with the rest of them, making sure that every last recruit made muster. Grinning, he waved them back to bed and bade them a good night's sleep.

Paul lay in the dark listening to the squeak of springs and the murmurs of relief of those settling back into the warm nests of their bunks. The wood stove popped and sputtered and soon the voices ceased, replaced by the long drawn, deep breathing. Outside he knew that the temperature was still dropping. Icy fretworks grew on the barracks windows as the fire in the stoves, more slowly now, consumed the heartwood. In another hour, the stove detail would come through to load on more fuel.

Sleep nearly had him when he heard the first dull shudder. It started way over on the far side of Hyde Pond and ran straight for the camp, ending as a muted pop, raising the ice another inch over the dense, cold water. A series of muffled chugs followed, like the sound of stones colliding under water.

Coming awake, Paul crawled slowly out from under the covers and despite the incredible cold coming through the floor, made his way in darkness to the window. Just outside the thermometer read minus 18 degrees Fahrenheit. A tree limb cracked sharply somewhere up on the ridge as he caught sight of a figure standing alone on the company street, head cocked upwards toward the pinpricks of light in the pitch sky. Paul knew it was Harwood, but why was he out there when the entire camp lay asleep? Since the hurricane, he'd noticed that Harwood had kept much more to himself and had more shadows under his eyes from lack of sleep. So what was he doing out in this cold in the wee hours? What could he be thinking? Feet nearly numb from the shins down, Paul couldn't take any more and shifted across to the warmth of the stove, his captain's odd behavior slipping from his mind.

Somewhat thawed, he dove into his bed and fell back towards slumber. He heard the swish of large predator wings just outside the window, then a rabbit's high-pitched death squeal ending abruptly as feathered talons pierced, then crushed air and life away. Paul mumbled a short prayer recognizing what he read as God's plan and squirmed more deeply into his blankets.

Walsh glanced malevolently at the flurries dancing up and down in the eddies around the library windows. They might well have been mating summer midges but for the brutal cold. That winter it snowed and snowed like there was some perverse shortage of moisture not only in Vermont, but all over New England. Walsh hated cold weather and longed for an early spring, not that the mud season pleased him any more. But the elements, although making life in camp a bit less convenient, was no hindrance. Coping was becoming easier for everyone as camp routines were well established and adequate supplies and resources, particularly firewood, had been laid up beforehand.

In their free time, many of the recruits had started skiing, using borrowed gear from families back home or donations from local town folk. A farmer over in Londonderry even rigged up a rope device to allow skiers to climb back up one of his mountain cow pastures hand over hand rather than using the traditional side step or fishtail clamber. In a moment of genius, he hooked the rope to a Model T Ford he'd put up on blocks so that the rope formed a continuous belt between the rear drive wheel of the Ford and a return wheel at the top of the hill. A number of CCC boys had spent several weekends helping with this project, erecting support posts, attaching bogey wheels and the like. It quickly became the place to be for those skilled enough to handle the makeshift tow and the swift descent.

Rafferty quickly mastered both skis and tow and became the chief advocate for the sport. Following his lead, more than a score of recruits were spending all of their free time at Londonderry. Even Johnson, the forester, couldn't resist a good time and convinced Paul to come along. He'd found them some skis back in Amherst and they had glided around camp, swiftly mastering the short slopes. Paul wasn't too keen on mixing with Rafferty's crowd, but knew there was protection in numbers.

After a frigid ride in the back of the Army supply truck, they arrived in Londonderry prepared to do battle with the cow pasture. The Model T chugged away at the foot of the hill as each skier took his turn grasping a large knot on the endless rope. Several fell flat on their faces, unable to achieve the rigid body coordination and control of their skis needed to be whisked up the hill. Amid hoots of laughter, they were cleared away for the more experienced whom, although wobbly, skittered their way up the slope. Rafferty was the smoothest of all and was soon rifling his way down, ending in a swirl of thrown-up snow onto those waiting their turns.

Paul was next up and watched for his knot. He'd been cautioned to ride up only as far as the red flag, then let go. A few of the experienced masters were allowed to go the extra 50 yards to where the tow rope rode up to the return wheel and cycled overhead. To his dismay, Rafferty took the knot immediately behind him. There was no time to drop out, so he grabbed the knot and lurched off, leaning back and keeping his legs firmly planted. The climb was exhilarating and his body quickly adjusted to the challenge. He'd nearly forgotten about Rafferty when he heard the sneering voice behind him.

"Think you'll make it all the way down, Frenchy?"

Paul turned slightly to gauge the distance between them and missed the red flag.

"Let go now, you damned little fool!" came the hated voice again. Paul clung even harder to the rope in both fear and anger.

"I said drop it, right now!" Rafferty was shouting.

Paul glanced up to see the return wheel spinning closer. He tried to let the rope go, but his gloves were frozen to it. He could now hear the squeal of the return wheel as it twisted the cold rope nearly back into itself and shot it backwards down the hill. The rope quivered behind him. Rafferty was coming up hand over hand. Rafferty let go the rope and lunged at Paul, taking him down in a pile of twisting skis, ripping his hands free from the frozen gloves which continued around the wheel, shooting out the other side in four nearly even pieces of frayed fabric. They got untangled and each rose separately, beating off the snow and adjusting their traces. Rafferty said nothing and pushed off down the slope. Paul watched him and followed, executing a competent, if undramatic run.

Only two of Rafferty's cronies had seen what had happened and were muttering among themselves when Paul approached. Paul confronted Rafferty squarely and uttered just two words.

"Merci beaucoup."

"Don't let him use that French blab on you!" retorted the Irish giant beside Rafferty as he took a step toward Paul. Rafferty caught his arm.

"Let him be. Canucks like him don't know any better." "Besides," he added scornfully, "he just had the shit scared out of him. Didn't you, Frenchy?"

Paul remained silent, but his insolent glare lingered on Rafferty's face for a full half minute before he nonchalantly turned his back and pushed off, fully expecting they would pounce on him. But they didn't and he borrowed some gloves and took another turn at the rope as if to prove that mulishness was not the sole province of the Irish.

33

By the end of February, the Vermont mud season was nigh. Days were growing longer, like the icicles hanging off the barracks roofs in the northeast shadows. The chickadees had changed their chuckling to plaintive "pee-wee" calling. Chickarees were coming up from their subnivian chambers to give chase to one another in the forest while other sleepers rolled over for another few winks. The leafless trees were still buttoned up in their dormancy, but Paul knew that the new slant of the sun was calling up their sugary life.

Hurlburt, too, smelled change in the air and suggested to the mess hall cooks that some maple syrup might improve their flapjacks. He needed a project to keep the recruits busy and was sure that up on one of the ridges there must be a sugar bush. It didn't take Paul long to get wind of this and soon he and Fred were sloshing and sliding over the tonsured hill to the rock maples.

The second Monday in March Fred sent Walsh and Paul out with a small crew to begin tapping. By noon they had wooden spiles dripping sap into buckets hung on the south face of three dozen trees. Another contingent of men started building fire trenches in the old gravel pit beyond the orchard. Down in the pit, out of the wind, they built a lean-to for temporary storage and comfort against foul weather. Iron pipes were laid over the fire trenches to support the evaporators, then 55-gallon drums cut in half and their ends removed were positioned on the pipes. Into the drums went steel 10 gallon cans to hold the boiling sap. Three of these units were placed over each fire trench.

Another large crew commenced cutting and hauling the slash and slabs left over from clearing Hyde Swamp. Most of this was pine and spruce capable of generating the hot fire needed for the evaporation. Sugar maple sap is 3% sugar and 97% water. It takes a lot of fire and boiling to reduce the volume 50 times, driving up the sugar to the 66% found in syrup.

By most standards the whole operation was not very efficient. Everything, from the dumping of sap buckets into milk cans on the stone boat transporter, to keeping the fires going all day required hand labor. But that was Hurlburt's strong suit. By mid-week the fires were started and the first sap run was bubbling. At the end of the day a quart of rich, amber syrup was sent to Hurlburt for approval.

Despite the March winds and bitter cold in the early morning, the project became so popular that Walsh and Paul had to restrain their crew from tapping too-small trees and over-extending the supply line. Each night, under the sap moon, the temperature dropped into the high teens, perfect for a continued sap run. But getting in and out of the sugar bush to dump buckets was a challenge as the previous day's melt and heavy snow remaining in the woods made for treacherous footing.

Long before the sap runners made their first morning stumble over the hill, chickadees were at the spiles stoking up on free energy. The arrival and shouts of the haulers scattered them, but in emptying the buckets, the recruits found a gray, speckling scum floating on the sap.

"Damn birds have been shitting in the buckets," growled several of them and this seeming unshakeable logic was soon spreading like gospel. Every time a chickadee came near, it was barraged with snowballs.

Walsh picked up on it first and told them to knock off the horseplay and tend to the buckets. "Just trying to keep the bird turd out of the sap," one of them groused. Walsh gave him a stare somewhere between severity and incredulity. "It's true. Look here," was the yelped defense. Walsh took one look, then brushed a mittened hand over the gray, teeming surface, removing half of the scum and shaking it on the snow. The flotsam soon separated and tiny points began jumping wildly. "Snow fleas," snorted Walsh. "Nothin' to do with birds. Just a bunch of bugs that come out of the ground about this time. Adds a little meat to your syrup." He was grinning now as the recruits licked their lips, remembering the recent breakfast. "When you see 'em this thick, do just what I showed ya. Skim 'em off and keep the sap. We need all the juice we can get."

After three weeks, the maple buds began to pop and Paul shut down the supply, removing the spiles and tapping in wooden pegs to stanch the oozing. They had harvested 40 gallons of syrup and 10 pounds of Indian sugar.

Walsh stamped about in the truck garage, blowing on his fingers and muttering. "No end to this damnable weather. You'd think that winter was coming back, 'cept for the leaves out there. Cussed Vermont. More like Siberia, but at least there they don't have a mud season."

Paul glanced up from his task of replacing spark plugs on the Ford dump trucks. His fingers were clumsy with cold, but he was glad not to have Walsh's job of flushing the radiators. Walsh had on a winter coat, but he was drenched to the elbow.

"We have job done quick, then we go to get cocoa," Paul offered.

"Yeh, I guess so, but that don't keep the cold out for long."

Paul smiled. "These days in May we name after the saints, Mammertias, Pancras and Gervais, the three chilly saints. Help us to remember dat even holy men have bad day. You wait, you see, we have good weather real soon now."

Walsh looked at him quizzically over the hood ornament, but said nothing. Bending, he grasped again for the petcock at the base of the radiator and twisted. Nothing happened. He lay down on one shoulder under the vehicle and tugged again. Around the engine, Paul could see Scooter scowling at the reluctant radiator.

"Cold do not seem to bother Captain Harwood. Last winter I see him out in the middle of the night when cold was killing. Why he stand outside on parade ground by himself and do this?"

Walsh remained silent for so long, sighing and grunting with effort under the truck that Paul thought he had not heard.

"War." came the muffled reply from below. Walsh skittered out from under the chassis to get another pair of pliars and, rising, caught the perplexed look on Paul's face.

"Dirty, damn war! Lots of men come out with all their parts intact, but scrambled eggs inside. Shell-shocked they were. Some of them fellers are spending the rest of their time locked away. Others are just real nervous and don't sleep right." he turned to rummage in the tool box. "I know cause it takes one to know one."

Walsh slid back under with his tool and clamped it on. Suddenly, the valve loosened and rusty water and anti-freeze shot into his face and down his neck. Walsh rolled out from under the truck with an agility that surprised Paul. His accompanying howl made Paul's ears red.

"God damn good for nothing whore mother!!!!" He threw the set of pliers clear across the garage where they fell beneath a storage bin.

Paul busied himself over the engine while Walsh stripped off his coat and wiped his face with a soiled towel. Then he went looking for his pliers as Paul finished up and put his own tools away.

"We go for cocoa now?"

"Sure," said Walsh, putting his pliers in the box and throwing down the towel. He couldn't suppress a wisp of a smile as he muttered, "Lucky for you them damn chilly saints."

They were interrupted by the throaty hum of a vehicle coming up the camp road. Paul knew at once it was the Harley and gave a whoop before bolting to headquarters, leaving Walsh with his mouth open. McGarry had returned.

34

It had been a glorious summer day full of bright sun, dry air and blobs of cloud making infrequent tack across an immaculate blue sky. Near sunset McGarry prepared for the final sortie to finish spraying the test plots laid out by the bug crews according to Stone's plan. Even the mild breeze began to die down as the loading crew pumped the viscous mixture of Paris Green and fish oil into the DeHaviland's holding tanks. When topped off, the crew withdrew and Walsh spun the propeller. The Canuck fired almost immediately and McGarry urged it to a healthy, full-throated purr, then gave Walsh the thumb's up signal and adjusted his flight helmet. The biplane lumbered effortlessly down the field to the end of the runway. McGarry revved the engine preparatory to take off. It had never sounded better. The windsock on the control shack was completely limp. McGarry glanced at the perfect sky, then opened the throttle. He was airborne a little more than halfway down the runway, the big engine in full voice, its propeller snatching great swathes of sunset. The crew cheered and waved as McGarry roared over their heads scarcely twenty feet up, climbing rapidly. He cleared the tree line at the west end of the runway by a comfortable margin and continued climbing a bit slower, putting the biplane into the first turn. At two thousand feet, McGarry leveled off and began to search for the test plot by dead reckoning. Proceeding east with the sun at his back he spotted the bright panels marking the hillside and banked slightly to align himself for the spray run. He cut the engine's revolutions and dove until the altimeter read five hundred feet as the foliage rose to meet him, the occasional fir poking up like a stiletto at his silver bird. He would do a dry run over the marked area to check air speed and handling, then return to apply the insecticide. Well into the run, he noted for the first time the panel marking the end of the plot. It was accurately placed, but beyond was a granite cliff falling off several hundred feet to a ravine. The other side of the ravine rose sharply again before leveling out at approximately the same height as the test plot. He would have to be sure to maintain altitude throughout the application and remember to start his climb directly over the marker. He made another dry run to test this procedure. Directly on the marker he gunned the engine and pulled back on the stick. Effortlessly, the Canuck lifted him and the tanks of spray up over the ravine and cliffs.

"If she can do it that easy with full tanks, there's no question about doing it with reduced weight," he said to himself as he banked around once more.

Coming in at twenty-five feet above the canopy, he snapped open the valves precisely above the starting marker. Insecticide and fish oil spewed outward and behind from a dozen cannulas, evenly coating the foliage. At the end of the run he snapped the valves closed, gunned the engine and pulled back on the stick.

He felt a small shudder, almost imperceptible at first. Chalking it up to an errant local turbulence from the ravine, McGarry poured on full throttle. The Canuck responded as before and hurtled skyward. Out of habit he checked the instrument panel. Nothing was amiss, but God, how the fish oil stunk.

Four runs later he was turning for the last time when again he noticed the alien shudder. McGarry checked the gauge showing insecticide level in the tanks. Hurlburt had calibrated the system well. There was just enough for the final run which would complete Stone's experiment. From here on in it would be up to the bug teams to collect data on the effects of the lead arsenate. That hesitation would have to be the shifting liquids in the tanks. Still, he kept an experienced ear tuned to the DeHaviland's growl. Never sounded healthier. He was halfway through the last run when the whole airplane shook violently from nose to tail, as though it were a rabbit seized by a terrier. The engine emitted a loud pop and McGarry's head beat against the padded lip of the open cockpit, his view temporarily blurred. Cruising at quarter power so close to the canopy, he had few options, but seized upon what he could. Quickly jabbing shut the tank valves; he reduced drag caused by the spray dispersal. He must gain altitude and very quickly, but what would the Canuck do under acceleration? Despite the vibration, the plane continued on a straight course and with great difficulty McGarry kept control. He had to get away from the trees, even if it meant losing some control and getting further beaten about by the vibrations. His windscreen was becoming smeared with oil that was oozing back from the wounded engine and scattered by the slipstream. Slowly, he opened the throttle and for a time, though in great labor, the craft responded. He pulled back on the wobbling stick and gained ten, maybe twenty feet. The end marker was coming up rapidly. He crossed it and shot out over the ravine, nose slightly up, still gaining height. Suddenly the fight went out of the engine and died completely. The eerie silence after the hellish noise and shaking surprised him, but he was too good a pilot to be stunned inactive. With no power, he had to decide whether momentum alone would carry him over the cliffs. He knew he was losing altitude rapidly and peered out around the useless windscreen to check his position. Nothing but green stilettos, yet over to the left a bit was a grassy bald on the edge of a ravine. "God, it'll be tight, but maybe," he said in near panic while easing back a notch in the stick. For a second the pale glow of the sunset swung into view over the top of the cliff. Then he realized that the bald was too short. Best now to stall or to slip sideways in hope of reducing airspeed to minimum when impact occurs. It was a near perfect stall, and the biplane plunked down almost gingerly in the center of the grassy postage stamp. But centrifugal force set in motion the remaining fluids in the tanks causing the DeHaviland first to totter, then throwing it onto its back into the boulders at the bottom of the ravine.

The impact stunned McGarry and when he came to he was aware of the crushing dead weight of the craft on his right side pinning him fast. He could see light above him through the open cockpit although leaves were mashed against his cheek. His right arm was useless, broken he knew in several places. Yet he could move his head and left arm and to his amazement, his left leg, which was dangling outside of the crumbled fuselage. "At least the patched leg is O.K.," he chuckled. The fish oil smelled rank, and then he heard the gurgle of petrol and the hiss as it splashed on the hot engine. A small funnel of smoke curled over him and he was gripped by fear. "Oh God, not by fire," were his last words as the DeHaviland ignited like a torch.

35

Walsh heard it first, the stuttering engine, then the silence and became agitated. Then, as the silence continued, he was near frenzy as he grabbed the phone and called Hurlburt at the camp. In less than twenty minutes Hurlburt pulled in with a camp truck and cobbled together a search team. Walsh made sure that Paul stayed behind to man the phone and communicate with Harwood should he arrive back at the camp. The team, including Rocco who might be needed for emergency aid, lumbered off to the test area, hoping to encounter a spotter who probably had a fix on where McGarry went down. It took about an hour to reach the ravine and one look told them to forget the charred remains and concentrate on burning brush now spreading outward from the smoldering wreck.

Harwood signed the papers for the removal of what was left of McGarry's body and handed them to the mortician's agent. There would be no services. The funeral director would notify the next of kin and publish the obituary. As the agent's car rolled down the company street towards Grafton and civilization, John snapped off the lamp on his desk, leaned back and closed his eyes. No denial of Pel's demise was going to ease this pain. He got up, fumbled in his pocket for the key and went to the whiskey cabinet. The first glass of Scotch went down like a hairball, but the second and third were smoother as he stood in the dark staring at nothing.

"To you, Pel." He said out loud, raising his fourth tumbler to the chair where McGarry always sat. Then he grabbed two bottles and went to his room, locking the door behind him.

The morning fog above the meadow was soft, fragile and deceiving. With the Boche on the run at last, Lieutenant Harwood led his platoon carefully across the open ground. Advancing like this was unthinkable only weeks before, but whole areas of the German front were now collapsing and the Americans were stunned to find that some parts of France were just like the picture books the Army had provided as propaganda. After months in the Brueghel trench landscapes, this was a sudden Eden. There were occasional shell holes among the fall flowers, but this sector had always been quiet.

Harwood was euphoric, but the quiet gave him a mild case of nerves. He had no choices; his orders were clear. Take the ridge just beyond the wood line he could now see across the meadow. Actually the ridge was a mere hummock, much smaller than his map indicated, but the land dropped sharply away on the far side, giving the holder of the high ground a solid defensive position. The meadow stretched on before the platoon, the fog making the flanks appear open and endless, the objective even closer than it really was.

The first chatter of machine gun fire on the right confirmed Harwood's worst dread—his men on open ground in an enemy pocket. He yelled one command, "Down," before another chatter started on the left. The fog swirled among them as the uncanny quiet returned. "Perhaps no one was hit," he hoped as his mind raced. But the silent lull was like that of a child who falls hard while playing and is stunned voiceless, yet within a minute regains enough air to scream like a banshee. The wretched wail of several wounded gave him his answer. Harwood knew that this would be the cue for the German gunners. Only the blessed fog was their ally now and he mustn't panic.

"Into the shell holes," he barked, just as the gunners, perfectly interlocked with carefully laid fields of fire, crisscrossed the meadow with their lethal seed. Most of the men reached the shallow safety of the craters, dragging with them their wounded buddies. Harwood and his platoon sergeant shared an irregular dimple in the earth with about a third of the platoon. German lead soon began to concentrate on the moans and cries out of the fog and in short order only those in the shell holes were audible. A few men fired back at the chatter, hoping to kill or at least scatter the gunners, but it soon became clear that this drew ever more accurate fire onto their positions. They lay in the terribly shallow depression, which probably had resulted from two simultaneous airbursts of their own artillery.

Harwood watched the fog swirl and the sun get brighter. It would soon burn off their only protection. The men knew this too, and were digging furiously with anything they had to pile up even a little mound of protection around them. Panic was in their eyes and Harwood, although he could do nothing, must keep them calm.

"Keep digging," he ordered. Doing anything, no matter how futile, would help stave off thoughts of the inevitable. Harwood counted his men and quickly checked the wounded. Several were already dead and a number of the wounded would never last to receive medical treatment.

"These men," Harwood said, touching the dead, "push them up to the edge."

The men balked, preferring not to hear.

"C'mon, move," he shouted harshly. "These lads will have to help save us. There's no protection here no matter how we dig once that fog goes.

Reluctantly, they pushed the bodies of their comrades up to the lip of the crater. A stray shot took the platoon sergeant in the back, tearing a grisly opening where it exited his chest. Harwood slid over to the unconscious man and tried to stanch the flow of blood. He felt the fluttery pulse, then grabbed hold a vacant-eyed corporal, saying "Help me hoist him up."

"But, sir," the corporal whimpered, "he's still living."

"Unless we put him up there, everybody in this hole will be dead!" Harwood yelled frantically, fire in his eyes.

They pushed the sergeant on top of the other dead just in time as a hail of shot ripped through the corpses and the wounded man, splashing hot blood and brains over those hunkering for their lives inches away.

"Oh, God," cried a man nearby, crazed with fear. He stood up and ran for the wood line, but got only forty feet from the crater when he was cut nearly in half by the German grim reaper. Harwood rose to a crouch, yelling, "No, come back!"

Walsh held Harwood's shoulders and glared at Liebowitz. "Help me hold him! This is going to be a big one," he said softly. Liebowitz was white. He had heard enough to last him a lifetime. He grabbed Harwood's sweaty legs and hugged them tight.

John woke to birdcalls. He opened his eyes only a slit and could tell that the sun was low in the west by the angle of rays filtering around the drawn window shade. He stirred and immediately squeezed out the light by clasping his hands over his forehead. The pain was terrific.

"You O.K., sir?" The quiet voice came from the doorway. Raising on an elbow, Harwood tried the eyes once again, finally coming to focus on Walsh standing beside the door which hung partly off the hinges, smashed and askew.

"What are you doing here?" John asked in a hoarse, hushed whisper.

"Just making sure you are all right. You had a bad time of it," he said gently.

"That door. What the hell happened to the door?" John managed.

"That's where Liebowitz came through. It took two of us to get in here."

"Oh, sure," Harwood sighed, uncomprehending. He laid back and felt his body juices trying to catch up. He grew nauseous and thought for a moment he would heave, but the crises subsided and he just moaned.

"Now, just stay put, Captain. You've been shot at and missed, shit at and hit. You're in no shape to move anything. I'll stay right here til you've got hold of yourself. No one comes into headquarters today with Liebowitz out front deflecting visitors. Most everybody thinks you're away from camp for a few days and no one but the two of us knows you're here in bed. Tomorrow or next day you'll feel more like yourself."

"Did . . . did I talk and carry on like a damn fool, Walsh?" Harwood groaned.

"You said nothing we already didn't know," he lied.

"Besides, ain't nobody but Liebowitz and me ever going to know what you said."

Liebowitz brought in some supper, but Harwood just grunted and faced the wall. They both managed, however, to get some water into Harwood.

"Not too much," cautioned Walsh, "or he'll start going through it again. Just enough to keep him from drying up like a year-old cow turd." By sunset, Harwood had sunk into a deep, undisturbed sleep and Walsh knew that the crisis had passed.

"Go to bed, Liebowitz. You were up most of the night with him. I'll stay down in the office in case he needs help." Walsh checked on Harwood every half-hour the whole night. To busy himself, he took off the remains of the door and threw them out behind the building. Taking care to keep the desk light low, he nodded off from time to time, but never once forgot Harwood. Towards morning, just as the sun came up, he pulled the blanket over Harwood and went to his own barracks.

John felt wretched, but he knew he'd better be out for reveille. His mouth tasted of copper and standing was a major accomplishment. Liebowitz came out of his quarters and gave him a silent once-over.

"Don't say it, Liebowitz. Just let me wash up and get the right clothes on for the ceremony." With the little Jew's help he managed to put on an acceptable appearance for the assembled camp. Despite an incredible head, he was hungry and went to breakfast. He returned to his office and acted as if it were another regular day. Hurlburt came by later and, without a word, replaced the door. As he was packing up his tools, John looked up from the report he was completing.

"Thanks, Fred. Sorry to be a bother to you, but it won't happen again."

Hurlburt grinned. "Good to have you back with us, Captain."

It took a while, but Father Mercier, still harboring reservations about the aviator's lifestyle, was finally convinced by Paul and Rocco to lead a memorial service for McGarry at the camp. It was a bland and mercifully brief afternoon prayer service with nearly everyone squeezed into the sweltering recreational building to hear short eulogies by Rocco and Liebowitz followed by a moment of silence. Professor Stone, his voice quaking a bit, spoke fondly of his work with the aviator. Walsh, Hurlburt, and Sarah were there in the front row along with Gladys from Springfield, dabbing her eyes now and then. Harwood had quietly left for Burkett right after breakfast, not to return to camp until well after dark.

Stone and Sarah went to the headquarters building after the service where Liebowitz and Hurlburt arranged to have lemonade brought in. No one commented on Harwood's absence, but Sarah left him a message expressing concern at having missed him. She never did get an answer, but learned later that John had paid all expenses for his friend's burial and had sent a donation to Father Mercier for his services.

36

"Has Hurlburt given you that lumber order yet?" Harwood asked.

"Yeh, he give me that this morning." Paul responded only slightly fracturing the English. Since coming to camp two years before and working with Sarah and Liebowitz, his conversation had markedly improved.

"I need to pick up some mail at the Bellows Falls post office, so let me ride with you. When are you leaving?"

"About a half-hour, I'll be ready."

John tossed the mailbag and several packages into the cab of the Ford flat-body and he and Paul drove down to the lumberyard near the banks of the Connecticut.

While Paul took care of the paper work in the office, Harwood made a turn around the wood yard, noting the variety of the building materials. The freshly cut lumber smelled clean and resinous. At the end of the yard a small sawmill was doing custom work, the blade periodically whining its lament. Rounding the corner of a woodshed, he almost ran into men stacking two by fours. One of them, tall, bearded and slack-mouthed, looked a lot better than when he'd been carried off to the hospital several years prior. Bush recognized Harwood at once and a half-sneer, half-smile crossed his face. John nodded and stepped out of their way. But as he continued walking, Bush dropped his end of a pile of studs and announced loudly, "We can knock off for a bit now, boys. The Army is here."

Harwood ignored the sarcasm.

"You need some help finding lumber, soldier? Maybe we can fix you CCC boys up." He called to Harwood's back, chuckling.

John turned to answer and saw Bush and his crew loitering, not about to lift a finger.

"I'll wait. There'll be a truck out here soon and a man with an order."

Bush raised his eyebrows in mock astonishment. "Oh, you got men out there in Grafton? Well, that's news. I thought they was seasonal campers."

The men guffawed at this and Bush looked like he had eaten a canary.

Harwood smiled and turned towards the sound of the sawmill. He hadn't gone ten paces when he heard an ear-splitting crack next to his right shoulder and saw his service cap skittering its way into the dust. He flinched and instinctively dropped to all fours, his heart pounding. Turning, he saw Bush rolling up a nasty looking bullwhip. His cronies were covering their mouths, barely holding back the laughter.

John picked up his cap, dusted it off and strode right back to the loiterers. Two men stood aside, but Bush held his ground.

"You handle that tickler pretty well, Bush, but it seems every time we meet you've got a big mouth so long as lots of fellows are behind you. Too bad it cost you your jaw last time."

"Listen you," Bush growled, his face reddening, "nobody makes a fool out of me for nothin."

Harwood's face was passive, but his eyes bored right through the big man's facade and careless bravado. "No one has to, Bush. You do a fine job on your own."

Bush made a fist and raised the whip over his head just as the ton and a half came around the corner of the woodshed. The men had to move out of the way and this broke up the confrontation. Paul had seen some of the encounter and emerged from the cab a bit puzzled by the frayed tempers, looking first at Harwood then at Bush fingering the whip.

"Looks like you finally have some legitimate work, Bush." Harwood said evenly and turned away toward Paul. Bush threw down the whip and grabbed the work order, barking out commands to his cronies.

Paul kept a sharp eye on the lumber being loaded and complained when Bush tried to palm off some inferior stock. Bush gave him a severe look, but Paul leaped onto the truck bed and told the men to take away the knotty, twisted studs, pointing out the fine print of the work order. Bush glowered, but had no recourse. It was Harwood's turn to stifle his amusement.

As they pulled away from the lumberyard, Paul asked why the bearded one was so obnoxious. He wanted to relate his encounter with the poachers on Johnnycake Hill, but decided to hold his tongue.

"Pettiness." Harwood responded, rather off handedly. "Before you joined us, he used to work at the camp and got into trouble. I discharged him, but he still has a chip on his shoulder. Nothing to worry about."

Paul wasn't convinced by Harwood's sang-froid, but remained silent as John dismounted and went into the post office. Returning with mail in hand, Harwood shuffled the envelopes absently as Paul headed up the main street towards camp.

"Stop here and let me grab a paper." John instructed as they passed the corner newsstand.

Harwood stared at the bottom block on the front page in disbelief. "HITLER AND STALIN SIGN COMMERCIAL TREATY." He fumbled in his pocket for change while glancing at the date—August 20, 1939.

Back in the truck, he read the short article from beginning to end, oblivious to Paul's presence. He searched the entire paper for more information or editorial comment. Finding none, he whistled through his teeth, sat back and said nothing the whole way to camp. Paul knew it was not the time to ask questions. The Captain would tell him more in due course.

They drove into camp just before Retreat. Harwood went directly to headquarters and chucked the paper on his desk. Liebowitz, who was freshening up for supper in the adjutant's office, came out to ask Harwood for some shaving cream.

"Be my guest." John responded reaching into his drawer and laid a jar on the desktop. "And you might as well read this now rather than later. I can't imagine that when we get more details either of us will have much to crow about." He thrust the folded paper, bottom block up, into Liebowitz's hand and watched the color drain from the small man's face, the disbelief widen his eyes.

Harwood grabbed for his cap, lips meeting evenly as he shook his head and went out the door to join the assembled men.

On August 23, the full impact of the Hitler-Stalin Non-Aggression Pact became known. Within a week, Nazi Panzers were pouring across the Polish border and Europe was at war.

37

Paul left the mess hall and strolled down the camp road as was his custom just before supper. The truck bringing in the forest crews would return in a half hour and he might try to hitch a ride back with one of his friends who was on driver duty. The cooks didn't mind his late afternoon break for he always finished his kitchen chores way ahead of schedule. This permitted them a little extra time for a smoke and talk out on the loading platform.

A short way out, Paul left the road and took to a narrow trail. After crossing the brook flowing from Hyde Pond he doubled back and ascended a rocky knoll sparsely clad with hemlocks. From here he could see a stretch of the highway leading to Chester. The brook splashed down through a steep and narrow glen, noisy even in this dry season of the year. Several lower cobbled ridges made the water snake east slightly, but eventually it would fall away to Saxton's River.

He found a seat on a blowdown and retrieved the stub of a Lucky Strike from his shirt pocket. A persistent breeze blew out his first two matches, so he turned towards the glen, shielding his last match. The butt caught and Paul drew strongly on his bit of fire, letting his eyes focus on the small copse a quarter mile down the dingle. A spot of color attracted his attention, then disappeared into the understory. Someone was moving along the old tote road towards the brook. Then on the other side of the ridge, he saw a Model A parked beneath some big maples. A careful driver could traverse the tote road from the highway to the glen by auto. Many of the recruits used this route as a shorter hike to camp after getting a lift back from Chester on Saturday nights.

His curiosity was whetted, but as it was none of his business, Paul continued to draw slowly on his cigarette in the late afternoon sun. Presently, Rafferty emerged from behind a rock and bent over the brook to wet his hair. Paul snubbed his smoke and slid swiftly behind the blow down to avoid being seen by his archenemy. Fortunately, Rafferty was too busy preening himself. Carrie Bush soon joined Rafferty at the edge of the stream where they lingered, chatting, their words muffled by the gushing cataracts. Rafferty drew Carrie close in a rather ruthless bear hug, disengaged her with equal roughness and leaping from rock to rock across the stream, disappeared up the trail to camp without so much as a backwards glance.

Paul breathed a sigh of relief and watched Carrie stand wistfully by the glen for a moment, then turn and walk towards the maples where the Ford was hidden. Paul snuffed out his butt, scattering the contents and was about to return to camp himself when he noticed another car parked away off on the shoulder of the Chester highway. Old, rusty and looking abused, Paul had the feeling it had been there some time. But few cars passed this way on late afternoons in mid-week and Paul gave it no other thought as he scrambled down the ridge and bushwhacked due north to Hyde Pond to purposely avoid Rafferty. When he hit the access road he double-timed it up to the mess hall.

Carrie never made it to the Ford. Her assailant was waiting beneath the maples. Weeping openly through bitten and bloodied lips, he grabbed her from behind and with one angry stroke, the deer knife flashed up and pierced her heart. Only he heard her brief, stifled scream. Withdrawing the knife, he kissed her unresponsive and cooling lips, ran drunkenly to the old car on the highway and sped away.

The mess hall was quiet that night. Long hours of scouting and salvaging hurricane timber had taken the starch out of the boys who where now glad to be putting away whole flocks of fried chicken. A quick shower and early bed was the goal of most who knew that tomorrow meant more of the same work. Paul sat with Rocco and avoided Rafferty who seemed in unusually good spirits, but refrained from rousing his cronies with characteristic sarcasm or innuendo.

Halfway through desert, Liebowitz and Harwood came in the side door and stopped at the enlisted men's table. Harwood looked positively haggard as Blantin pounded the table for attention. The little Communist walked behind Harwood to the center of the mess hall. A glance at Liebowitz's scowling face told them that something serious was afoot and the pieces of blueberry pie stopped moving from plate to mouth. The heavy silence was broken only by the clang of a dropped fork as Harwood told them how Liebowitz had found Carrie's body in the woods. The police were now investigating and everyone would remain in camp until further notice. Paul's eyes were on Rafferty whose face transformed from stunned disbelief to twisted rage. He nearly rose off his bench leaning menacingly toward Liebowitz.

Like everyone else, Paul was overwhelmed by the murder. After K.P. he returned to his barracks and stretched out fully clothed on his bunk thinking back over the tryst between Rafferty and Carrie. He hated the Irishman, but knew he was innocent. A third person had been waiting in the forest and it wasn't Liebowitz, who had no motive. He barely knew the girl and was not the type to lust after gentile lasses. No, the communist was too idealistic and wary to get involved, even briefly, with Carrie. Then, he realized with a start, that should his late afternoon walk come to light, as surely it must, Paul himself would be a suspect. His mind sharpened by this vulnerability, he began to analyze events more diligently. Could Rafferty have doubled back? He doubted it, as Paul had spotted him on the baseball diamond immediately after his own return. No, he wouldn't have had time. Who could get to the Model A and back without being spotted by Rafferty, Liebowitz or himself? He tussled with these thoughts as darkness fell. Then, his heart skipped a beat a second time as he recalled the rusty car parked on Route 35. Whoever was in it might have been trailing Carrie's Ford, then followed her up the tote road. Paul swung his feet to the floor and walked out of the barracks into the dark towards Harwood's office knowing that the Captain was the only one who could piece this thing together.

He waited in the reception area outside of Harwood's office and watched Constable Snow leave, then rapped on the door.

"C'mon in," said Harwood wearily. Paul stepped in and was surprised to see Liebowitz there.

"What have you got to say, Paul?" Harwood was impatient. He noted Paul's discomfort and furtive looks in Liebowitz's direction.

"Mr. Liebowitz is with me because of the investigation going on. No one is above suspicion until the police get to the bottom of this awful thing. Besides, Rafferty and his cronies have threatened him."

Paul's eyes widened as he shook his head. "Neither of them killed that woman," he declared in even tones.

Both Liebowitz and Harwood were stunned by Paul's report. Harwood kept insisting, "Are you sure of what you saw, Paul?"

When Paul had finished, Harwood tucked his hands behind his head and stared at the ceiling. Liebowitz continued to stare incredulously at the boy.

"O.K., dammit," John said suddenly. "Let's go out there. Liebowitz, you tell Sargeant Blantin that he's in charge for a while. And then go to bed in the adjutant's office with the door locked."

He grabbed a 5-cell flashlight from his desk drawer and they went out.

Paul jumped into Harwood's car and they made the circuit around Grafton's hills, up Route 35 to the end of tote road. Harwood stopped on the macadam, leaving the engine running and lights on. He took a second flashlight from the glove compartment, gave it to Paul, and the two of them crossed the road to the shoulder where Paul had seen the car. There were many marks going in and out of the tote road made by the police and the ambulance which finally took Carrie away, but the roadside above and below was undisturbed. Spreading out, each of them worked the shoulders. Paul headed north trying to get a perspective of where the car had been parked. He was ready to give up and join Harwood when he noticed the weeds crushed in two parallel lines. Tire tracks. He signaled Harwood who came up and the two of them followed the track back along the side of the road. The grass between the tracks was unbent, but Harwood spotted a patch of oil indicating that a car had rested there for a period of time. Paul could feel the hairs on his neck raise slightly as he realized that the killer might have stood right where they were.

"We can't see much more tonight. Perhaps in the morning we'll get Constable Snow back up here for a look."

They were about to cross the road when Paul spotted the bloodstained rag. Tiny and molded tightly, it lay partially buried under some ferns. Harwood carefully placed it in a box in the trunk of the Ford, exclaiming, "This will prove Liebowitz's innocence if it's Carrie's blood. I'll see that Snow gets it to the state police lab first thing in the morning."

Driving back to camp, Harwood asked Paul to describe the car again and afterwards shook his head in frustration saying, "There are probably dozens of old heaps like that which leak oil. Finding it and the owner will be next to impossible."

38

As is often the case, trouble begets trouble, but this time it came from an unexpected quarter. One evening, three days after the murder, John was alone in his office writing up his monthly material accountability report. All day he had successfully fended off reporters who infiltrated the camp from every direction trying to get a new slant on the killing. Harwood was dog-tired, but drove himself to finish his report despite the hot, sticky nightfall. Only the occasional twitch of the curtain in the open window presaged change. The smell of rain was in the air. John heard the purr of a Chevy motor as it came up the company street and stopped on the dark side of the officers' quarters. He finished his page, then, exasperated by both the interruption and the lack of a knock on the door, stormed out of his office, crossed the reception area and reached for the outside knob.

"At least this stringer has decided to come in the front door," John mumbled to himself. No matter, he would have to get rid of him as unceremoniously as the others. Harwood flung open the door to confront Bush standing on the dimly lit stoop wearing a menacing grin. A little way off in the dark stood two other figures.

"Hullo, Captain," Bush spat out quietly. "You got someone here we want."

John didn't move a muscle, but felt his neck hairs prickle at the edge of his undershirt. The Sam Browne belt with revolver and holster was hanging on the peg back in his office. He realized he was snared as the smile rapidly disappeared from Bush's face.

"We know Liebowitz is in that there other office where the light is. Me and these other boys want to take him for a little ride."

"You're crazy, Bush. Liebowitz is innocent and so are all the boys in this camp. Neither you nor anyone else is going to touch

Liebowitz while he's confined to quarters. In due time it will be established that he had nothing to do with the girl's death."

"Don't get in my way, soldier boy," Bush's voice rose harshly. In his hand a blunt-nosed police revolver appeared. "That girl was my brother's flesh. Just because he's too broke up about losing her and the kid she were carrying to come get that Yid in there don't mean he's going to go free. In these parts, kinship means a lot and no anti-Christ is going to get away with what he did." The revolver moved slightly in Bush's hand as he motioned for John to open the adjutant's door and turn Liebowitz over. Seeing no choice and deciding against any nonsense like raising an alarm, John did as he was told.

Liebowitz came out when John called and froze when he saw Bush with the pistol. They were trapped and Bush knew just what he was doing.

"You and the Captain are going for a ride with us." Bush had returned to his quiet tone and the grin split his slightly misshapen face once more. "Just act natural and if we see anyone on the way out, soldier boy here will give the password and get us through."

Harwood and the Jew looked at one another helplessly. John turned toward his office saying, "I'd better get the rest of my uniform."

"Don't bother," Bush snapped. "Just get out to the car, both of you and we'll be off." The two anonymous Vermonters now stepped into the room and gave Bush the high sign that he should hurry up.

Paul had struggled through his history reading in a corner of the mess hall. The other students working on high school courses had called it a day and were preparing for bed over in A barracks. He finished making notes of the events leading to the Mexican War and decided to go to the officers' quarters to type them out. Planning to return in a few minutes, he left his books and did not turn out the single light hovering over the corner table. Paper in hand, he strolled out the mess hall door and across the reviewing area towards Harwood's office. By the flagpole, he paused, feeling with relief the breeze on his face, then noticed the car with only parking lights on turning off the company street towards the officers' quarters. The car stopped in shadow, and a tall figure emerged. Paul recognized trouble as the man moved furtively from one window to another and his gut twitched as Bush crossed into the patch of light coming from Liebowitz's window.

Soundlessly as a cat, Paul crossed the dark square and put some trees between himself and headquarters. If there was time, he must get around to Harwood's window and let John know of Bush's strange visit. But before he could make the warning, Bush was inside. Not sure of what to do next, Paul carefully pressed himself to the building and inched his way to the corner. Fortunately, the night was black as pitch and someone even a few feet away would not have noticed Paul peering at the two Vermonters on the stoop. Retreating quickly back from the corner, Paul returned to John's open window, hitched himself noiselessly onto the sill and swung his feet into the room. He pressed his ear to the door which John had left slightly ajar and heard Bush's demands. Then he saw Harwood's Sam Browne belt on the peg.

Harwood and Liebowitz walked towards the Chevy in front of Bush. One of Bush's cronies ran ahead to open the door while the other went around to start the engine. As the three of them crossed the same light patch where Paul had first recognized Bush, the light went out on the stoop and Paul, Harwood's revolver in hand, told Bush to freeze where he was or have his back blown out.

"He's got a gun, Paul," John warned quickly.

"Then, throw it into that patch of light where you're standing, Mr. Bush." Turning, Bush blurted out, "Who the hell . . . ," but never finished the sentence as the Smith and Wesson barked twice, squirming in Paul's hand like something wild straining to be free. Bush caught both slugs and spun past both Harwood and Liebowitz onto the hood of the Chevy. He clung there a moment, then, dead weight, slid down and lay on the fender curve like a bagged deer.

Harwood relieved Paul of his revolver and brandished it through the window of the Chevy only inches from the man frantically trying to start the car. Bush's other henchman froze, his back to the unopened door. Liebowitz, meanwhile, turned to Bush, who was still grasping the blunt-nose, shook it loose and checked the man's vital signs. He was bleeding heavily, but his pulse struggled on and the breathing, though shallow, was regular. Liebowitz ran quickly to telephone the hospital for a doctor. Lights came on and the cooks swarmed over from the back of the mess hall. One had a powerful flashlight and after assessing Bush's condition it was decided to move him onto the loggia to await the ambulance from Bellows Falls. There they slowed Bush's blood loss, but could do nothing for the internal bleeding which was quickly changing his complexion to a sickly gray.

Harwood knew what he had to do next. For the second time in a week he called the State Police and old constable Snow. As he placed the black earpiece back into its cradle, he couldn't suppress the twitch in his hand.

The two would-be kidnappers sat horrified next to Bush's prostrate form, the camp cooks keeping a watchful eye on them as two troopers and the ambulance arrived. While the police took testimony, the doctor examined Bush thoroughly and guessed that one bullet had gone through a lung and grazed the ribs, but had exited rather harmlessly, tearing away a sizeable piece of flesh just above Bush's hip. He would have to perform surgery right away in Bellows Falls hospital for the second slug, check for other internal damage and remove any shrapnel and cloth fragments. With minimal infection and luck, he thought Bush would survive.

The troopers put handcuffs on Paul and sat him in their vehicle. When Snow arrived, they filled him in on the details and arranged for Paul's incarceration in Newfane. Snow was hopping mad. He paced in front of Bush's now-meek cronies, shaking his finger and chewing tobacco violently.

"I told that dumb son-of-a-bitch to stay away from here and you two horse's asses stood right behind him and heard me. Who the hell do you think you are, Ethan Allen's Green Mountain Boys?" After a withering glare, he added, "Yup, cut out of the same cloth, I expect, but with only half the brains." He spat a terrific load of tobacco juice onto the floor right in front of them, the ricochet spattering their trousers.

"Now get on your feet and into my sedan. You're going to spend some time with the Canuck down in Newfane, out of harm's way until the legal system decides what to do with you."

Before driving off, he turned to Harwood. "I'll send a man over tomorrow to pick up Bush's car." Then in hushed tones, but with feeling, he added. "I sure don't envy you and that Canuck lad. It's bad enough for you these piss-ants want the kike's neck over that tart, Carrie. If the court does indict Liebowitz and find him guilty, these Vermonters may accept it, but they'll never forget what happened here tonight. They'll never forgive the shooting of one of their own, worthless though he may be."

John looked away with no response. He shook Snow's hand and thanked him for taking care of things, then turning, headed for his office. He felt very old and extremely tired. Snow got into his car and watched Harwood go up the steps, noticing for the first time the sagging shoulders.

"God," he mused, "the man's been worn out by all this nonsense."

Then, turning to his passengers, he snarled, "You two horse turds better enjoy your ride down country. It'll be your last for a while." He gunned the motor and took off down the company street.

39

Father Mercier recited his evening breviary in the privacy of his study just as he had done for years untold. Canonical hours were always his time of recuperation from the tedium and scramble of administering his parish and the unrelenting responsibility of saving souls. He moved his lips silently through the ancient rite, slaking his thirst for distance and peace.

The telephone rang, but he chose to ignore it. Yet, a cloud of irritation crept across the bucolic landscape of his encounter with the Lord. Again it rang, and again. He would be patient. The caller would soon tire and ring off as had happened before when parishioners had forgotten his routine. But this caller was different, as Father Mercier had concluded by the tenth bell. He reached for the receiver.

"Allo," he answered rather gruffly. It was Constable Snow. Less than a minute into the conversation, Father Mercier sat down in the hard-back chair at his desk, all thoughts of the breviary long gone.

"Who did the boy, shoot?" Snow's hesitation and refusal to be forthcoming troubled the priest.

"Well, you might as well know now as later," Snow finally said. "It's Cy Bush."

Father Mercier ran his hand through the few strands of hair he had left, and uttered in a whisper, "Holy Mother of God."

"Look, we both know that Bush is the boy's father, but I'm sure the lad has no idea. This wasn't anything premeditated and was probably an accident, although the circumstances don't look very good. That fool Bush should have never been out at that camp looking for trouble."

"Will Bush live?" the priest asked breathlessly.

"That's hard to say. Right now he's getting all the help the doctors can give."

Father Mercier's mind raced wildly, yet his single focus was on the future of Paul.

"I must talk with the boy right away."

Father Mercier made the trip to Newfane in record time, the old Plymouth belching oil smoke as never before. Snow had the boy brought to his office, then left them alone. While Paul was relieved to see his former mentor and felt better after they had prayed together, he refused to buy the priest's suggestion that his involvement was an accident.

"But Father, that man was going to harm Captain Harwood and Mr. Liebowitz," Paul declared, his voice rising.

"Yes, yes, my son, you had nothing but good intentions to help, but the weapon must have slipped in the upset of the moment, don't you think?"

Paul looked the old priest in the eye. "I intended to pull the trigger, Father, and would do it again to protect Captain Harwood." His coolness took the priest aback and he decided to try another approach.

"Your Grandmere doesn't know where you are or what has happened, but tomorrow, I will bring her here and you can talk. Things will be better then."

"Please don't tell her or bring her. She will know soon enough, but right now I don't want her upset. Constable Snow is good to me and I know that he and Captain Harwood will find a way to return me to camp. Then we can tell her when things are better."

The old man looked at Paul and suddenly realized how much he had changed. While still very naive, the boy had grown far beyond the parish confines and his influence. Recognizing the inevitable, he suffered pangs of sadness for his star pupil and his own loss of influence.

"All right, Paul. But remember that I am ready to help in any way. Tomorrow will be better, God willing. Now join me in prayer to our Holy Mother."

After the priest had left, Paul lay on the prison cot and shut his eyes very tightly, thinking about the bizarre happenings, stunned that the kaleidoscope of his life had changed so abruptly.

Late that evening, the Constable sat in his cramped corner office looking out at Newfane Common. He was edgy and an old injury made his back ache. He'd put many a felon away in the lock-ups across the hall and had seen more ne'er-do-wells go to the state penitentiary than he'd care to count. But knowing what he did about this shooting, Paul Boisvert was not resting easily on his mind.

He got up, went to the cells and looked in. Bush's boys sat on their bunks cowering in the dim light, watching for an opening to bully or con the old man. The door at the end was Paul's cell, but the boy did not acknowledge his presence and continued to stare out the small barred window, his back to Snow. The old man had seen this type before—young, angry and self-righteous. He actually preferred these to the manipulators and whiners, but this one was different. Snow developed the deep-down feeling that the boy was miles away and that no prison in the world would rehabilitate him.

He went back to the front desk and told the jailer to keep an eye on the prisoners. He was going home to bed. As he stepped outside, heat lightning split the sky and he hesitated in the heavy, humid air. He cranked up the engine, but knew that bed would wait. Even at this hour, Miss Pyle would let him in. She always did when he needed to talk. And he had a lot to get off his chest.

40

The murder and violence at Camp Grafton galvanized 1st Army Headquarters into action in record time. The day after the story hit the Boston papers a board of inquiry was appointed whose first task was to relieve Harwood of his command. The board had not even met when the officer in charge had the order cut, effective immediately. Dr. Porcini and the young lieutenant in Headquarters personnel came to Harwood's defense, but were outgunned by the Commanding General himself. The lieutenant later learned that Major Butler, back in Boston after two years of distinguished service as field inspector, was advising the board.

The story refused to die when Bush's friends circulated rumors that CCC recruits were being armed. That was enough for the general. He closed the camp almost overnight. All recruits and civilians were to be sent home or transferred elsewhere, leaving a small cadre of Army personnel to keep an eye on camp property until it could be disposed of through government channels.

Harwood, now without authority, remained at camp headquarters until the discharges and transfers were completed. Everyone knew his diminished status, but carried on as if nothing had changed. More confusion was added when no new replacement officer was appointed. The top brass had removed Grafton with the stroke of a pen then forgot about it. War in Europe was fast overshadowing anything in Vermont.

John woke to the hiss of a light September rain and following usual routine, prepared for reveille only to remember that it was no longer required. He sat down at his desk in his shirtsleeves to put some records in order when a knock at the door stirred him. As Hurlburt and Walsh walked in, he gave them the eye.

"Up a bit early, aren't you? With this place closing down, you must have better things to do."

"Put your tunic on, Captain," Hurlburt ordered. "There's a crowd out here wants to see you."

When he stepped out onto the loggia, the whole company was on the parade ground in dress uniform, at attention in the misty rain. No reveille, no bugler, just spruce green clad figures waiting silently. He removed his cap and walked among them, making eye contact with every recruit, but saying nothing, the rain on his face. When he had done every row, he returned to stand in front, facing them. He had no appropriate words. As if on signal, Rocco stepped forward and handed him a foot high figure. It was the Grafton Mule's mascot, the rough maple jackass carving done by the Vermont recruit, earlier discharged.

"From the company for you, sir." He hesitated, then added, "And it's not a donkey, despite what you may say!"

A ripple of laughter ran through the ranks and changed to applause as Harwood's perplexed frown shifted into a smile and he held the statue high for all to see.

"At ease, everyone. You'll get no speeches from me, but thank you all and may the best of fortune be yours wherever you go from here. Now let's get out of these wet uniforms and this damned Vermont mist. The cooks have got a hot breakfast waiting for us."

But they refused to move and snapped to attention the best they knew how. Harwood took their salute as the rain intensified.

John packed his leather suitcase and duffle bag, absently thinking how he had arrived in Bellows Falls with the same luggage three years before. The camp was now nearly deserted. Sergeant Blantin was over in the mess hall with the skeleton crew left to police the area preparatory to closing.

"A good time to be going. No fanfares or farewells," he thought to himself as he tidied up the desk for the movers. Still he did not hurry and found himself looking out across the reviewing area, as was often his habit at sundown. He shook his head and pulled down the shade.

After throwing his belongings in the Ford, he took a turn around the little rock garden Sarah had planted. The myrtle and herbs were doing well and the columbine and coltsfoot violets clung bravely to the scant soil. The pasture rose she had given him last spring had budded anew and within a week would bloom one more time. He made a mental note to have the next commander's boys prune it and heel it in for the winter. Then, remembering there would be no one to do it, bent and pinched as best he could all but the single bud and scraped some soil and leaf litter up around it with his boot.

As the sun slipped behind the hill, he ambled down the access road to the earthen dam and felt the evening breeze off the pond lave over him. The pangs of recalling his first meeting with Sarah hit him like a brick. By the overflow, he lay on his belly and drank the cool water, letting it run over his face and down his neck. The brook ran away to the meadow where timothy grew high and strong, undulating in the early evening wind. Maples on the ridges across the valley were showing scarlet. Those in the swale were already ablaze. He savored the peace and tranquility, yet was swept away by the awareness of being utterly alone. He lay on his back and watched low, slate-like clouds crowding in from the west, soon to wink out the faint diamonds trying to punch through at the eastern horizon. Surges of emotion wrestled in his brain, peaks and troughs of joy and sadness wrenching his gut, knotting his throat. It was always the same when he really let go. But this time was different. His hand gripped the Smith and Wesson and slid it out of its holster. How easy it was to make the grand gesture.

Sarah drove north into the dusk. She had tried to give John plenty of space since McGarry's accident, gathering only bits of information from Professor Stone on how he was coping with the debacle at Camp Grafton. Hurlburt and Walsh had been discharged, Walsh going to stay at the Belchertown camp until he could find another job. Screwing up her courage, she had called Mary Grout to learn more and had been told of the camp retirement. It was Mary's urging that put her on the road.

Hyde Pond had become gray silk, reflecting the on-coming storm. Ripples out in the deep reminded Harwood of Sarah's best and only dress. He squeezed his eyes momentarily, thinking "Sarah! How long since we have seen each other." But that too had come to naught. A common merganser, unaware of Harwood's presence, set out boldly from the near reeds, her arrowhead cleavage of the rumpled surface pointing out her destination, a pine-arched cove on the far shore. Small gusts twisted her wake, ballooning the north angle and scattering the south until, in time, the entire track was erased by tiny drumlins of dark water.

The pond suddenly became still. Even the old gangly-headed pine across the way had ceased its sway. Harwood watched the bird until she was no more than a speck while tears of release flowed copiously onto his tunic and Sam Browne belt. In disgust, he replaced the revolver in the holster telling himself, "We sure as hell don't need any more blood in this place." Later he made his way back to camp surprised by how cool the pond air was on his wet cheeks.

He slammed the headquarters door shut for the last time, then dropped in on Blantin for a brief farewell. By the time he re-crossed the parade ground it was pitch dark. His key was not even in the Ford's ignition when he knew that he was not the sole occupant of the car.

41

"Sarah, what are you doing here?", he managed to whisper hoarsely.

"John, since Pel's horrible accident you've done your best to avoid me. And now with the camp closing and all that, you're making a fast getaway. Did you really expect that I would let you depart without a word?"

"My mind is made up, Sarah. I've botched things here and it's time to move on."

"That's just an excuse for the wounded ego behind that damned shell you grow around yourself," she said angrily.

"What do you expect me to do," he shot back. "Tell you lies about getting a steady position somewhere and building a rosy future? You don't need that kind of bullshit and hassle from anyone."

"Don't talk to me about hassle," she continued coldly. "You haven't even looked for something else, John. With your ability, you could manage most anything if you'd put your heart in it."

"It seems I've tried my hand at quite a few things," he said carelessly.

"That was only because of, of . . . . ," she couldn't find the words. "It had nothing to do with your ability."

"For God's sake, Sarah, I'm a damned loner who seems to do best out here in the woods where no one else can interfere . . . and I even bungled that."

There was a silence, then Sarah began again, softly this time. "What happened here was pure chance and some nefarious troublemakers. You're not a bungler, John, just too hard on yourself. There wasn't a man in this camp who wouldn't have followed you to the ends of the earth, if need be. The government had to cover itself by relieving you of command, but anyone who counts knows that the way Boston headquarters did it was an arbitrary decision. You've got to accept that it was political and be done with it."

"Politics or just being in the wrong place at the wrong time matters little. The fact is I'm out of a job. You and I both know that Butler will see to it that I don't get another real soon. I just need a bit of time to think over what to do next. That's why I'm going to the summer place on Lake Saint Catherine for a while."

"You really want to run off to a new adventure, don't you?" Her voice was soft, yet like steel and John winced. "You can't face yourself unless you are completely self-sufficient. You never confide and really fear being owned by me, by anyone. You wear this like some badge of honor. Not open on your chest where everyone can see it and beware, but inside, hidden where only you can warm at its cold, cold light. If we part, will you find another who will understand and love you just the same?" She was wanting and demanding words from him for a thin skeleton of reason, however brittle.

But John had no response to reassure her. He gripped the steering wheel and touched his clenched hands with his forehead.

"Oh," she keened softly to the dark. "I worry so about you and what you'll become."

The heavy silence between them was broken by an owl's call up behind the cistern.

"You may as well start the car, John, because I'm going to Lake Saint Catherine with you." He knew by the tone of her voice that she would have it no other way.

They covered the fifty-odd miles of backroads in less than two hours, stopping only in Manchester for groceries and ice. Theirs was the only vehicle going north at this hour and the katydids were calling loudly among the mists on the lake road leading to the Harwood retreat. John pulled up next to the cottage, killed the engine and snapped off the lights. It was pitch black. The vista toward the lake framed by its thick canopy of hardwoods was curtained in with fog, obscuring the few pale lights on the distant shore. Only the sounds of the insects pierced the silence as they sat unspeaking in the Ford, neither wishing to break nature's tempo.

Huge drops of dew, sounding like acorns, plinked irregularly on the Ford's metal roof. John shifted slightly in his seat and Sarah, thinking he was about to open the door, laid her hand on his, murmuring, "Stay for a moment more. We need to remember this."

He pressed her hand gently to his lips, then to his cheek for a long moment. Disengaging, he reached in the back for his flashlight, stowed it in his pocket and left the car. She joined him as he ascended the cottage steps and fumbled with the padlock, trying several keys before succeeding. Throwing open the door, they were greeted by the close, oppressive atmosphere of disuse within. He groped for the lantern near the hearth, lit a match and held it to the wick. The soft light spread over the old furniture he used to climb on as a child. Nothing had changed. His father never permitted additions or new arrangements and, after the funeral, his mother could not bring herself to alter anything. In fact, the cottage had been rarely inhabited since that summer in 1930 when the Harwoods had last been together. John shuddered anew with the glacial emptiness that seemed like permafrost in him now. He quickly found some kindling in the wood box and soon had several small licks of flame going.

Sarah stood silently in the doorway, watching him.

"Come sit here by the fire," he said, "while I get some bigger wood, then we'll have something to eat." When he returned from the woodshed, she was on her hands and knees, coaxing the fire. Sparks of desire started their ancient semaphore within him, but he quashed them with forced resignation, knowing in the same instant that whatever the future had in store for them, neither would find it easy.

The little handful of fire greedily consumed the pine slabs he brought and quickly dispelled the dankness and gloom. They basked in the growing warmth until it became nearly uncomfortable, then John banked the hearth level with well-seasoned maple and oak. He found a spider in the kitchen and heated up beans and franks. They ate this simple fare in silence, Sarah not finishing her small portion. She offered to clean up, but John forbade it and washed all their utensils himself in a roasting pan of water heated over the fire.

"How long will you stay here, John?" she asked finally. "About a week, maybe less. Canada can't seem to make up her mind about joining Britain, but it won't be very long."

He grasped her hand and, noticing that it was cold, threw his jacket around her shoulders, his arm lingering around her for a time. But he did not draw her near and after a little while he got up, apologizing for the cottage's lack of amenities.

42

Father Mercier got another call from Snow who got right to the point.

"In serious cases like this, bail is usually set pretty high, but under the circumstances I'm willing to release him into your custody. We've done this before with other of your boys who have gotten into trouble and you've done me the service of keeping them out of sight and the news off the front pages of the paper. I'm really sticking my neck out on this one, but I think if anyone can talk sense to the boy, it's you. Meet me at the Newfane jail in an hour."

Paul slumped in the passenger side of the Plymouth, mute and seeing nothing, as the priest drove them back to the rectory in Springfield. Father Mercier was a model of self-control, but his inner turmoil had left him speechless. Perhaps after Grandmother Boisvert joined them in the safety of the rectory parlor, the words would come, but this fear for her was as great as for Paul. Her reaction to the shooting, like his, was sure to provoke anguish and perhaps even hysteria. He silently consulted the Lord and his secret prayers were answered when they arrived at the rectory and found that she had retired early. He ushered Paul into the kitchen and offered him food which, to his surprise, Paul consumed ravenously. While Paul ate, the priest tried to find words to explain the conditions that he and Snow had struck. Paul said nothing, but after he'd finished a glass of milk, he fixed his eyes on Father Mercier.

"How could Constable Snow let me come here?"

"It is not an unusual arrangement, Paul, with young persons of our heritage who find themselves at odds with the law. The offices and sanctuary of the Church are always here to help."

"But my shooting that man Bush was more than a minor offense. And should he die, there can be no chance of me staying here."

Father Mercier was visibly taken aback by the boy's coolness and logic.

"That may be true, but we must wait. Constable Snow tells me that his wounds are not too serious," the priest lied, trying to lend some comfort. Long years of counseling had allowed him to use small untruths for a greater good. He caught Paul's eye and continued.

"Besides, you had no intent to inflict harm. You were trying to prevent a foolish and terrible thing from happening when the pistol went off accidentally. There will be no . . . ."

Father Mercier saw the youthful face turn dark, the jaw set tight, the hands clench as his protege cut him off.

"But that is not true," Paul spat out, his voice rising. "I hate that man so much. He is truly evil. I wanted him dead!"

"Now, now, Paul, you don't mean that. You are very excited and upset." Father Mercier did his best to curb the black anger he saw and his own anxiety as well, but neither was working.

"You'll have some sleep and tomorrow will be better. You must let go this anger. Come, we'll go to the church and pray together. God will see your plight and come to you."

"Who is this Mr. Bush? Why does he seem to be everywhere doing things to cause harm to Captain Harwood's camp . . . to me?" Paul's voice was tight with emotion, his eyes showing the shine of tears.

His grandmother's arms came around him and he sobbed openly. She had heard everything, but refused to let anything show beyond the hurt she felt for Paul. She saw the confusion in the priest's eyes as she held her grandson ever closer.

"Grandmere, will you tell me about that ugly man? Who is he and why does he go about wrecking things?" Paul managed.

Grandmother Boisvert again caught the priest's eye and saw his panic as he began to shake his head and raise his fists to his breast. But she ignored him.

"Paul", she began slowly, "Cyrus Bush is your father. Someday you had to learn this and it is better here than from others. Your mother left you with us because she felt that there would be nothing but trouble if she stayed anywhere near him. And she knew we would give you what she could not. We forgave her in time and you must, too. As for Mr. Bush, he wanted little beyond his animal passions and, to his credit, has never scorned you or us. He kept his distance . . . until now."

Paul hugged the old woman as he had done countless times, then held his head, covering his eyes and rubbing out the tears.

"Why did you wait so long to tell me?" Paul asked quietly after he had regained his composure.

The priest came over to him and laid a kindly hand on his arm. "Do not question so. Your grandmother and grandfather, dear departed, have given you so much of their life and love."

"That is very true, Father, but had I known, all this might have been avoided. I truly do not wish that man dead, but I hate him with all that's in me and would smile to see him beaten and trampled if ever we should meet again."

Paul crossed his arms in smoldering anger and raised his chin in defiance. The priest then realized that there was more than just youthful bravado here. He recalled something from more than eighteen years before when the boy's mother had called him to task for his lack of compassion and courage.

"And isn't there something in Canon Law about candidates for holy orders to ensure that those marred by serious sin and legal flaws are disqualified?" Paul continued, "If my father dies, it will be very hard to explain away what I have done. All that I have prepared for is now in doubt. What is there left for me but to do as my mother did?"

"Don't be so hard on yourself, Paul," Father Mercier counseled. "The fate of Cyrus Bush is not settled. There are dispensations available in cases like this and I will help you as I always have . . . ," he trailed off, his voice becoming unsure and less than convincing.

Paul confronted him. "You will, I'm sure. For all you've done I'm truly grateful, but those decisions will take a long time and will likely be out of your hands. And how can I stay here where everyone knows whose son I am?"

"We must not forget to trust Jesus, our Lord. He will give us the strength when we need it." Father Mercier was straining to get his confidence back. "Now let us all go to the sanctuary and pray together for peace of mind, Cyrus Bush's health and the souls of all who are troubled by these events."

Paul glanced at his grandmother. Her head was bowed and her shoulders looked as if she were holding up the world. She arose and meekly followed the priest across to the darkened church. He did the same, his feet responding to old habits. Inside, the many votive candles glowed in their glass enclosures. Despite the gloom, they each knew the way and quietly took their places at the altar rail. For a long time, Paul studied the perpetual flame on the altar. Then as the priest silently mouthed his requests and adoration and Grandmother Boisvert, with eyes closed, fingered her rosary, Paul rose and left. The closing of the door caused the tiny flicks of votive flame to jump and gutter. Father Mercier squeezed his eyes tight and laid his forehead on the rail, but neither kneeler followed the boy.

Paul made a telephone call to the Grafton Camp and learned that Harwood had left for Lake Saint Catherine. He emerged from the rectory only minutes later with a few belongings, but hesitated, looking over at the church. They were still at prayer, but he knew they would not emerge until he had gone. There would be the denials and manufactured stories of his whereabouts, then the search, but with luck, he would be in Canada by then. A breeze had sprung up, washing through the maples behind the rectory, the same trees he had climbed as a child and in whose shade he had lain beneath as Father Mercier had taught him the wisdom of the Church. There was less than a full moon, but clouds were closing in, darkening, pushed by the wind, now brisk and chilly from the south. Rain soon. He raised his collar up around his ears, took a deep breath and turned into the wind, crossing the silent street before disappearing into the dark lane that would take him west cross-country to the Green Mountains and the lakes. He never once looked back.

43

"I'll fill the roaster so you can have a warm wash. I'm going down to the lake."

She shrugged slightly and suddenly realized how exhausted she was. John leveled the coals once more and put on the pan. He rummaged in a closet and found towels, an old feather bed and pillow which he placed on the table.

"In the dresser you'll find a nightgown. You have the choice of the big bed in my parents' room or one of the cots. There are extra blankets in the cedar chest. I'll say good night now," he finished, throwing a towel over his shoulder and scooping up the bedding.

She opened her mouth to protest, but he cut her short.

"I want you to lock the door when I leave. The keys are there on the mantle. I'll be in the gazebo."

With that, he snapped on his torch and left. She watched the door close and heard him getting his toilet kit from the car. She stared dully at the dying embers for a time, then went to the mantle and fingered the keys. In a sudden pique of anger, she raced to the door, locked it and threw the keys into the far corner of the room.

Cooler air was coming in. She heard the wind rising ever so slightly and the tapping of twigs on the side of the cottage. Sleep was out of the question and she knew that lying alone in John's parent's big bed was a mockery of her turmoil. She remembered her conversation with Mary Grout and began to think that coming here with John was a foolish mistake. She rose and found the keys. Stepping onto the veranda, she was surprised at how the fog had been whisked away, how bright the stars. Down the path to the lake on a small promontory stood the gazebo, dimly outlined, the water beyond lapping at the shore. For a long time she sat in the glider. Finally, shivering from the fresh drafts rounding the corner of the porch, she made her way carefully down the path towards the gazebo.

"I'm awake," he uttered, sensing her presence.

"John, come up to the cottage. It's getting much too cold for you here."

Harwood shifted in the feather bed laid out on the gazebo floor. She was standing in a corner looking out over the lake. The catch in her voice told him that she was trembling. The ill-fitting nightgown did nothing to dampen his overwhelming desire as his arms went around her waist and his body pressed against her posterior. She leaned back her head on his shoulder.

"Oh, John, be easy with me," she murmured as they sank down to the feather bed.

And he was. All the cares and frustrations of the years, all the women he had known, even Hazel, simply vanished in the slow, warm tumble of the feather bed. He played her body in three-quarter time, like a Chopin waltz and when he entered her she was more than ready. Savoring her cries of bliss, he felt her release as she pulled him even closer. His climax, seconds later, burst a dam inside him and he was carried on the torrent far away to some unreal place that only he and Sarah inhabited. When they caught their breath, they went at it again, more slowly, but with no less zeal. Later, locked together, they drifted off to sleep that nothing would or could disturb.

She woke first. The steely gray light of early dawn was seeping into the gazebo. She was lying partly on him and could feel his vibrant organ between her legs. Lake waves powered by a stiff northwest breeze over the three-mile fetch of water were now crashing on the dock down the hill. Sometime during the night rain had blown into the gazebo, soaking a corner of their feather bed. He stirred slightly as she caressed his eyes and lips, then opened his eyes and smiled, sending thunderbolts through her as he wiggled closer and held her fast.

"If you keep that up, I'll be sore for weeks," she cooed, clasping him hungrily.

"Weeks, months, how about years?" he said carelessly.

"Oh, now that's a new tack for the famous commander. I thought you were about to go adventuring." She chided with delight and veiled irony, back to her old bantering self.

"Yes, I suppose you're right. I'd quite forgotten about that." He kissed her eyes and breasts and raised his eyes to hers, still smiling, then turned over on his back so that she might sit astride.

"Oh, God," she thought as euphoria and pure pleasure swept her away, "let this never end."

Harwood prepared breakfast in a light mood. She had never seen him so spontaneous. She hung the feather bed on the clothesline out back and drank in the fresh morning air. When the bacon and eggs were ready, he called to her, but when she failed to appear he went around to find her bent over, cutting flowers from the long swatch of garden, which stretched nearly to the gazebo. He leaned against the cottage rather taken aback at how perfectly she fit into the Harwood locale, as if she had always been a part of it. He marveled at the way she seemed to notice every growing thing, straightening a leggy tangle of blooms here, dispatching a weed there. Upon spying him, she turned and came up the path, cradling a small bouquet, her face radiant.

"This is such a lovely place, John. I'll bet the garden was your mother's favorite," she smiled perceptively. "It just gets inside me and makes me wish I had been here those summers years ago," she continued a little sadly.

The wind blew her hair and her eyes shone as he took her in his arms and held her gently. She was so happy and for all the painful memories the cottage held for him, he felt just as she did now that she was here.

They went in to eat and Sarah set the bouquet in a small vase between them on the table. They said little during the meal, silently noticing the minute behaviors, which endeared them to each other as lovers have done since time can be remembered.

They were both surprised at how easily they returned to their love-making in the big bed, like a long-married pair, adroitly responding to one another, ending in a blessed nap before the sun was overhead. As Sarah drifted off, locked in John's arms, she heard the far-off chimes of a bell, sweet and clear, yet passing into silence. The thought danced across her mind and was gone.

Later that afternoon they found the canoe in the boathouse and paddled northward not far from shore exploring tiny inlets. The water was warm and flat and protected from the wind. As the sun slipped away behind the Adirondacks, mist appeared hovering over the water.

"Better we get back before dark," John announced simply. She could not see his face, but nodded approvingly as they glided through the twilight calm. A waning moon rose pale in the east.

That evening, they sat close in the glider on the cottage porch. The night was crisp so they huddled under the featherbed in the dark, the moon's light no challenge for the stars. Orion's lopsided rectangle stood out like a beacon, the jeweled belt aglimmer. Talking quietly of their long ago lives, avoiding the future, enjoying the now familiar touch and warmth of the other's body, the near monastic quiet was broken only by the chilled call of a katydid. They needed no lantern to return to the big bed where they slept like little children.

John rose first and made the fire, then set about putting together a breakfast. Sarah got up and after stretching like a cat, sidled up to him at the stove for a squeeze. They clung together, the warmth seeping between them and were about to sit down for coffee when John spotted Paul coming down the cottage road. Harwood met him by the car as he stumbled into the yard.

"You're telling me that you walked here from Father Mercier's rectory?" John asked in disbelief, but knowing that Paul was not one to fabricate.

"Got a short hitch-ride, but mostly I walk. Glad to find you, Captain Harwood." Paul breathed a sigh of relief and sat down on the running board of the Ford.

"C'mon in, you're in need of some breakfast."

Paul brightened at the prospect and rose smiling just as Sarah stepped out on the porch. Looking first at Sarah, then at Harwood, his face darkened.

"No, no. I keep going. Sooner I get to Canada, the better."

As he turned, Harwood caught him by the shoulder and Paul nearly lost his balance from exhaustion.

"Hell, no you don't!" Harwood barked. Now get in there where Sarah and I can get some grub into you. You need to tell us more about how come you're not still in the Newfane lock-up."

Paul ravenously devoured everything that was put before him, then told them about his release to Father Mercier and the hike over the spine of the Green Mountains. Sarah only listened and tried to make the boy comfortable, but Harwood's brain had pretty much sketched out the near future before Paul had finished his story.

"O.K. Right now I want you to go into the next room and get some sleep before you drop in your tracks. When you get up we'll talk some more."

His belly bloated and barely able to crawl into a pair of Harwood's pajamas, Paul was asleep as soon as he hit the pillow.

Sarah and John walked down to the lake and watched the clouds gathering in the west. He dabbled his hand in the water among yellowed leaves, early drops, victims of the recent storm. She knew from his silence that he had changed.

Her voice seemed not her own when she broke into his isolation with calm analysis. "You've made up your mind and are on your way to Canada, aren't you? Paul provides a good excuse. And in no time you'll both be with the Canadian Army as it falls in line behind Britain. They'll be needing every experienced officer and recruit they can lay their hands on."

Then, in tones coming from her very core, "But why go, dearest, when it is none of your affair and when the things you do so well at are crying to be set right here at home?"

"This war will be ours soon enough," he responded quietly.

She grasped his hands and confronted him. "Doesn't being with me mean anything to you?"

He looked away out at the lake for a while, then he turned to her, still holding one of her hands and brushed the honeyed hair, caressing the delicate strands on her neck.

"Yes, you are all of life to me, for I love, you, Sarah Chapman," he said slowly. "The good nature and generous heart that was sorely left out of me makes you so wonderfully complete." He hesitated. "But I fear that a year with me would start to corrode all that you are and leave us both dry husks". He smiled ruefully. "My grandmother used to say of me that I burned like a brick of peat, all smoky and charred, throwing out a flame or two only when the flue was open. Lost souls give grudgingly and can offer little more than a cheerless, guttering hearth. But then she never dreamed that you would be the oxygen. Nor did I."

She opened her mouth to protest, but he embraced her, burying his face in her hair. In the tiny cell of silence she could feel his tension mounting, the muscles on his back tightening.

"Oh, yes, Sarah, you are truly all the fire a man would cherish. Had fate but given us our chance back when."

She shook her head and tried to draw free, but he held her fast. "I'm so afraid of what comes next, but I can't avoid this grinding debt that's been run up these past twenty years." Then, with a slight moan, he continued. "All that was decided so long ago. I am so sorry. I won't ask you to forgive me, but please try to keep these wonderful few days here special."

She said nothing more, but held him close for a long, long time and looked out across the lake, searching for the light, for the bell of yesterday. But there was nothing, only the smack of small waves among the floating leaves. Mary Grout had been right. She thought of the foggy evening at another lake, now seemingly so long ago and began to hum softly an old love song. He could feel the vibrations with his lips pressed on her throat. The only other sound was the dry shifting of sand in the leaves beneath their slowly dancing feet.

By late afternoon they were ready to depart. Paul at first insisted that he go on alone, but Harwood's plan won him over. They would take the twilight run of the Champlain excursion steamer moored at Whitehall, New York about a dozen miles from the cottage. Using the Granville road, they would be out of Vermont in minutes, counting on the Vermont State Police to limit their search for Paul to the main roads. This would prove to be easier than they knew for Father Mercier had not yet informed Constable Snow of Paul's flight. This tactic had worked more than once in assuring that Father Mercier's charges would reach Canada safely. If Snow ever suspected, he never let on.

Harwood insisted that Sarah have the Ford free and clear and drew up a bill of sale for one dollar despite her protestations. He donned work clothes similar to Paul's and Sarah drove them to Whitehall. To avoid any questions by the few late season passengers on the run, Sarah dropped them in town away from the dock area. Paul and Harwood kept to themselves, mumbling guardedly in French as they boarded.

Driving up the edge of East Bay, Sarah reached an overlook about three miles beyond the town. She stayed in the car to avoid any attention, but waved as the vessel chugged by on its northerly course. Both Paul and John spotted the car and leaned on the port rail, their arms half raised in acknowledgement. A stiff wind from the Adirondacks had sprung up and temperatures were dropping suddenly, a not unusual event on the lakes. Just as the vessel rounded a bend of the bay to go out of sight, a snow squall showered the lake for a time, nearly obscuring the boat. Then they were gone.

44

Camp William James was a unique CCC camp established in early 1941 in upper Vermont. From the start it was a star-crossed experiment, all too short-lived, a victim of bad timing and political maneuvering. The camp was the brain-child of Frank Davidson, a recent Harvard graduate and Eugene Rosenstock-Huessy, a Dartmouth College professor of social philosophy, who, well aware in the late 1930's of the imminent threat of another world war, tried to fashion an antidote for the recurrence of hostilities. Their ideas were built on the writings of the turn of the century American philosopher, William James who believed that war, widely held to be the event that brings out the high human virtues of battlefield courage and sacrifice, was actually a sham which would ultimately lead to chaos and the destruction of civilization. He suggested that the human propensity for physical combat be channeled into constructive deeds which could enhance civilization rather than decimate it. Conscription for war would be replaced by conscription into an army of builders willing to improve human society and its environment. This was his idea of "the moral equivalent of war" for which he is most often remembered. In time, he said, the allure of masculine combativeness would wane and more civilized virtues would prevail.

Huessy extended James' philosophy into practical schemes and Davidson would test them in the real world. He and the professor recognized that young Americans, perhaps accentuated by crisis conditions of the Great Depression, were sliding into a segregated society of haves and have nots, separated economic class, education and race. Both saw the CCC camps as a venue for their experiment. Davidson, from a family of the relatively well-off, was ineligible for regular CCC enlistment, but in 1939 convinced the CCC leadership to allow him regular CCC enrollment. He soon verified the social differences between regular CCC enrollees and himself and came to appreciate the value of manual labor in support of his ideas of the civilizing nature of constructive work. In the summer of 1940 he sent a report to the Assistant Secretary of Agriculture arguing that restricting CCC ranks only to enrollees from low-income families was limiting the effectiveness of the program. Initially, Davidson's ideas were championed by the Washington D.C. establishment, particularly by the CCC itself. He soon was appointed to staff in the Department of Agriculture where he developed a plan to inaugurate a civilian conservation corps staff college. By 1940, it was becoming abundantly clear that the War Department would soon be withdrawing their reserve officers as CCC camp commanders. Washington bureaucrats liked the idea of establishing training centers where college men would learn principles of CCC leadership and take over running the camps when the military left.

The godfather of the CCC, Robert Fechner, died in service on January 1, 1940. His assistant, James McEntee succeeded him as CCC Director. Although part of Roosevelt's team and an able administrator, McEntee appeared not to be reading off the same sheet of music as the President. Roosevelt endorsed the scheme, which was supported by notables like Dorothy Thompson, a celebrated news columnist, and even by his wife, Eleanor. Thompson, in particular, pressed for quick action to open a closed CCC camp on Mount Sharon in Downer State Forest near Tunbridge, Vermont. A small group of enthusiastic Harvard and Dartmouth men would make up the implementation staff of the model program. Huessy was recommended as a training consultant and agreed to accept the camp administrator's post. A Council of Nine Towns made up of local inhabitants would have input into the camp's activities and a federal government Supervisory Committee was established to monitor progress.

The aim of the CCC staff college was the development of leaders who thoroughly understood the spirit of service and democratic processes. Military control and indoctrination were to be banned from camp life and camp management was to be subject to majority vote of the enrollees. Community service by the college student company was to consist of agricultural and conservation projects in the central Vermont area. These goals were a bit lofty and impractical, at least in McEntee's eyes, but the plan was the first and only one geared to making the CCC a self-perpetuating program. In the previous seven years the corps had served unemployment and conservation purposes admirably, but its leadership was, of necessity, makeshift with the Army in the driver's seat. Run largely by reserve officers, discipline and order were well maintained, but the camps lacked formal leadership training. Despite the alleged intentions of a few high ranking Regular Army officers, the military, to its credit, never viewed the CCC as an arena for armed forces training and indoctrination.

Despite a political line-up of public and private heavy hitters supporting the Mount Sharon experiment, trouble brewed almost from the very beginning. McEntee did not voice opposition at the outset, but gradually cooled to the idea of a special CCC unit run by college students, citing the original purpose of the CCC as a welfare program for destitute families. He insisted that the structure of the camp retain the control and direction as laid down by Fechner. Since the camp would have to rely on government support for its existence, camp planners could not bolt from McEntee's influence. As is often the case with bold, new ventures, there was not total consensus among the planners either. Much time and effort was spent trying to cobble together a scheme which satisfied both the Davidson/Huessy theory and the day to day practicality of making the camp work.

The camp opened on January 1, 1941 with 42 members, about half of which were college students, the remainder consisting of regular CCC recruits drawn from other camps as volunteers. Three days later, opponents of Roosevelt requested information on the Sharon Camp from the Secretary of Agriculture with the alleged motive of embarrassing Roosevelt's administration. Despite the Secretary's clear and open description in reply, opponents continued their sniping against the camp, citing unfounded, unfavorable news articles which even suggested that Dorothy Thompson and Huessy were admirers of Hitler. A rebuttal by the venerable Republican Senator from Vermont, George Aiken, failed to quell the frenzy of negative publicity. A U.S. House subcommittee investigation concluded that McEntee's support for the camp was lacking as continued charges in the full House fanned anti-German sentiments.

The public had known very little about the camp until late December, 1940 when editorials began appearing in prestigious newspapers which, while praising the CCC and its work, questioned the experiment at Mount Sharon. Congressmen became increasingly rankled by the use of tax dollars to support a camp of privileged Ivy League students, reminding their colleagues that relief of the poor had always been the cardinal objective of the CCC.

Then the bomb dropped. Professor Huessy, it was learned, was an alien and had helped set up youth labor camps in pre-Hitler Germany. Given the anti-German hysteria of the time, no allegation could have been more damaging. Despite Huessy's solid credentials, professed anti-fascism (he had been driven out of Germany by Hitler) and his steadfast refusal to initiate anything remotely resembling the Nazi camps, the project was consumed like wax in the fiery public outcry. Roosevelt, desperately trying to balance the country's neutrality and in the midst of delicate Lend-Lease negotiations needing support in Congress, quickly saw the writing on the wall and turned the project over to McEntee. On February 21,1941, the War Department was placed in complete charge of the Mount Sharon Camp. Regular CCC enrollees were either transferred or given discharge and by March 19 any semblance of the "CCC Staff College" was gone. A number of students, dismayed, but idealistic to the end, set themselves up in an old farmhouse nearby in Tunbridge with the help of some local, private money. They petitioned the U.S. government for financial support, but obtaining none, they eventually disbanded.

So ended perhaps the only chance to develop a cadre capable of continuing the CCC. Less haste, more planning and better publicity might have resulted in broader political support to make the project a success. But fickle fate also played a major role. Timing couldn't have been worse with the world moving into another World War. A little more than a year later, in 1942, the nation was quickly becoming fully employed and embroiled in combat to again make the world safe for democracy. Congress failed to appropriate monies to continue conservation activities and, although understandably distracted, never formally disbanded the CCC. It simply withered away.

45

Sarah drove from Northampton to Amherst in a chilly downpour. She was delayed on both sides of the river by the storm's unusual intensity and pockets of high water. Rain hammered the cold earth as she turned into Professor Stone's driveway and cut the motor. Stone probably hadn't heard her arrival and there was still time to terminate this visit, back out of the driveway and never return.

She sat for a while, grasping the wheel tightly, pondering how what she must say would appear in a letter. Cowardly, she decided. With renewed determination she got out and trudged up the wet walk. In the near dark of the porch she grappled again with her failing resolve. Rain pelted clear through the wool cap and jacket she wore. Shivering, she reached for the knocker and raised it slowly. But before she had a chance to release it, Stone flung open the door, a look of bewilderment on his face.

"Sarah, what are you trying to do, catch pneumonia? Come in here and take off those drenched things."

His confusion and disbelief moderated as he led her into the living room where a roaring fire in the hearth provided cheerful refuge.

"Now stay right here and give me that hat and jacket. You'll need something warm to drink."

The heat quelled her shivering, but her heart was leaden, the tears welling dangerously close. She must not cry, she told herself. She bit the inside of her cheek and turned her back to the fire. Ashley was rummaging in the kitchen for tea and heating the kettle.

"This encounter will be difficult," she told herself, "but he must not be put to unfair advantage by tears."

By the time Ashley returned, her shoulders had lost their droop and her eyes met his squarely. He smiled warmly as if to say, "Now, that's my girl," and put down a tray of biscuits and jam, then returned to the kitchen for the tea kettle, cheerily announcing its readiness. He poured the tea and sat down in an easy chair, bidding her to do the same across from him. He said nothing for a time, but his eyes twinkled, the more from genuine pleasure of her company than from any mystery about her unexpected appearance.

"Damn his eyes," she thought without rancor and turned toward the fire once more to warm her hands.

When she faced him again, the twinkle was gone, the hazel eyes expectant, but revealing nothing of what was going on behind them.

"Go on, tell me," he said at last. There was more kindness in his tone than she had ever expected. She sat down in the chair and took a biscuit, realizing suddenly that she was very hungry.

"Ashley," she began slowly, "it's going to be difficult for me to tell you this."

Her eyes searched his for any hint of disapproval. There was none, only the unwavering hazel question marks.

She grasped her arms firmly and leaned a little forward, hoping her voice would be strong enough.

"John has gone. He and Paul Boisvert left nearly two months ago from Whitehall, bound for Canada. I tried to change his mind, Ashley, but he would hear none of it." The words came surprisingly easy as she went on, her voice gaining strength as the tension eased.

"The only information I have is that the Canadians may send a contingent of their 1st Division to England soon for likely deployment in France with the British Expeditionary Force. This I read in a Montreal paper, as I've heard nothing from either of them. You know as well as I that they'll be with that contingent. The British are begging for Canadian officers and men who are bilingual to interface with the French."

Ashley just nodded slightly and sipped some tea. Great gusts of wind blew the deluge into waterfalls down the windowpane.

Sarah changed the subject abruptly. "I've decided to take the whole year off instead of just this semester and try to get my thesis completed by summer. I've come to ask you for an extension of time."

"But what will you live on, where will you stay?" Ashley asked gently.

"I have enough saved to get me through and I've gotten a promise of a permanent post in the high school beginning next September. Even if I have a small debt by summer, there is really nothing to worry about."

"I see," said Stone, again very quietly.

Sarah shifted uncomfortably and stared into the fire.

"There's more, Sarah." Ashley's voice was commanding, yet barely audible.

"Yes." The tiny word came out quietly, but slowly.

Sarah stood and crossed her arms once more, not daring to look at Ashley. After a long pause, during which the rain let up its loud drumming and only the clock and the hissing fire could be heard, Sarah told him of her pregnancy.

"Are you sure?" Not a decibel higher than before.

"Yes, my periods are as regular as that clock on the mantle. I've never missed."

"And Harwood's run off like some poltroon in the guise of a hero." Ashley's voice rose for the first time and Sarah looked at his face, stormy at last with repressed anger.

"Perhaps he'll return, I don't know. For weeks I really expected word—a letter, a card—but none came. I do know that I shall never force him. I feel so senseless about it. After all, I'm not a lovesick schoolgirl. I'm 28 years old." Her voice rose and she became self-indicting. "Me, who knows all about biology and how babies are made, to perpetuate such a colossal blunder. Ashley, I was like a trapped animal and didn't care about dignity or propriety."

"You loved him very much, Sarah." The sound of velvet, tinged with sadness.

Her composure left her at this and the tears began. She turned her head away so he would not see, but continued on, her voice small and unsure.

"Yes, I wanted this child so very much, but with him here beside me. Why do you think he left, Ashley? God, I'd have done anything to make him stay. I'd set my cap for him and he knew it, but refused to take me as a lover. He simply told me to stay locked in the cottage at the lake while he slept under the stars."

She hesitated, then continued, "Finally, out of self-pity and feminine silliness, I went to him and begged his love. He never pursued me. He didn't have to. I was his. The moment he walked out of the forest more than a year ago, I was his. Do you remember that, Ashley?"

He did indeed remember. With sinking heart he had observed the subtle, yet powerful chemistry between the two. He had always hurt from that wound, but felt powerless to do anything about it. She was, after all, his old friend's niece—no, more than that, a surrogate daughter. Propriety and age made him subvert his own furtive romantic feelings for her. What a fool he had been. But what a bigger fool had he declared himself.

Stone rose slowly from his chair like some overburdened animal and went to the window. The storm was now going away and a few lingering rays of sun were caught in the frigid raindrops clinging to the glass. He stood there a long time while Sarah waited, staring into the fire, feeling purged, yet miserable for all the flotsam she had heaped on her old friend.

"His reasons for running probably go back a long way, Sarah. It's easy for us to try to make others out as perfect, but we forget that we're an unfinished species." Ashley's voice had lost its ire and sadness now taking on the solid ring of something coming from down deep.

"John is a tortured idealist. He just couldn't forget the horrors of the last war, but detested even more a peace that made a mockery of all those battlefield deaths. And when McGarry died, he couldn't live with anyone, especially himself. His abandoning you may have been due more to this than he would ever care to admit."

Sarah was amazed and touched by his perception of John.

"So you knew about his inner hell?"

"Only by intuition, which isn't much. McGarry shared a few things with me—the brother and his father's death after the Crash. Once you got behind John's seamless exoskeleton, could there be much doubt?"

Stone became silent, his hands clasped behind his back. After a time, he continued softly. "He's doing what he is best at. The Canadian Army is just another challenge to him like the CCC was. When Germany is beaten once again, he'll return, perhaps this time purged of his demons. And until then no human force will change him, although, God knows, if anyone could, it would be you."

He ended in barely a whisper, turning slightly to look at her.

Sarah kept her eyes on the embers, the tears again heavy and leaking from the corners of her eyes. The silence was broken only by the hiss of wet wood in the guttering fire.

Stone tried to remember how many evenings he had stood alone before this window watching the sun weave its way down between the trees as it was now doing. Strangely, all those years seemed not to matter now.

"Sarah," he began slowly, but confidently, "please think this over before you answer. You know I'm not a young man and have many of the foibles of age. Years of teaching and caring only for myself have given me some wretched baggage you wouldn't find in other men. But I have hung onto my integrity and humor, such as it is. My great need is for companionship and to shed a loneliness hardly bearable at times." He paused. "Right now you need me, too. That child needs a father, if in name only. As my wife you would find in me the loving husband and father that Harwood dared not to be."

Sarah bit her lips and met Ashley's eyes. No mystery now, but windows to a spirit loving, vulnerable and proud. She had no words.

"Think of me not as a desperate old fool," he continued, his voice rasping slightly from emotion.

"Nor me as the wanton woman crawling out of the mire to your door with some deceitful surprise in her belly, using you as a handy port in the storm." She said this through tears, but with a hidden strength, never averting her eyes from his.

"Sarah, my dear, only a damned fool would ever accuse you of easy virtues or barnyard morals. You're no light-o-love and, anyway, real love is never wanton," he ended softly.

At this she broke and the tears slid freely down her cheeks. Her body shook with half-repressed sobs and she rummaged in her bag for a handkerchief.

"But your reputation, this short-term child, people talking; it just wouldn't work," she said through bitter tears.

"It is true, my colleagues will snicker and some may deride. But my mark in life has been made. They will learn to overlook this and take me as I am, as must you."

"My God, Ashley, I feel like a cowbird in a thrushes nest," she mumbled, blowing her nose.

"That's how the cowbird's survival is assured, my dearest Demmie."

She hadn't heard herself called that since Sam had gone.

He continued, "As for John, trust me to release you when he returns."

"You would do even that?" cried Sarah in disbelief.

"Yes," then more briskly, "now be sensible. As soon as your condition begins to show, the school committee will drop you like lightening and there won't be another school who'll even consider your credentials." She did not respond to this and looked into the fire, dabbing her eyes. After a pause, he added, "For Heaven's sake, Sarah, think of the child."

His frankness completely disarmed her and she rose and went to him by the window, taking his arm in hers. No words were needed as together they watched the night descend on the birches.

46

On Friday, January 28, 1943, Stone arose late and turned on the radio for the news. It was mostly wartime propaganda, but he discerned that the Nazis must be in serious trouble at Stalingrad, even as the U-boats continued to take their toll in the North Atlantic shipping lanes. He conjectured a bit on the obvious paradox—he and Sarah, their comforts, her music and the drowsy child in the next room—the brutal war now raging in distant places all over this beautiful planet. So many lives being twisted, destroyed. He exhaled forcefully, hoping that those he knew—young Paul, Rocco, even Harwood—were not among them. Yes, humankind evolution was showing itself as terribly complex and far from any assured success.

He shut off the set and looked out the living room window at the overcast sky. "A good morning, none-the-less," he thought, anticipating a productive day and a happy weekend with Sarah and the child. Sarah had waked much earlier, fed her son and gone to teach her classes at the high school. After peeping in on the sleeping child, Stone quickly prepared his own breakfast, ate and settled down at his desk to write up his research notes. The day grew more gray and bleak as morning wore on. The wind rose and drove sleet hard against the windowpanes.

The young boy awoke shortly, and jabbering to himself, climbed out of his crib and toddled into the living room where Stone had built a fire on the hearth. After the child had his porridge and toast, Ashley put a Paul Whiteman record on the phonograph and danced around the room, holding the boy in his arms. Then the two of them erected block towers and watched them topple. This was always a delightful morning event and Stone savored their time together. The professor wrote while the child had his bottle, then at noon he made them a simple meal and afterward read the boy a picture book.

Warmed by the fire, they listened drowsily to the wind moaning in the firs behind the house. The velocity had increased and the temperature had dropped, changing the tiny shards of ice to blinding snow. Inch piled on inch throughout the early afternoon. When the boy fell asleep, Stone gently laid him in his crib, well bundled against the cold with the wool comforter Sarah had made.

Returning to his work, Stone huddled a bit nearer the fire and continued to write, setting his lamp on low to pierce the unnatural gloom. The storm's intensity grew and by mid-afternoon, he began to be concerned about Sarah's return. About seven inches of snow had accumulated and gusts of wind made walking difficult. He decided to get the car out and go after her about three-thirty. The boy was still asleep, so Stone put on cap and mackinaw and went out, grabbing the snow shovel on his way. He would dig out the car, warm it up and return for the child.

The wind was now blowing with a vengeance, casting snow in every direction. Drifts had formed across the driveway where the wind cut around the corner of the house. After finishing the walk, Stone tackled the drifts and was making good headway when a tingling sensation began in his left arm. It crept up the biceps and pressed on his shoulder and chest. Stone ceased shoveling and stood up, but the pressure turned to pain and quite suddenly bore down on him with a great weight. His face flushed and he staggered, breathing heavily and reaching out for the support of the garage wall. The flame under his breastbone was a roaring inferno and, helpless, he sunk to his knees in the drift, then pitched sideways, his knees drawn up to his chest in the womb position. His last energy was pathetically spent twisting his body sideways far enough so his face was towards the sky. The pain slowly ebbed into numbness, only the swaying of the firs telling him he had not lost consciousness. In a twilight world he saw Grace riding out of the lake waters once more. But, unlike past dreams, he did not go under the flailing hooves. She halted her steed, dismounted and put her hands out to him. The delicate mouth was not twisted in pain, but smiling and the joy about her face was the same he had seen when they had lived in the little bridal cottage on the edge of town. The vision faded and he was aware of intense cold trickling upwards from his groin. He tried to lift an arm, but got no response.

"So this is how it is," he thought, "wretchedness and eternal ice." An overwhelming sense of loneliness and panic gripped him as consciousness slipped away.

Sarah quickly tidied up her classroom after the students left and prepared herself for the brutal outdoors. Perhaps Ashley would be waiting for her near the side entrance as he often did. In the corridors, students and teachers alike were hustling into their coats and jackets so as to get home in the remaining daylight. Seeing no Ashley, she bravely charged the cruel wind and drifts. By the time she had gone the quarter-mile to the corner of Main Street, she was flushed with exertion. A Model A slid silently up beside her and she was ordered to get in by Millie Lewis, one of the history teachers at the high school.

"You must be out looking for pneumonia."

"Thank God you came along. I expected that Ashley would pick me up at the school. He must have had trouble."

As she said these words, Sarah became slowly aware of a tiny, silent alarm ringing persistently, deep within her brain.

"Perhaps you have time to stop at my house for something warm. You could call Ashley from there."

"Thank you, but no. I'd really appreciate your dropping me at the house." The gong in Sarah's mind was really clanging now.

As they drove up the side street past the neat row of middle-class homes, Sarah noted that nearly all had lights on in the parlors and kitchens. They approached the Stone homestead, which was set on a little hill and apart from the nearest neighbor. The pasture behind their property was now heavily blanketed and the birch clumps that Ashley loved were bent and muted with snow. The house was dark except for a single light burning in the living room. No tire tracks were in the driveway. Millie turned the car around to head back towards town. Sarah thanked her friend as she jumped out and, promising to call later that evening, hurried up the walk.

The wind swirled tiny flakes in a frenzy and the daylight was nearly gone as she let herself in the front door. She called for Ashley and, hearing nothing, raced into the living room. There the fire burned low behind the screen and the lamp shone on the incomplete page of Ashley's journal.

Instinctively, Sarah ran to the child's bedroom. There, bundled and warm, lay the sleeping boy, perfect peace written on the tiny face. She closed the door quietly and went to the front entrance, calling up the stairs. Throwing open the closet door, she noticed that Ashley's mackinaw was gone. Her breath became labored as a premonition savagely gripped her heart. She flung open the back door, crying out, "Ashley," only to be answered by the satanic moaning of the wind. Frantically, she ran into the storm, making for the garage. Then she saw the shovel handle sticking out of the drift and beside it a section of Ashley's mackinaw nearly buried in the snow.

Ashley, through blurring eyes, saw her coming and lapsing back into reality realized that the drifting snow had nearly buried him. Only his shoulder and cap remained visible and had shielded his eyes and nose against the driving storm. He knew there was nothing to be done now, but strove to remain conscious as Sarah came to him, her eyes full of love. She pushed away the encroaching snow, fell to her knees and, knowing she could never move him, ran to the telephone for help. Returning at once, she opened her coat in a futile attempt to revive his freezing body with her warm breasts. His images were coming fast now, tumbling over one another—working with his father in the wintery Berkshire milk room, milk-white gypsies clustering on tree trunks, smelling Sarah's warm milk being let down, even above the scent she wore. Entwined in her arms, he could only smile weakly to himself as he realized that this woman, mated to another man, really loved him as no other person ever had. Harwood may have given her the child, but he, Ashley Stone, had loved her better and had made that motherhood whole. What matter that another man's genes sang within the boy ? The two fathers were needed and now gone, but he had outlasted Harwood and like an upwelling of the sea, had given both Sarah and the child the thrust, the necessary energy to crest a wave all the way to shore.

Stone felt the threads of life snapping throughout his body, the cells winking slowly out, one by one. He could swear that someone was humming a sweet, old love song as he passed for the final time into the unreal world of fantasy. Before sucking down into the fatal swoon, he entered a never-land where he thought himself a young swain who leaped onto the horse behind Grace and, the two of them laughing, the wind blowing through their hair, disappeared forever beneath the waves.

47

The faculty committee looking for Agnes Hewitt's replacement was at impasse. The old woman, a venerable professor of biology for some thirty-five years, had retired and wisely stood aside as the interviews proceeded over the summer. It was now near September and no decision had been made. If much more time were lost, there would be no one to meet the new and returning students. Professor Hewitt was having afternoon tea with Catherine Harwood when the committee chairman, a kindly, but harassed man named Jones, sought her out.

"We just can't agree on the candidates, Miss Hewitt. If you could give us some direction . . ."

"But I've told you, Russell, that the choice has nothing to do with me. I'm retired and want no voice in who replaces me. Why, it would be just unfair and in very bad taste to weigh in on your decision."

"Our time is so very short and you've got a better view of what our students need than any of us. You wouldn't be required to vote, just sit with us for the final interview."

Professor Hewitt looked dubiously at her friend who now spoke up.

"It's up to you, Agnes, of course. But if you decide, you're welcome to use this house for the interviews. That way, you'll be able to stay out of the limelight and avoid all those questions as to why you're back on campus. And I'll feel like I'm doing something more than just taking up space on the trustees' board."

"That's very generous of you, Mrs. Harwood," said the chairman, and turned expectantly to the old professor.

"Well, that might work, if you really don't mind the inconvenience, Catherine."

"Not at all. Just let me know when you want to meet."

"Then of course you'll sit with us, too, Mrs. Harwood," added the chairman.

Four finalists were to be interviewed on Thursday afternoon. Sarah was delighted when the letter came informing her that she was to meet with the committee. Only the closing paragraph stating that the session would be at Trustee Harwood's house left her unsettled, but she knew there was no way to back out at this point. Nor did she have any intention of doing so. She called Millie Lewis asking her to come along for moral support and to watch her son.

Late in the afternoon on the appointed day, the two women and the boy drove into the Harwood grounds in Millie's venerable Model A and parked near the fountain.

"You go right along, Sarah. Robbie and I will stay here and take a little walk by the goldfish pond while you're being interviewed."

Sarah patted her son's hair into place, then braced herself and walked up to the front door, recalling vividly the last time at the house. Mother Harwood evinced genuine surprise when she opened the door. Nothing had passed between them since that summer evening in 1938, but Mother Harwood recognized her instantly. She took Sarah's hand in hers and welcomed her from the heart.

"It is so good to see you again."

Sarah nodded her assent.

"The interviewing committee is on the terrace. I was going to let them use the study, but it's too clammy in there. This summer heat will just have to break soon." She paused, noting Sarah's discomfort, and spoke kindly. "Don't let the committee frighten you. You've got as good a chance as the others. Would you like a glass of cool water before you meet them?"

The old woman couldn't possibly know that the greatest difficulty in this visit lay with the memories of John and the secret of their child. Sarah demurred graciously, then squared her shoulders and replied, "No, thank you. I'd better just go right out."

Led by Mother Harwood, she made her way through the parlor to the back terrace, trying not to remember that magical summer evening of fireflies. The committee was arrayed near a large low table on which sat a huge pitcher of lemonade. The chairman welcomed her to the circle and bade her sit down. The silent scrutiny was terrific, but Sarah weathered it well, waiting for the chairman to finish his discourse on the merits of teaching at Burkett. Mother Harwood had taken a seat near the veranda where she could look out across the lawns.

Sarah summarized her training and experience in precise terms and handled the questions to the satisfaction of all except a humorless, middle-aged professor who took a dim view of Sarah's research thesis and public college education. Sarah cast her a benign look and saw her sharpening her claws.

"Just what was the research you and Professor Stone did on the mating attractant of gypsy moths?"

"It's not clear-cut as yet, but our work suggests that the chemical cues secreted by the female may not only be air-borne, but also effective over long distances, perhaps up to a mile or more. Some U.S.D.A. scientists have taken up where we left off and . . . ." The clawed cat pounced without letting her finish.

"Under what conditions did you conduct those studies?" The question was harsh.

"During the last big defoliation in Vermont we did a number of field studies and later duplicated many of our findings in the laboratory at Mass. Agricultural College."

The cat's upper lip raised in a microscopic sneer. "Isn't that putting the cart before the horse? Most research is done the other way around—laboratory studies, which are then verified in the field."

"You are correct, but Professor Stone was never one to let convention get in the way of research. The massive outbreaks in 1937—38 provided an ideal study population. The opportunity was too good to miss."

I'm surprised that others have not corroborated such an important find."

"Oh, but others have," Sarah returned sweetly.

"Really? Who?" The question was loud and blunt, expectant of victory.

"Jakes at Harvard for one," Sarah said evenly and watched the cat run.

"Harvard, you say?" The voice was weak, deflated; the question was nonsensical.

The chairman shifted uncomfortably and asked if there were any more questions. Hearing none, he launched his final volley. "Would you please tell us, Mrs. Stone, just what you think you can do for our students should you be hired?"

Sarah paused before answering and caught Mother Harwood's eye for a split second. Then she began.

"I love learning and became a teacher because I like to see others share this love. Some might think this egotistical or selfish, but if there is anything that I can do well, it is to help others learn, not just by what I say or do in front of the class, but by how my students value their knowledge and themselves as they learn. Teaching biology is important to me, but I am less concerned with what I teach than with students wanting to develop the discipline and passion they need to explore the truth for themselves and to realize the many wonderful things of this earth. If I can help them find some of that beauty and dignity, much of which is right there inside them knocking to get out, I will have done my job."

No one said anything for a time and Sarah felt Mother Harwood's gaze resting on her from across the terrace.

A child cried once from the side yard and Sarah rose slightly by instinct, but before she could move, Robbie came dashing across the yard towards the terrace, his little bare knees beating quick time.

Mother Harwood was on her feet, her face taut with incredulity. As Sarah excused herself to pick up the child, she saw the old woman silently mouth one word, "Jack!"

Robbie had found an apple in the grass and picked it up, not knowing a yellow jacket had found it first. The hornet had stung him on the hand and this major catastrophe required his mother, not Millie Lewis. Sarah cuddled the boy who was quiet now, being courageous in spite of the pain. He peered shyly at the committee as his mother wiped away the tears. Millie came up to take him back to the car, but Mother Harwood interrupted and ushered them inside to dress the child's wound with ice and baking soda. Sarah again faced the committee, apologizing for the interruption. Several more questions of no consequence were asked as the interview wound down. Mother Harwood returned to her seat by the veranda.

"We are just about concluded," the chairman announced a bit stiffly, but with finality. "That will be all, Mrs. Stone. You will hear from us presently."

Sarah nodded and expressed her gratitude to the group for giving her the interview.

"And thank you, Mrs. Harwood. No, don't bother to show me out. I'll just go around to where my son waits."

Mother Harwood's face bore a strange look, as if searching for some words to say, but which wouldn't come. Yet, her eyes were bright and glistening with joy as she smiled her assent to Sarah.

After Sarah had gone, the committee sat down to deliberate. The cat arched herself and announced that she didn't think a mother with a child so young could possibly do justice to the position.

"And she clearly fails to recognize the value of research. Why she's published only one paper. And her degrees! Music education and entomology, both from cow colleges." She looked around for support, the smile standing out for all to see.

Professor Hewitt remained silent and merely looked at the woman over her small wire frame glasses.

The chairman coughed in embarrassment and asked if there were any further comments.

"Yes." Professor Hewitt turned to address the chairman. "For thirty years I've seen young women come and go from our program, many of whom excelled here and then led successful, productive lives. Yet I could count on one hand the number who have taken their training beyond the confines of biology. In the early years it always seemed necessary to steep our students in the discipline to assure that they learned all the important facts. We wound them up, so to speak, and turned them loose to march faithfully into the future. Their futures consisted of positions with people who thought and acted just like us. It worked amazingly well, but it won't work any more. The world's changed and that includes *our* world." She looked severely at the cat, then continued.

"We need new blood and new breadth in this department. Too many of us, and I include myself, have Ivy League degrees. Oh, that's hardly a handicap. We're good, it's true, and do we know it! But sometimes we forget that real learning and the ability to impart it may occur when and where we least expect it, and by others equally as good or better than us." She paused, then continued. "Good God, what would old Pasteur and Mendel do to hear us talk so? They must be rolling in their graves." Smiling benignly, she looked at Mother Harwood. "Catherine, could I have another glass of your delicious lemonade?"

The subsequent vote on offering Sarah the contract was unanimous.

Months later, Mother Harwood encountered Sarah and her son walking on campus. She inquired into the boy's health and Sarah remained on her guard as the old woman took the child's bee-stung hand in hers and examined it. "And how is this doing?"

Her gentleness disarmed the boy's shyness and he gave her several small seeds he'd been carrying.

"Oh, I see he's a biologist already," she remarked with delight. "He'll soon be taking right after his parents."

Sarah relaxed a bit.

"Yes, I expect so, especially his father."

"He was a fine scientist and teacher, wasn't he, Sarah?"

"He was a good man," Sarah said simply, her eyes never wavering.

Mother Harwood's mouth softened in a smile and the crow's feet near her eyes seemed to disappear.

"You and the child must come visit me sometime."

48

Paul couldn't believe it. The old orchard hadn't changed and Hyde Pond shimmered as if it had been there forever, but not a building remained. Or so it seemed. Then he spotted the officer's quarters whose yard along with the parade ground was now overgrown with weeds. In just six years, the trees had nearly blocked off the loggia. Part of the roof over the offices was holed, perhaps from some windfall. He'd go there later. First, he wandered to where the recreation hall and mess had been. Gone, all but the footings. The emergency mobilization after Pearl Harbor had meant that every remote government structure known was uprooted and used elsewhere for the war effort. He hesitated briefly on the concrete apron of the truck garage, then traversed the Hyde Pond dike, stopping to cup his hand in the overflow for a drink. Beneath the dike he could see pipe which led off in the direction of Grafton, fulfilling Hollis' early plan.

The orchard basked in the sun, the apples about ready for picking. But up close, Paul noted that the fruit were rather small and misshapen from human neglect and repeated pest attacks. Stooping, he was heartened to see Johnson's grafts firm and well-embedded in new wood. He picked up a drop and smelled its wine of decay, then pitched it as far as he could towards the ridge. Only then did he see that the ancient pine up by the boulders was missing. The hole it left was now being crowded in by young maples. He had the sudden sense that more than just the old conifer had gone. Way back in the sugar bush he heard the fluting of a wood thrush. He took a step in that direction, then changed his mind. He might go there later, but first he wanted to visit his and Harwood's old quarters.

The place needed maintenance badly, but structurally was still sound. The myrtle they'd planted next to the loggia had thrived and run off towards the pond. He paused on the front step with a twinge of foreboding, but then pushed the door and went inside. Gutted, like he expected. He'd seen enough. No point in going up to his old room. Anyway, the stairs did not look too sturdy, having soaked up the years of rain and snow from the holed roof. But the closed door to the Exec's office intrigued him. He turned the handle and it swayed open to reveal a short man sitting at a crude table. Paul let out a startled gasp as he breathed in the dank, fetid air and met dark, piercing eyes that bore right through him.

"Hell, you're here. You might as well come in," rasped the surprisingly deep voice with the tell-tale quiver of years of heavy drinking. The exasperated edge told Paul that its owner was exerting more effort than he wanted to. A partially consumed bottle of Four Roses sat on the table along with some frayed technical manuals. In one corner of the room was a jumble of wires and boxes, which Paul had seen often enough. Dynamite caps. Next to the far wall was a pile of soiled clothes and blankets perched on an old couch. Only then did Paul notice the two-fingered hand. The man ignored Paul's stare and poured a bit more whisky into the cracked cup at his elbow.

"So, you must be one of them CCC boys. A few come up here every now and again to see what's left of the place. I sort of keep an eye on things here for the county. Gives me a place to shelter." He nodded to nothing particular in the room. Paul was pretty sure he was lying.

"They shut this place up in a hurry after that kid who was here shot his father," the little man continued. "You here then, kid?"

Paul shook his head, but said nothing, still stunned by finding this squatter in the old camp.

"Well, don't amount to a piss-hole in a snow bank anyway. The old man was a worthless son of a bitch. Thought his brother's little girl was knifed by one of you boys. Found out later it was his own nephew done it. That boy went and hung himself like a jacked deer right out by the pond and left the whole story in a note pinned to his shirt. Helped cut him down myself, so I know. But don't many others here know about it and those that do keep it to themselves."

The voice suddenly stopped, but the piercing eyes still continued to bore into Paul's face, then sensing something in Paul's demeanor, shifted away.

Paul had heard more than enough. Without a word, he turned and left, shutting the door behind him. In a moment of sudden exhaustion, he took a deep breath and leaned back against the jamb. Through the main entrance whose door he had left ajar, he spotted Sarah's rose carefully tended, incongruous amid the encroaching weeds. Someone had recently mulched and watered its space. "The squatter? Who else?", thought Paul absently.

On his way across the loggia, he saw for the first time, the battered truck pulled up close nearly out of sight under the saplings. He walked down the company street, the musky perfume of the Old Garden rose in his nostrils, past the unkempt parade ground, never once thinking about the old pine or the sugar bush. Soon, several miles of the Grafton Road were behind him.

The ringing at the front door roused the curate from his reading. The young man who stepped inside was unfamiliar and the request to talk with Father Mercier was odd.

"Father Mercier has been gone for nearly two years now, in Canada at the Grand Seminary. I can give you his address."

Paul waited in the parlor while the curate went to his office and copied. Handing the paper to Paul he asked, "You knew Father well?"

"He was close to me and my family, the Boisverts. I'm the only one left now." He turned to go, but the priest stopped him.

"If you are Paul Boisvert, Father Mercier left something here for you. Please, just a minute."

He disappeared again, this time upstairs and returned with a small sealed package, clearly marked with Paul's name.

"In packing up, Father left this thinking you might one day return." The curate eyed Paul carefully. "You were in the war?"

"Yes. In Europe." He sized up the priest, only a few years

older than himself, noting the starched white collar at this throat and the long, smooth fingers, unroughened by physical tasks. He smiled at the irony. With a few less detours, their roles could be reversed.

"You may sit and open the parcel here if you like," offered the curate, hardly concealing his interest. "Perhaps the housekeeper will make us some coffee. It's been a long time since we've had any in the house."

Paul settled into a familiar chair and undid the wrapping. On top was a letter written in French in the old priest's formal script, below that a small trophy. He knew at once what it was. He took his time with the letter.

> *Dear Paul,*
>
> *I despair that I shall never see you again, but if you should read this, know that you are forever in my prayers. The Heavenly Father loves you and has much work for you on this earth. Do not be disappointed that it is other than what you and I once thought. And please do not think less of me for my many faults and errors which have caused you to suffer needlessly. Like you and all our human brothers and sisters, I am but a simple pilgrim on the way to the Lord.*
>
> *This trophy was given to me by your mother at the time of your grandmere's death. One of her acquaintances knew Pelham McGarry well and he had asked the woman to give it to you should anything ever happen to him. This man always thought highly of you despite (perhaps because of) his rough and dissolute life. With all his imperfections, I believe McGarry was a lover, not just in the flesh with this woman and perhaps others, but of most people he knew. Captain Harwood never shared his grief over McGarry's horrible end, but I could read it in his eyes. Recognition of wounded hearts is a thing we priests become good at. Both he and Harwood survived harrowing experiences, yet prevailed. When a loved one departs, such resilient sinews break. Life*

may persist, but the loss remains. I pray that Harwood will not carry this wound green to his grave.

As a man of God, I was fortunate to have a more serene life, yet the distress of mind and shadow of sin have been my companions, too. You see, long years ago I loved your mother. I was careless and desperate, a behavior totally inappropriate for my position. She was astute and mature beyond her years in many things and I clung foolishly to the happiness she brought me during our weekly lessons in the rectory. Yet she could only guess at my feelings for they were never expressed to her through our many hours together.

When you were born, I became insane with jealousy and disbelief. In one evening she had tossed aside all virtue and reason and destroyed forever my foolish dreams for her. I became craven and cruel, wishing to hurt her to salve my battered ego. Too late I learned that he who yearns for revenge digs two graves. I shall never comprehend her rejection of God's love, but it was because of me that she abandoned you to live her life of the streets. Yet mine was the greater sin, for I did not know love, denying utterly the wisdom of your namesake. I shall never forgive myself and only through your beloved grandmere have I learned to love and forgive what your mother did to you. They both have been and will always be in my prayers.

And now you, too, must forgive both her and Cyrus Bush. Hate the sin, but love the sinners. Their mistakes and passion must no longer continue the Devil's work in you. A heart overburdened with anger and hate wears itself out long before its time. Yours is a good heart and strong. Give it peace to do the Lord's work.

I was relieved to learn through Professor Stone that you and Captain Harwood are together somewhere in Canada. I pray God's protection for you both in this ghastly war. Your love and admiration of this man is not misplaced. He knows failure and the demons unleashed when he falls short of his own

impossible measures, but he also understands the power of human
love and loyalty. Before becoming overly critical of him, look
twice in the mirror and realize that you are much alike.
        May He who knows and loves all things bless you all the
days of your life.

                                        Affectionately,
                                        Father Mercier

He slowly folded the letter and slipped it in the box with
McGarry's trophy. The curate had returned with the coffee and
they shared some cookies and conversation about changes at Saint
Boniface. As Paul rose to go, the curate remembered something
else and went upstairs, returning with Pierre's old violin.

"Father Mercier kept this in his room and said it belonged to
your family, so it's now yours."

Paul ran his right hand over the old wood, feeling the grain
while at the same time being aware of the stiffness and numbness
in the wrist of his fingering left hand. A surge of awareness swept
over him not unlike the feeling he had experienced up near the old
pine at the Grafton Camp. The manitou? Grandmere had always
warned him of its constant presence.

"You must keep it", Paul said, handing the instrument back to
the curate. "Someone, perhaps yourself, may need it to add a little
life at the annual church fair." No refusal by the curate was tolerated
as Paul took his leave.

49

Paul got off the bus at the Burkett town common. It was a particularly pleasant mid-September late afternoon. Indian Summer was ascendant, yet the leaves were still crisp and green on the maples and sycamores vaulting the sleepy common. Across the main route to the east rose the towers of Burkett College. Young women were leaving classes for the afternoon, chatting their way to gracious dinner in the dormitories. He paused to drink at the fountain behind the granite Civil War soldier, becoming aware that the most enterprising place in Burkett was the pharmacy at the end of the common next to the filling station. Light meals as well as toiletries were advertised in the slightly dusty window. Paul entered and ordered a hamburg and milkshake, disregarding the sidewise glances of the local folk. Once upon at time, this small town curiosity and too often downright hostility would have made him uncomfortable, but no more. He finished and tipped the old gentleman who waited on him. Stepping outside, he noted the soft lemon light casting their horizontal shafts between the gothic towers. He smiled, knowing that Sarah would have watched this same play of the sun many times. He hoisted his backpack and set off up the street rising before him.

Ten minutes later he turned in at the stone gate and saw for the first time the old Harwood place at the end of the long drive. The large, rambling structure with yellow clapboards was done New England style with a "River Gods" flair. Porches faced every side but the east, this face being reserved for the porticoed front entry. He hesitated, put down his pack and hoisted himself onto the stone wall flanking the gate. He'd come too far to quit now; yet he could not bring himself to continue. After a time, he slid down, and using the pack as a pillow, put his back to the wall and closed his eyes, reconstructing the years before since the Grafton forest camp. The light was beginning to fade.

Paul easily outflanked the patrol and was able to make rapid headway. But the front caving in at every point by the punching German armor moved faster. He found himself having to double back many time to avoid capture and to slide between the Nazi tank thrusts. His gravest danger lay not with the enemy armor but with running into a "hold or die" French unit whose officers might accuse him of deserting. His Canadian uniform was of little consequence given the elan of some of the French officers he had observed. The distinct possibility of his being pressed into one of these rearguard units was unnerving. He decided early that his best ploy lay in joining a group of fleeing refugees who were generally ignored by the German Panzers. When a contingent of French troops appeared, Victor abandoned his cluster of civilians and hid in some convenient spot only to be picked up by another refugee wave in short order.

Pandemonium reigned among these homeless, helpless people. No one was in charge and like blinded, confused beasts, hordes of civilians and deserters rushed to and fro over the land with what few accoutrements they had left, responding with panic to each fresh rumor of tank or bomber attack. The Stuka dive-bomber was particularly feared with its long screaming whistle as it dropped from the heavens to release its deadly load. The Luftwaffe concentrated on troop clusters, gun emplacements and airfields, and regularly destroyed bridges useful to the retreating French. It was at these points that the refugee tide became constricted in its rush to the west and where the most hellish events occurred.

In a pack of perhaps 3,000 refugees, Paul reached the last remaining bridge over the Authie River. All other spans had been destroyed by either Stukas or French sappers. A virtual crush developed as the head of the column approached the ramp. A French lieutenant barred the way and as the crowd surged toward him he drew his revolver and leveled it at the leading individuals. The mob stopped and was told that the bridge was rigged for dynamiting and would be blown up immediately to prevent its being taken by the Germans. Time was essential to the French High Command and the officer was duty-bound to carry out his orders to the letter. Everyone was to disperse and return home. They were too late. Mumbling and milling commenced in the crowd, but just then two German photo-reconnaissance aircraft came in low over the hills. The refugees mistook them for the dreaded Stukas and, made lunatics by their fear, became a single, senseless brute, which rushed madly at the officer. He fired once, but was so shaken that his shot went wild and struck a young girl on the fringe of the mob, killing her instantly. Her mother's screams generated a groan within the multitude and eight burly men with rude farm implements converged on the hapless lieutenant. In seconds he was slashed and beaten to a quivering mass of broken and ruptured flesh as the crowd swirled on around the scene and rushed for the west side of the river. The lieutenant's men, realizing what might be in store for them, jumped into the river and swam for the far shore. Concealed in the clump of shrubs, Paul watched as the mob madly dashed to their freedom. Only the girl's mother remained, holding her dead daughter in her arms, wailing openly. Sensing nothing could be done to help her and numb with revulsion, Paul stepped onto the bridge to follow the crowd. Shame or morbid curiosity made him turn to look at the sorry scene a final time. He saw the woman, crazed with grief and despair, spitting on the officer's corpse, kicking the still-warm flesh and stamping in his blood as if to dishonor and destroy every part of the man's body.

Paul eventually reached the Somme River west of Abbeville on the evening of June 5th only to find the city and all of its bridges in German hands. Artillery and small arms fire from the south bank told him that the collapsing front had momentarily stabilized here. Fires were raging out of control in Abbeville. Fortunately, the Nazis had not had time to secure the riverbank at all points and in darkness he was able to slip unnoticed between outposts and swim the slow, meandering stream, pushing his pouch with Harwood's belongings before him.

Noiselessly, Paul approached the dark shore. He had carefully selected a bend of the river in deep shadow, then drifted downstream several hundred yards to another turn whose opposite bank grew rank with tall grass. On his belly, he slithered into the muck between the clumps and was nearly out of the water when a pair of iron hands grabbed his shoulders. Quick as a weasel Paul spun away, but other hands pinned him fast and a hoarse whisper sent chills down his spine.

"Not so fast, my lad, or you'll never see your mother again."

Against the fire-lit sky Paul recognized the outline of British Tommy helmets. His hands were painfully snugged behind his back and he was tethered to a giant private. Despite the searing pain of the rope burns, Paul kept silent, secretly pleased with his fortune at having been captured by a British unit. The patrol took him to the battalion headquarters located in a small copse two miles south of the river. To his great surprise, he learned that his captors were the same Highlanders with whom he had served at Longwy. The Scots captain recognized Paul in the dim light of the blacked out lean-to, ordered the ropes cut and the patrol dismissed. After telling of Harwood's death and his escape from St. Omer, Paul learned that the 51st Highlanders as well as the rest of the B.E.F. had been reorganized into the Tenth French Army whose job it was to defend the coastal flank of France. After many skirmishes, they had been pushed back south of the Somme River and it was rumored that a strong frontal Panzer thrust towards Rouen fifty miles to their rear was imminent. The Scots, strung out to the English Channel, were vexed by the French who seemed unperturbed by these reports. A successful split of the French Army would create yet another situation like the one at Dunkirk which had just fallen. The French seemed intent on taking everyone they could down to defeat.

On June 7th the blow fell and the Highlanders with four French divisions were cut off, their backs to the sea. They fell back to Dieppe, desperately trying to shorten their front. The commander of the Scots, Major General Fortune, was finally given orders to move with all possible speed to Rouen, still thirty-five miles away, and link up with a rescue force from the main Allied body striking northward. But the Germans moved faster and reached the sea before the would-be rescuers had even left their tents.

General Fortune moved to secure a port of departure from which his men might board rescue vessels of the Royal Navy. He and the French remnants moved into St. Valery-en-Caux. Defensive positions were hastily organized the more to buy time than to pose any serious obstacle to the Panzers.

Paul was assigned as a rifleman to a platoon supporting two anti-tank guns near a section of the coastal railway leading to Dieppe. The raised rail bed provided an ideal position from which to fire on troops and armor approaching St. Valery form the north and east. Marshes shouldered the single road leading to the position forcing attacking Panzers to go single file. Machine gun nests were planted on a wooded cliff adjacent to the anti-tank guns, which were in defilade behind the rail bed. Mines were laid in the road several hundred yards in front of the guns to stop a sudden rush by tanks.

They had barely organized when a German scout car was spotted probing the road far beyond the marshes. The Scots were told to hold their fire until the vehicle was within 300 yards, but a nervous machine gunner up on the hill squeezed off a burst at 700 yards. The bullets went extremely wild, but kicked up enough dirt to alert the driver who turned quickly and beat a retreat.

"Fire," yelled the gunnery sergeant and both guns roared out. One shell raised a plume of muck and water in the marsh, but the other projectile caught the scout square in the rear, causing a brilliant flash as the petrol ignited. The vehicle careened sideways, smoking, rolled over onto its top in the marsh and lay still, one wheel turning lazily in the sun. Paul fingered his rifle eagerly as elation surged within his breast. Small revenge at last for his captain's untimely death. A shout went up from the gun crew, but was cut short by the observation officer who commanded silence and ordered reloading of the weapons.

Nothing stirred for what seemed an hour. Soldiers relaxed over their weapons and wiped sweaty foreheads beneath their flat-lipped helmets. A few even closed their eyes and stretched out in the sun. Only the observation officer remained taut and motionless, his binoculars fixed on the road across the marsh. Suddenly they all heard it. Faint at first like a freight train far off and coming down a valley, then louder and more menacing. The officer wiped his lenses and peered more intently, but there was not mistake, tanks were coming up the road, fast. Their speed and audacity clearly spelled that the Germans knew the weakness of the Scots position and the B.E.F.'s dearth of tanks and artillery. Paul's late elation turned instantly to fear as the iron monsters ground angrily toward them at 30 miles per hour. Back in the tree line beyond the marsh, flashes of light appeared as yet more tanks provided artillery support. Shells almost simultaneously crashed into their position raising much smoke and debris, but with flat trajectory, not really doing much harm. The rail bed proved to be a well-chosen position. As soon as the tank column came into range, the Highlanders' weapons leaped back in recoil. Six Panzers looking like giant, lethal turtles churned rapidly on, closing the gap across the marsh. The observer shrieked above the din, "Get the first and last tanks," his plan being to bottle up the middle four on the narrow track. Several direct hits were scored by the Scots on the front plates of the lead tank, but no penetration was made and it lumbered on at a terrifying speed.

"The tread, the tread," roared the gunnery sergeant. Small flashes were now winking from the Panzers and a sound like the passage of a mowing machine went through the platoon. The machine gunners and riflemen on the points took the brunt of this fire for they were least protected by the embankment. Soon the cries of the wounded added an infernal dimension to this desperate scene. Still onward came the tanks. A well-placed shot finally dismembered one tread of the lead vehicle which spun sideways in a vain effort to continue. Its main gun was now brought into play and at short range began to wreak havoc on the anti-tank guns. Despite the defilade, two Nazi shells in rapid succession poured into one of the gun positions, knocking it out and killing the crew.

Among the dead was the gunnery sergeant whose order had stopped
the behemoth. The second gun, now under the direction of the
officer observer, swiftly pumped shells into the Panzer, striking its
more vulnerable side. A sudden flash of orange told that a mortal
wound had been dealt. The tank stopped firing and black smoke
began to pour from hidden seams. Paul positioned near the
remaining gun and overwhelmed by the ferocity of the clash, had
in pure panic, plunged retching to the ground at the height of the
Panzer's shelling. Rising unsteadily to a crouching position, he
gazed at the smoldering monster. The other tanks had come to a
halt behind it. The Scots officer yelled at the top of his voice for his
men to get the rear tank—any tank, but the hulk in front of them
blocked the field of fire. Two tanks now turned around and sped
back to the forest edge. The remaining three stayed buttoned up
behind the wreck. Suddenly the hatch of the smoking tank opened
and a horribly burned figure began to emerge, being pushed by
others inside the wreck. Its face and trunk were burned black and
parts of limbs fell away as it rolled out of the turret onto the fender
and into the marsh. Flames now rose from the opened hatch and a
series of explosions ripped the air as the ammunition went off.
Paul noticed that others besides him were retching at this hideous
end of the tankers.

The second tank now started forward again and bumped the
wreckage. The officer, knowing it was just a matter of time until
the hulk was pushed off the track, rallied the men at the gun to
continue their fire. Shells again screeched into the charred mass,
but not one hit the second tank which quickly and cleverly, using
the wreck as a shield, was moving the debris out of the way. The
other tanks, meanwhile, had backed down the track far enough to
bring their guns to bear on the Scots' position. Soon shells and
machine gun fire were again raking the gun emplacement. Their
position becoming less tenable by the minute, the officer ordered
the rifle platoon to carry the wounded to the rear and to occupy a
second prepared position beyond the wooded cliffs. Paul's squad
was to protect the retreat of the gunners after they had fired their
last rounds and spiked the gun. This done, the squad and gunners

beat a hasty path up the cliff and into the forest as a hellish hail beat on the embankment.

The wreck with its roasted crew now lay out of the way in the marsh. The number two tank quickly swept up over the railway bed and flattened the spiked gun. The Panzer following ran out of luck and hit one of the mines, immobilizing it immediately and tearing a gash in its belly.

Under the cover of the forest, the Scots officer halted the squad and motioned them into hiding, yet where they might survey the carnage below. The Highlanders were not overjoyed with this order, but had to admire their officer's steel nerves. Momentarily, they were safe as the tanks could not climb the escarpment and any information on the number of tanks and their probable direction was invaluable. Paul felt the taste of nausea once more as he saw the dead sergeant's body go under the Panzer treads like some cast-off doll. As the officer had expected, the tanks halted once they had secured their objective and took up defensive positions in the brush beside the road. Several tankers dismounted and sought out the wounded in the disabled vehicle.

The officer's attention was drawn to the marsh road once more, for out of the woods-line had emerged several more tanks and infantry in half-tracks led by another scout car in whose open hatch stood an officer with goggles banded to his cap. The Scot trained his binoculars on this vehicle and followed its approach. The driver carefully stayed in the track made by the tanks and halted beside the gutted vehicle. Engineers from the lead half-track dismounted and swiftly began to comb the road for additional mines. Once a route had been cleared, the scout car climbed the railway embankment and joined the lead tank. The officer, of middle-age and high rank, dismounted and waved the waiting tanks and infantry through, pointing out positions for them to occupy. Paul, camouflaged in some brush about forty feet from his leader, observed all this clearly, but failed to ascribe any importance to it. Suddenly, the Scots officer dropped his binoculars and breathlessly sidled over to Paul's hideaway.

"That man in the scout car is a general officer. You've got to bring him down with your rifle. I don't know what he's doing this far forward, but we can't miss this opportunity. Hurry up and fire."

Paul's nausea from all that had happened had left him weak and dull-witted. He looked blankly at the officer, but knew enough to mechanically check his rifle for chambering and to release the safety lock. Remembering the horrible end of the sargeant and his men at the anti-tank position, his anger flared as he snapped the rifle to his shoulder. When he drew a bead on the German, however, he noticed the man stooping to talk to a wounded tanker beside the road. Paul's rifle wavered as he breathed deeply, trying to steady himself.

"Shoot," rasped the Scotsman. "What are you waiting for?"

The German stood up and placed his hands on his hips. Paul could see the goggles pushed up on the cap, the heavy binoculars around the neck and the camera hanging by the side pocket of his blouse. The man removed his cap to mop his brow revealing an intelligent face with its resolute jaw. Paul's bowels churned and his mouth went dry for he no longer saw the man as his enemy. The hatred he felt towards his father that evening at the CCC camp was gone. A strong presence came over him much like the morning at the old pine. "Listen to the manitou", his grandmere's voice seemed to be saying. He could not squeeze the trigger. This man was different and might just as well have been his company commander reviewing work in the Vermont woods. He remembered Harwood's anguished embrace near the pillboxes and noticed that his hands were trembling He lowered the barrel slightly as the man looked up at the escarpment. To Paul it seemed that he was looking right into the muzzle of the rifle.

"Shoot, lad, for God's sake," hissed the officer at his elbow. "We've got to move."

Paul raised the barrel again and squinted across the sights. The officer was right. With German infantry beginning to fan out into the woods, the squad would have to run like hell as soon as the round was squeezed off.

The German was still standing, looking straight at Paul. Had he frozen like this out of fear when he had seen the deadly weapon ranged on his chest? Moving the sights ever so slightly from the man's breast to a tree trunk behind the motionless figure was easily accomplished without the knowledge of the Highland officer who by now was in a frenzy. Paul pulled the trigger, the shot sounding like a bomb. The Nazi officer dropped to one knee and pointed in the direction of the cliff, yelling words Paul did not understand. The Scots officer barked several swift commands and the squad melted deeper into the forest making for the defensive perimeter of St. Valery. Just before he bolted, Paul caught a glimpse of the German standing once more, brushing off his immaculate trousers.

Several bullets pruned the leaves and mortar rounds burst in the forest as Paul stumbled after the Scots. A burning sensation like a bee sting crept up his left arm and he saw his own blood dripping down onto his trousers. Strangely, there was no pain, only a heavy weight, as he clutched the arm to his chest and continued running.

The next 36 hours was a hellish eternity for the surrounded Highlanders and the decimated French forces. General Fortune had neither the troops nor the firepower to stave off the German juggernaut. The Luftwaffe raked everything that moved by daylight in both St. Valery and the English Channel. Hitler was not about to let this pocket of resistance escape as had the one at Dunkirk. General Erwin Rommel, Wehrmacht commander, relentlessly probed the perimeter of the town seeking a soft spot for his wedge.

The Channel lay choked in fog on the night of June 11th. Fortune knew that he could hold no longer than the next day and begged the Royal Navy to take him off posthaste. But the navy, blinded in the fog, could not maneuver in the tricky shore currents and had to lay far off shore to avoid groundings and collisions. Only a few intrepid civilian captains with small, shallow-drafted excursion vessels ventured close in to the beach as they had at Dunkirk.

Paul, his arm bandaged and useless, was one of about 1,000 British evacuated. The Scots officer had seen that he was among the evacuees. As the clammy night closed behind the tiny rescue packet, he could hear muffled explosions and see fuzzy lights on the shore. Incongruously packed into plush passenger chairs and on the carpeted deck, the tattered, grimy men were silent and grave. Friendships born in the danger and stink of battle were being torn asunder. With the dawn, the unlucky men on the beach must again seek shelter from the Luftwaffe and try to hold out yet another day against the grim Panzers.

Sharing this sense of helplessness and anger, Paul stared back at the thickening darkness. These Scots whom he had so roundly cursed in garrison were now his comrades. Had only a week passed since burying the Captain? Less than a year ago had he stood inspection in Vermont under the watchful eye of Hurlburt? A whole lifetime had intervened and the days he had thought immutable were now gone forever. His only tie with that past was the bundle in the waterproof pouch at his feet. The captain was now just a missing in action statistic. Only Paul knew the truth. He would send the pouch with a letter to Dr. Stone who would know best how to break the news to next of kin.

Dimly, he began to see things in a new pattern. He knew he would never go back to those bittersweet times in Roosevelt's Tree Army. The people and events which shaped him had left their indelible marks, but their time was gone. He winced as someone lost footing and caught hold of his arm for balance. No one could see the tears in his eyes as he turned and carefully picked his way over disillusioned soldiers to the ship's bow cutting its way towards England's coast. He had no hope in what was to come, but for better or for worse, he would survive.

The sea cliffs south of St. Valery fell to German infantry early on the morning of June 12th. From this position, Rommel gained total control of the battle zone. The hapless French surrendered shortly after daybreak and General Fortune, unable to squeeze out another day's grace, capitulated several hours later. He met Rommel on the harbor dock where photos were taken for propaganda purposes. For the few mauled men disembarking at Folkestone, neither bands nor bagpipes played. The other remnants of the 51st Highland Division, B.E.F., were on their way to a POW camp in Germany.

50

He'd just about convinced himself to forget about Sarah, Harwood and the rest and return to Amherst when barely audible music issued from the big house. Trudging up the long, gravel drive, past rows of sycamores, he knew it was Schubert.

He laid his bundle at the entrance and let the knocker fall just once. An elderly woman with a cane opened the door. Behind her, hanging back in shyness was a young boy of about six years. The woman stared at him in silence for a moment, eyes widening, then comprehending as a smile appeared. The boy turned to retreat to another part of the house, but not before Paul recognized the rather special eyes and cheekbones. The child was definitely a Harwood.

The music stopped and a door opened to the left of where they stood. Sarah gave a small cry of recognition and took Paul's hands. Her eyes burned fiercely and he could see the tears welling up, but they never left his. Mother Harwood finally broke the silence.

"Come, come. Let's go sit on the porch while there's still some sun. I'll get us all some tea." She hobbled off towards the north wing while Sarah led Paul to the huge veranda facing the sun and the Berkshires. They sat looking at each other, saying nothing, like an old couple who, understanding silence, were content to let it be. After a time, Paul blurted out softly.

"You know, I . . . I couldn't come sooner . . . and almost decided not to come at all, but . . ."

"Oh, Paul, you are here now and that's what matters." That gracious, loving voice nearly raised tears in Paul's eyes and he looked away at the setting sun on the hills.

"This will not be easy for any of us, Paul, but we can't change anything, not you, not me, not Mother Harwood. Just talking will help the healing."

Mother Harwood came out with the tea and took her favorite wicker chair next to Sarah. Paul turned to them and began his tale, telling of the trip to Canada, the ocean voyage to Britain, their assignment to the French forces during the Phony War. Carefully skirting John's death and the terror of the fall of France, he related the trek to St. Valery on the coast, the collapse of the defense there, his evacuation to Folkstone and reassignment to the training regiment in Scotland.

Sarah gently encouraged him from time to time, but Mother Harwood said nothing. As Paul was about to close, the old woman, speaking just above a whisper, asked him the question he dreaded.

"How did John die?" Paul looked her in the eye and saw steel and courage there.

"A single bullet, no suffering, instant death," he responded directly.

She held his eye for a long time, as if trying to test him for an alternative answer or perhaps hoping for him to say that none of this happened. She turned and for a long time faced the sun over the Berkshires, her lips moving, some silent, private incantation pouring forth.

"I'm very sorry," Paul whispered hoarsely. Mother Harwood took Paul's hand.

"No. Never apologize for the truth, Paul. My heart is so very sad, but you've given me, us, a resting place for the thoughts we lacked the courage to face."

She continued to hold his hand for a while, then rose quietly and went inside. They could hear her and the boy talking in the kitchen, then a door closed and it was quiet. Paul and Sarah remained until the soft autumn light was gone and the cool nip of frost, a portent of the coming winter, eased up from the river bottom.

They retired to the south parlor which served as Sarah's study and music room. A large desk in the corner was filled with her teaching materials for biology and a piano stood in the center of the room, set up for the private lessons she offered young women at the college. Some violins and a cello lay to one side in their half-opened cases. The minor clutter and odor of Sarah made Paul comfortable and he took a seat on the couch near them.

Sarah explained her marriage to Professor Stone and the birth of Robert. She learned of Paul's plans to enter college to train as a teacher of vocational agriculture in Nova Scotia. He told her more of his assignment to the Commando Training School in Scotland, then in 1944, to guard duty for German prisoners working the farms. Earlier he'd carried the message of the 51st Highland Division's demise and POW incarceration to the Scottish captain's family. There he had met the younger sister, Anne, and a mutual attraction had blossomed. She had accompanied the British Evacuee Children to Canada during the worst of the blitz and had remained in Halifax during the hostilities. Paul had followed after his discharge and both had decided they loved the fertile Annapolis Valley enough to settle there.

"Paul, I am so happy for you," beamed Sarah upon learning this.

"The bundle I brought is for you, Sarah," he added when their stories were told. He explained the strange odyssey of John's personal effects and the burial map, their discovery by Johnson in Ashley's office after the professor's death and how the forester decided to return them to Paul. Sarah's eyes became moist.

"I'm most grateful," she stammered. "Ashley always wanted me to believe that things would be right for me and tried to keep John's fate out of our relationship. He must have known that someone would find your bundle eventually, but death took him so suddenly there was no time to let me know of it." She removed the items from the pack one by one, slowly and in silence.

Paul rose and went to the window to allow her a bit of privacy. He ignored her courteous plea to stay with her. At the bottom of the pack was John's letter. She slid it open carefully and read.

December 29, 1939

Dear Sarah,

Please pardon the long delay of this letter. As you may have guessed, it has suffered many fits and starts, but I'll make no excuses for my shabby exit last October or for the thoughtless

silence since. Paul and I are well and in France, waiting for this
phony war to end. And it looks now that it will be sooner rather
than later. Paul and I hunker down among the poilu and
simply serve our time while the politicians rant and rave.

Despite the unusually harsh winter we've had, it has rained
all week giving us a soggy and sultry Christmas season. The
unusually mild wind now gusting from the east is welcome, but
tonight, alone in this wet village with this creaky, old typewriter,
trying to keep cadence with banging doors and window blinds,
I think what a far cry from our winters in Grafton. Yet, all the
other winter cues abide—bare willows, rattling brown leaves
clinging to the oaks, the long nights—so much out of phase.
Nothing much like our evening under the stars at the homestead
in Burkett or that chilly night at the lake. You know that our
time then will live in me forever. McGarry put it right by
telling me how often I have failed to see the chances for happiness
and fulfillment in life until long after the opportunity has come
and gone.

Paul closed his eyes, but stood at near military attention by the
window. He'd read and reread Harwood's awkward, unfinished letter
many times since 1940 in France and knew every word. He had no
wish to intrude on her. Let John and Sarah be together again. He
slowly opened his eyes and caught the tiny dust motes floating leisurely
in the soft light. Focusing across the lawn and the swale to the hills,
he thought of Mother Harwood's quiet soliloquy and another evening
of soft light in a tiny French townhouse with another woman.

No, there were no words of any import now. No need for Sarah to
know of John's frequent visits to take his pleasure with that woman in
Longwy or of his own loss of innocence to the same woman. How he
wished that could be different for both of them. How disgusted he
became in the Phony War with the bored and drunken Scots in garrison,
their brawls and use of easy women. Yet he, too, finally fell to their
taunts, the lonliness and the inferno in his blood. The deceit of others
and their self-delusion to get or to keep what they wanted galled him.
Still, he knew now that he was no different.

No need for Sarah to know that the letter in her hand had more than one author, and that he, Paul, had written the second page not two weeks ago. Here he was foisting more deception on the person he most admired. Had he finished the letter in disguise to further some end of his own ego? Perhaps he even hoped that Sarah would see through the ruse and suddenly become beholden to him. How miserable and easy that genuine affection between people becomes twisted by embroidered truth, a lack of candor or just plain lies. Had not even Professor Stone deliberately withheld John's letter from Sarah? Not for a minute did Paul believe that Stone's sudden death was the reason for her not getting it. After all, the parcel must have been in his office for at least two years. Yet, had the professor not hesitated, the completed letter she now held would have never been. Closure would have never had a chance.

Sarah continued to read.

> *Sarah, the longer we dwell in this barren and empty place, the more I long for the life, the music, you offered me. I was awfully wrong to try to rid myself of the past. All that should have been clear to me when first we met at Camp Grafton, but I foolishly fought it, long and hard, and to no avail. I see now that this albatross has become just another dead duck and ready for burial. Life is too long and tough for me to go solo. If you can forgive, we still have time to live and make something of our future. Somehow, someway, we will choose to be happy and get beyond the misgivings and foolishness. At the very least, I want to be a comfort to you in our years ahead. I want to come home to you, Sarah. Trust me and think of us now and then.*
>
> *All my love,*
> *John*

Paul knew from the crinkling sound that she was done. She must have scanned the letter many times. He closed his eyes to the growing gloom and quietly breathed his relief. Yes, he had done the right thing after all. Hate the sin, love the sinner. He was done deceiving and would never play God again. He could face her now.

Her head was bowed for a long time. When the moment of angst had passed, their eyes met. Fear and bewilderment was written on her face.

"Oh, Paul," she gasped in the very small voice of a child, "what does it all mean for us?"

Reeling from guilt and relief, he would not and could not speak. She moved away to the piano and played a few chords ever so softly, breaking the tension.

"Do you remember the musical show we did, Paul?"

"Could never forget it," he returned with a slight smile.

"Play something with me now." The light in her eyes caused his heart to tumble, but he shifted uncomfortably.

"I've given up the fiddle, Sarah. Had to after the operations . . . ." He bit off the rest of his words.

Her eyes widened. "You were wounded? I didn't know, couldn't tell . . ." she murmured in that tiny voice. Paul saw the eyes turn tired and the shoulders slump slightly.

"It was a very lucky near miss, but two slivers of German steel from the mortar went into the shoulder and arm. I spent a bit of time in hospital where they tried to put everything back together. They got the infection, but after the healing I found that the shoulder stayed weak and the lower arm wouldn't rotate. That was the end of my fiddle playing, but I count my good fortune. It kept me off the roster for Dieppe and Normandy."

She rose and stood before him, her cheeks wet. Leaning over, she buried her face in his good shoulder, trembling with repressed sobs. He made room for her on the couch, took her in his arms and held her close. When her body became still, she found the buttons of his shirt and carefully undid them. He could feel her warm hands on his scars, the sensitive fingers searching the handiwork of the British surgeons, then the even warmer lips and wet cheeks tracing the new flesh of the rippled skin. After a little while, she got up, crossed to a small table and poured two drinks from a small carafe. She held one of the glasses out to him.

"To dear John's memory, to you and me and to all of us who have come through this damned war," she murmured without rancor. "We are all just dancing in the dark." She wiped a tear from the corner of her mouth and sipped from the glass. "Taxi-dancing survivors, Paul—you, me, Robbie, Mother Harwood. Yet the fray never really ends for us, does it? We commit thoughtless deceptions, then live with them forever. We are so vulnerable, but if we can only keep our balance we can make small things right in the time we've got left. The four of us aren't much against the great lies and treachery of this world or the roaring greed and hatred that will always be out there. But if we love, pardon and give quarter again and again, we can be proud in the petty skirmishes, insignificant though they may appear."

She had regained her teacher's composure. He could feel it pervading the room as surely as the brandy was warming his innards.

She reached for his left hand and held it gently, slowly rotating the wrist in its limited arc, saying, "Yes, yes!!" and led him to the cello, urging him to cradle it and finger the strings. She faced him squarely, "Professor Stone often said that human evolution is terribly incomplete and our lives will always need healing, especially when we cannot show what is in our hearts. And there will be more unspeakably terrible times for us when we must bind each other's wounds as best we can. Promise me, Paul, you must make music. It's as life giving for us mammals as mother's milk. We give up the teat, but the need remains, sometimes bent or broken and so often corrupted and misunderstood. But when we let music's nourishment flow, we find strength and joy. And joy is what we are here for . . . . ," She trailed off, eyes wide and moist. "But you already know this, Paul. I shouldn't carry on so."

He recalled Walsh's earthy take on music years before, smiled warmly and shook his head lightly from side to side. "Oh yes, the music will stay, for you have shown me what joy is, Sarah." He had never spoken her given name before, but now it seemed so natural and he used it without hesitation.

He looked away and buttoned his shirt. A chapter was closing and there was nothing either could do about it. But when he met her eyes, she was smiling as she had when they danced to the scratchy Lehar tune at the side camp in the forest on Johnnycake Hill.

He went out to the huge kitchen to pay respects to Mother Harwood and the boy. Ready for bed and eyes full of sleep, Robbie was less reticent than before and chuckled when Paul ruffled his hair. After bidding Sarah a final farewell, he made his way down the long sycamore drive. The farther he went, the lighter his tread became so that by the time he reached the huge stone gate, his pace was regular and rapid, as if some force at his back was driving him on. He'd catch the last bus to Amherst and tomorrow would begin the journey north to the Black River, to Lake Champlain, to Montreal, then to Nova Scotia and to Anne.

EPILOGUE

Despite Stone's reservations, people's lives and river water do have things in common. To be sure, there's a lot we don't know about rivers and a whole lot more we don't know about people. But lives sometimes rush heedlessly headlong in melt water torrents, at times tortured, at other times slowing down, eddying in a sheltered pool or meandering in an inextricable backwater. Some lives become revered, special places of beauty and strength, if only for a moment. Others end quickly, like intermittent streams, evaporating in the summer's heat or dropping suddenly out of sight, to percolate into some underground cavern or aquifer to lie dormant and forgotten. But whatever life they are dealt, with an inward eye these river swimmers inevitably paint their life's scroll in tones personal if not always familiar. Bold or barely audible; forthright, but more often enigmatic, rivers and swimmers are like lovers whose hearts, even between the beloved, may never be totally understood.

Fred Hurlburt and Mary Grout were wed in June 1944, shortly before D-Day. He'd sold his timber in Belchertown to the government and made enough for a down payment on a dairy farm in Tyringham over in the Berkshires. With typical Yankee thrift and hard work, the two were successful. Mary was able to supplement the farm's earnings by working for many years as the school nurse in the nearby town of Lee. With his own hands, Fred built a cabin on the height of land in Belchertown and, as he and Mary aged and the farm prospered, they spent some time there each fall enjoying the Quabbin wilderness just as his father had wished. Over the years, Fred and Mary saw the healing of the Swift River Valley and took heart as the bald landscape inexorably returned through biological succession to the climax forest. Fred had to admit that Boston's puddle, now nestled between his hills, was lovely.

Scooter Walsh never left Vermont, despite his long-standing complaints about the vagaries of the climate. Shortly after the Grafton camp was inactivated in 1939, he was hired on as a member of the public works crew in Bellows Falls, thanks to a word in the right place from Mary Grout. He gave good service until his retirement 20 years later. He never married and lived alone, a near recluse, in one of the apartment blocks not far from the Tamarack Hotel. On Sundays in summer he could be seen sitting on the banks of the Connecticut River, seemingly lost in thought, watching with the patrolling swallows for the rise of insects from the unseen turbulence below. Passersby thought him vacant or possibly scouting out the best fishing holes. But for Walsh, in his hobo stare, the swirls and eddies condured up a kind of comic irony. When the breezes blew north, stubbornly driving that inexorable current a few inches back toward its source, he would often crack a rare smile, perhaps recalling the Grafton Mule or a hint of self-recognition. Only when the late afternoon freight rumbled up from the south, its plaintive hoot calling, did he stir, perhaps tugged by his old life in the hobo jungles. They found him in his bed in early Spring 1960. He had died peacefully in his sleep.

Joshua Lieberman returned to Chicago to continue as a social worker. When the films on the 1937 Memorial Day massacre were finally made public, opinion shifted dramatically to the side of the workers and no charges were pressed against those responsible for the demonstrations. As war became more evident, Lieberman enlisted and became an officer in the propaganda section of the U.S. Army. As one might expect, he was good at his job and was discharged a major at the conclusion of hostilities in 1945. He then enrolled at the University of Chicago to earn a PhD in economics and spent several years teaching at mid-western colleges. Called up during the Korean War, he became an infantry battalion commander, earning an honest Silver Star for heroism under fire during the calamitous retreat from the Choshin Reservoir. Upon discharge, he replaced his old mentor at Columbia as professor of economics and political science.

Lieberman had early championed Paul Robeson's call for social justice, a futile attempt to challenge that worst evil of U.S. white racism, the lynching of blacks. In the half-century ending in 1950, nearly 1,800 blacks, mostly below the Mason-Dixon Line, were mutilated and hung, their bodies then often publicly burned to a crisp. Yet the U.S. Congress blocked every move to make lynching a federal crime. Robeson, the artist, after an incautious flirtation with Communism, paid the Cold War price of being the walking point man against black injustice. Public scorn, government harassment and subsequent loss of bookings and income by blacklisting were to be his fate. Just when he thought that the nadir was reached, a depraved, racist mob openly confronted and vilified Robeson in Peekskill, N.Y. in 1949. But the cruelest blow to the college "All-American" was to be libeled "Un-American" by the McCarthyites.

Lieberman, himself, barely escaped the dragnet of communist hysteria and only his impeccable war record silenced the rabid senators. He worked tirelessly for the relief of victims of the Holocaust and, as special consultant to the United Nations, assisted the migration of Jews trying to escape the tyranny of Communism. But he never forgot the lesson the steel mills—that arrogance and misuse of power by capitalists was equally tyrannical. He was relentless in his intent to help heal a corrupt and tortured world and challenge those whose inherent mendacity and greed exploited others, causing misery and injustice. They would feel the lash of his tongue wherever they befouled the human nest.

Rafferty returned to Boston and served as an aide to his father in the legislature. Soon tiring of this, he enlisted, was sent to Officer Candidate School and then to Camp Hale in Colorado where a mountain division was forming. He excelled, both as a ski trooper and platoon leader, and was in the first battalion of alpine troops sent to the Italian Theater. His unit was held in reserve for months as the Allies and Germans battered each other slowly up the bloody Italian boot. By pulling strings and politicking, he wangled TDY to a front line unit and a month later in a nasty engagement on the flanks of Monte Casino, he was shot through the head by a sniper. His body and unused skis were sent back to Boston where the now Colonel Butler had a bogus Silver Star cut for him and arranged a hero's burial. While truly decimated by the tragic loss of his son, the new U. S. Senator from Massachusetts shrewdly grasped the mourning event to gain some needed publicity and political mileage.

Rocco Donnelli did well out west. With help and mentoring from Dr. DiMaggio, he trained to become a male nurse, somewhat of a rarity in the medical profession of the time. Despite his unorthodox indoctrination to flying with McGarry under the French King Bridge, he suffered repeated losses of bowel control and jumped as a medic with the 82nd Airborne Division at Normandy. After the war he married an Oregon woman and for many years served the rural counties as a physician's assistant before retiring to the California wine country in the early 1980's.

Lester Gilpin went back to New York City and began studies for the ministry, qualifying for a military deferment early in the war. As a newly ordained minister, he spent 1944-45 with an all-black U.S. Army stevedore unit in San Diego loading munitions. Returning to Harlem after the war, he was called to the Buelah Baptist Church whose chorus was already well known in the black community. Within two years, Lester had honed it to perfection and over the next quarter century, every city and many college campuses, including Burkett, up and down the eastern seaboard had hosted and acclaimed his efforts.

He remained a mostly peaceful, gentle man, but on rare occasions could become powerfully angry. In 1939, Marion Anderson, the sublime black operatic contralto was denied the use of Constitution Hall in Washington, D.C., which was owned by the Daughters of the American Revolution. He wrote to President Roosevelt and others decrying this injustice, then stood with the thousands of others at Anderson's epic performance on the steps of the Lincoln Memorial. A number of years later, when Carnegie Hall also refused to host her performances, he again roundly and publicly castigated the cultural and political community, then invited her to come sing in his Harlem church. She came and brought Robeson with her and many shared the bittersweet memories of that visit.

He always hoped that the WWII sacrifices rendered by blacks would at last result in equal rights only to see the Old Harry racial barriers return with the peace. But despite the repeated injustices, Lester remained a powerfully happy man and was never more pleased than when Jackie Robinson became the first black in the major leagues. In April 1948, he was part of the crowd that watched the Dodgers take the Braves at Ebbets Field. Even after the heart-rending racial conflicts of the 70's and 80's, he continued to sing of the goodness of the human spirit, knowing that in time . . . . much too long, long time . . . . things were better.

Grandmother Boisvert died in her sleep at the rectory on Christmas, 1944. Father Mercier gave one of the most moving eulogies of his career at her funeral, but it was heard by a mere handful of old women, ritual mourners who had braved the brutal cold. Burial next to her beloved Pierre had to wait until the spring thaw. Paul's mother refused to participate in the services, but drove her friend's blue Chevrolet to Springfield to assure that the funeral expenses were paid and that the marking of the tombstone was accurate.

Father Mercier continued his pastorate in Springfield throughout World War II, kindly ministering as best he could to parents and kin of servicemen sent overseas and fulfilling his time-honored function of intermediary between his French-Canadians and the Yankee small town power holders. He served God, his parish and his bishop well with complete loyalty and obedience.

A grand jury had convened in the spring of 1940 to consider the evidence against Paul. Father Mercier was called to testify. He took full responsibility for Paul's escape to Canada, cleverly presenting it in terms of a young man rushing to serve with his relatives in the Canadian Army against the Nazi menace. Given the patriotic fervor of the times, it was not surprising that a finding of "no case" was rendered, thus effectively exonerating Paul. After the war, he was assigned to the Grand Seminary in Montreal as confessor and novice master. A stroke felled him only months into this office, leaving him frail, nearly speechless and alone. When Paul visited him in the small retirement home for priests, he was greeted by a husk of a man who could only mumble, "God is good. God is good."

Cyrus Bush lingered near death for almost a month, then inexplicably improved. Showing amazing strength and thoroughly confounding the doctors, he sat up in bed one day and demanded a drink. Receiving none, he rose and threatened the shift nurse, then lurched as far as the front entrance of the hospital and collapsed. By the time he was returned to his bed, there was no pulse. The official certificate of death noted cerebral-vascular accident as the cause. Mary Grout made sure of this. Not that it changed the minds of any of Bush's other relatives. For them, Cy Bush had died at the hands of a crazy Canuck kid who was guilty as hell. There would never be forgiveness.

Through her representative in Washington, D.C., Mother Harwood contacted the United States Ambassador to France who, with the help of Paul's map, located John's grave and arranged to have his remains returned to Burkett. In a simple ceremony attended by only her, Sarah and Robbie, he was laid beside his brother and father in the family plot on the Harwood estate.

They placed a small stone bench close by which offered a view of the Berkshires across the river. Carved into its seat was this inscription:

> *The more the earth there are of loving hearts*
> *The more worth loving, and the more the love*
> *Which like a mirror, each to each imparts.*

Dante's Purgatorio, Canto XV, verses 73-75

Myrtle grows beneath this pleasant seat, thrusting forth its purple blooms in May. And to one side slightly hidden, is a wild pasture rose which scents the air from mid-summer until the first frost.

On warm summer evenings, the slightly fetid tang wafts up from the swale and the lightning bugs come out, then the stars in the obsidian night. The demons ? They are long gone, blown away on the battlefields of France or was it in the forests of Vermont?

ACKNOWLEDGEMENTS

Credit is due to the many former CCC men who generously shared camp factual information and personal experiences with me through scores of oral and written recollections. Whatever insight I may have gained into the spirit of the times and how events of the Great Depression challenged and shaped these men has been because of them. I hope that my fictional embellishments and interpretations have done them justice. Looking back at their history after nearly 60 years, many of us stand humbled by and in awe of what they did.

In particular, I wish to thank the late Clifford Richards and Charles Lord who recalled for me in great detail their own experiences regarding camp organization and work schedules as well as Francis Derwin who generously shared information on the CCC in New England and elsewhere.

A number of sources were consulted in preparing this book:

An overview of the New England invasion by the gypsy moth and its establishment in the Northeast United States was found in:

Forbush, E.H. and C.H. Fernald. 1896. *The Gypsy Moth*. Wright & Potter, Boston. 495 pp. and from various United States Department of Agriculture and U. S. Forest Service bulletins and state government brochures.

A summary of CCC accomplishments in the nine year period 1933-1942 was found in:

Leake, F.E. and R.S. Carter. 1983. *Roosevelt's Tree Army: A Brief History of the Civilian Conservation Corps.*(5th edition) National Association of Civilian Conservation Corps Alumni, Arlington VA. 7 pp.

Merrill, P.H. 1981. *Roosevelt's Forest Army: A History of the Civilian Conservation Corps.* Northlight Studio Press, Barre, VT. 206 pp.

Stetson, F.W. 1978. The Civilian Conservation Corps in Vermont. Proceedings of the Vermont Historical Society. Vol. 46, No. 1, pp. 24-42.

Data on the WWII Battle of France and the surrender of the 51st Highland Division, B.E.F. on the French coast at St. Valery-en-Caux in 1940 was obtained from:

Horne, Alistair. 1969. To Lose a Battle: France 1940. Little, Brown & Co. Boston. 647 pp.

Williams, T. 1969. France Summer 1940. Ballantine's Illustrated History of World War II, Balantine Books, New York. 160 pp.

A history of Camp William James was found in:

Preiss, Jack J. 1978. *Camp William James*, Argo Books, Norwich VT, 256 pp.

Information on the workings of a single CCC camp was reported in:

Bailey, Jackson, Faculty Advisor. Report of First Ealham College Vermont Off-Campus Study Group. 1970. *The Civilian Conservation Corps in Vermont: A Study of Camp Calvin Coolidge, Plymouth, VT*, Unpublished manuscript.

I am also indebted to persons at the Holyoke Community College Library, Holyoke, MA, particularly Elizabeth Sheehan, Judith ⌐ ˺pbell and Claire Wheeler who provided research assistance.

nk you, Peggins, for research assistance and computer ˥, as well as patience and support when most needed.